DB

D0527006

THE LOST FLEET

RELENTLESS

**ALSO BY JACK CAMPBELL AND
AVAILABLE FROM TITAN BOOKS:**

THE LOST FLEET: DAUNTLESS
THE LOST FLEET: FEARLESS
THE LOST FLEET: COURAGEOUS
THE LOST FLEET: VALIANT
THE LOST FLEET: RELENTLESS
THE LOST FLEET: VICTORIOUS

COMING SOON:

THE LOST FLEET: BEYOND THE FRONTIER:
DREADNAUGHT

THE LOST FLEET

RELENTLESS

JACK CAMPBELL

TITAN BOOKS

The Lost Fleet: Relentless
ISBN: 9780857681348

Published by
Titan Books
A division of Titan Publishing Group Ltd
144 Southwark St
London
SE1 0UP

First edition: March 2011
10 9 8 7 6 5

This is a work of fiction. Names, characters, places, and incidents either are the product of the author's imagination or are used fictitiously, and any resemblance to actual persons, living or dead, business establishments, events, or locales is entirely coincidental. The publisher does not have any control over and does not assume any responsibility for author or third-party websites or their content.

The right of John G. Hemry to be identified as the author of this work has been asserted by him in accordance with the Copyright, Designs and Patents Act of 1988.

Copyright © 2009, 2011 by John G. Hemry writing as Jack Campbell.

Visit our website: **www.titanbooks.com**

What did you think of this book? We love to hear from our readers. Please email us at: readerfeedback@titanemail.com, or write to us at the above address.

To receive advance information, news, competitions, and exclusive Titan offers online, please register as a member by clicking the 'sign up' button on our website: www.titanbooks.com

No part of this p_____ system, or transmitted, in a _____ permission of the publisher _____ g or cover other than that _____ tion being imposed on the _____

A CIP catalogu_____ rary.

Printed and bou_____

FIFE CULTURAL TRUST

FCT30273	
DONATION	11.8.15
AF	£7.99
SFI	DB

To Doug Tillyer (aka "Hellfire"), a man who loved books, ideas, and people, who brightened many a convention and panel with his remarks, and who left his wife and the rest of us far too soon and will be deeply missed.

For S., as always.

THE ALLIANCE FLEET

CAPTAIN JOHN GEARY, COMMANDING

As reorganized following the losses suffered prior to Captain Geary assuming command in the Syndic home system.

Second Battleship Division

Gallant
Indomitable
Glorious
Magnificent

Third Battleship Division

Paladin (Capt Midea) (lost at Lakota)
Orion (Capt Numos)
Majestic (Capt Faresa) (lost at Lakota II)
Conqueror (Capt Casia)

Fourth Battleship Division

Warrior (Capt Kerestes) (lost at Lakota II)
Triumph (lost at Vidha)
Vengeance
Revenge

Fifth Battleship Division

Fearless
Resolution
Redoubtable
Warspite

Seventh Battleship Division

Indefatigable
 (lost at Lakota)
Audacious (lost at Lakota)
Defiant (Capt Mosko)
 (lost at Lakota)

Tenth Battleship Division

Colossus (Capt Armus)
Amazon
Spartan
Guardian

First Battle Cruiser Division

Courageous (Capt Duellos)
Formidable
Intrepid
Renown (lost at Lakota)

Eighth Battleship Division

Relentless
Reprisal (Capt Hiyen)
Superb
Splendid

First Scout Battleship Division

Arrogant (lost at Kaliban)
Exemplar (CDR Vendig)
Braveheart (lost at Cavalos)

Second Battle Cruiser Division

Leviathan (Capt Tulev)
Dragon
Steadfast
Valiant
 (Commander Landis)

Fourth Battle Cruiser Division

Dauntless (flagship)
  (Capt Desjani)
Daring (Capt Vitali)
Terrible (lost at Ilion)
Victorious

Fifth Battle Cruiser Division

Invincible (lost at Ilion)
Repulse (lost in Syndic home system)
Furious (Capt Cresida)
Implacable (CDR Neeson)

Sixth Battle Cruiser Division

Polaris (lost at Vidha)
Vanguard (lost at Vidha)
Illustrious (Capt Badaya)
Incredible (Capt Parr)

Seventh Battle Cruiser Division

Opportune (lost at Cavalos)
Brilliant (Capt Caligo)
Inspire (Capt Kila)

Third Fast Fleet Auxiliaries Division

Titan (CDR Lommand)
Witch (Capt Tyrosian)
Jinn
Goblin

Thirty-seven surviving heavy cruisers in seven divisions

First Heavy Cruiser Division
Third Heavy Cruiser Division
Fourth Heavy Cruiser Division
Fifth Heavy Cruiser Division
Seventh Heavy Cruiser Division
Eighth Heavy Cruiser Division
Tenth Heavy Cruiser Division

Minus
Invidious (lost at Kaliban)
Cuirass (lost at Sutrah)
Crest, War-Coat, Ram and **Citadel** (lost at Vidha)
Basinet and **Sallet** (lost at Lakota)
Utap, Vambrace, and **Fascine** (lost at Lakota II)
Armet and **Gusoku** (lost at Cavalos)

Sixty-two surviving light cruisers in ten squadrons

First Light Cruiser Squadron
Second Light Cruiser Squadron
Third Light Cruiser Squadron
Fifth Light Cruiser Squadron
Sixth Light Cruiser Squadron
Eighth Light Cruiser Squadron
Ninth Light Cruiser Squadron
Tenth Light Cruiser Squadron
Eleventh Light Cruiser Squadron
Fourteenth Light Cruiser Squadron

Minus
Swift (lost at Kaliban)
Pommel, Sling, Bolo, and **Staff** (lost at Vidha)
Spur, Damascene, and **Swept-Guard** (lost at Lakota)
Brigandine, Carte, and **Ote** (lost at Lakota II)
Kote and **Cercle** (lost at Cavalos)

One hundred eighty-three surviving destroyers in twenty squadrons
First Destroyer Squadron
Second Destroyer Squadron
Third Destroyer Squadron
Fourth Destroyer Squadron
Sixth Destroyer Squadron
Seventh Destroyer Squadron
Ninth Destroyer Squadron
Tenth Destroyer Squadron
Twelfth Destroyer Squadron
Fourteenth Destroyer Squadron
Sixteenth Destroyer Squadron
Seventeenth Destroyer Squadron
Twentieth Destroyer Squadron
Twenty-first Destroyer Squadron
Twenty-third Destroyer Squadron
Twenty-fifth Destroyer Squadron
Twenty-seventh Destroyer Squadron
Twenty-eighth Destroyer Squadron
Thirtieth Destroyer Squadron
Thirty-second Destroyer Squadron

Minus

Dagger and **Venom** (lost at Kaliban)

Anelace, Baselard, and **Mace** (lost at Sutrah)

Celt, Akhu, Sickle, Leaf, Bolt, Sabot, Flint, Needle, Dart, Sting, Limpet, and **Cudgel** (lost at Vidha)

Falcata (lost at Ilion)

War-Hammer, Prasa, Talwar, and **Xiphos** (lost at Lakota)

War-Hammer, Prasa, Talwar, and **Xiphos** (lost at Lakota)

Armlet, Flanconade, Kukri, Hastarii, Petard, and **Spiculum** (lost at Lakota II)

Flail, Ndziga, Tabar, Cestus, and **Balta** (lost at Cavalos)

Second Fleet Marine Force -
Major General Carabali commanding (acting)

Originally 1,560 Marines divided into detachments on battle cruisers and battleships. Approximately 1,200 surviving following losses in ground actions and on destroyed warships.

1

The structure of the Alliance heavy cruiser *Merlon* shuddered again and again as hell-lances fired by Syndicate Worlds warships ripped into and through her. Commander John Geary grabbed for support as a volley of Syndic grapeshot struck *Merlon*'s port side, the impacts of the solid metal balls vaporizing part of the hull. Wiping a hand across his eyes to clear away sweat, Geary blinked through the fumes the overloaded and failing life-support systems couldn't clear out of the atmosphere left inside the ship. His first real combat action might also turn out to be his last. *Merlon* tumbled helplessly through space, unable to control her motion, and the final hell-lance still working on the Alliance warship went silent as more enemy fire ripped into her.

There wasn't anything else he could do. It was time to go.

Geary cursed as he got the emergency destruct panel open and punched in the authorization code. Another volley of hell-lances sliced into *Merlon*, and more indicator lights on the bridge went out or shifted to blinking damage status. Geary pulled on his survival suit helmet, knowing that he had only ten minutes before the power core overloaded and *Merlon* exploded. But Geary paused before he left the bridge. He'd ordered the remaining members of the crew off once it was clear that he alone could handle the few operational weapons and the final act of self-destruction. He'd bought all the time he could for his crew to get clear.

But *Merlon* had been his ship, and he hated to leave her to her death.

Another rumble and *Merlon*'s out-of-control tumble rolled sideways and up as more Syndic grapeshot slammed into her, the passageways around Geary rotating dizzyingly, bulkheads thrusting suddenly toward him, then away, sometimes slamming painfully into him. His search became more desperate as he kept passing escape-pod berths either empty or with mangled remnants of their rescue craft still wedged in place.

He finally found one with a yellow status light, indicating damage, but he had no choice. Inside, seal the hatch, strap in, slap the eject control, feel the force of the acceleration pin him to the seat as the escape pod tore away from *Merlon*'s death throes.

The pod's propulsion cut off, much earlier than it should have. No communications. No maneuvering controls. Environmental systems degraded. Geary's seat reclined automatically as the pod prepared to put him into survival sleep, a frozen state where his body could rest safely until his escape pod was recovered. As Geary's consciousness faded, his eyes on the blinking damage lights of the escape pod as they winked out into dormant status, he knew that someone would come looking for him. The Alliance fleet would repel the Syndic surprise attacks, reestablish control of the space around the star Grendel, and search for survivors from *Merlon*. He'd be picked up in no time.

He opened his eyes on a blur of lights and shapes, his body feeling as if it were filled with ice and his thoughts coming slowly and with difficulty. People were talking. He tried to make out the words as the blurry shapes began to resolve themselves into men and women in uniform. One man with a big, confident voice was speaking. "It's really him? You've confirmed it?"

"DNA match with fleet records is perfect," another voice said. "This *is* Captain Geary. He's been badly physically stressed by the duration of his survival sleep. It's a miracle he came through this well. It's a miracle he came through at all."

"Of course it was a miracle!" the big voice boomed. A face leaned close, and Geary blinked to focus, making out a uniform that was the color of the Alliance fleet but otherwise different in details. The man beaming at him bore the stars of an admiral, but Geary didn't recognize him. "Captain Geary?"

"C... C... Com... man... der... Geary," he finally managed to reply.

"*Captain* Geary!" the admiral insisted. "You were promoted!"

Promoted? Why? How long had he been out? Where was he?

"What... ship?" Geary gasped, looking around. From the size of the sick bay, this ship was much larger than *Merlon*.

The admiral smiled. "You're aboard the battle cruiser *Dauntless*, flagship of the Alliance fleet!"

Nothing made sense. There wasn't any battle cruiser in the Alliance fleet named *Dauntless*. "Crew... my... crew?" Geary managed to say.

The admiral frowned and stepped back, motioning forward a woman who wore captain's insignia. Geary's gaze left the woman's face, unsettled by her expression of awe and distracted by the number of combat-action ribbons on the left breast of her uniform. Dozens of them, but that was ridiculous. Topping her rows of ribbons was the one for the Alliance Fleet Cross. He couldn't even remember the last time one of those had been awarded. "I'm Captain Desjani," the woman said, "commanding officer of *Dauntless*. I regret to inform you that the last surviving member of the crew of your heavy cruiser died about forty-five years ago."

Geary stared. Forty-five years? "How... long?"

"Captain Geary, you were in survival sleep for ninety-nine years, eleven months, and twenty-three days. Only the fact that the pod had a single occupant enabled it to keep you alive so long." She made a spiritual gesture he recognized. "By the grace of our ancestors and the mercy of the living stars you lived, and you have returned."

One hundred years? A wave of shock rode through Geary's slow-moving thoughts as he tried to absorb the news, not even trying to grasp why the woman had apparently seen some religious significance in his survival.

The bad news having been delivered by someone else, the admiral leaned forward again with another big smile.

"Yes, Black Jack, you have returned!"

He'd never liked the Black Jack nickname. But if Geary managed to show his reaction, the admiral didn't notice it, speaking as if he was giving a speech. "Black Jack Geary, back from the dead, just as predicted in the legends, to help the Alliance win its greatest victory and finally put an end to this war with the Syndics!"

Returned? Legends? The war was still going on after a century? Everyone he had known must be dead.

Who were these people and who did they think he was?

John Geary bolted awake in his stateroom aboard *Dauntless*, gazing up at the overhead, breathing heavily and sweating even though his insides felt a lingering memory of the ice that had once filled him. It had been a while since he'd had flashbacks to the last moments of *Merlon* and his awakening aboard *Dauntless* a century later. He sat up, kneading his forehead with one hand while he tried to calm his breathing. Around him loomed the darkened outlines of his stateroom.

The admiral with the big voice had died in the Syndicate Worlds' home star system after his plan to win the war had turned out to be an ambush by the Syndics. A lot of other people and Alliance warships had died with him. The survivors had turned to the legendary Black Jack Geary to save them, and despite Geary's abhorrence of the impossibly heroic figure that legends claimed Black Jack had been, he'd been forced to assume command of the fleet. After all, his commissioning date to captain had been almost a century earlier, and no other surviving officer in the fleet had anywhere near that much seniority. A number of them had doubted he could do it, doubted that he was truly the hero out of legend, but even though Geary privately shared those doubts, he'd known that he had to try.

And so far he'd done what seemed impossible. He'd brought the Alliance fleet back through Syndic space, a long, fighting retreat using every skill he'd learned a century ago, kills lost to the fleet in the decades of bloodbath the war had become after *Merlon*'s destruction.

His eyes went to the star display floating over the table in his stateroom. He'd left it active when he went to sleep, centered on the star Dilawa. Still inside Syndic space, but only three more jumps away from reaching safety in Alliance space. He was so close to saving those who had believed he could save them. But the fleet was still inside enemy territory, still had to fight its way past the Syndic flotilla that would surely be waiting at the end of one of those jumps, and the loss of the *Merlon* had come back to haunt him.

Geary exhaled wearily, then dug in a drawer for a ration bar. He eyed the bar dubiously. Like most of the food left in the fleet, the bar had come from Syndic stockpiles abandoned in place when marginal star systems had been deserted after the introduction of the hypernet. It was food even the Syndics didn't think worth hauling away. While no doubt long past its expiration date, the bar and the other food they'd picked up had been frozen in airless vacuum since abandonment and technically remained edible.

The bar had a propaganda wrapper featuring impossibly heroic-looking Syndic ground troops marching from left to right. He tore the wrapper open, trying to avoid reading the ingredients, then started biting off and swallowing chunks of it. Despite his best efforts to avoid tasting the thing, he still ended up wincing at the flavor. Sailors in the Alliance fleet often complained about the food they got, but one of the few virtues of these Syndic supplies was that (aside from keeping you alive) they also made the Alliance rations taste wonderful by comparison.

And, as the ancient joke went, not only was the food terrible but there wasn't enough of it. The bar sat like a lead ball in Geary's stomach, but that wasn't why he didn't get another. A fleet cut off from resupply and trapped in enemy territory had to get by on short rations. He wouldn't eat better than his sailors. Though considering the quality of the Syndic food, "better" probably wasn't the right term.

His comm panel buzzed urgently, and Geary hit the acknowledge button.

"Captain Geary, enemy ships have arrived at the jump point from Cavalos."

He slapped another control, and the star display winked out, to be replaced with a display showing just the Dilawa Star System and the ships within it. There hadn't been much in the way of Syndicate Worlds' warships left in the Cavalos Star System when the Alliance fleet departed, unless you counted the wreckage of the Syndic warships that orbited Cavalos in slowly spreading clouds of debris.

But there were plenty more Syndic warships hunting Geary's fleet, and the Alliance fleet was increasingly feeling the strain of the long retreat through Syndic space. Not all of the wreckage left at Cavalos had belonged to Syndic warships. The Alliance battle cruiser *Opportune*, the scout battleship *Braveheart*, and nine Alliance cruisers and destroyers had also been lost in the battle there, some torn apart in the battle and some blown to pieces on Geary's orders because they had been too badly damaged to keep up with the retreating fleet.

The pressure was wearing on him as well. His mind kept dwelling on the losses suffered thus far by the Alliance fleet, which was probably why he was getting post-traumatic-stress flashbacks again.

With an effort, he focused on what was happening now. "Only one HuK and two nickel corvettes," Geary commented.

"That's right," Captain Desjani replied, her image popping up next to the display. She was on the bridge, of course, watching over her ship. "Too bad they're almost three light-hours away. *Dauntless*'s hell-lance crews would enjoy the target practice."

"Not that your hell-lance crews need target practice, Tanya," Geary agreed, his remark earning him a proud grin from Desjani. As she'd noted, the jump point was three light-hours distant from where the Alliance fleet was located deeper inside the star system, which meant the images he was seeing of the Syndic warships were three hours old. "No one's following them in. They must be scouts."

"Agreed. We expect to see one of the nickels brake to stay near the jump point. The other nickel and the Hunter-Killer should accelerate toward the jump points for Kalixa and Heradao." She paused. "This is the first time I've seen a nickel corvette outside a Syndic-occupied star system. Those things are so obsolete I'm surprised they risk them in jump space."

So obsolete, in fact, that nickel corvettes had been operating a hundred years ago, back when they'd been given that nickname by the Alliance because they were seen as cheap and easily expended in battle. Back when the war began. Images from his flashback returned, of nickel corvettes making firing runs on *Merlon*.

"Sir?" Desjani asked.

Geary shook his head, startled to realize he'd let his mind drift like that. "Sorry."

Only Geary might have been able to see the concern in the look Desjani gave him, but she went on speaking as if everything was routine. "The first nickel corvette may jump back for Cavalos in a little while to let them know we're still here." Her expression shifted, now professionally unrevealing. "Since we are still here."

"We need everything we can salvage from the materiel the Syndics left behind when they pulled the last people out of this star system decades ago," Geary replied, trying not to speak angrily in response to Desjani's prodding.

"We've lifted all of the abandoned food already." Desjani made a face. "If I can use the term 'food' loosely. The fleet is still going to have to reduce rations again to stretch out what food we've got left." She shrugged. "That's one good thing about the slop we're getting from the cast-off Syndic stockpiles. No one really wants to eat a lot of it, so shortening the rations doesn't bother the crews as much as it would if the food were edible."

"I guess there's a bright side to everything." Geary smiled briefly as he rechecked the information on the raw minerals being loaded into the bunkers on the fleet's auxiliaries, then realized that Desjani had first made her point about the need for the fleet to move and then deliberately changed the subject to defuse his resentment.

I shouldn't be angry. It's a legitimate concern for every commanding officer in this fleet. When are we leaving Dilawa, and where are we going? We've been here for almost a day and a half, and that's probably at least one day too long.

There weren't any good reasons for staying at Dilawa. A star without any habitable worlds orbiting it, Dilawa had once boasted only a small human presence, perhaps several thousand judging from the facilities the Syndics had left behind. Those humans had been here because the old faster-than-light system jump drives could only take ships from star to nearby star, requiring ships to pass through every star system on the way to their objectives. The hypernet had changed that, allowing ships to go from any gate in the net directly to any other gate, leaving the human presence in many unexceptional star systems to dwindle gradually as the interstellar traffic bypassed them.

But those old jump drives were getting his fleet home, one star system at a time, and the hypernet had proved to be a threat to the very existence of humanity. *Dauntless* was also carrying a Syndic hypernet key, which could provide a decisive advantage to the Alliance if it could be safely delivered into Alliance space. If he didn't get the fleet home, that key and the knowledge of the threat posed by the hypernet would be lost along with the warships and their crews. The costs of failure seemed higher every time he thought about them. "Let me know if anything changes," he asked Desjani.

"Yes, sir." Desjani's image disappeared, but not before her expression and her tone somehow conveyed the message that something needed to be changing and wasn't.

He sat there, the star display centered on Dilawa once again floating above the table before him. No matter how long he stared at it, though, the display refused to perform like a crystal ball and offer answers from its depths to the questions he had to resolve.

Primarily, where to go from Dilawa.

Just make up your mind, Geary told himself. He'd done it many times already during the fleet's long retreat through enemy space. It shouldn't have been that hard a decision. There weren't that many jumps left before the fleet reached a Syndicate Worlds' border star system from which it could jump back to Alliance space. It should be easy, with safety so close. Instead it felt harder every time he approached the decision. He kept hesitating, each possible choice running hard into visions of what had gone wrong at Lakota and the losses suffered at Cavalos. And now memories from the destruction of *Merlon* were adding to the mix.

He'd considered asking Victoria Rione, Co-President of the Callas Republic and a member of the Alliance Senate, for her opinion. But the Alliance politician had refused to offer advice of that nature for some time. Outwardly, Rione claimed it was because she'd been wrong so many times in what she wanted the fleet to do. If there was another agenda driving Rione in the matter, he wasn't sure what it was. Though for a while they'd been off-and-on lovers in the physical sense, Rione had kept much of herself hidden from him even during that phase of their relationship, before they both ended it.

In any event, he'd seen little of her in the last couple of days. "I need to concentrate on employing my in for mants throughout this fleet," she'd told him. "We need to find which Alliance officers have escalated their opposition to your command of the fleet to the point of employing malicious worms in the fleet's operating systems." Since those worms had once nearly caused the destruction of some of the fleet's ships, Geary couldn't argue with her priorities.

There were others he could ask. Intelligent, reliable, and thoughtful officers like Captain Duellos of the *Courageous*, Captain Tulev of the *Leviathan*, and Captain Cresida of the *Furious*.

But Geary sat alone and eyed his star display, feeling a strange reluctance to seek advice, despite knowing that further delay could be fatal.

His hatch alert chimed, identifying the person seeking entry as Captain Desjani. He authorized entry, wondering what could have brought her here. Given the widespread rumors about his being involved with Desjani, she didn't come to his stateroom very often.

The truth was that they were involved, though neither would, in any way, speak of or act on the feelings they hadn't sought. Not while he was fleet commander and she was in his chain of command.

"Has something happened?" he asked.

Desjani nodded toward the star display. "I wanted to talk with you privately about your future operational plans, sir."

That should have been welcome, because he knew how well Desjani could handle a tactical situation, but this was an operational decision. Or so Geary told himself, wondering why he was reluctant to hear what she had to say. But how could he put her off? Admitting uncertainty would only justify Desjani's request to discuss the matter. "All right."

She walked in, seeming unusually distant, then stood before the star display, not directly facing Geary. "You seemed a little off earlier, sir."

"Bad dream." Desjani looked his way with a wordless question, and Geary shrugged. "About my old ship, and waking up and everything."

"Oh." Desjani's eyes went back to the star display. "We were so caught up in finding you that we didn't realize how badly shaken you were. I've often wished we'd handled it differently, telling you how long it had been, the fate of your crew. I must have sounded very callous."

"I don't think there was any good way to tell me all of that, and no, you didn't strike me as callous. It was obvious you knew I had to be told, and no one else was going to do it."

"Certainly not Admiral Bloch," Desjani agreed. "I've often wondered what your first impressions of me were."

He grimaced, trying to remember. "I wasn't thinking clearly at all. There was so much. I remember wondering how you could possibly have accumulated so many battle ribbons. And the Fleet Cross. How did you earn that, anyway?"

Desjani sighed. "At Fingal. I was just a lieutenant on the old *Buckler*. We'd fought until the ship was a wreck, and the Syndics boarded."

"What did you do?"

"I helped fight them off." Her gaze lifted, focused somewhere else.

"Any actions worthy of the Fleet Cross must have been a great deal more than 'helped fight them off,' " Geary commented.

"I did my duty." She fell silent for a moment.

Geary respected Desjani's right to tell that story where and when she wanted. There might be a lot of trauma behind the events that had led to the medal. He watched her, surprised by the topics she'd brought up. "Did you come down here just to talk about those things?"

"Not just that." She paused and took a deep breath. "I'm aware that you don't usually discuss your plans in advance," Desjani began in much more formal tones.

"Sometimes I do," Geary admitted.

She waited, but when he didn't say anything else, didn't offer his thoughts on what he intended, Desjani's brow lowered slightly. Her voice still didn't betray any emotion, however. "I've been reviewing the information we have on Syndic star systems we can reach from Dilawa. I assume you intend going to Heradao Star System, but you haven't yet communicated that intention even though the fleet needs to leave this star system."

If he'd heard right, that was one of the closest things to a rebuke that he'd ever gotten from Desjani. Geary frowned a bit. "I haven't decided on our next destination." There. He'd said it.

Desjani waited again for him to elaborate, then spoke firmly. "The other star systems accessible from here are back to Cavalos, which wouldn't accomplish anything but getting us farther from home, Topira, which leads down and back into Syndic space, Jundeen, which is isolated and would offer no destinations within jump range except back here, and Kalixa, which has a Syndic hypernet gate. Heradao is the only reasonable objective given the threat posed by that hypernet gate at Kalixa and the lack of advantages in going to Cavalos, Topira, or Jundeen."

"I'm already aware of the situations in all of the star systems we can reach from here," Geary replied. "Is there anything else?"

She gave him a hard look, apparently ignoring his implied dismissal. "Some of the Syndic records we captured at Sancere indicate there are Alliance prisoners of war in a labor camp at Heradao."

"I'm aware of that as well."

"Captain Geary," Desjani said in a low voice, "I am a fleet officer and the commanding officer of your flagship, and both of those positions require that I communicate my opinions and advice when I deem it necessary."

Geary nodded. "I don't deny that. You've given me your opinion. Thank you. There are a lot of other factors for me to consider."

"Such as?"

He stared at her, startled by the abrupt question. "I'm still ... formulating them in my own mind."

"Perhaps I can help."

A wall of resistance rose in Geary, though he didn't understand why. "I appreciate the offer, but I'm not ready to discuss options yet. There are advantages and disadvantages to all possible star systems we can reach from here."

"Captain Geary, it's not like you to avoid making a decision."

His frown returned, deeper this time. "I'm not avoiding making a decision, and this conversation isn't helping things. Is there anything else?" he repeated.

"What about the Alliance prisoners of war at Heradao?" Desjani asked, her tone getting more clipped.

"For one thing," Geary replied, getting aggravated himself, "we don't know that they're still at Heradao. The Syndic records we've acquired are all old. That POW camp might have been relocated a long time ago. For another thing, the Syndics will know that the presence of Alliance POWs in the system will increase the chance that this fleet will go there, and that means they could be laying a trap in Heradao right now."

Desjani stood silently, her breathing unusually controlled, then finally spoke. "How would the Syndics know that we knew a POW camp was at Heradao? They don't know what Syndic records we've picked up."

That was a legitimate question, but for some reason it made Geary even more irritated. "You know full well that I'm willing to take reasonable risks to rescue Alliance POWs."

"Yes, sir."

No matter the literal meaning of the words, Geary had learned that a simple *yes, sir* from Desjani meant that she was unhappy, that she was disagreeing with something. "I'm not at all certain that the advantages of going to Heradao outweigh the risks," Geary added, growing aggravation giving extra warmth to his words.

"Sir, I must *respectfully* point out that there are risks no matter where we go, and the longer we linger here, the worse those risks will become."

Geary heard her tone and felt his jaw tighten. "And I must *respectfully* point out that I, not you, have responsibility for the survival of this fleet."

"I'll try to keep that in mind, sir," Desjani stated crisply.

Geary glowered at her. "You know, that sort of attitude and this conversation aren't exactly making my life easier."

She turned slightly to face Geary and glowered right back. "Not to be too blunt about it, but at the moment the question of how easy your life happens to be is rather far down the list of priorities. That's true of a ship's commanding officer, and it's even more true of the fleet commander. I repeat that I have a duty to give the best advice I can to the commander of this fleet, and I will damned well do so even if he chooses to disregard it."

"Fine." Geary made a sharp wave at the star display. "What's your advice?"

"I told you. Go to Heradao."

"And I told you that I've already considered that."

She waited for him to continue, then shook her head. "You're afraid. I've seen it growing since Lakota and Cavalos."

Geary stared at Desjani, shocked to hear those words from her. "Is that advice supposed to be helping me? Why are you talking like Numos or Faresa?"

Desjani's face reddened alarmingly. "Don't you dare compare me to those individuals! *Sir.*"

Geary tamped down his own temper and swallowed a biting response. She had a right to be upset. He never should have even implied Desjani was like those two officers. She wasn't political, she'd never questioned his status as commander of the fleet, and she was a fine commanding officer of her ship. All of which made her totally different from under-arrest Captain Numos and now-dead Captain Faresa. "My apologies," Geary said in a stiffly proper voice. "Why did you accuse me of being afraid?"

"I didn't *accuse* you." Desjani made a visible effort to control her own anger. "I'm not trying to establish which of us was conceived with the bigger gonads. But in talking with you and observing you, I have seen subtle changes, which have increased since Cavalos." She nodded abruptly toward the star display. "Ever since assuming command of this fleet, you've used a mix of cautious and bold actions to keep the enemy off-balance and win victories. I think you depend on your instincts for when to proceed boldly or cautiously, because neither I nor anyone else has been able to identify a pattern. But I can see a pattern now in you, and it tells me that you're afraid."

If anyone but Desjani were telling him this... If Rione were saying it, or one of his known opponents in the fleet... But it was Desjani. He'd had no firmer ally than her, no more reliable and capable supporter since assuming command of the fleet. She believed in him, originally because Desjani was one of those who thought the living stars themselves had sent him back to save the fleet and the Alliance, but now also because of what she said she'd seen in him. If he didn't listen to Desjani, he'd be a fool. Geary took a couple of calming breaths. "What pattern?"

She seemed to have calmed as well, speaking determinedly but without heat. "I've tried to see things through your eyes as the fleet commander. In the Syndic home star system and afterward, the odds of this fleet getting home seemed very small. Risks were easier to take because every possible course of action held serious threats. Caution often didn't make sense because boldness was necessary, and the obvious result of too much caution would have been the destruction of the fleet. But we're close to home now." She pointed at the representation of Dilawa, then swung her hand to indicate Alliance space. "So close. And now risks *seem* more dangerous, because we've made it this far, against all odds, and you're looking at that and the small distance left to Alliance space and thinking how awful it would be to get the fleet this close and have it destroyed *now* because you made a serious error."

"I have made serious errors," Geary stated heavily. "Such as taking this fleet to Lakota—"

"Which was a calculated risk, and in the end it worked! And taking us to Cavalos was a risk because we might encounter the Syndics there, and we did meet them, and we beat them." Desjani clenched one fist and kept her eyes fixed on his. "The losses we took at Lakota and Cavalos were the worst since you assumed command. That wasn't your fault. Any other commander I know of would have lost a lot more ships in those battles, and would have

32

lost the battles for that matter. Those losses weren't in vain. We've hurt the Syndics badly, and we're close to home."

The words finally came out from deep inside him. "The ships we lost at Lakota and Cavalos won't reach home, and neither will most of their crews."

"They died so their comrades would make it! Don't negate their sacrifices by becoming so fearful of more losses that you end up losing all! The time for risks is not past. I can understand how you fear failing now, after bringing the fleet this far, but we are still in enemy territory, and excess caution carries a great danger in itself. You can't win unless you try to win, but you can lose by trying not to lose."

She had a point. Had fear of failure after succeeding this far caused him to shy away from the sorts of risks he knew had to be taken to win, to survive? Geary gazed at the star display, trying to sort out his feelings and his thinking. "Do I follow my instincts or not?" he finally said, as much to himself as to Desjani.

"What are your instincts actually telling you?" she asked.

"The consequences of getting caught in a bad position again—"

"Those are your *fears*. What are you instincts saying?"

Geary met her eyes again, realizing she was right. "Heradao."

"Then follow them," Desjani urged.

He exhaled heavily, pointing to where the fleet's status was displayed. "Dammit, Tanya, you know the state of the fleet as well as I do. We've only got twenty battleships left, even if we count in *Orion*, and *Orion* appears determined to see how long it can possibly take to repair battle damage. There are only sixteen battle cruisers remaining in the fleet, and of those, *Courageous, Incredible,*

Illustrious, and *Brilliant* are barely combat-capable after the damage they sustained at Cavalos. The scout battleship division is down to one surviving ship, there are exactly forty-one specter missiles and fifteen mines left in the entire fleet, and every cruiser and destroyer in the fleet has at least one weapons system jury-rigged to keep functioning despite battle damage. *And* fuel-cell reserves on the fleet's warships are down to an average of only fifty-two percent. That's no way to go into a battle."

Instead of answering immediately, Desjani reached over and highlighted the status of the four fleet auxiliaries. "I know you've already checked this. *Goblin*, *Jinn*, *Witch*, and *Titan* are working all out to manufacture what this fleet needs to keep going. But from the beginning their efforts haven't been enough to gain ground on our logistics situation while we were facing constant threats inside Syndic territory. Even with all the risks we've taken to keep those auxiliaries supplied with the raw materials they need, they simply don't have the manufacturing capacity to keep up with this fleet's combat consumption of fuel cells and expendable weaponry. Not with all of the maneuvering that your tactics demand."

He couldn't deny that. "You're right. I've already checked that."

"So you already know that, until we get back to Alliance space, it's not going to get better." Desjani hammered home. "The fuel-cell situation is at the point where the auxiliaries have to devote everything they can to making new ones, meaning they can't manufacture new missiles. They can give us new grapeshot, and stocks of that are rising to acceptable levels right now. But the missile and mine situation will not improve, and until we make it home, we're going to keep using fuel cells faster than we can make them. There won't be a better time to fight the Syndics than Heradao. We're low on everything, and we do have accumulated battle damage, but they've taken terrible losses. Given time, the enemy will recover faster than we can inside their own territory."

He looked at the star display again, his eyes going from Heradao across the light-years to Alliance space.

Desjani watched him for a few moments, then spoke again, her voice softer. "You're also worried about what happens when the fleet gets home, aren't you?"

Geary shifted his gaze, his eyes locking on her again, as Desjani continued.

"You're worried about facing a place you knew as home a hundred years ago and all the changes since then." Desjani nodded toward the region of Alliance space. "Most importantly, you're much more worried about what most of this fleet expects you to do once we get home."

Did he have no secrets from this woman? Had he ever actually discussed those things with her in those terms? Geary shook his head, though not in denial of her words. "I won't do it, Tanya. I don't care if most of the fleet, and most of the citizens of the Alliance for that matter, want the great, legendary Black Jack Geary to ride in on a white horse and toss out the elected leaders of the Alliance. I won't destroy what makes the Alliance worth fighting for in the name of defending the Alliance. But a lot of people are expecting that; some of those people will probably try to force my hand, and I have no idea how to deal with that."

"Yes, you do." Desjani's gaze held his. "You already know what you *won't* do. You have a strategic goal, to preserve what makes the

Alliance worth fighting for and to end this war. Consider ways to implement that strategy, and the tactics will follow."

"It's not that easy—"

"Not if you try to do it alone! Ask for advice! Is there no one you trust in this fleet except the politician?"

That made Geary look away for a moment. Just as Rione had long since stopped using Desjani's name, Desjani herself had started referring to Co-President Rione only as "the politician." On one level, the job description was true enough, but politicians were also despised by a fleet that, after a century of war, had come to blame them for the failure to achieve victory. "Do you want to know why I haven't asked you for advice on that?" he asked.

"It might be a refreshing change of pace for you to tell me."

Damn. What had gotten into Desjani? Geary met her eyes once more. "Because I'm afraid you'll agree to whatever I say, that you'll break your own oath and follow me no matter what I do, because you believe that the living stars sent me to this fleet and are guiding me."

Desjani nodded, her expression resolute. "Yes, I would follow you." As Geary openly winced, she held out a forestalling hand. "Because I *know* you were sent to this fleet with a divine mission and that you do benefit from special guidance. Because of that, I also *know* that you will not do something that you have sworn not to do. I know you will not destroy the Alliance, and therefore I know I can follow you and help you, *if you will let me.* There are others who will help you figure out a course of action if you confide in us, and I'm sure you know who they are. Give us credit for loving the Alliance as much as you. I admit that at one time I could have been talked into accepting a military coup, but not now, not after the things of which you've reminded us all. Our own attempts to match Syndic brutality have only served to convince the Syndic populace of the need to keep fighting hard against us, and there wouldn't be much point in winning if victory meant becoming the mirror image of our enemies. But like the problems with the Syndics, political problems within this fleet and at home will not get better if you defer dealing with them."

A host of retorts and rebuttals came to Geary, but he knew every single one of them would either deny what he knew to be the truth or avoid the real issues. He sat staring at the stars once more as the fragments of what he knew and what Desjani had said fell into place inside his own mind, forming a picture he recognized as accurate, then he finally nodded. "Thank you. You're right. About everything. I've been avoiding a decision. I was seeing it all, but I wouldn't put it together because I was haunted by the thought of losing this fleet on the threshold of safety and because I was letting worries about what would happen when we got home further paralyze me."

Desjani grinned, the tension having suddenly fled from her. "We're going to Heradao?"

"Yes, Tanya, we're going to Heradao. We're going to get those Alliance prisoners of war, if they're still there, and we're going to defeat what ever force the Syndics might have gathered at Heradao. And I'm going to work on that strategy for when we reach Alliance space."

"You can ask Captain Duellos, Captain Tulev—"

"And you," Geary interrupted her list. "It seems you're a very important part of my 'special guidance.'" Desjani actually flushed slightly at the praise. "I wouldn't have reached these decisions on my own, and I've been avoiding anyone who would make me confront that. I needed you to push me into it because you know me a lot better than I realized you did and because you're a tough enough bitch to make me see what I was doing."

She smiled wider. "This tough bitch has had to deal with a lot of difficult sons of bitches in her time. You're one of the more reasonable ones. Sir."

"Thank you." He hesitated. "Tanya, none of the other senior officers in the fleet seems to have picked up on what was bothering me."

"You never openly spoke of your growing caution. Knowing you well, from all the talks we've had, from all of the experiences we've described to each other, did make a difference. But from watching you I also knew that you were smart enough to realize how important advice from others can be. The fact that you were recently working to avoid such advice told me something, too."

"I guess I need to thank my ancestors that you're the captain of my flagship. Thank them again, I mean."

One corner of Desjani's mouth curled up in a half smile. "I'll take that as a professional compliment. Now, by your leave, sir, I have other matters to attend to, and you need to formulate the orders for the fleet's movement to Heradao."

"Certainly, Captain Desjani." He wrenched his eyes away from her smile and his mind away from wondering how her lips would feel against his. That wouldn't happen, not while he was in command of the fleet, not while this war lasted. She'd earned his respect countless times, and even if he'd failed to maintain proper professional feelings toward her, he could still be sure to grant her that respect in both public and private. So Geary simply stood up and returned her salute.

But she paused just before leaving and looked back at him. "I hope you don't take adversely anything I said, sir. I did feel obligated to speak honestly and forcefully."

"Thank you, Captain Desjani. I hope you will continue to speak with as much honesty and force whenever you feel it is appropriate, and I will listen when you do so. I've been told that I am one of the more reasonable sons of bitches in the fleet."

"That's probably true, sir, but don't let it go to your head."

He managed not to laugh until the hatch had closed behind her.

2

The fleet conference room on *Dauntless* wasn't all that large, and the table and seats it boasted could have held no more than a dozen people at the most. But the virtual conferencing software made the apparent size of the table and the compartment expand to accommodate the numbers of people in any meeting, so that Geary stood at the head of an extremely long table with hundreds of officers seated around it. Aside from him, Captain Desjani, and Co-President Rione, none of the other individuals were actually physically present. As much as he disliked fleet conferences, Geary had to admit the software was an impressive piece of work, and the fact that most of those "present" weren't actually here had kept anyone from going for anyone else's throat during arguments in the past.

Unfortunately, there didn't seem much chance of open argument this time. As much as he had disliked bandying words with the likes of Numos or Casia or Midea, at least the straightforward hostility of their attitudes had made it clear who needed to be watched. He would have welcomed that now, as a chance to identify the remaining opposition to his command of the fleet. But whoever was driving that effort seemed to have expended most of their human shields yet was remaining frustratingly hidden. If the only threat they posed was to his command, he wouldn't have expended much worry on them since after the second battle of Lakota his standing with the sailors and most of the officers of the fleet was as firm as hull armor, but his hidden foes had repeatedly demonstrated a willingness to endanger some of the fleet's warships in their attempts to strike at Geary. The game had shifted from trying to topple him to trying to assassinate him and his firmest supporters, which, in practice, meant trying to destroy the ships they were on.

Geary called up the star display over the conference table. "My apologies for the delay in communicating my intentions. We've stripped Dilawa of everything of use to us. I've already ordered the fleet onto a course for the jump point for Heradao." On the display, the projected path of the Alliance fleet curved in a graceful arc through the empty reaches of Dilawa Star System. "We hope to find that the Alliance prisoners of war are still at Heradao, in which case we'll liberate them."

"We need to liberate more food along with them," Captain Tulev stated bluntly. "What we have is inadequate."

Commander Neeson of *Implacable* shook his head. "We can't loot enough unless we occupy a planetary-surface ware house district, and that's beyond our Marines' capability. We also can't trust any food the Syndics give us under duress, and we can't test it all thoroughly."

"Two thousand prisoners at Heradao according to the old records we have," Tulev pointed out. "We must liberate them, I agree. Physically, we can hold them. Some of our ships are still slightly understrength from battle casualties even with the survivors we've picked up from ships we've lost, and the others can take on extra personnel for the time needed to reach Alliance space. But the food situation is growing critical."

"You mean like the fuel situation?" Captain Armus of the *Colossus* grumbled.

Geary held up a hand to quiet everyone. "We're short on everything. However the logistics systems project that even if we pick up two thousand liberated Alliance personnel, we'll be able to make Alliance space without running out of food, though rations will have to be reduced again."

"And if we're delayed?" Tulev asked.

"We can't afford any more delays," Geary replied. "Fuel and food are at critical levels, and the only source we can count on for resupply is back in Alliance home space. We're going to keep moving and fighting. We've had to be very concerned with keeping the Syndics guessing as to our route home, but from this point on we're heading straight there." Relieved smiles appeared on many faces as Geary shifted the scale on the star display, but then the smiles faded on most faces.

Armus put the worry into words. "A direct route increases the chances of running into Syndic blocking forces. How can we fight through those forces if we're low on fuel?"

Pray to our ancestors for a miracle occurred to Geary as an answer, but hoping for divine intervention wasn't a sound basis for tactical planning. "By fighting as smart as we can to minimize fuel-cell usage. If necessary, we'll try to blow past the blocking forces and leave them in our wake." That intelligent and reasonable idea drew grimaces around the table. It was too contrary to the primitive concepts of honor and courage that had controlled the fleet's actions for at least a generation and led to horrendous losses as well. But Geary had gained enough experience with those attitudes to know how to satisfy them. "We can always come back and destroy those Syndic ships once we've refueled, or leave them for the Alliance warships that have been defending our home space in our absence and deserve an opportunity to get in their own blows."

The grimaces lightened, and some smiles reappeared as Geary continued.

"There's a strong possibility that what ever the Syndics have left to try to stop us will be waiting at Heradao, because it's a straight shot back home for us. If a Syndic flotilla is at Heradao, we *will* fight them there because our fuel stocks will be as good as they're going to be until we get home."

He glanced at Captain Desjani, who betrayed no sign that Geary was practically quoting her own advice. *I can't afford to feed rumors of favoritism toward Desjani now, but once this is over, I'll make sure that she and people like her get the credit they deserve.* Outwardly, Geary just indicated a bright white star. "After Heradao we'll go on to Padronis, and from there to Atalia."

A sigh seemed to run around the table as Captain Badaya of *Illustrious* spoke the thoughts probably on everyone's mind. "And Atalia is within jump range of Varandal."

"Right," Geary agreed. "Alliance home space, and the biggest concentration of fleet support facilities in the region. Once we reach Varandal, we can get all of the supplies we need."

"Boldness is certainly called for," Captain Caligo of the battle cruiser *Brilliant* agreed. "The Alliance needs us and every Alliance prisoner of war we can liberate from within Syndic territory."

That unobjectionable statement drew nods of agreement as Geary took a moment to look at Caligo. He'd been mostly silent at these meetings until recently, but had begun speaking up. Not that Caligo had yet said anything exceptional, just things that found concurrence with almost everyone.

"Our intelligence personnel believe the Syndic mine inventories must still be very low after all of the mines they laid in the star systems around Lakota to try trapping us," Geary continued. "We'll still do a preprogrammed evasive maneuver upon arrival at Heradao and be ready for combat coming out of the jump exit. Are there any questions?"

"What about Kalixa?" Captain Kila asked. "It's on the way home, too, and it has a Syndic hypernet gate." Her tone seemed to be intended to be mild but was still sharp. Diplomacy definitely wasn't Kila's strong suit, but then he already knew that.

"We're not going to Kalixa," Geary replied. "The risks posed by a Syndic hypernet gate are too great."

Kila pretended puzzlement. "Are risks a problem for this fleet? We're not afraid of what the Syndics can do, Captain Geary, but this would be a good opportunity to inflict more damage on them by eliminating another star system of theirs."

Commander Neeson sounded incredulous. "Excuse me, Captain

Kila, but you were at Lakota with us, weren't you? Our own fleet could have been destroyed."

"It wasn't," Kila pointed out. "Avoiding actions out of exaggerated fears of the enemy response isn't what's expected of any commander in this fleet, let alone a battle cruiser commander."

Neeson's face flushed with sudden anger. "Are you accusing me of cowardice?"

"Quiet," Geary ordered. "Everyone. Captain Kila, your statement was out of line."

She shrugged. "I didn't mean offense, merely to point out—"

"That's enough." He could see the flare of defiance in Kila's eyes as he cut her off. "Commander Neeson has demonstrated his courage many times. I will not tolerate attempts to question the abilities or the bravery of anyone in this fleet without good cause."

Captain Cresida, who had clearly been waiting for an opening, jumped in. "Commander Neeson is also right. The energy discharge when the hypernet gate at Lakota collapsed was on the low end of the theoretical range. I'll remind Captain Kila that the high end runs up to a novascale burst of energy. No ship in the same star system could possibly survive that even if located as far as possible from the gate when it collapsed."

"In *theory*," Kila replied sarcastically. "We didn't see anything like that at either Sancere or Lakota, so perhaps the *theory* is wrong, and the gates may be safely used by us as weapons to eliminate Syndic star systems and finally make them pay in full for what they've done in this war!"

"That statement," Cresida returned with growing heat, "reflects a total misunderstanding of what is known about the hypernet gates and the data we collected at both Sancere and Lakota!"

"That's enough." Geary broke in again. "Captain Cresida is right. We don't need to debate the science here. Captain Kila, I recommend you familiarize yourself with what is known before you make suggestions for courses of action." Kila reddened at the barely veiled rebuke.

Daring's captain nodded. "As for being able to ride out taking down a hypernet gate, we all saw what happened to the Syndic warships that took down their own gate at Lakota."

"Our ships—" Kila began.

"At Sancere my ship was right up there while it was collapsing, and *Inspire* was a long ways distant! I know exactly what it's like to be near a collapsing hypernet gate, and I don't want any part of that again no matter what you say. Only luck and the living stars saved us at Sancere and Lakota."

"Luck, courage, and brains," Geary added. "As long as this fleet continues to use the last two, we can save the first for emergencies. And as for using the hypernet gates to destroy enemy star systems, I've already stated that I will not order such an action. Neither the living stars nor our ancestors could possibly approve of such an atrocity and on such a scale."

"It appears," Captain Duellos observed, "that there's no reason to go to Kalixa then."

Kila shot him an ugly look as Captain Caligo chimed in once more. "We're one fleet. We all believe in the same things. Arguments like this only serve the goals of the enemy by driving us apart."

That brought many more nods of approval. Geary couldn't find fault with Caligo's words, either, and for some reason they even shut up Kila, who finally subsided.

"Are there any other questions?" Geary asked dryly.

There weren't, and the meeting ended in a flurry of images vanishing and the room apparently shrinking back to normal dimensions again.

Captain Duellos lingered for a moment. "I have to confess I was starting to wonder why we hadn't headed out of Dilawa before now."

"I needed to have my head pounded with a brick," Geary admitted.

"Ah, I see. How fortunate that you had Captain Desjani handy for that task."

Desjani gave Duellos an annoyed look. "Don't you have better things to be doing right now, Roberto?"

Duellos nodded, then smiled. "Call me if you ever need another brick, Tanya."

"I'll do that. He's got a hard head. I bet you've saved up quite a supply of bricks so they'll be handy for arguments with Kila."

"She's not worth our time," Duellos said dismissively. "I only speak with her when duty requires it."

Geary grimaced in response. "I'm just glad she shut up before I had to outright order her to do that."

"Even Kila couldn't object to what Caligo said."

"Yes, she could've," Desjani insisted. "Even the blandest statement can be twisted. I was surprised she accepted it so quietly."

Duellos pursed his lips in thought. "That's a point, but you're implying that Kila and Caligo have some sort of agreement. They don't socialize, I don't know of anyone who's even seen them together except in meetings like this one, and they're not exactly soul mates."

"I won't argue that," Desjani conceded.

"How well do you know Captain Kila?" Geary asked.

Desjani shrugged. "I've had little contact with her, but that's been by choice based on what I've heard from friends. And I've heard plenty."

"What did your friends say?"

Another shrug. "They say that Kila's bitch-switch is locked into the 'on' position and comes with a power-boost setting that activates at the slightest provocation."

Geary managed to convert his laugh into a cough. "That sounds like good justification for avoiding her."

"As well as an accurate description," Duellos observed.

"How did she make rank with a personality like that?"

Desjani gave Geary a skeptical look. "Are you serious? Her personality only comes into play with people junior in rank to her, or with peers who are rivals for promotion. As far as her superiors are concerned, she's always as fine as a micron filter."

"Oh." It had been a dumb question. He'd encountered a few people like that in his career a century ago, and somehow wars usually managed to avoid causing the loss of such individuals.

"So you can see," Duellos continued, "that Kila isn't the sort to buddy up to a bland sort of officer who can do nothing for her ambitions. Caligo is the sort of officer that Kila snacks on for fun."

"That doesn't mean they couldn't end up in bed together," Desjani pointed out.

"Ouch." Duellos made a pained face. "I know you meant it

metaphorically, but now I have that image in my head. Oh, please, make it go away. By your leave, Captain Geary, I have to go take a shower."

After watching Duellos's image vanish, Geary shook his head at Desjani. "I'm glad you two are on my side." He held up a hand as Rione started to leave. "Can you wait a moment, Madam Co-President?"

Rione stopped, her eyes going from Desjani to Geary. "I thought you two might want to be alone."

Desjani's eyes narrowed, and the corners of her upper lip curled to bare her teeth. "Perhaps Co-President Rione would care to repeat that to me in private?"

"I was hoping"—Geary broke in before Rione could offer Desjani her choice of weapons—"that you could let me know if you've found out anything?"

This time Rione let her gaze linger on Desjani, plainly indicating a question about her presence, but Geary just waited. He needed another set of eyes on this, another mind double-checking his own. Eventually, Rione shook her head. "What I've learned can be summed up in one word— nothing."

"Not a thing?" Geary rubbed his forehead, trying to hide his disappointment. "I know how good your spies in this fleet are, Madam Co-President. I'd hoped—"

"Since they're working on your behalf, you should call them agents, Captain Geary." Rione gestured angrily. "Whoever has been behind the most recent challenges to your command and the attempts to sabotage some of the ships of this fleet has hidden their involvement exceptionally well. They've left no trails to follow. Even

Even the interrogations you authorized of that oaf Captain Numos after the last attempts to insert worms into the operating systems of your warships produced nothing because Numos doesn't have a clue who was actually goading him on. Faresa might have had some idea, but she died at Lakota. The same is true of Falco, assuming he could have managed to separate fantasy from reality long enough to provide anything useful. Captain Casia and Commander Yin can't talk because they're dead as a result of a convenient accident. If you've been underestimating your remaining enemies in this fleet in any way, stop doing so now. Whoever they are, they're very capable and very dangerous."

"So are we," Desjani said.

Rione looked amused. "Bravado may be useful against the Syndics, but it isn't what you need against this enemy."

"We know that." Geary intervened before Desjani could fire another volley. "What about Kila? She's grown steadily more open in her dissents."

Now Rione's amusement faded to annoyance. "As your fellow officers reported and my agents confirmed, Kila is too widely disliked to have a hope of being accepted as commander of this fleet. But she's also too arrogant, and— unlike Numos— too capable, to allow herself to be used by others. Apparently this is just her normal personality asserting itself now that she's realized you won't fall for the usual ways she tries to suck up to her superiors. She never tried to seduce you, did she?"

"What?"

"There's indications it might have been one of her tactics for advancement, though that could also just be gossip fed by the general dislike for Kila among her peers. You're saying she never tried that with you?"

"No!" He could see Desjani out of the corners of his eyes, and she was looking daggers at Rione. "We haven't even physically been on the same ship!"

Rione nodded. "That might explain it, then. In any case, your reputation is such that she probably would have realized such an attempt would have been futile."

"Thanks." Rione always seemed to know how to keep him off-balance.

"But Kila wouldn't work as a human shield for those pulling the strings in these actions against you and the fleet," Rione continued. "If she were behind this, why would Kila be drawing attention to herself?"

"If my hidden foes are as smart as we think, she wouldn't be." Geary shook his head. "The systems-security people are watching for more dangerous worms but can't guarantee they know every possible back door into fleet control systems. What else can we do?"

"I don't know." Rione's frustration was easily apparent. "I understand you haven't received any more offers to become dictator."

"Not in the last few days."

"The only thing between you and being able to do that," Rione noted, "is the distance remaining to Alliance space and what ever Syndic forces are left to get past."

"And me," Geary replied. "I won't do it."

Rione gave him a weary look. "Why do you think that is a critical factor? When we reach Varandal, those who want you to seize authority from the elected leaders of the Alliance will expect you to act."

Desjani replied this time, her voice cold. "Captain Geary will not violate his oath to the Alliance, no matter how badly the politicians leading the Alliance do their jobs."

Rione ignored her, speaking pointedly just to Geary. "They won't accept your denials forever, and they know the vast majority of the fleet would support them if they acted allegedly on your behalf. They don't need your approval to launch a coup in your name. You have to expect that they will do that and try to present you with a fait accompli. You need to have a plan for how to deal with that *before* the Alliance government is overthrown."

"All right." He couldn't help noticing that Rione was essentially offering the same advice as Desjani had earlier. No way was he going to be foolish enough to mention that, though. "Do you have any suggestions on a plan?"

"If I were dealing with other politicians, it wouldn't be too hard to come up with ideas," Rione replied with an exasperated scowl. "But my grasp of the military mind is still limited."

Geary gave Desjani a sidelong glance. "Perhaps we should run with the military angle. Think of it as a military problem, a matter of strategies and tactics."

Rione's expression altered as she pondered the idea. "That might be very useful."

Unseen by her, Desjani flashed a very unmilitary smirk.

Geary tried to flick a cautioning look at Desjani, which, of course, Rione noted, and she turned slightly to watch Desjani with narrowed eyes, though too late to catch the mocking expression.

"Can you do that?" Rione asked Geary. "Explain it to them in their terms in such a way that they won't act?"

"I'm trying to, but I haven't yet thought of any argument powerful enough."

This time Rione snorted in derision. "Think in terms of disasters, because that's what a military coup would be. A very big disaster, the biggest you can bring to mind."

Desjani lifted one eyebrow toward Geary. "That sounds like a description of the results of the attack on the Syndic home system that trapped this fleet far inside enemy territory."

"That's good," Rione conceded. "Very good. Something recent enough that the memories and emotions are fresh, and something that sounded attractive but was actually a debacle that could have lost the war. Surely you can come up with something drawing on that."

Geary nodded. "I just need to figure out who the enemy is in that scenario."

Rione exhaled in exasperation. "That's the easiest part. Ask your captain, there. She'll tell you. Or ask Captain Badaya. Who's the enemy at home? I am, and every other politician. That's what they believe." Desjani nodded once, her eyes on Rione and all trace of mockery fled. "You see? Your strategy should be based on what people like Badaya already consider to be the truth. They'll be much more likely to accept it if you do that. Then you can test out your ideas on this one. She has a military mind, and you haven't got anyone more trustworthy." That praise startled both Desjani and Geary into letting their reactions show. Rione smiled, her lips a thin, tight line. "I'm neither blind nor stupid. If you don't keep that woman guarding your back, you're an idiot, Captain Geary. However, will she tell you if she doesn't think your ideas will be effective?"

Geary's mouth twisted into an ironic return smile. "I feel confident that Captain Desjani will let me know if there are any shortcomings on my part."

"Good. I don't want the government of the Alliance overthrown by anyone claiming to act in the name of the great hero whose legend the government created, and I don't want to have to deal with you if that does happen and you decide you like it." Rione turned and left, the hatch sealing behind her.

"Did she just threaten you?" Desjani asked.

"Yeah. It's not the first time, though I think it's the first time she's done it in front of someone else."

"Why do you tolerate it?"

"Because," Geary replied, his eyes on the hatch, "there are times when I wonder if I can trust myself, and at those times I'm glad to have a threat hanging over me."

Desjani considered that for a few moments. "I have to admit that she was right about a number of things. Among them that I have your back, sir."

"I know that, but you have an oath to the Alliance, too."

She shook her head. "We already discussed this. You won't violate your oath, so I won't have to violate mine. Why do you trust her?"

That was a reasonable question given that Rione was a politician, but more than that Geary had been shocked to learn that in the century of war fleet officers had developed a corrosive distrust for the elected leaders of the Alliance. So now Geary inclined his head toward the hatch through which Rione had left. "Because despite all that she has hidden from me and everyone else, I am absolutely certain that Victoria Rione deeply loves two things. The first is her husband, who we discovered may still live and be a prisoner of the Syndics somewhere, but the second is the Alliance. She'd die for the Alliance, Tanya, just like you and I would. Don't think that because she doesn't wear a uniform that isn't true. Rione is loyal to the Alliance, and I think she's as incorruptible as a person can be. She's often a royal pain in the butt, too, but we can trust her."

"One good thing about Heradao," Desjani remarked, "is that our enemies there will be easy to identify." She shrugged with an uncharacteristic air of melancholy. "Sometimes I miss the days before you were found, when the answer to everything was killing Syndics in any way we could and as fast as possible. They were the enemy. Victory would come when we'd killed enough of them. It didn't work, but it was much simpler. You've made things much more complicated."

"The Syndics are still the enemy," Geary pointed out. "As long as we stay focused on that, it shouldn't be too complicated."

"You're asking me to respect a politician," she reminded him. "That is not going to be a simple or easy thing."

He watched her for a moment, trying to understand how fleet officers like Desjani could be loyal to the Alliance yet disdain the elected leaders of the Alliance. Part of it was doubtless a very human need to find someone else to blame for the failures in the war, but Rione herself had admitted to him that the Alliance's political leaders deserved a full share of culpability for their own actions over the last hundred years. Maybe he himself was just a living anachronism in that way, an officer who believed respect was automatically due to the leaders of the Alliance and the idea of things being otherwise was simply too hard to accept. "I guess you'll just have to trust me that we can trust her."

Desjani made a contemptuous noise. "I will do my best to treat her with due respect since that is my duty as an officer and you vouch for her, but I don't ever expect to trust her." She stepped back, toward the hatch, her eyes on him. "I'll accept your judgment because I trust you."

Hundreds of warships and their crews were trusting him to get them home, the fate of the Alliance and perhaps humanity itself rested on his decisions, but it was the trust of this one woman that really mattered to him. Rione had told him once that people didn't really fight for grand causes or great purposes, but for the closest and most personal of reasons. They might say they fought for the high ideals, but in practice they fought for the comrades beside them and their loved ones at home. Geary looked back at the star display, centered on Heradao, then beyond that star to Padronis, Atalia, and finally Varandal.

So very close. They'd come so far. He'd have to make sure they made it the rest of the way no matter what awaited the fleet at Heradao.

Because a lot of people trusted him to be able to get the fleet home. And one of those people was Tanya Desjani.

He had to hold one more meeting before the fleet left Dilawa. Once in jump space, only simple and short communications could be passed between ships. There was a small and select group with whom Geary had to consult before then.

He sat in the conference room once more, but this time the table didn't seem much larger than it really was. Around it sat the images of Captains Duellos, Tulev, and Cresida, as well as the real presences of Geary, Desjani, and Rione. "We're getting close to home," Geary began. "We're not there yet, and I anticipate a nasty fight at Heradao or one of the other Syndic star systems we still have to get through. But we can feel reasonably confident of handling the Syndics. What we still don't know is how the aliens might react to this fleet's getting home."

Tulev resembled a bull as he nodded slowly and stolidly. "The aliens tried to ensure this fleet's defeat and destruction at Lakota. That argues that they will not be pleased by our making it home."

"But what will they do?" Cresida wondered. "If our speculations are right, they could trigger the collapse of every hypernet gate in human space. Will they actually do that when we get home?"

"That's one of the things I'm worried about," Geary said.

"We'll have a little time," Rione stated quietly but confidently. Everyone else gave her a questioning look, so Rione waved one hand at the star display over the table. "Consider first of all what we know of their tactics. They don't appear to have acted directly against either us or the Syndics. Instead, they've tricked us into doing harm to each other."

"True enough," Duellos agreed.

"Now, what do the aliens know about this fleet?" Rione continued. "That we have learned that the hypernet gates make extremely powerful weapons. Do these aliens have agents or sources of intelligence, even if only automated worms and 'bots, within Alliance space? We have to assume so."

"They had them threaded through the systems on our ships," Cresida noted. "Those quantum-level probability based worms. We think we found and cleared them all out, but for all we know they can activate new ones, or new ones can be triggered by certain events."

"Exactly." Rione pointed to the star display again, beyond Syndic space. "They've been watching us. They've been seeing how we act. Based on that, the aliens can reasonably conclude that when presented with the existence of such weapons, the Alliance will choose to use them."

Cresida bared her teeth. "I think you're right, Madam Co-President. They'll wait to see if we do that, if we tell our political and military superiors that the hypernet gates in Syndic star systems can be used to wipe out the Syndics. And if our political authorities then order that such actions begin. If I'd been watching the progression of this war over the last century, I'd believe it was just a matter of time before one side used those weapons and the other retaliated in kind."

"Thank you, Captain Cresida. After which," Rione said, "the aliens will sit back and watch as the Alliance begins wiping out Syndic star systems, and the Syndics respond with the same tactic. The aliens wouldn't have to lift a finger as humanity wiped itself out using weapons the aliens provided."

Geary nodded, tasting something acidic in his throat. "So they'll wait a little while to see what we do. That does give us some time."

"Not too much time, Captain Geary." Rione gazed at the star display, her expression somber. "I've been considering this in light of what we've guessed about the start of the war, that the aliens tricked the Syndics into attacking us by pretending to ally with the Syndics. But did the Syndics attack out of greed, or did the aliens tell them things that led the Syndics to believe an attack on the Alliance was a good idea?"

"What could they have told the Syndics?" Desjani demanded.

Rione gave her a look cold enough to liquefy oxygen. "Anything and everything. False intelligence that the Alliance intended to attack the Syndics, for example."

"We didn't have the forces in existence to allow that," Geary objected.

"Not as far as the Syndics knew," Rione stated sarcastically. "Why shouldn't the Syndics have been ready to believe that the Alliance was hiding forces? But the specifics don't matter. Stop focusing on that. They tricked the Syndics into attacking us. They can do that again."

"Again?" Captain Cresida leaned forward, her eyes intent. "How?"

"If we don't seem to be acting, the aliens might try to goad us into using the hypernet gates as weapons. There's a good chance that they know we're learning things, and they probably don't want to give us time to apply that knowledge. We've speculated that the aliens have a means to cause hypernet gates to collapse. A trigger signal, somehow propagating faster than the speed of light." She indicated different stars in the display, one by one. "Suppose a few hypernet gates collapse within Alliance space, one by one, destroying the star systems they served? Who would the Alliance blame?"

"Damn." Geary could hear the others softly cursing as well. "If we don't start genocidal attacks, the aliens will provoke us or the Syndics into it by making us think the other side is already doing that."

Rione's gaze seemed distant, but it was still fixed on one star far off to one side of the display, on the far-distant fringes of Alliance space. "Sol Star System has a hypernet gate," she added. "Even though it stands apart from the Alliance and remains weak from the ancient wars that raged there, old Earth abides in that star system, along with the first colonies on the other planets of Sol. The homes of our most ancient and revered ancestors, circling the star we view as the foremost symbol of the living stars. It was given a hypernet gate out of respect and to ease pilgrimages there, even though economically Sol system couldn't justify such an investment." She looked around at the others. "What if the people of the Alliance believed that the Syndics had destroyed *that* star system?"

Duellos answered, his voice unusually harsh. "Nothing would stop them, no argument would dissuade them. They'd want every Syndic dead by any means possible."

"Bloody hell." Geary wondered why most of his contributions to these discussions were curses. "All right. We can guess that we have some brief grace period after getting home in which the aliens will wait to see if humanity takes the poison bait. If we don't go for it within what ever period of time they think reasonable, the aliens will start trying to trigger what could well be humanity's last offensive. I wish I knew what they wanted or intended."

"We have no way of answering that," Rione said. "We believe we know what they've done. They seem very comfortable with placing weapons in our hands and waiting for us to use them on each other. But we don't know if they're avoiding direct actions against us as some sort of strategy or if it reflects some moral or religious aspect of their thinking."

"What could possibly be moral about that?" Cresida wondered.

"From an alien perspective? They could believe that simply providing the tools places no guilt on them as long we're the ones who pull the triggers. I don't know that, it's just a possible explanation."

"Or," Tulev stated, "it could be equally possible that it is a totally amoral strategy to ensure humanity is eliminated or contained as a threat or rival in the most efficient manner possible for these aliens. We have no way of knowing, so we must base our assumptions of future actions on what they have done in the past."

"You're right. Unfortunately, if our guesses are accurate, what they've done in the past has been very bad for us." Geary turned back to Rione. "Co-President Rione, can you put together a list of the stars with the highest symbolic importance? We'll have to make sure those star systems get the highest priority on safe-collapse systems for their hypernet gates."

"Do you think such a thing could be done? Opinions on levels of symbolic importance will vary." She eyed Geary for a long moment. "If they wish to incite a massive retaliation against the Syndics, the aliens might target the home star system of the fleet commander and legendary hero Black Jack Geary."

His breath caught, his eyes suddenly seeing not the compartment they were in or the companions with him, but the world where he'd grown up. The world where his parents and other family members were buried. Home, even though it had surely changed a lot in the century he had been in survival sleep. He imagined a shock wave hitting it like the one that had devastated Lakota Star System, instantly turning a pleasant, well-populated world into a corner of hell and a charnel house.

How could he accept a low priority for his home world? Geary's vision cleared and he looked at those with him. They all had their own home worlds. Which one did he bump down in priority for his home? Geary sighed, shaking his head. "I'm not very good at making the sorts of decisions reserved for the living stars, I'm afraid. Madam Co-President, if you could just make your best appraisal—"

"You think *I'm* qualified to play at being a deity? Or desire to do so?" Rione cut in, her voice clipped with anger.

Tulev spoke into the awkward silence that followed. "I will make the list." He gazed into the star display, his eyes distant. "I have nothing left to bias me."

The image of Duellos on one side of Tulev leaned forward, resting a hand on Tulev's wrist, while from the other side Desjani wordlessly did the same. Cresida, farther away, nodded once to him, her expression conveying understanding. Tulev nodded to each of them, then to Geary. "I'll do it," he repeated.

"Thank you, Captain Tulev," Geary said. "At some point I'm going to have to tell the fleet the aliens exist, but for now I think we should continue pretending that the danger posed by the hypernet gates is simply an unintended technological side effect."

"That's all it has to be," Cresida agreed. "If it's presented as a possibility of any hypernet gate's spontaneously collapsing at any time or subject to the Syndics causing a collapse, backed up by images of what happened at Lakota, then people will have all the reasons they need to act."

"Okay. We'll talk again before we jump for Varandal. Thank you for coming to this meeting, thank you for your advice, and thank you for your continued discretion on what we think is true about these aliens."

"If only we knew more," Cresida commented. "I'm still working on my design for a safe-fail system we can install on hypernet gates as quickly and easily as possible. I think I'll have it ready by the time we reach Atalia."

"Let's hope so." Duellos sighed. "Since we know so little of what these creatures may do or what they want."

"Feathers or lead?" Desjani asked, invoking the ancient riddle in which only the demon asking the question knew the right answer and could change it at any time. As Duellos had once pointed out, the aliens, too, were riddles in which both the answers and the questions did not just remain unknown but also reflected thought processes estranged from the humans trying to understand their purposes and meaning.

"That's my question, Captain Desjani. I'll thank you not to play demon with my riddle. Just out of curiosity, though, what was the right answer this time?"

She smiled unpleasantly. "Wouldn't you like to know? Women can be just as enigmatic as demons."

"You don't honestly think I'm going to touch that line, do you?"

As the images of Tulev, Cresida, and Duellos disappeared, Desjani frowned down at her personal data unit. "Excuse me, sir, but I'm needed in engineering." She hastened out, leaving Geary and Rione alone.

Rione, seeming uncharacteristically subdued, turned to go as well, but stopped before leaving. Standing near the hatch and still facing it, she spoke to Geary. "What happened to Captain Tulev? He said he had nothing left."

Geary nodded, recalling the personnel files he had read. "His family, wife, and children died in a Syndic bombardment of their home world."

"Oh, damn." Rione shook her head. "That's horrible, but it should've left something. Some other relatives. What world was it?"

He tried to remember. There were so many worlds. "Elys... Elysa?"

"Elyzia?"

"Yeah, that's it." Geary stared at her, bothered that the name had come so readily to her. "What happened to it?"

"Syndic bombardment," Rione murmured so low he almost didn't hear. "But prolonged, part of a very large strike at the Alliance. Most of the world's surface was devastated, the great majority of the population killed. After the Syndics were repelled, the world was written off, the survivors evacuated except for a few who insisted on staying to occupy rebuilt defensive installations, in case the Syndics ever came back. Captain Tulev spoke the literal truth. He has nothing left." She looked directly at him. "Except the fleet. Did you realize that you and he share that?"

"No." Geary searched for other words and couldn't find any.

"We retaliated at Yunren," Rione continued, as if speaking to herself. "A Syndic border star system. There's nothing left of Yunren, either, except a few defenses occupied by diehards who continue to live only for the chance to kill some of those who wiped out their world. Both sides have avoided repeating that since then, though I don't know if that's because it takes so much work to devastate an entire world or because everyone was horrified at how low we had sunk."

Geary shook his head, feeling sick inside. "How could anyone give such orders?"

"Oh, it's easy enough, Captain Geary. You just have to form your plans somewhere far from the enemy while looking at a large star display with lots of little planets on it. Just dots with strange names. Targets. Not the homes of people like you, but targets that must be wiped out in the name of protecting people like you. It's very easy," she repeated, "to rationalize the murder of millions or billions."

"That's strange," Geary commented. "I've talked to Marines. They say they have to dehumanize the individuals they kill in order to be able to fight, and they have to worry that the process will go too far and they'll kill individuals who aren't really a threat. But on the other end of the scale, the highest-ranking individuals, who'll never confront an individual enemy, have to dehumanize them by the hundreds, thousands, or millions."

She turned to look at him. "I sometimes wonder if the aliens are right, and that humanity can be counted upon to wipe itself out someday."

"I hope not. Personally viewing the events at Lakota seems to have impressed a lot of people in this fleet. There's no way to distance yourself from events when you watch a habitable planet be devastated that way by a single blow."

"It does appear to have had a strong impact. What about Captain Cresida? The way she looked at Tulev as if they shared something. Was her family from Elyzia as well?"

"No," Geary replied. "Her husband was a fleet officer. They were married about a year before he died in battle."

"How long ago was that?"

"Two years."

Rione nodded. "After ten years I still expect to see my husband sometimes. Would Captain Cresida accept condolences from me?"

"I think so. She's never spoken of it to me, but you do share that kind of loss."

Her sigh came out slow and long, like the last breath of a dying runner. "I don't know if the living stars truly arranged for you to be here now, John Geary, but there are times when I think about this war and pray desperately that they did, and that you can bring an end to this."

She left then, leaving Geary looking at the closed hatch.

3

Heradao. As the ships of the Alliance fleet flashed into existence at the jump exit from Dilawa, Geary's first thought was that only three more jumps would bring the fleet home.

His second thought was to wonder how hard it would be to get through Heradao Star System, but he'd have the answer to that soon enough. The fleet's sensors, sensitive enough to spot small objects across light-hours of distance, scanned their surroundings and rapidly updated the display before Geary.

"They're here," Desjani noted calmly, even though her eyes were lighting with enthusiasm at the prospect of combat. "But nowhere close by."

Geary kept his breathing slow and calm as enemy warships multiplied on his display in a flurry of updates. The main Syndic flotilla, arrayed in their customary box formation, was almost four light-hours away, loitering in an orbit around Heradao's star. A second and much smaller flotilla orbited a bit farther off, about five light-hours from the Alliance ships. As Desjani said, that wasn't close. Even if the main Syndic flotilla turned directly toward the Alliance fleet for an intercept, it would still be more than a day before the opposing forces got close enough to fight. "I thought we'd see more in the way of system defenses since we're getting closer to the border."

Desjani made a noncommittal gesture. "Yes and no. The warships assigned to defend this star system would have been substantially more in quality and quantity than we've been encountering deeper in Syndic space. The smaller flotilla we're seeing may be made up of those system-defense forces. But I'm not surprised to see nothing significant in the way of new fixed defenses. We're still two jumps from a Syndic star system right on the border. The border star systems get priority on defenses. I'm sure the Syndics would like to be able to place more defenses in star systems farther from the border, but they face the same constraints on resources and funds that we do." She popped up a display spanning a huge region of space, centered on the border. "That's especially true because as you get one jump in from the border, you greatly expand the number of star systems that need to be defended. Go two jumps from the border, and the number of star systems in the zone increases exponentially. It's simply too huge an area with too many star systems to disperse strong defenses across evenly."

"We assumed Kalixa would be more heavily defended," Geary agreed, "since it has a hypernet gate and is a wealthier star system than Heradao."

"Yes, and when we get to Padronis, we'll probably find nothing there because there's nothing there worth defending. Atalia will be a much harder nut to crack." Desjani made an annoyed sound, then gestured at her display. "I ran out the course to the jump point for Padronis. The Syndics are in orbits which allow them to intercept us if we head for that jump point."

Geary frowned, his mind locked on the main enemy force. Against the Alliance fleet's twenty battleships and sixteen battle cruisers, the Syndics had a flotilla containing twenty-three battleships and twenty-one battle cruisers, plus enough heavy cruisers, light cruisers, and destroyers to give them an advantage there as well. The second enemy flotilla was much lighter, consisting of an even dozen heavy cruisers and a score of light cruisers and destroyers. The coming encounter wouldn't be easy, and could be worse than Lakota and Cavalos if he screwed up. "Why are you bothered by that?" he asked Desjani. "We expected them to block us from reaching the next star system home."

"Because from where they are, they couldn't stop us from reaching the jump point for Kalixa," Desjani pointed out. "If our estimates are anywhere near accurate, then after the losses this fleet has inflicted in the last few months, the flotilla here must have almost all of the Syndics' surviving major warships. Why aren't they worried about our going to Kalixa? Its system defenses can't be *that* good."

He got it then, his frown matching hers. "Kalixa has a hypernet gate. Maybe they're planning on blowing it when we arrive." Geary couldn't keep from wincing at the idea, imagining another inhabited star system devastated or completely destroyed by a collapsing hypernet gate. It wasn't unthinkable, though, given the sort of tactics the Syndic leadership had employed in the past.

"Maybe," Desjani agreed with visible reluctance. "They're leaving us an open path there, almost as if they want us to go that way. They could follow us to Kalixa with an idea of mopping up what ever survived the hypernet gate collapse. But the Syndics know we survived the collapse of the gate at Lakota without serious damage, so they should realize that they couldn't be sure that would cripple this fleet. If it didn't hurt us badly, the flotilla here would be in a stern chase and couldn't catch us unless we deliberately lingered to wait for them. Why take that chance?"

She was thinking it through, and her questions sounded uncomfortably close to those Geary was coming up with. "What else could be at Kalixa?"

"I don't know, but if the Syndics *want* us to go there..."

"Then we don't want to go there." Had the Syndics struck a deal with the aliens? Would they let the Alliance fleet use the hypernet gate at Kalixa with the understanding that the aliens would divert the Alliance warships from their chosen goal to some location deep within Syndic territory? The fleet couldn't possibly fight its way out of some place far within Syndic-controlled space again. "What ever the explanation, our questions add up to more reasons for getting past these guys and going to Padronis instead of heading for Kalixa."

"I couldn't agree more," Desjani concurred. "Besides, I hate leaving Syndic warships in one piece. Their formation is a little unusual this time around."

"I'd noticed that." Even though the Syndic flotilla was formed into an overall box, that box was formed from five distinct subformations, one at each corner and one in the center. "Interesting."

"I wonder where they learned that," Desjani said mockingly.

"The question is whether they're actually going to try maneuvering those five subformations in dependently, or if they're just groping toward doing that and will keep the subformations slaved to their places in the box." If the Syndics did try moving each formation separately, it would probably be a fiasco on their end since such skills were hard-won by training and experience he knew the Syndics couldn't yet have gained. If they didn't move them independently, the five subformations were within supporting distance of each other, but barely.

He pulled his focus off the Syndic flotillas so he could evaluate the entire star system. "They've got pickets out." Geary indicated the jump exits for Padronis and Kalixa, where the Alliance fleet's sensors had identified Syndic Hunter-Killers. It would be several hours before any of those HuKs saw the light waves carrying images of the Alliance fleet, but once they did, some of them would surely jump to carry the news to other Syndic star systems. "No nickel corvettes this close to the border, I guess."

"I'd never seen one operational before Corvus," Desjani reminded him.

Mention of the first star the fleet had reached during its retreat from the Syndic home star system jerked Geary's mind back to that time, and his eyes went to the portion of the display showing the Alliance fleet. At Corvus he'd been appalled to see the Alliance fleet falling apart as every ship raced to engage the weak Syndic defenders. But those days were past. The Alliance fleet held its formation now, trusting to Geary's command to ensure that the Syndic flotilla would be crushed. He wondered how much small gestures like reintroducing saluting to the fleet had helped forge that discipline. Their bravery had never been in question, but now these Alliance warships fought as intelligently as they did courageously.

The field of battle where they'd be engaging the enemy this time mostly involved empty space, of course, and, for the rest, Heradao wasn't too unusual as habitable star systems went. Four planets orbited in the inner system, the closest to the star only about two light-minutes out from it in a fast orbit, as if the small world were trying to outrun the heat and radiation pummeling it. The other three inner system planets orbited about four light-minutes, seven light-minutes, and nine and a half light-minutes from the star. Given the intensity of the star Heradao, the world at seven light-minutes out had not perfect but endurable conditions for human life, and humans had taken advantage of that even though at that distance from its star the radiation bombardment was probably high enough to cause extra health problems. Cities and towns dotted the surface of that planet, and even though Heradao had been bypassed by the Syndic hypernet, that third world was apparently attractive or wealthy enough to sustain a decent population. Surprisingly for a star system bypassed by the hypernet, the cold fourth world had more human activity than had once been the case according to the old Syndic records the Alliance fleet had seized at Sancere. "Are there any indications regarding the POW camp on the third planet?"

The operations watch-stander nodded. "Yes, sir. It's still there, still occupied, and we're picking up message traffic that indicates it still holds Alliance prisoners."

"It looks like we will be visiting the third planet after we deal with these Syndic flotillas, then." The middle ranges of Heradao Star System were empty except for a few asteroids and the Syndic craft. The next planet out was a super gas giant well over three light-hours distant from the star. With all of its moons, the super gas giant resembled its own solar system, and was nearly big enough to have become a brown dwarf star itself. Apparently the giant had sucked up everything else in the outer reaches of the star system. Geary wondered if its larger moons in wide orbits had once been planets themselves before the giant captured them.

A lot of Syndic activity could be seen around the gas giant, currently orbiting on the other side of Heradao's star from the Alliance fleet, indicating substantial off-planet mining and manufacturing under way. But diverting to that gas giant to loot its mines for raw materials to fill the bunkers of the auxiliaries would take the fleet too far from the path to the jump point for Padronis.

"Do we have to fight?" Rione suddenly asked. "Can't we just race past the Syndic defenders? You've told me that velocities above point two light speed cause so much relativistic distortion that Alliance and Syndic targeting systems can't compensate well enough to reliably hit other ships. If this fleet heads for the jump point for Padronis at a high enough velocity, the Syndics won't be able to do damage to us."

"Or us to them," Desjani muttered too low for Rione to hear.

Geary thought about it, then shook his head. "It'd be too easy." Before an incredulous Rione could say anything else, he pointed at the display. "The Syndics know how badly we need to reach that jump point. They know we could try blowing past them, and they've had time to prepare for that."

"What could they have done?" Rione asked, then frowned. "Mines?"

"Yeah. Mines. Look at that small flotilla there between the main Syndic group and the jump point for Padronis. They're in a perfect position to track our trajectory past the main flotilla and plant mines along our path. If we were going fast enough that the Syndic targeting systems couldn't hit us, we'd also be going so fast that our own systems wouldn't have any chance of spotting those mines, or any others already laid along our probable tracks between the jump exit where we arrived and the jump point for Padronis. They could drop the mines right in front of us along our track in as dense a pattern as they could manage."

Desjani was frowning now. "They shouldn't have that many mines left, but they could have transferred everything from the other warships onto that small flotilla."

"If we did strike a minefield, there's no telling which ships might get hit," Geary added, "and the higher impact velocity would increase the force of the mines."

Rione stared past him for a moment, her brow furrowed in annoyance. He didn't have to say openly that *Dauntless* could be the victim of such a mine strike, and *Dauntless* had to get home. "What's your plan then?"

"I don't know yet."

"You knew we were likely to encounter the Syndics here. You must have planned something."

Geary felt a familiar headache starting, while, unseen by Rione, Desjani rolled her eyes. "Madam Co-President, I knew I'd probably find the Syndics here, but I didn't know in what strength or how they'd be positioned. Unless we found them waiting at the jump exit and had to fight right off the bat, I knew I'd have to develop a plan once I saw the situation."

"How long will that take?" Rione pressed.

"Madam Co-President, has anyone ever told you that sometimes you can be extremely demanding?"

She smiled with mock sweetness. "Thank you for the compliment. But we were talking about your plan, not me."

"I'll let you know. We've got time to think, and I won't waste that." Geary stood up and nodded to Desjani. "We'll stay on course for the jump point for Padronis. I'm going to walk around and think a bit. If you get any ideas, or the Syndics react to our presence, give me a hail."

"Yes, sir."

He gave Desjani a suspicious look, but this once "yes, sir" appeared to mean nothing but that.

Geary walked the passageways of *Dauntless*, returning salutes and greetings from the crew almost absentmindedly as he thought. The basic problem was that the Syndics had been learning and adapting to his tactics. He couldn't count on any more brainless charges straight for the center of the Alliance formation that would allow the Alliance fleet to bring to bear all of its firepower just where Geary wanted it.

There were ways around that, ways to confuse and out maneuver the Syndics, but all of those ways required more use of fuel cells. A fleet wasn't supposed to find itself in a situation where fuel-cell reserves were so low. But like many other things that weren't supposed to happen, he had to deal with that reality.

His steps took him through many passageways, across the width of the ship more than once, past living areas and hell-lance batteries, and no inspiration struck. Neither did Desjani call with some concept that might work. He thought that in some ways she still had too much confidence in him, too much certainty that the great Black Jack Geary would manage with the help of the living stars to pull yet another rabbit out of his hat just when that rabbit was desperately needed.

Finally, Geary paused, took his bearings, and headed for the one place where he might receive wisdom beyond that of anyone in the fleet.

Down here, as deep within *Dauntless* as any compartment could be, as well protected as any part of the ship, were the small rooms where comfort and guidance could be sought. Geary didn't know for certain why he'd come here now. It never hurt for the crew to see their fleet commander displaying proper piety, but anything that might smack of public displays of worship had always bothered him. It could also backfire if the fleet concluded that he was not so much pious as desperate for advice. Especially since there was some truth to that.

Geary closed the door and sat in one of the tiny, private rooms on the traditional wooden bench, his eyes fixed on the flickering flame of the candle he had lit to help warm the spirits of his ancestors. "As far as I know," he finally said out loud, "none of you were legendary military commanders. I'm still not sure how I got stuck with the title. The odds are against us here, the fleet's fuel supplies are so low that I can't afford fancy tricks to sucker the Syndics, and the enemy has clearly been studying what I've been doing in battles and are trying to counter that. I fear that the best outcome here would be a bloody engagement in which this fleet would be victorious but decimated. The worst outcome..."

He shrugged. "I need something new. Something unexpected. The only thing I can think of that the logistics situation would allow is surprising the enemy with an attack in the style this fleet had grown accustomed to, straight into the teeth of the Syndic flotilla. But even if that worked, the cost could be huge. My battle cruisers can't take that kind of engagement on top of the damage they're already carrying, and I don't have enough battleships to form a shield for the battle cruisers."

Geary sat for a while, watching the candle grow shorter. "Too bad I can't just throw the battleships at the Syndics, but even they need support against that much Syndic firepower. The battle cruisers would have to be right beside them even though it doesn't make sense for them to charge into that kind of hornet's nest. But I've already seen that my battle-cruiser captains will still do that even against orders because they think their honor requires it. I need the battle cruisers to avoid direct charges at the enemy, I need to hit the Syndics with my battleships, and I need to keep the Syndics guessing. But how do I do all of that, especially without complicating the battle beyond my ability to control it? I lost the bubble at Cavalos, let myself get overwhelmed by the complexity of the battle and couldn't make any decisions for far too long. If that happens here, the results could be a lot worse. I need some different approach."

A different approach. How to build it? What were his advantages?

Not numbers, not firepower, not munitions, not fuel. No friendly bases within reach. Ship for ship, the Syndic warships were roughly comparable to their Alliance counterparts, although Syndic Hunter-Killers were identificantly smaller and less capable than Alliance destroyers. But then the Syndics tended to have superior numbers of HuKs on hand because they were smaller and cheaper. The Alliance warships had a lot better onboard capability for damage control and repair, but even that required time for repairs to be made before the Syndics hit a badly damaged Alliance ship again.

It took a minute to come up with an advantage for the Alliance fleet. *The quality of my sailors is superb. They're more experienced than has been the norm in the last several decades since crews tended to die before they acquired too much skill. But I've kept mine alive.*

Most of them.

And they'll fight like hell, and they'll fight to the death. Some of my subordinates are also good leaders. All of the ship commanders will listen to me now. I can count on their carrying out my orders. Within limits. He paused, trying to come up with something else, then remembered the Syndic guard flotilla destroying the hypernet gate at Lakota when the Alliance fleet was light-hours distant. *And the Syndics are scared of me. Admit it. It's an advantage for us. They expect me to do something unexpected, to do things that no one else can do.*

How to use that? What unexpected things are still left to try with the force limitations I have to deal with? Too bad I can't figure out a smart way to fight the kind of battle this fleet was used to fighting before I took command, charging straight into the enemy. After watching me command engagements at stars from Kaliban to Cavalos, the Syndics would never expect...

Can I do that?

He watched the candle flame dance, ideas swirling through his mind. *There might be a way. It wouldn't be cost free in terms of fuel cells, but it wouldn't cost nearly as much as any alternatives, if the ships and the maneuvering systems can handle it, and if I can construct the necessary orders before we reach the Syndics.*

And if Desjani doesn't kill me when she finds out what my plan would mean for Dauntless.

Thank you, ancestors. I heard you.

Rising, Geary bowed toward the candle, snuffed it out, and hurried toward his stateroom. He had a lot of simulator work to do.

It took a while. He had to keep trying different approaches, and the maneuvers were far too complicated for any human to have worked out unaided by the fleet combat systems. When he viewed the resulting maneuvering commands, the dizzying mix of vector and speed changes didn't produce any coherent picture at all. But when he ran the commands for the final product through the simulator, the results looked right even though his professional experience and training cringed at the idea of so many ships weaving through each other at high speed immediately prior to contact with the enemy. Still, everything was within the performance capabilities of his ships, even the lumbering fleet auxiliaries and the damaged warships because he'd minimized their required changes in courses and speeds.

He could imagine how his old instructors would have reacted to his plan. *The concept is far too simple and the execution far too complicated.* His protests that it was the best option left to him would have produced stern lectures to avoid getting into situations where the best option was something like this. Which advice was all very well in theory or peacetime practice, but the real universe, a century of war, and the long retreat from the Syndic home star system had left him this harsh practical reality to deal with.

He checked the time and the location of the Syndics, for once grateful for the long delays caused by the huge distances in space. Desjani had called to tell him that once the Syndics had seen the arrival of the Alliance fleet four hours after it exited the jump point, the enemy flotilla had turned onto a vector that would intercept the Alliance warships if they continued toward the jump point for Padronis. A light-hour behind them, the smaller enemy flotilla had eventually turned onto a similar course. Both Syndic formations had held their velocity to point zero eight light speed, the same velocity at which the Alliance fleet was moving, the forces closing on each other the entire time in which Geary thought and ran simulations. At a combined closing rate of point one six light speed, the Alliance fleet and the Syndic flotilla would require about twenty more hours to come into contact.

The downside of the Syndic decision to hold their velocity to point zero eight light was that they were obviously trying to improve their chances of getting good hits in when the fleets clashed. They were willing to wait a little while to ensure maximizing damage on the Alliance fleet.

Geary sat down, calling up the commands for the battle and reviewing them again anxiously before calling *Dauntless*'s bridge. "Please tell Captain Desjani that her presence is requested in my stateroom."

He waited, watching the enemy, wondering how these Syndics

would maneuver to contact and during the battle, until his hatch alert chimed and he allowed Desjani to enter.

Her eyes went immediately to the display above the table. "What's the plan?" Desjani asked. From the look of her, she'd reined in her curiosity as long as she could.

"It's... complicated." True enough. Especially once Desjani saw where *Dauntless* would be when the fleets clashed.

"I can check it."

"I'd appreciate it if you did." He grimaced, not happy with knowing how she'd react. "I'm trying something new." Geary fell silent, gazing at the display.

"All right, sir," Desjani finally said. "That's not a problem. But if you want my input, I need to see the maneuvering plan."

Just as he'd once been told, when Desjani locked on a target she didn't let go. Besides, he did want her input. Best to get it over with now. "Okay. I just caution you again that this is a new approach."

She was obviously puzzled. Geary looked down, sighed, then punched the commands to play out the intended maneuvers during the initial encounter with the Syndics. Desjani watched, her eyes widening with disbelief as the Alliance fleet's formation dissolved into an apparently chaotic swarm as it approached contact with the enemy. As the warships of the Alliance fleet re-formed at the last moment, she watched intently, then her expression froze. "You're—" She didn't seem to breathe for a moment before speaking in a tone so flat it sounded almost lifeless. "Sir, I must respectfully inquire as to whether I or my ship have lost your confidence."

"No. Not at all."

"Sir, this plan—"

"Will allow the battleships to do what they do best."

Desjani's face reddened. "Battle cruisers do not go into combat behind other ships! We lead the way!"

"Not this time." He could see how tightly her hands were clenching into fists. "Captain Desjani, I need to hit the Syndics in a way they don't expect without getting my own fleet wiped out in the process. I am not putting the battle cruisers in a secondary position in this engagement. Run the next set of commands."

She didn't look at him as she did so, then took in a long breath. "As you say, this is an unusual plan."

"That's the idea."

"I understand why you don't wish to communicate this to the other battle cruisers in advance. They'll be extremely unhappy. As am I. But I will follow my orders, Captain Geary." Desjani seemed slightly mollified but still sullen, and didn't look at him.

"Thank you, Captain Desjani. I would not wish to be on any ship but *Dauntless* in any circumstances." She didn't respond, and he wondered if he should say more, but he'd said what he believed. "Do you think the plan is sound?"

He could see her trying to control her emotional reactions, trying to focus on the plan as an abstract. "If our ships can actually carry out these maneuvers in the time and distance allotted, then it will certainly surprise the Syndics... as much as it does some of our own ships."

"The maneuvering systems say our ships can do it."

"In theory." She gave Geary a hard look. "This will have to be done totally on automatic controls. No ship-handler in the fleet could possibly execute this without disastrous results."

"I understand."

"Sir, please, *Dauntless* can be farther forward."

"She will be when we split the formation. Tanya, it's one lousy firing run. How many battles have we fought on this ship together? How many times has *Dauntless* led the way, held the center of the formation while the Syndics aimed right at us?"

Desjani kept her head bowed, glaring at the deck. "I don't suppose I should have expected you to understand."

"Dammit, Tanya, in a perfect world I'd bend the heavens to make you happy, but I have responsibilities to this fleet and to the Alliance. This would be one hell of a lot easier if I was on any other ship talking to any other captain, but I can't let my personal feelings dictate this decision." Desjani stiffened, and he gritted his teeth. His last statement could refer to professional respect and friendship, but could also be seen as a careless allusion to something neither he nor she could admit to, talk about, or base any actions on. Geary refocused his argument onto impersonal reality. "*Dauntless* has to make it home, because *Dauntless* carries the Syndic hypernet key, and that can't be duplicated until we reach Alliance space. I cannot put *Dauntless* in a position that would virtually guarantee her destruction. Nor do I have to, since no one could possibly claim that *Dauntless* and her commander have been anything but honorable and in the forefront of every fight."

She stayed quiet for a while, then glanced sidelong at him. "You'd bend the heavens?"

Startled, Geary nodded. "If I could."

"I may hold you to that." Desjani straightened and saluted.

"*Dauntless* will do her duty, as will her captain. It's a good plan, sir. It'll surprise the enemy, and more importantly, it should hurt them."

"Thanks." He returned the salute, sighing with relief as Desjani left.

Though he did feel a twinge of worry as he wondered just what "hold you to that" might mean.

"I assume you now have a plan?" Rione asked.

Geary, once more seated in the fleet command position on *Dauntless*'s bridge, turned to nod at her. "It's a surprise."

"Wonderful, but apparently it's intended as a surprise to your own ships as well as those of the enemy?"

"To some extent."

"Since we're less than an hour from contact, I suppose we'll all find out what you intend before much longer." Desjani was maintaining a poker face, but it appeared even that gave something away to Rione. "Those of us who aren't already in your confidence that is." Rione settled back, looking outwardly unconcerned.

Desjani waited a few minutes, then leaned close to Geary to speak inside his privacy bubble. "I need to apologize to you."

"No, you don't. I expected your reaction to be a lot worse, if you want to know the truth."

"That's not what I mean." She glanced toward Rione. "I wondered if you'd held *Dauntless* back at her urging, to keep the Syndic key safe. I should have realized you wouldn't do that. I'm sorry for thinking it."

"That's all right. Now keep your head in the game, Tanya. This is going to be a tough one. I need you at your best."

"You always get my best, sir." She grinned and settled back into her captain's seat.

Half an hour to contact. Twelve hours ago Geary had deliberately set up the Alliance formation as virtually a mirror image of the Syndics', with four subformations flanking a central subformation. He'd have to move soon, but not too soon. The Syndics had held their own course and speed, swinging in toward a head-on encounter with the Alliance fleet's own central formation even though they surely expected Geary to make some last-minute changes to his fleet's vectors.

"Do you want to address the fleet?" Desjani asked in a way that implied he did whether he realized it or not.

"Good idea." He paused for a moment to order his thoughts, then hit the fleetwide circuit. "All ships in the Alliance fleet, this Syndic flotilla stands between us and home. What we lack in supplies we make up for in experience and spirit." He wasn't following in the footsteps of Captain Falco's sort, who thought "fighting spirit" magically multiplied the capabilities of a fighting force. But it did matter, it did make a difference, as long as you didn't assume it provided mystical protection against enemy firepower. Experience, on the other hand, could make a tremendous difference. "These Syndics won't stop us here because this day we will add another victory to the annals of the Alliance fleet."

He ended the transmission, feeling uncomfortable at using such high-sounding words, then saw Desjani looking at him approvingly. "You always give good speeches before an engagement, sir. Short, direct, and powerful."

I do? "Thank you, Captain Desjani. I meant every word of it."

He wondered if the last part sounded defensive.

She seemed startled by it, though. "Of course you do. We all know that. You've proven it. In any event, we've all had plenty of experience with hearing long speeches. It always seemed to me while listening to them that anyone who really believed what they were saying could get it said in a lot fewer words."

"You may have a point there."

Rione unexpectedly chimed in, her tone dry. "She does have a point."

Not looking back, Desjani frowned, then, with a glance at Geary, gestured everyone on the bridge to silence.

He barely noticed, concentrating on the movements of the opposing forces sweeping closer to each other. The maneuvering systems were counting down a recommended time to initiate the maneuver, but Geary was matching that against his own experience, his own gut feelings for the right moment, factoring in the time required to send the command to begin carrying out the package of commands he'd already forwarded to all of the other ships in the fleet.

Still no change from the Syndics. They'd done that at Cavalos, too. Whether or not the CEO in charge of their flotilla knew that it had given Geary problems at Cavalos, he or she was following the same tactic here, holding off on a course change until the last possible moment to frustrate what ever plan Geary had developed.

One minute to recommended time to initiate maneuver. He frowned at the countdown, feeling a nagging instinct that it was a little too tight. He had to time this right, not perfect-world right but real-world right, all while not knowing how the Syndic CEO would react. But he'd fought the Syndics enough now that he had good grounds for guessing, so Geary waited, letting his instincts speak as his eyes watched the Alliance fleet and the main Syndic flotilla rushing together. Waiting. Waiting.

At ten seconds before the recommended time to pass the command his thumb twitched without conscious thought, activating the comm circuit. "Formation Indigo Two, Formation Indigo Three, execute maneuvering orders package one effective immediately." He paused, then called out again. "Formation Indigo One, execute maneuvering orders package one effective immediately." Wait. Seconds ticked by as *Dauntless*'s bow pitched upward. "Formation Indigo Four, Formation Indigo Five, execute maneuvering orders package one effective immediately."

On his display, Geary could see the smaller subformations above and below the Alliance fleet's main body losing their shapes and collapsing toward the main body as that formation rose to meet them, its warships also leaving their positions as they altered course. The Syndic CEO would see all that beginning to happen, a few minutes delayed since the fleets were still that far apart, and either believe that the Alliance fleet was aiming for a firing pass above the Syndic box or trying to vault past the top of the Syndic flotilla. That CEO would have to decide whether to alter course slightly upward as well, and know that there were only minutes to decide.

The one thing he wouldn't expect was for the Alliance fleet to steady out and aim straight for a head-on intercept against the center of the Syndic flotilla. That was the sort of damn-the-missiles, straight-up-the-middle charge that had become common on both sides as the training and skills needed to carry out more complex maneuvers were lost in increasingly bloody battles. Commanders who knew only one way to fight had followed that way, depending on "fighting spirit" to overcome bad odds and enemy firepower. Courage and honor were the watchwords, making possible horrible slogging matches in which one side or the other eventually prevailed at awful costs in ships and personnel.

Geary had never done that. He'd brought with him from a century before the expertise to fight intricate battles across vast reaches of space, coordinating the movements of different formations despite time lags of seconds, minutes, and even hours in communications and information. Despite its initial resistance, the fleet had followed his lead. Most of the fleet, anyway. The closest he'd come to ordering an attack into the teeth of the enemy had taken place at the first battle of Lakota, and it had been only after a series of maneuvers had fooled the Syndics into spreading their formation so wide that their middle was weak and unsupported by flanking units.

No, the Syndics knew that Geary didn't attack up the middle in the opening of an engagement. They knew that of all the options available, he wouldn't do that.

So that's what he was doing.

The Alliance fleet's main body and the two upper subformations kept dissolving and merging together, every ship breaking from its position relative to *Dauntless* and swinging onto a wide variety of course and speed vectors as *Dauntless* herself kept her bow swinging past up, over, and down slightly. The battle cruiser's main propulsion units slammed into action briefly, slowing her and allowing other Alliance warships to take up position on the side closest to the oncoming enemy.

Beneath them, the other two Alliance subformations had also dissolved, their ships rising to meet the main body and moving toward their own new positions.

"Can we really get this done before contact?" Desjani inquired tonelessly.

"I hope so."

"Why do you think the Syndic flotilla will rise to meet what seemed to be your path?" Rione asked.

Geary kept most of his attention on the movements of ships as he answered. "It's a natural human instinct. If someone tries to rise over us, we try to rise to match or overreach them." Even humans raised entirely in space showed the same bias even though the designation of up and down in star systems was purely arbitrary, *up* being above the plane of the star system and *down* being below it. "If the Syndic CEO follows their instincts in the very short time they've got to react, we'll have them."

With the rest of the fleet's ships braking, the massive hulls of the Alliance battleships were passing through them and forming up into a slightly curved wall leading the fleet, around them clustering a swarm of Alliance destroyers and heavy cruisers.

All around *Dauntless*, other battle cruisers were sliding into place, their commanding officers only now realizing that they were positioned well behind the battleships. Geary had no trouble imagining the outrage that would be blossoming on those battle cruisers, but they wouldn't have time to do anything about it before contact with the enemy.

Just behind the battle cruisers, the four auxiliaries were surrounded by the shapes of the four most badly damaged

Alliance battle cruisers, other battered Alliance warships, and every heavy cruiser.

"Estimated time to contact twenty seconds. We have incoming transmissions for Captain Geary from *Daring*, *Victorious*, *Implacable*, *Illustrious*, *Inspire*, *Intrepid*—"

He'd obviously underestimated the outrage of his battlecruiser captains and how quickly they'd move to vent that outrage. Desjani was being obvious about not saying, *I told you so*, as Geary hit his command override on the communications controls, his eyes on the Syndic formation, which had tipped upward slightly, just as he'd expected. The Syndic commander had hoped to bring a lot of firepower to bear on the Alliance fleet as it tried to rush past above the Syndic formation on one of the slashing firing passes Geary had often used, the heaviest Syndic firepower concentrated at the top of the formation. But the latest Alliance maneuvers had brought the concentrated Alliance fleet on a vector aimed straight at the center of the Syndics instead.

And the Syndics had no time to react.

"All units, we are less than twenty seconds from contact with the enemy. All battleships are to concentrate their fire on enemy capital ships. We need their shields down. Battle cruisers are to strike the death blows on those capital ships. If all capital ships within range have been eliminated, engage targets of opportunity as they enter weapon envelopes but conserve specter missiles." Geary's eyes flicked toward the time readout. He had to give the next maneuvering order before the fleet passed through the enemy flotilla even though it wouldn't be executed until afterward. "All units, execute maneuvering package two at time one four."

"Estimated time to contact ten seconds. Five seconds."

The Syndics were ahead, then behind, the moment of contact incredibly brief, automated targeting systems aiming and firing as the warships tore past each other at a combined speed of almost sixty thousand kilometers per second. *Dauntless*'s hull shuddered as enemy hits registered on her shields. Geary tried to remain focused on the big picture as watch-standers called out reports.

The Syndics had volleyed missiles and grapeshot at the expected position of the Alliance fleet, the great majority of those shots passing overhead as the Alliance warships went beneath them. By contrast the Alliance grapeshot couldn't miss, slamming straight into the comparatively weak center of the Syndic flotilla. At short range and with the Alliance formation so compact, the dense barrage of steel ball bearings it had fired annihilated the light cruisers and HuKs in its path, blossoming flashes of light marking the deaths of the escorts. More lights flared as Alliance grapeshot slammed into the shields of the Syndic heavy cruisers, battleships, and battle cruisers in the center of the flotilla. As the opposing warships shot past each other, hell-lances tore into targets and from the Alliance battle cruisers and battleships null fields blossomed to engulf parts of the Syndic combatants.

Syndic counterfire had lashed out, pummeling the massive shields and armor of the Alliance battleships. After the battleships had absorbed the first volleys, Syndic fire had flailed at the following Alliance warships, weakened but still deadly.

It had all taken only a fraction of a second, in which humans could only trust to the strength of their defenses, the accuracy of their automated targeting systems, and their luck. Now, as the

Alliance formation and the Syndic flotilla raced away from each other, Geary watched as the fleet's sensors evaluated the results.

The seven Syndic battleships and three battle cruisers anchoring the center of the enemy flotilla had faced thirty Alliance battleships and battle cruisers. Outgunned three to one and without the null fields, which gave the Alliance an advantage at very short range against ships whose shields had been weakened, the Syndics had suffered the inevitable result. All three Syndic battle cruisers had exploded, along with two battleships, another battleship had broken into three large pieces, and the remaining four battleships were drifting, badly shot up, displaying the huge bites in their hulls that marked null-field hits, and showing few systems left operational.

The list of disabled or destroyed Syndic cruisers and HuKs was gratifyingly long. The center of the Syndic flotilla had simply disappeared.

"Executing maneuvering package two at time one four," Desjani announced, the excitement of battle finally breaking through her aggravation with Geary.

He simultaneously checked the Alliance fleet's status and the movements of the Syndic flotilla. The Syndics were swinging their formation to the right and around, keeping the four corner formations slaved to each other, probably expecting the Alliance ships to keep heading for the jump point. But instead, the big Alliance formation was dissolving again, the battle cruisers, light cruisers, and many of the destroyers angling down as they coalesced into a new formation, while the battleships, heavy cruisers, auxiliaries, damaged warships, and the rest of the destroyers closed up on each other and bent their track upward.

Geary felt like he'd swallowed grapeshot as his display pulsed with alerts reporting heavy damage or destruction of Alliance warships. A bright symbol in the wake of the Alliance fleet marked the spreading debris field that was all that was left of *Exemplar*, his last scout battleship. Smaller than battleships, bigger than cruisers, the scout battleships must have made sense to somebody but had suffered from the compromises in their design. Like her sister ships destroyed in previous engagements, *Exemplar* had been large enough to draw extra enemy fire but too small to withstand it.

None of the Alliance battleships were out of commission, but the Syndics had concentrated their fire on *Resolution* and *Redoubtable* as the Alliance battleships engaged them, and both of those battleships had taken major damage forward. *Resolution*, having also suffered propulsion damage, was trying to keep up with the fleet but sliding backward relative to the other warships.

In the wake of the fleet, the battle cruiser *Incredible* drifted, having suffered even more damage as she protected the auxiliaries. She still had some weapons operational, but otherwise was a sitting duck, her crew doubtless praying that the battle would remain clear of *Incredible* until they could get some propulsion units back online.

Heavy cruisers *Tortoise*, *Breech*, *Kurtani*, and *Tarian* were knocked out, with nothing left of the first two but pieces of wreckage. Light cruisers *Kissaki*, *Crest*, and *Trunnion* were gone, and destroyers *Barb*, *Yatagan*, *Lunge*, *Arabas*, and *Kururi* had been destroyed.

There was simply no time to review all the lesser damage inflicted during the first firing pass.

Where the formations had clashed, swarms of escape pods filled space, Alliance survivors of destroyed ships intermingled with

Syndics who had abandoned their own disabled craft.

Worst of all, with a second volley of missiles fired just as the forces passed through each other, the Syndics had finally scored serious hits on one of the ships Geary could least afford to lose. "*Goblin* has lost all propulsion units," the operations watch reported. "Serious damage aft from two or three missile hits. Estimated time to regain partial propulsion is at least one hour."

Geary watched the auxiliary's track through space as, unable to alter its course or accelerate, the stricken *Goblin* followed the path of the wreckage and derelicts from the engagement, curving away from the rest of the Alliance warships. Running out *Goblin*'s path and comparing it to the movements of the Syndics produced a simple and unpleasant result. "*Goblin* doesn't have a chance. Can anyone confirm for me that the most probable estimated time to the Syndics hitting *Goblin* is twenty-five minutes?"

"Confirmed, sir," the operations watch responded immediately. "I have twenty-four minutes on my estimate."

Way, way short of the hour *Goblin* needed to get moving again, and in any event the lumbering auxiliary couldn't have escaped even if half of her propulsion units miraculously popped back online at this moment. Nor could the Alliance fleet get back and around in time to try to prevent a Syndic firing pass on *Goblin*. Geary sighed and tapped his controls. "*Goblin*, this is Captain Geary. Recommend you begin abandoning ship immediately and set power core for overload in about twenty minutes." He planned to win this battle, but the outcome remained in doubt, and he couldn't risk the Syndics' capturing *Goblin* intact.

Goblin's answer came half a minute later. "Sir, we're trying to load what fuel cells are left on board onto our heavy-lift shuttles. We might be able to get them out. Our repair crews are trying to get one of the propulsion units back online."

Desjani made a disbelieving sound. "Those heavy-lift birds can't get clear of the Syndics. They don't have the speed even if they're empty."

Geary nodded. "*Goblin*, the heavy-lift shuttles are far too slow and will be magnets for enemy fire. They cannot escape, and anything on them will be lost. One propulsion unit can't save your ship, and the fleet can't get back to you in time to cover you. You're an engineer. Do the math. Get your people off that ship while there's still time. You may regard that as an order if that makes the decision easier."

This time *Goblin*'s reply took an extra minute and sounded resigned. "Yes, sir. I'm ordering all personnel to the escape pods now. Setting power core to overload in... eighteen minutes."

"Sir, *Incredible*'s commanding officer informs us that he has given orders for nonessential personnel to abandon ship."

"Very well," Geary responded. The situation didn't leave any other choice.

"*Resolution* cannot keep up with the fleet. She's declaring her intention to close on *Incredible* and provide support."

"Approved. Tell *Resolution* and *Incredible* that we're going to try to keep the Syndics busy." Geary concentrated on the movements of the Syndics and his own two formations as the three groups of warships swung through the huge turns required at velocities still close to point zero eight light speed. As the Syndics came around to the right, a cluster of battleships began sliding over to fill the gap where the center of their flotilla had been, then apparently halted halfway between its old positions and the center.

"They're confused," Desjani said scornfully.

"That's the idea."

Rione's voice came from the back of the bridge. "Why are they confused? You've put our fleet into only two formations instead of up to six as you have in the past."

"It's how those formations are constituted," Geary advised her. "One is built around all of our battleships, slower and massive, obviously configured to slam right into the heart of the Syndic flotilla again. But the other formation contains all of our battle cruisers, swift and agile, obviously configured to hit the edges of the Syndic flotilla."

"I see." Rione smiled with one side of her mouth. "They don't know where you'll hit, so they don't know where to put their heaviest firepower."

"Exactly." Geary shook his head as he watched the Syndics. They'd been expecting the Alliance fleet to turn back toward the jump point for Padronis, but instead found themselves lining up with the Alliance battleship formation to one side and above them, while the Alliance battle cruisers were to the other side and beneath. "I don't think I should punch the battleship formation through the middle of the Syndics again. Not yet, anyway. If the Syndic commander reacted quickly enough and collapsed his flotilla around the center he could hurt our battleships badly."

Desjani thought about it, then nodded. "I agree. May the Alliance battle cruisers lead the way *this* time, Captain Geary?"

"Yes, Captain Desjani. Let's do that, while I bring the battleships around to hit the Syndics from another angle."

"Captain Geary, sir, *Resolution* and *Incredible* request that you leave plenty of Syndics for them."

Desjani laughed, and even Geary grinned despite his tension. "Tell them that shouldn't be a problem, Lieutenant."

Led by Captain Tulev's Second Battle Cruiser Division, the fifteen remaining operational Alliance battle cruisers and their light cruiser and destroyer escorts angled upward and to the right, while Geary ordered the battleships to come left and accelerate. The battleship formation moved much more sluggishly, both because of the massive battleships and because it included the three remaining auxiliaries in the fleet. Hopefully, he'd compensated properly for that in his orders.

The Syndics were continuing their turn, angling slightly downward. Geary adjusted the track of the battle-cruiser formation to counteract the Syndic maneuvers, increasing the angle of the Alliance attack so it was climbing almost straight up toward the enemy.

The Alliance battle-cruiser formation screamed upward at the rear bottom corner of the Syndic flotilla. "They're braking!" the operations watch-stander shouted at the last moment before contact, too late for anyone to react. At the velocities they were all traveling, both sides noticed the changed vectors too late for either group of warships to compensate.

Instead of racing past outside the corner of the Syndic flotilla, the Alliance battle cruisers slammed through that corner. The automated maneuvering systems managed to avoid collisions, which would have instantly vaporized the ships involved, but the Alliance battle cruisers still ended up enduring close passes against enemy battleships.

The four Syndic battleships anchoring that corner threw out a barrage of hell-lance fire that tore apart *Steadfast*, riddled *Intrepid*, and hammered *Inspire*, while *Illustrious* took more damage on top of that suffered at Cavalos, and *Courageous* spun out of control as the Alliance warships cleared the Syndic formation.

"*Intrepid* thinks she can keep up but all of her combat systems are out," *Dauntless*'s combat watch reported. "*Inspire* has full maneuvering but has sustained heavy damage to weapons systems. We can see escape pods leaving what's left of *Steadfast*."

"What about *Courageous*?" Geary demanded.

"No communications, sir. She's off the fleet net. Sensors register all systems dead."

Along with who knew how many of her crew.

"Roberto Duellos is very hard to kill," Desjani commented.

"Let's hope so." Geary shoved his worries for Captain Duellos to the side and grimly focused on the Syndic flotilla. The Alliance battle cruisers had been hurt, but had also been able to hit the corner of the flotilla with a lot of firepower. The two Syndic battle cruisers there were both too badly damaged to keep fighting, and one of the enemy battleships had taken enough hits that it was falling out of formation, while another seemed as badly off as *Intrepid*, able to maneuver but otherwise badly hurt. Most of the Syndic light cruisers and HuKs in that corner of the flotilla had been knocked out or destroyed, but there were more Alliance escorts also missing now or helplessly falling behind.

Fortunately, the Syndic maneuvers that had put the Alliance battle cruisers badly out of position had also positioned the Alliance battleship formation to hit another corner of the Syndic flotilla head-on. This time the four Syndic battleships there were not only badly outnumbered locally but facing warships as heavily shielded and armored as they were. *Gallant* and *Indomitable* were the focus of the enemy fire, and both suffered damage as their shields failed in spots and Syndic grapeshot or hell-lances made it through to their hulls. But as the Alliance formation opened the distance again, they left three of the four Syndic battleships out of action and three Syndic battle cruisers in pieces.

"That more than evens the odds," Desjani remarked.

The rest of the Syndic flotilla swept toward *Goblin*, which vanished into a ball of fragments a moment later as its power core overloaded. Beyond where *Goblin* had been, *Resolution* and *Incredible* threw out everything they had left at the approaching Syndics.

Geary involuntarily closed his eyes as a corner of the Syndic flotilla tore past *Resolution* and *Incredible*. When he opened them, he was astonished to see that both Alliance ships were still there. "They survived? That's..."

"Incredible?" Desjani murmured. "*Resolution* shielded *Incredible* as much as she could. She got shot to hell, and *Incredible* took more damage, but the Syndic intercept must have been far enough off to save both ships."

Luck had saved *Resolution* and *Incredible*, but a moment later the gods of war favored the Syndics. "Damn," Desjani commented. "There goes *Intrepid*." Missiles had leaped out from the Syndic formation during the last firing pass, aiming at the projected course for the Alliance battle cruisers. Because of the last-minute vector changes, most of those missiles had been too far off the Alliance track to get hits and had curved through space, chasing the Alliance ships. Many of the missiles were destroyed as their slow relative speeds in a stern chase made them easier targets for the Alliance escorts, but one made it through to the already heavily damaged *Intrepid*. The stricken battle cruiser seemed to buck as the missile hit her dead astern, smashing her propulsion units. *Intrepid* spun off to the side, her weakened structure visibly buckling under the stress of the impact and the sudden changes in course and speed. "She's not going to be recoverable, sir."

Desjani didn't seem shaken by the losses of *Intrepid* and *Courageous*, but then Geary knew that she'd seen far worse. "Let's avenge her." He tried to relax, watching the tracks and projected paths through space, attempting to factor in the seconds of time delay in the images he was seeing. "Formation Indigo One, come right two five degrees, down one six zero degrees at time five three." The Alliance battle cruisers came up and over, swinging down and to the side for another pass at the Syndics.

The Syndic commander was trying to concentrate what was left of his flotilla, bringing the ships together until the group of enemy warships once again almost resembled a square box, though a much smaller one than the Syndics had started with. At the same time, he tried a tight maneuver, rolling the entire formation up and around to the left to face the Alliance battle-cruiser formation.

"Bad move." Desjani bared her teeth. "We look like an easier target, but we're faster than he is. That's not a very experienced commander."

"Neither are some of his captains, apparently," Geary replied, watching the Syndic warships scramble to get into position and carry out the major changes of their vectors. One of the Syndic battleships blundered into a Syndic heavy cruiser, causing most of the heavy cruiser to disappear in a flash of light while the battleship reeled away with major damage. "One more down."

The intended compact Syndic square spread and warped out of shape as the Syndic flotilla failed to make the turn.

"Formation Indigo One, come right two zero degrees, up one five degrees at time zero six." The Alliance battle cruisers raised their bows slightly as they turned, sliding around to aim for an intercept of one side of the flailing Syndic flotilla. "Formation Indigo Two, come left two eight five degrees, up two one zero degrees at time zero eight." The battleships, now well below the Syndics, began turning upward as the Alliance battle cruisers closed on the enemy again.

This time, with the enemy caught in temporary disarray, the Alliance battle-cruiser formation roared past one corner of the Syndic flotilla at almost perfect range, lashing out at the exposed Syndic warships with a large local superiority in firepower.

Dauntless shuddered heavily in the wake of the firing pass. "One Syndic missile got through, Captain. Damage aft. Hell-lance battery six bravo out of commission. Reduced capability from main propulsion unit alpha."

"Can we keep up with the formation as it maneuvers?" Desjani demanded.

"Engineering is boosting output from the remaining main propulsion units, Captain. Damage control teams are reinforcing damaged hull sections. Damage control central requests we avoid major maneuvers for the next ten minutes."

"Tell them to make it five!"

"Yes, Captain. Five minutes."

Illustrious, still carrying plenty of damage from the fight at Cavalos, took more hits, along with *Valiant* and *Daring*. But the outnumbered Syndics in that part of the flotilla had lost three more battle cruisers.

"What the hell are they doing?" Geary burst out with as the Syndics continued to swing up and around in a corkscrew movement.

"Beats the hell out me," Desjani confessed.

"They're just continuing the same— We got the CEO. They're following their last orders because no one else has established themselves in command yet."

"Nice," Desjani almost purred, watching the Alliance battleship formation rip through the diminished Syndic flotilla. Only ten Syndic battleships and battle cruisers remained operational after that, though the Alliance formation shed *Gallant* as it bent back for another firing run.

"Propulsion damage on *Gallant*, but she can still defend herself. They're concentrating their fire," Desjani noted with grudging approval. "Throwing everything they can at the battleships that have already taken the most damage. Look at how badly *Redoubtable* got hit, too."

"At least she can still keep up with the formation."

Desjani spun to face her engineering watch-stander. "Five minutes are up. Can I maneuver?"

"One more minute, Captain," the engineer pleaded.

"I don't have one minute!"

"Ready for maneuvers," the relieved watch-stander gasped as he received the report.

"Good," Geary approved. "Let's go." On the heels of his words, the Syndic flotilla altered course radically, bearing back around and down. "Where... ?"

Geary brought the battle-cruiser formation toward the Syndics in as tight a swing as he could, trying to guess on which vector they'd steady out. The answer became clear after several minutes. "They're going after *Resolution* and *Incredible*."

"We'll get at least one more pass at them before then," Desjani pointed out, "and so will the battleships."

"Any updates from *Gallant*?" Geary asked. He could scroll through the display looking for that information himself, but he needed to spend that time and concentration on the big picture.

"*Gallant* reports about half of her combat systems remain active," the operations watch reported. "Shields weak but regenerating, several major breaches in hull armor being sealed. Estimated time to regain some maneuvering control is twenty minutes."

Deciding that *Gallant* could look out for herself for the time being, Geary lined up the battle cruisers on another intercept with the Syndic flotilla and adjusted the track of the battleships so they'd hit the Syndics again.

The wait to contact was agonizing this time. *Resolution* and *Incredible* drifted helpless, both ships too badly damaged to have any hope of surviving another Syndic attack and neither having enough working weapons to have much chance of inflicting any damage on the enemy. The Syndic box, even smaller now, was curving in from above and the left. Farther to the left and slightly higher, the Alliance battle cruisers were swooping down on the Syndics. Off to the right and roughly even with the Syndics, the Alliance battleships were boring in steadily.

It must have become apparent to the Syndics that they didn't have a hope of rendering death blows to *Resolution* and *Incredible* before being savaged by the rest of the Alliance fleet. As the two Alliance formations drew close, the Syndic flotilla abruptly dove, greatly increasing its down angle and steadying out toward where the smaller Syndic formation was holding off from the battle.

Geary rapped quick commands to the battle cruisers and the battleships, correcting for the Syndic moves.

As the Alliance ships steadied onto their new vectors, collision-warning alarms blared. Geary barely had time to jerk his gaze to the alerts before the Alliance battle cruisers raced through the Syndic flotilla from one side and above almost at the exact same instant as the Alliance battleship formation tore through from the other side and slightly above.

For that heart-stopping instant, a lot of warships going on widely different vectors at very high speed threaded past each other, automated maneuvering systems screaming alarms in protest as they tried to avoid collisions in the maelstrom of warships. Meanwhile, the automated combat systems on every combatant saw a suddenly target-rich environment and gleefully hurled out shots in all directions.

Then the three formations were diverging again. Geary inhaled heavily as he realized he'd forgotten to breathe for a moment.

Even Desjani looked pale. "Sir, have you considered the possibility that there could be such a thing as being too good at compensating for the movements of the enemy?"

"Not until just now." He took another breath and checked his display, then checked it again. "We lost some more destroyers, but that was probably to enemy fire. No collisions?"

"All the same, let's not do that again, sir."

"Okay." The Syndic flotilla's box, subjected to so much firepower at once from different angles, had disintegrated. Two battleships were still slogging along their track, but both had sustained identificant damage. No Syndic battle cruisers remained, and the escorts had been slaughtered. Conversely, with so many targets at once, the Syndics hadn't been able to concentrate their fire. Aside from some unfortunate cruisers and destroyers, the Alliance fleet had avoided more serious damage.

Geary breathed a sigh of relief. "Formation Indigo Two," he ordered the battleships, "break formation and get those two remaining Syndic battleships. Formation Indigo One, general pursuit. Avoid the two surviving Syndic battleships until they've been reduced by our battleships." The last thing he wanted was another loss like *Opportune*.

To his surprise, Desjani didn't instantly whip *Dauntless* around to go after a target. She saw his reaction and shrugged. "The only thing left worth killing is those battleships. Besides"— she pointed to her ship's status display— "we're down to thirty-five percent fuel-cell reserves."

"Thirty-five percent?" In peacetime he would have been court-martialed for letting fuel-cell reserves get that low on ships under his command.

"Good thing we saved *Titan*, *Witch*, and *Jinn*," Desjani observed. "We're going to need every fuel cell they can squeeze out between here and Varandal."

4

The butcher's bill after a battle was always the worst part. Geary read through the names. *Courageous, Intrepid, Exemplar, Goblin*, heavy cruisers *Tortoise, Breech, Kurtani, Tarian*, and *Nodowa*. Light cruisers *Kissaki, Crest, Trunnion, Inquarto*, and *Septime*. Destroyers *Barb, Yatagan, Lunge, Arabas, Kururi, Shail, Chamber, Bayonet*, and *Tomahawk*.

At that they were very lucky. If they'd had to flee the star system with the Syndics in pursuit, easily three times that many cruisers and destroyers would have been lost, plus more battle cruisers and battleships. As it was, the Alliance fleet had time to make repairs and get the ships moving again.

Resolution, though shot to hell, would be able to keep up with the fleet, but he didn't yet know if he'd be able to save *Incredible*. *Gallant* had enough maneuvering control back to fight once more, though many of her weapons remained out of action.

They'd have to linger here a little while, whether they liked it or not, to get the propulsion on damaged ships repaired, along with other critical systems, to collect escape pods from Alliance ships abandoned during the battle, and to distribute the all-too-few fuel cells manufactured on the auxiliaries since the fleet left Dilawa.

Desjani was grumbling. He followed her gaze to the smaller Syndic flotilla, which had torn off toward the jump point for Padronis after the destruction of the large flotilla. Now the cruisers and HuKs of that flotilla were fanning out, some continuing on toward the jump point and others heading for the jump points for Kalixa and Dilawa. "We'll never get them now," Desjani complained. "I was hoping they'd make a stand at the jump point for Padronis so we could trash them."

"Odds are they've laid their mines and are now rushing off to report what happened here," Geary commented.

"They abandoned their comrades! They didn't even try to hit us while we were fighting the main Syndic flotilla!"

So that was what was really bothering her. To Desjani those Syndics had let down their comrades, and even if they hadn't been Syndic scum, they deserved to pay for that. "Tanya, I'd bet you that small flotilla had orders to stand off from the engagement so it could form a last-ditch defense if we ran for the Padronis jump point."

"That's no excuse."

"At least they're not darting in trying to snap up any of our damaged ships."

Before Desjani could reply, an image popped up before Geary, showing Captain Cresida grinning. "I thought you'd like to know, sir, that we've recovered the escape pods from *Courageous*, including the one carrying a slightly banged-up but still-operational Captain Roberto Duellos."

Geary smiled back so broadly his cheeks hurt, then looked over to Desjani. "Duellos is safe on *Furious*."

"I told you he was difficult to kill," Desjani replied serenely, then she smiled, too.

"Here he is, Captain Geary," Cresida announced.

Her image was replaced by that of Duellos, his uniform torn and scorched in a few places. "Captain Duellos reporting for duty, sir."

"I..." His words stopped coming, and Geary just looked at Duellos for a moment. "Damn, I'm glad you're okay. I'm very sorry about *Courageous*. And *Intrepid*."

"Thank you on all counts." Duellos looked down for a moment. "It's hard to lose a ship, but then, you know that as well as I do."

"Yeah. It hurts like hell. Get yourself checked out and get some rest."

"I need to look after my crew, sir." Duellos gestured vaguely to one side. "Make sure they're being taken care of. The crew from *Courageous* and those off *Intrepid* on the ships that picked them up."

Geary started to say that Cresida could be trusted to do that, then stopped himself. He remembered his own sense of helplessness after his cruiser *Merlon* had been destroyed, the wish that he could do something, especially for the crew that were forever beyond his aid. Of course Duellos wanted to see to that himself. It would give him something to do besides dwell on the loss of *Courageous* and those crew members who hadn't made it off the ship. "Certainly, Captain Duellos. Let me know if you or your crews need anything."

Duellos moved to break the connection, but then hesitated. "You know what I need, Captain Geary, and you know you can't provide it. But I thank you, because I know you understand."

As soon as the window showing Duellos closed, Geary checked the fleet's status again, unwilling to let his mind dwell once more on the loss of *Merlon*. Unfortunately, *Dauntless* wasn't alone in having fuel-cell reserves in the 30 percent range.

Unable to do anything about that at the moment, he called *Incredible*, getting an image of her captain, Commander Parr. "How's it going, Commander?"

"Could be worse," Parr replied, smiling for a moment as he focused on Geary. "You didn't need to save quite so many Syndics for us, sir."

"Sorry about that. I've seen the updates from *Incredible*, but I want a personal assessment from you. Can you get her going again soon?"

Parr hesitated. "How long do we have, sir?"

"Maybe a few days. I can't spare any more than that, and we've only got that much because we need to pick up the POWs on Heradao's third planet."

Commander Parr looked around, as if his personal appraisal of this small portion of *Incredible* could give him an answer. "Sir, I'd like to try."

"Two days, Commander."

"I think we can do it, sir." Geary gave him a questioning look. "I *know* we can do it, sir."

"Okay, Commander. Let me know if I can assist with anything."

"*Titan*'s closing on us, sir. She's going to help *Incredible* and *Resolution*."

Geary smiled encouragingly. "You can't get better help than that. Commander Lommand on *Titan* is a good officer. He'll do everything that can be done. I look forward to seeing *Incredible* under way in two days."

He slumped back, rubbing his forehead, after the conversation ended.

Desjani gave him a sympathetic look. "Will *Incredible* make it?"

"Beats the hell out of me. She deserves a chance, though. When is *Intrepid* going to be scuttled?" As they'd feared, that battle cruiser had suffered so much structural damage in addition to other injuries that there was no way to get her fixed up enough to accompany the fleet from this star system. Instead, her power core would be overloaded, blowing the ship into pieces too small for the Syndics to exploit.

Desjani bounced the question to her engineering watchstander, who answered quickly. "Tomorrow, Captain. Late. They're sure they'll have everything salvageable off her by then. The two biggest pieces of *Courageous* are scheduled to be blown up to night."

"Should we tell Duellos?" Desjani asked Geary.

He thought about that. "Have you ever lost a ship?"

"A destroyer at Xaqui, a battle cruiser at Vasil, another destroyer at Gotha, a heavy cruiser at Fingal—"

"You were commanding officer of all those?"

"Just the second destroyer and the heavy cruiser after the one at Fingal."

Geary stared at Desjani. She'd discussed some of her combat experience, but had never dwelt on her own actions or provided details of what had happened to the ships she'd been on. "I'm sorry. You don't talk about them very much."

"No," she admitted. "I don't. We both know why. And that

answers my question about Duellos and *Courageous*, doesn't it?"

"Yes. *Courageous* was his ship. He can decide if he wants to see her final moments."

"I'll pass the word to Cresida, then."

"Thanks. If you ever do want to talk..." Geary offered.

"I know. Same here."

"I'll remember that." He pulled out the scale on the display to view the entire star system. Syndic merchant shipping was still fleeing for any relatively safe place. There didn't seem to be any fixed-orbit defenses in Heradao to worry about, though he suspected they'd find a number of those on the third planet. As Desjani had pointed out, the smaller Syndic flotilla had broken up, its component ships heading in different directions, none of those vectors anywhere near the Alliance warships.

There were still the Syndic HuKs standing picket duty at the jump points, of course, but they weren't a threat and couldn't be caught anyway. Geary leaned back, willing himself to relax now that the hard part was over. Maybe it was over not just in the sense of Heradao, either. What could the Syndics have left to contest the fleet's return to Alliance space? No, the hardest part would be trying to block out more memories of exploding warships.

The only remaining contact with the enemy that the fleet had to handle would be what ever was needed to pick up the Alliance prisoners of war held in the labor camp on the third planet. The fleet's sensors had confirmed that the camp was still there and apparently still occupied by a couple of thousand Alliance prisoners of war. Getting them liberated would require some negotiations, and doubtless some threats, but they'd been down this road before. "Madam Co-President," he asked Rione, "could you get in contact with the Syndics and see how difficult it's going to be to get our POWs off the third planet? Use any necessary threats, and you're free to promise them that we won't bombard the planet if they play nice."

Rione gestured to the communications watch. "Please set up a link to the Syndic command net. When the link is ready, I'll send them a preliminary message." She then settled back herself to await the establishment of the link to the Syndic authorities in this star system.

And waited.

Desjani finally intervened. She might not personally like Rione, but failing to provide proper support to a member of the Alliance government would reflect badly on her ship. "What's the difficulty? Why haven't you established a link for the co-president's transmission?"

"Captain, the Syndic net we've observed since entering this star system doesn't seem to be working right." The communications watch-stander seemed baffled. "It's still there, but we're seeing very strange activity."

"Strange activity?" Desjani pressed.

"Yes, Captain, it's ongoing, so it's hard to assess. It's almost as if..." The watch-stander's apparent bafflement increased. "We just received a transmission addressed to us. Someone calling themselves the Heradao governing council has sent us a message from the third planet. They insist on speaking with Captain Geary."

Geary covered his eyes with one hand, unwilling to bandy words with Syndic CEOs right now. "Tell them that Captain Geary isn't particularly interested in talking at the moment." The third planet was a little over two and a half light-hours away at the moment. Conversations in which an exchange of information required five hours had never been his favorite pastime.

"But... sir, they say they've established a new government here, and they want to negotiate the status of the star system with you."

His hand came down and Geary swiveled to stare at the watch-stander, but Rione spoke before he could. "These people didn't identify themselves as the Syndic commanders in the star system?" she asked.

"No, Madam Co-President. The Heradao governing council. That's how the message ID shows up."

"Are there still transmissions coming from the Syndic authorities in Heradao?"

"Uh... yes, ma'am." The watch-stander shook his head in puzzlement. "The system just identified another new transmission ID, this time from the Free Planet of Heradao Four, whoever that is. Captain Desjani, the Syndic command and control net in this star system seems to be *shredding*. I've never seen anything like this. It's as if—"

Rione had moved to stand by the watch, peering at the readouts and patterns on the communications display. "As if people are grabbing whichever pieces of it they can get their hands on and trying to break those pieces out from the command net." She turned to look at Geary. "I've seen something like this. This star system is dissolving into civil war."

"Where could you have seen something like that?" Desjani demanded, shocked into speaking directly to Rione.

"At Geradin. In Alliance space," Rione added calmly. "I wasn't there, but the records were provided to the Alliance Senate. I studied them."

"Geradin?" Geary questioned. "Where's that?"

"A backwater system, low population and fairly isolated, especially since the hypernet was established, which nonetheless kept sending its best to the Alliance military." Rione made a gesture of distaste. "Which left the field open for the far-from-best to foment trouble. An attempted silent coup turned into open fighting and the subsequent collapse of central authority." She faced Desjani. "And, no, you never heard about it. Security. It wouldn't do to let the people of the Alliance know what could happen even in a place like Geradin."

"Collapsing authority," Geary muttered, eyeing his own display. "Are we seeing signs of open fighting among the Syndics?" No one answered, so Geary punched a control. "Lieutenant Iger. We have indications that central authority in this star system is collapsing or being challenged. I need an assessment and reports on what's happening on each planet as soon as possible."

"Yes, sir! We're working on it."

Geary watched the information available to him, gratified to see more of the Alliance escape pods being picked up. Around the Alliance escape pods, much larger swarms of Syndic pods headed for the nearest refuge. He wondered how the survivors of the Syndic flotilla would align themselves within the star system. For a central authority that might be disintegrating? With any of at least two rebel factions? Or fort up on bases and try to ride out the rebellion until Syndic enforcers arrived in warships to bombard the rebels into submission?

"There aren't many Syndic warships left," Geary said to himself.

Desjani frowned, then nodded as she grasped his meaning. "Not much left to wield the whip. We've gradually turned the Syndic whip hand into fragments of broken warships stretching all the way back to the Syndic home star system."

"Yeah. And we apparently aren't the only ones to realize that." Geary slapped his controls again. "Lieutenant Iger! Don't you have anything yet?"

A window popped up with the intelligence officer's face within it. Iger's expression revealed perplexity. "Sir, the situation is chaotic."

Geary waited for a moment. "Thank you, Lieutenant. I never could have figured that out without intelligence support."

Iger's face flushed in embarrassment. "I'm sorry, sir. We can't give you a clear picture yet because there isn't one. Everything seems to have fallen apart here, like a garment in which every seam fails at once. There are indications that the fourth planet may have gained population in recent decades because dissidents unhappy with the government were moving there. We have no idea who's got real power or how much. No one may know that, including the various parties fighting for control of parts of this star system."

"There is fighting going on?"

"Yes, sir. We've identified explosions, vehicle movements, signal traffic, and other indications of ongoing fighting on the third and fourth planets. We can't tell yet if the fighting is intensifying. Since everything elsewhere is under cover, it's much harder to tell if there's any fighting going on inside buried cities or orbital installations." Iger paused and looked to one side, nodded to someone, then faced Geary again. "We've just detected a substantial blowout affecting one of the Syndic orbiting facilities near the third world, which indicates that they're fighting up there, too."

Desjani had been listening and now shrugged. "Not our problem, sir. We aren't an occupation task force with several hundred thousand ground troops along for the ride."

"I guess not," Geary agreed, then saw Iger shaking his head nervously. "Yes, Lieutenant?"

"The prisoner of war camp, sir, the one on the third world."

He'd actually forgotten that for a moment as the collapse of Syndic central authority grabbed attention. "It is our problem."

Iger was clearly reading updates even as he reported them to Geary. "There are indications of fighting outside the POW camp, but no signs of violence within the camp. Our best estimate is that the guards have forted up to protect themselves."

"Is anyone attacking the camp, Lieutenant?"

"Not that we can tell, sir. But, well, it's early."

"What about orbital nuclear bombardment capability?" Rione asked. "We know the Syndics had that in other systems to help keep their people in line."

"We can't tell if they've got those here, Madam Co-President," Iger replied. "None have been employed."

"They may not have them, then."

"Yes, ma'am, or they may lack a decent target, or they may have temporarily lost control of the nukes due to the command and control net falling apart, or they may be waiting for the various rebel factions to inflict as much harm on each other as possible before the Syndic authorities step in with their big hammer."

Geary drummed his fingers on the armrest of his seat, thinking.

"I assume this is all going to take a while to shake out, and we don't have time to waste. Lieutenant Iger, I need special emphasis on finding out who controls the area of the third planet near the POW camp, and I need the best assessments you can come up with on the ground threat around there as well as any orbital and ground-based defenses this fleet would need to worry about or take out."

"Yes, sir." Iger saluted quickly, and his image vanished.

Geary tapped another control, and the image of Colonel Carabali appeared. "Colonel, are you familiar with the developing situation in this star system and in particular on the third planet?"

Carabali nodded. "Going to hell in a handbasket at hypervelocity, from what I've heard, sir."

"Right. But we need to get the Alliance prisoners of war out of the camp on that planet. We're going to try to find somebody to negotiate their release to us, but it's very likely that your Marines will have a tough job to do."

"That's why the fleet has Marines, sir, to handle the tough jobs." Carabali saluted. "I'll work up a plan, assuming hostiles outside the camp and resistance from the guards inside the camp."

"Thank you. The fleet will clear the way even if we have to crater the entire part of the planet around that camp."

Desjani sighed. "Ground actions. Ugh. I really prefer fleet battles."

"So do I, but we're stuck with this ground action." He frowned at the display. "Let's get the fleet broken up. Leave enough around here to defend the ships under repair and get the rest headed toward the third planet. Madam Co-President, as soon as intelligence identifies someone to talk to you around that POW camp, I'd appreciate it if you began negotiations. Make sure they know that trying to blackmail us by threatening the welfare of the prisoners would be a very bad idea."

"I'll do my best," Rione replied. "Assuming we find somebody who is actually in charge around there. What if I can't?"

"Then Colonel Carabali's Marines are going to come knocking on the door of that camp, and I wouldn't want to be somebody standing in their way when they do."

About twenty-four hours later, as Geary was reviewing the latest status reports from the fleet, Rione came to his stateroom. "We managed to get into direct contact with the POW camp on the third planet. The guards are scared of us and scared of the rebels outside their camp," Rione reported. "They see the Alliance POWs as their only powerup, and they want to ensure they get all they can from that. They're also scared of the Syndic authorities."

"Even with things falling apart and the Syndic fleet almost wiped out?" Geary asked.

"Since people at their level don't know the Syndic fleet has suffered so many losses, that's not a factor for them. Captain Geary, for them the equation is simple. If they resist us, they may die. If they don't resist us and the Syndics reestablish control of this star system, they *and* their families may die."

"So they're going to fight."

"That's what they say."

He glared at the display over his table. "Do you think there's anything we can do to change their minds? Threats? Promises?"

"I've tried both." Rione shook her head, looking weary. "Usually

I spend a lot of time trying to see beneath whatever Syndics are saying to guess what they really mean or what traps might be hidden in their words. The only good thing about this situation is that I feel confident the guards aren't playing us. They mean what they say."

"But how hard will they actually fight?" Geary wondered. "A token resistance or a scorched-earth battle to the death or something in between?"

Rione furrowed her brow in thought. "My own instincts say that any resistance will be more than token. The guards are very worried about how their actions will be viewed by Syndic authorities. But even though they're putting up a good front, I don't think they're eager to die."

"Something in the middle, then. Thanks. Colonel Carabali is going to brief me on the Marine assault plan in about an hour. I'd appreciate it if you let her know your assessment before then so she can factor it into her plan."

"Sorry it couldn't be more pleasant." She gestured to the display. "Any good news?"

"Some. Commander Lommand called from *Titan* to say that he's confident they'll be able to get *Incredible* repaired enough to accompany the fleet. On the other hand, engineers inspecting *Intagliata* found a lot more structural damage had been suffered than we realized, so we're going to have to scuttle that light cruiser, too."

"And the fuel situation remains critical?"

"Yup. After we distribute every fuel cell the auxiliaries have and every one we could salvage off wrecked ships, the fleet will average about thirty-seven percent reserves. We'll burn some of that slowing to orbit the third planet and accelerating away after we get the prisoners, so we'll probably be down to the low thirties by the time we leave Heradao. Fortunately, fuel-cell use in Padronis should be minimal."

"Can we get back with that level of fuel cells?" Rione asked quietly.

Geary shrugged. "In terms of distance, yes, easily. We shouldn't have to fight any more battles between here and Varandal."

"And if we do have to fight more battles?"

"Then it's going to get ugly."

She gazed at the display. "I have an obligation once more to point out your options in such a case."

"I know." He tried not to get angry. "We can load up some of the ships and abandon others. I won't do that. We need every ship. The Alliance needs every ship and every sailor."

"The Alliance needs *this* ship, Captain Geary. It needs the Syndic hypernet key aboard *Dauntless*."

"I never forget that, Madam Co-President. You know, we could save fuel cells by not going after the Alliance prisoners on the third planet."

She gave him a long, hard look. "I suppose I deserved that. You know that even I wouldn't suggest abandoning those people. All right, Captain Geary, use your best judgment, and let's pray the living stars continue to look after us. I will contact the Marine colonel about my impressions of the Syndic guard force at the POW camp and let her know that I am at her service if she wishes me to attempt any other conversations with the Syndic guards."

"Thank you, Madam Co-President."

* * *

An hour later, the virtual presence of Colonel Carabali stood in his stateroom, pointing to two images of the POW camp on the third planet, each bearing symbols displaying different plans for liberating the prisoners. Seen from overhead, the Syndic installation was an almost perfect octagon, each corner of its eight sides anchored on a substantial guard tower, with smaller guard posts spaced between them along the sides. A tall, solid wall of reinforced concrete joined the guard posts. Triple barriers of razor wire ran inside and outside the wall, the cleared areas inside the razor wire bearing every sign of being mined and doubtless under extensive remote sensor surveillance. Farther inside the wall, ranks of buildings filled most of the camp, many of them tagged on the images with probable identifications such as prisoner barracks, guard barracks, hospital, administration, and so on. The center of the camp was clear, a large open field that served as both a landing place for Syndic shuttles and a parade ground.

Geary imagined being locked in such a place, with no hope of release. Until now.

"We've got two basic options," Carabali began in her nononsense briefing voice, "both based on the fact that I've only got a little less than twelve hundred combat-capable Marines left in the fleet. That's far too few to occupy a facility this size and defend its perimeter, even if we don't end up facing any resistance from the guards inside the camp. I understand from Co-President Rione that our governing assumption has to be that the guards will fight."

Her hand swept out, and a finger rested on part of the first image of the POW camp. "One option is that we can concentrate the

Marines and roll through the camp sector by sector, occupying each portion, evacuating the POWs there, then moving on to the next. That has the advantage of keeping the Marines all within easy supporting distance and limiting their exposure to attack. The downside is that it will take longer on the ground, and once the enemy realizes what we're doing, it gives them time to try either pulling out our POWs in sections we haven't occupied yet or digging in among those POWs and using them as hostages. I don't recommend this option."

She faced the next map. "The other alternative is to drop the Marines along the perimeter of the camp, along with a force in the center of the camp to secure the main landing field. There aren't enough Marines to secure the entire perimeter of the camp and the whole interior, but we can block all of the best angles of approach on the perimeter. Then the Marines on the perimeter will proceed inward, sweeping any resistance before them or bypassing strong points, and picking up POWs as they go, concentrating everything toward the center of the camp. We'd be lifting people out of the middle of the camp as fast as possible. This has the advantage of not allowing the enemy time to concentrate or pull out some of our POWs, and as time passes our own forces will concentrate and be able to respond better to attacks. The disadvantages are that our forces, especially initially, will be widely dispersed and unable to support each other. Many of the initial drops will also be more perilous for the shuttles since they'll be spread out along the perimeter."

Geary studied the maps and the colonel. He'd had some training on Marine operations a hundred years ago, but his actual experience with ground actions was limited to what he'd seen since assuming command of this fleet. That hadn't included any operations on this scale, yet as fleet commander he was required to oversee the Marines and make the final decisions on their plans. Fortunately, he'd seen enough of Carabali to have a high degree of trust in her competence. "Despite the higher risks, the second plan is your recommended option?"

"Yes, sir."

"What do you consider to be the odds of success using the first option?"

Carabali frowned slightly as she looked at that map. "If success is defined as rescuing all of the POWs, then my assessment is that option one would offer a maximum of fifty percent odds of success and probably substantially less depending on the Syndic reaction. That option leaves us very vulnerable to what ever response the Syndics choose."

"And the second option?"

Carabali frowned again. "Ninety percent chance of success."

"But the second option has higher chances of casualties for the Marines and damage to the shuttles."

"Yes, sir." Carabali faced him, her expression impassive. "The mission is to rescue the POWs, sir."

That laid it out as plainly as possible. Geary looked at the maps again. To be certain of rescuing the POWs, to carry out the mission, he had to increase the risks to the Marines. Carabali knew that, and he suspected every other Marine knew it, too, on one level or another. And all of them accepted that, because that was what being a Marine meant. "All right, Colonel. I accept your recommendation. We will proceed with the second option. The fleet will provide the maximum level of fire support of which it is capable."

Carabali flicked a tight smile at Geary. "There's a lot of permanent buildings inside that camp. In an urban environment like that, there's likely to be very small gaps between enemy and friendly forces."

"How big a safety zone do you want?"

"One hundred meters, sir, but I don't want that written in stone. We may have to ask for supporting fire a lot closer than that to friendly forces."

"Very well, Colonel." Geary stood up. "You may proceed with detailed planning and execution of the mission. Let me know if anything you need isn't instantly forthcoming."

"Yes, sir." Carabali saluted, then her image disappeared.

The images of the maps lingered for a moment. Geary looked at them, knowing his choice had meant life or death for some of the Marines he was sending down onto that planet, and knowing, like Carabali, that he hadn't had any other real option.

"The fighting seems to have spread substantially on the third and fourth planets," Lieutenant Iger was reporting as the Alliance fleet settled into position above the third planet. An orbital fortress that had tried pumping out shots at the oncoming Alliance fleet had been blown apart by several kinetic-energy projectiles, and since then nothing had attempted engaging the Alliance ships.

All of the Syndic heavy cruisers left in the star system had jumped out, and the remaining light cruisers and HuKs were sticking close to the jump points for other stars. None had made any moves toward the region of the engagement where Geary had left his most badly damaged ships being repaired along with the auxiliaries and a strong escort. "There's still no faction that seems to be gaining control on the ground?"

"No, sir," Iger replied. "There are plenty of claims being made, but we're not seeing evidence on the planetary surface to back up those claims."

"The guard force in the camp has stopped responding to our transmissions," Rione added. "They either can't or won't negotiate any further."

Geary took a look at the display for the camp, imagery overlaid with symbology. In a few places concentrations of Syndic guards had been identified, but for the most part the guards seemed to have vanished. "We haven't spotted any guards leaving the camp?" he asked Iger.

"No, sir. They're all still in there, somewhere."

"What about the POWs?"

"They all seem to be in their barracks, possibly locked down."

Rione eyed the display suspiciously. "If they're going to fight, why haven't the guards taken our prisoners as hostages?"

"Good question." As much as he hated bothering subordinates preparing for action, Geary figured this was something Carabali would want to talk about.

The Marine colonel nodded as if unsurprised by the report. "The guards are getting ready to fight. If you compare the estimated number of prisoners to the estimated size of the guard force, sir, you'll see that the prisoners outnumber the guards. Just as we don't have the numbers to occupy the entire camp in force, they don't have the numbers to guard all of their prisoners and fight us. They're choosing to keep the prisoners locked down. That keeps the prisoners available as future hostages but also ensures the prisoners aren't running around threatening the guards. Our assault plan should forestall any last-ditch plans they have to make use of the prisoners, though."

"I don't understand, Colonel. It sounds like the Syndic guards know they can't win. If they can't fight us and guard all the prisoners at the same time, why the hell aren't they surrendering?" Geary asked.

"Probably because they've been ordered to hold on to the prisoners and resist any attempt to liberate them, sir."

Just as Rione had also guessed. Put up a good fight and maybe die trying to defend the prison camp, or let the Alliance have its personnel and certainly die at the hands of the Syndic authorities. "Looks like we'll be doing this the hard way, Colonel."

"Yes, sir. Request that the fleet carry out the preassault bombardment as laid out in the battle plan."

"Consider it done. Good luck, Colonel."

"They're not asking for much in that bombardment," Desjani observed after Carabali's image vanished.

"There aren't many targets identified yet." Geary indicated the real-time imagery of the camp far below *Dauntless* as the battle cruiser and the rest of the Alliance fleet orbited Heradao's third planet. "We can't just hit the whole camp because it's full of prisoners, and we don't know every building that holds them. The preassault bombardment is mostly aimed at eliminating fixed defensive sites, trying to overawe the defenders, and suppressing their response to the assault." He glanced at the time lines scrolling down one side of the display. Time to launch of Marine shuttles. Time to launch of evacuation shuttles. Time to launch of bombardment.

The aerodynamic chunks of metal formally known as kinetic bombardment projectiles harkened back to the earliest weapons known to humanity. Aside from their streamlined shapes, they worked like rocks, and fleet slang referred to them that way. Unlike rocks hurled with only the force of human muscles, however, these kinetic bombardment rounds were launched from orbit high above the planet, gaining energy every meter of the way as they dropped. When they hit, the results were as devastating as if large bombs had struck. Simple, cheap, and deadly, the rocks were almost impossible to stop once they were fired.

"Marine shuttles launching," the operations watch reported.

On his display, Geary called up an image of the launches, the shapes of the shuttles enhanced for visibility. "I've never seen this many launch at once," he commented to Desjani.

"Sir, you should have been at Urda. Thousands of shuttles coming down. Absolutely amazing." Desjani's eyes shaded for a moment in memory. "Then the Syndics opened fire."

"Bad losses?"

"Horrible." She forced a smile at him. "This won't be like that."

He managed to force a smile back, wishing that Desjani hadn't mentioned Urda.

"First wave of evacuation shuttles launching."

"We have enemy movement on the surface. Armored column heading for the prison camp."

Geary's display illuminated the line of armored vehicles crawling along the surface toward the POW camp. He reached and with careful deliberation tagged the column as a target, asked the combat system for an engagement solution, got it an instant later, then tapped approval. Rocks punched out of three Alliance warships, hurtling downward into the planet's atmosphere. The entire process to firing had taken less than ten seconds.

"Preassault bombardment launching."

A wave of rocks burst from Alliance warships, each projectile aimed at a specific point within the POW camp. With the shuttles coming down slower than the rocks would drop, the bombardment would clear the airspace over the camp before the shuttles reached it.

"Boom," Desjani muttered, as the armored column disappeared under a cloud of fragments and dust tossed into the air by the impacts of the bombardment aimed at it.

"Maybe they'll figure out that resisting us is a bad idea," Geary observed.

"I wouldn't count on it, sir."

"We have surface-based particle-beam batteries opening fire at five locations!" the operations watch called. "Near misses on *Splendid* and *Bartizan*."

Geary faced his display, tagged the batteries, got a firing solution, and launched another bombardment. "Good thing I already had the fleet doing evasive maneuvers."

The preassault bombardment slammed into the surface, some of the rocks aimed simply at trying to suppress unseen defenses but many smashing into identified enemy locations and every guard post or tower. Within moments, craters of rubble had replaced the guard installations, and the formerly solid wall between them had collapsed in many places.

"Do you think there were any of them inside those guard posts?" Desjani asked.

"I doubt it. Colonel Carabali figured they were planning on firing the weapons on the guard posts by remote if we left them standing. So we didn't."

The operations watch called out another report. "Marine shuttles are two minutes from drops."

The locations of the five particle-beam batteries went up in clouds of debris.

"Shuttles on final. Marines on the ground." The operation had a sort of beauty when seen from this high, the shuttles swooping down toward their objectives around the perimeter of the camp and at its center, Marines leaping out as the shuttles hovered, the tracks of fire from enemy troops painting flashing lines as they fired on the Marines or the shuttles. Unlike regular fleet shuttles, the Marine shuttles carried defensive combat systems, which started pumping out grenades and automatic fire at wherever the Syndics were firing from. As the Marines deployed and went to ground, they joined in the barrages, the firepower blowing apart any location holding enemy resistance. The battle sites formed small eruptions of violence at locations all around the perimeter of the camp and at a few places near the landing field in the center.

"We don't know where all of the POWs are," Rione protested, "and the Marines are blowing that camp apart!"

Geary shook his head. "Their battle armor has every known POW location painted. Other than that we have to trust that they'll ID targets before they fire." He pulled up the feed from the Marines.

"The enemy is dug in," a Marine officer was reporting. "Strong resistance around landing zone."

"This isn't going to be pretty," Desjani muttered.

5

"Conventional ground artillery firing upon the camp from locations thirty kilometers to the east and twenty kilometers to the south."

Geary tagged more targets and launched rocks at them. His main display floated to one side, showing the situation on a wide portion of the planet's surface below and orbital locations that could threaten the fleet. To the other side hung an overhead view of the POW camp, symbols crawling along it to mark the movements of friendly and enemy troops on the ground. Directly in front of him, Geary had positioned a string of windows for calling up views from the battle armor of Marines. He had to avoid using those too much, had to avoid getting sucked into the action on one tiny part of the battlefield when he was supposed to be overseeing the entire fleet, but sometimes those personal views from the Marines could provide a very good feel for how things were going for them.

At the moment, that was hard to figure out no matter how he viewed it. On the overall view, some of the Marine platoons and companies were pushing steadily inward toward the center of the camp, symbols for liberated POWs multiplying rapidly around them as they blew open prisoner barracks and collected the occupants. In other areas, the Marines were moving slowly, under fire from Syndic guards entrenched in the buildings on all sides. Evacuation shuttles were dropping down into the center of the camp despite occasional shots fired at them as they descended. On the landing field, a growing number of dazed, liberated prisoners were being hustled toward the first shuttles. The command and control feed from the Marines was filled with reports and warnings.

"Shuttles Victor One and Victor Seven badly damaged by ground fire. Returning to base ships."

"Target building desig five one one! Hit it!"

"They're on the left, too. Small structures bearing zero two one and zero two three true."

"Mines. We're in a field, two Marines down. All units watch for mines."

"Can't somebody do something about that damned artillery?"

"The fleet's on it. Bombardment hitting now."

"Lighting up a bunker. Put a round on it!"

Desjani, who was listening and watching as well, shook her head. "Are we winning?"

"I think so." Geary turned as the combat-systems watch called.

"Sir, we're getting a lot of bombardment requests from the Marines—"

"Every bombardment request outside the one-hundred-meter safety zone from our Marines is supposed to be approved automatically," Geary replied a bit irritably.

"Yes, sir, but we could respond to them a bit faster if they were one hundred percent handled by the automated systems, just like when we engage other ships."

Geary shook his head. "Lieutenant, we might shave some seconds off the response time if we did that, but the Marines asked that every bombardment be verified by a human set of eyes before final approval to ensure it's aimed at the right spot. I'm not going to overrule the preferences of the Marines in this." The lieutenant looked unhappy, so Geary took a moment to explain. "We have no choice but to leave targeting entirely up to the fire-control systems when we're engaging Syndic warships. It's physically impossible for human beings to react quickly enough at the velocities involved. But neither the Syndics on the ground nor our Marines are moving at any appreciable fraction of the speed of light. We can afford to have a human in the loop. If you get any reports of undue delays in approving bombardment requests, I want to know. I assure you that the Marines will be the first to let us know if they're unhappy."

"Yes, sir." Only slightly abashed, the lieutenant focused back on his tasks.

"You're tolerant of lieutenants," Desjani remarked, her eyes still fixed on her own display.

"I used to be one. And so did you." Like Desjani, Geary kept most of his attention on the situation but welcomed anything that might cut the tension slightly. He suspected she could see how wound up he'd become and was trying to relax him a little.

"Not me," Desjani denied. "I was born the commanding officer of a battle cruiser."

"That must have been painful for your mother."

She grinned. "Mom's tough, but even she didn't like having the sideboys in the delivery room." Then the smile vanished as a high-priority transmission came over the Marine net.

"Third Company is pinned down!"

Geary tapped windows until he picked up the lieutenant in command of that unit. The view from the lieutenant's combat armor showed broken, tumbled walls shuddering and blowing apart under the impact of enemy fire. "Heavyweapons emplacements and hidden bunkers," the lieutenant continued. "We must have stumbled onto some kind of citadel area. We're badly outgunned here, and we've taken substantial casualties."

Colonel Carabali's voice came on. "Can you withdraw toward the center of the camp by stages, Lieutenant?"

"Negative, Colonel, negative!" The view through the lieutenant's armor jumped as something exploded with enough force to toss around nearby Marines. "We cannot move without being targeted. Request all available fleet fire support." Geary watched the tactical maps pop up on the lieutenant's heads-up display, watched as the lieutenant tagged scores of targets in a rough circle around the friendly symbols marking the positions of the Marines of the Third Company. "Request bombardment support on the following coordinates. All available supporting fire as soon as possible."

"Sir," the combat-systems watch reported, "we've received another Marine fire-support request, but the targets are inside the safety parameters."

"How far inside?" He read the data, blowing out a long breath as he saw the distances.

As Geary was checking, Colonel Carabali's image appeared.

"Captain Geary, my Third Company needs fire support and it needs it now."

"Colonel, most of these targets are only fifty meters from your Marines. Some of them are within twenty-five meters."

"I understand, Captain Geary. That's where the enemy is."

"Colonel, we're dropping rounds through atmosphere. I can't guarantee that our own fire won't hit those Marines!"

"We know that, sir," Carabali stated. "The lieutenant knows that. This is what he needs. He's the senior officer on the scene. He's made the call that these targets have to be engaged despite the danger to own forces. Request approve and execute the fire mission as soon as possible, sir."

Geary looked into her eyes. Carabali understood the danger, too, but was accepting her on-scene commander's judgment. As fleet commander, he could do no less. "Very well, Colonel. It's on its way." He turned to Desjani. "How can we maximize the accuracy of a surface bombardment right now?"

Desjani spread her hands. "Through atmosphere and all the junk we've already tossed up? Get the bombarding ship in as low an orbit as you can manage. But that will expose the ship to fire from the planet."

"Okay." A quick scan of the display showed the right candidate. A battleship could deliver enough firepower and have the best chance of surviving counterfire from the ground. "*Warspite*, proceed to lowest orbit and execute following fire-support mission as soon as possible."

"*Warspite*, aye. On our way."

"Sir, we have detections of aircraft en route the POW camp. Aircraft assessed military profile, all using maximum stealth capabilities."

"Engage them," Geary ordered.

Hell-lances lashed down from orbit, forming webs of high-energy particles around the Syndic aircraft. With so many Alliance warships in space above the planet and able to fire on targets, the aircraft didn't have a chance. Hard to see though the aircraft were, even a glancing blow from a hell-lance was enough to knock them out, and a lot of hell-lances filled the atmosphere around the aircraft. "All aircraft assessed destroyed. *Warspite* opening fire."

On the view from the lieutenant commanding the Third Company, walls began blowing inward, and the ground jumped in a continuous wild dance as *Warspite* hurled hell-lances and small kinetic projectiles into her targets. The feed from the lieutenant hazed as the destruction continued, dust and charged particles filling the air around him, then cut off completely.

"We've lost comms with the Marine Third Company," the communications watch responded. "There's so much junk in the air from the bombardment and the hell-lance fire that we can't get signals through. We're trying to reestablish contact, but it'll probably be a few minutes."

Was there anyone left to reestablish contact with? Geary had just had time to formulate that thought when another watch-stander called out.

"Missile launches from Syndic orbital facility Alpha Sigma. Three missiles. Assessed orbital-nuclear bombardment warheads. Initial tracks toward site of POW camp. Combat systems recommend vectoring light cruiser *Octave* and destroyers *Shrapnel* and *Kris* to destroy the missiles, and launching kinetic rounds from *Vengeance* to destroy the firing installation."

"Approved. Execute the commands." Geary looked toward Rione. "So they did have nukes in orbit."

"These might not be all of them," she answered.

"More aircraft inbound toward POW camp. Assessed military."

"Engage them," Geary ordered.

"Surface-based Intermediate Range Ballistic Missile launches detected. Trajectories targeted on POW camp. Combat systems recommend engage missiles immediately with hell-lance fire and that *Relentless* bombard the IRBM launch site."

"Do it."

"Marine Sixth Company reports encountering a boobytrapped area. Several casualties." An alert sounded. "*Warspite* has taken a hit from a surface-based particle-beam battery. *Warspite* is undertaking evasive maneuvers and engaging the battery with bombardment munitions. *Warspite* reports fire-support mission complete."

Still nothing from Third Company on their circuit.

"IRBMs and launch site destroyed. *Octave* has destroyed two of the nuclear bombardment missiles. *Shrapnel* has taken out the third. *Warspite* reports surface particle-beam battery destroyed. Estimated time to kinetic-round impacts on orbital launch site is three minutes."

Carabali's image appeared again. "Sir, we've spotted two ground convoys heading for the camp under cover of the dust thrown up by the bombardments so far." Next to her, imagery of the convoys appeared. "Our recce drones operating under the dust identified uniforms and weapons in both convoys before we lost one of the drones to ground fire."

"All right, Colonel. We'll take care of those convoys." Geary passed the data to the combat systems and watched a recommended engagement pattern pop up an instant later. He punched approve and saw another wave of kinetic rounds burst out of several Alliance warships, headed downward. "Good thing kinetic rounds are cheap and plentiful," he remarked to Desjani. Was this what ancient gods would have felt like, hurling death and destruction from above onto the humans and their structures far below?

"Bombardment impacting Syndic orbital facility Alpha Sigma."

Geary saw a flock of escape pods heading away from the doomed Syndic facility, then the Alliance rocks began hitting and blowing apart huge pieces of the Syndic orbital base. Within moments, it vanished, replaced by a cloud of junk.

"Comms reestablished with Marine Third Company."

Geary tagged the window and saw a static-riddled vision of almost total destruction. The lieutenant sounded stunned as he reported in. "Enemy fire has ceased."

Carabali's order snapped back. "Withdraw immediately along line one zero five true. I'm sending forces to link up with you."

"Colonel, our dead—"

"We'll come back for them. Get you and your wounded out *now!*"

"Understood, Colonel. On our way."

Our dead. Your wounded. Geary looked at the status readouts for the Third Company. It had landed with ninety-eight Marines. Sixty-one were still alive, and of those, forty showed various degrees of injury.

The bombardments aimed at the two Syndic surface convoys reached their targets, and two sections of roadway and surrounding terrain rose toward the sky as everything within the strike zone blew apart under the tremendous impacts of the Alliance projectiles.

"Sir," Carabali reported, "we have indications of enemy pursuit organizing behind Third Company's withdrawal."

"Thank you, Colonel. We'll take care of it." Geary passed the target area to *Warspite*. After viewing the Marines' casualties, he wasn't interested in humanitarian gestures toward the enemy trying to kill his people. "Turn this area into a dead zone, *Warspite*."

"*Warspite*, aye. It'll be a pleasure, sir."

As *Warspite* hurled another bombardment toward the planet's surface, Geary pulled back his view for a moment. The region around and at the borders of the POW camp had been turned into a seething hell of craters and dust. Other areas on the ground showed craters where kinetic rounds had taken out surface launch sites or batteries, and here and there clusters of damage marked where Alliance hell-lances aimed at Syndic aircraft had gone on to strike anything on the surface in their line of fire. Parts of the city nearest the POW camp were burning, but so were substantial portions of other cities on the planet, and as Geary watched, a massive explosion obliterated a section of one of the biggest cities on the planet. "They did that to themselves?" he asked.

"On purpose or by accident," Desjani confirmed.

"More aircraft inbound."

"If they're assessed military, then engage. Weapons free on all military aircraft heading toward that POW camp."

"Yes, sir."

Rione was gazing bleakly at the display. "You think they would've figured out how useless this all was. Everything they throw at us is just getting destroyed, usually with damage to other things on the surface."

"If the command and control net is still as fragmented as it looks, no Syndic in orbit or on the surface may have a decent picture of what's going on," Geary pointed out. "We don't even know who's giving orders to these units. Some of them may be operating independently, following standing orders to resist any force attacking the planet."

His eyes went to the window for the lieutenant leading Third Company. The battle armor showed a gradual lessening of destruction as the Marines made their way out of the area flattened by *Warspite*. But as Geary watched, the image suddenly blanked, to be replaced by another of roughly the same scene but from another spot. "Lieutenant Tillyer is down," someone was saying. The window identified the new speaker as Sergeant Paratnam. A building to one side collapsed as Marine fire tore it apart. "We got the sniper."

"Understood," Carabali replied. "I read you one hundred fifty meters from a linkup with elements of Fifth Company. Do you have them on your HUD?"

"Yes, Colonel. Got 'em." Paratnam sounded immensely relieved. "Proceeding to linkup."

Geary tapped a control, getting the health stats for the Marines in Third Company. Lieutenant Tillyer's status readouts were all zeroed. "One hundred fifty meters," he murmured.

"Sir?" Desjani asked.

"It's funny, isn't it? In a space engagement, one hundred fifty meters is too small a distance to worry about. At point one light speed we cover that distance in a tiny fraction of a second. It might as well be nothing. Except for weapons targeting. Then it means the difference between a miss or a direct hit. And for a Marine on a planet's surface that small distance decides life and death. He takes the chance of calling in our own fire right on top of his own position, he leads his unit to safety, and just short of safety, he dies."

Desjani looked away for a moment. "The living stars decide our fates. It often seems random, but there's always a purpose."

"You truly believe that?"

Her eyes met his, and Geary thought for a moment that he could see reflections of every death Desjani must have witnessed in this war, every friend and family member she'd lost. "If I didn't," she said quietly, "I couldn't keep going."

"I understand." Not for the first time he remembered that the people around him had grown up with this war. So had their parents. He couldn't begin truly to feel the pain they must have endured as the casualty tolls mounted ever higher with no end in sight.

"You didn't always." She gave him a sad smile. "You couldn't handle even minor losses once. Now, you can endure them and keep on. But I felt sadness back then, seeing your reaction to the loss of a single ship, and wishing I hadn't been born in a time when such innocence could never be."

"I can't remember the last time I was called innocent. Back when I was an ensign, I guess." Geary took a deep breath. "Let's get this battle done with and make sure we lose as few more people as possible."

The watch-standers and automated combat systems would alert him to anything he needed to know, but Geary made a last check of the larger picture before diving back into a close-up of the action in the POW camp.

On the overhead image of the POW camp, a swarm of human bodies could now be seen clustered near the large, open center. Left open in the middle was the landing field where Alliance shuttles were touching down and lifting off in what appeared a calmly choreographed operation. Geary called up a screen for one of Marines controlling the evacuation and saw a scene of seeming bedlam, the sky painted with the aftereffects of Alliance bombardments and hell-lance fire, peoples rushing here and there, shuttles dropping fast, loading liberated POWs as quickly as they could pack the bodies in, then leaping back upward. It took a moment to spot the order hidden behind the frantic activity.

The officers among the POWs were apparently keeping the other POWs in clusters until called to send people for a shuttle, and the Marines were sorting out and guiding disoriented former prisoners while shouting everyone into maintaining discipline. To one side he saw battle armor labeled with Colonel Carabali's ID huddled next to a Marine shuttle with a couple of other Marines standing watch over her while she doubtless concentrated on the movements of her units.

"I wonder," Desjani remarked, "if those former prisoners are trying to figure out if they're being rescued or if the apocalypse has come."

"Maybe both. Colonel Carabali, when opportunity permits I'd like your assessment of the operation."

Her image appeared instantly. "Better than I'd feared, sir. We've taken casualties in almost every unit as we withdrew toward the center of the camp, but only Third Company got badly beat-up. Apparently they did stumble into an area intended as a last-ditch defensive zone for the Syndic guards. The evacuation of the liberated POWs is proceeding with no other holdups. I estimate forty minutes until the last POW is off, then another twenty minutes before the last Marine shuttle lifts."

"Thank you, Colonel. We'll try to keep the Syndics off your backs until then."

Carabali frowned in surprise and it took Geary a moment to realize it wasn't in response to his statement but to something that had come in to her over another channel. "Sir, we've got guards and their families trying to surrender in exchange for safe passage out of here."

"Families?" His stomach clenched as Geary thought about the bombardments hitting the camp.

"Yes, sir. We hadn't seen any, either. Just a moment, sir." Carabali turned to some nearby POWs and spoke quickly, then reactivated her circuit with Geary. "The former prisoners say the guards' families lived outside the camp. The guards must have brought them in for safety when the fighting started on the planet."

"And then invited a battle on top of their heads?" Geary barked in disbelief.

"Agreed, sir. Our personnel who were imprisoned here say there are extensive underground storage areas in the north portion of the camp and are guessing the guards kept their families safe in those."

Geary checked the display of the camp quickly, seeing that the northern areas were almost unmarked by fighting. "Thank the living stars they had the brains to do that and not to resist our

Marines in that area. What does safe passage mean? Where do they want to go?"

"Wait one, sir." Carabali passed on the question, then waited for it to be passed to the Syndics and a reply to come back. "Off-planet, sir."

"Out of the question."

"They say if they're left here, it'll be a death sentence. The revolutionaries in the city demanded the Alliance prisoners from them, and the guards refused to turn them over without proper orders. The guards claim they held off the revolutionaries until we got here, but with the camp shot to hell and so many casualties when they tried to fight us off, they can't hope to hold out once we leave."

"Damn." Geary turned and explained the situation to Rione and Desjani. "Suggestions?"

"If they hadn't fought us," Desjani pointed out with some heat, "they'd be able to defend themselves once we left. Besides, we can't lift them off the planet. None of our ships are configured for that many prisoners. And in any event we don't owe them any favors after they did their best to chop up our Marines. They dug this hole for themselves."

Rione looked unhappy, but nodded. "There doesn't seem any way to assist them at this point, Captain Geary."

"Yeah, but as long as they keep fighting, we keep losing people." Geary sat and stared at the display for a moment, letting options cascade through his mind. One caught his attention, and he focused on it, then called Carabali back. "Colonel, here's what you offer them. They stop all resistance and we stop killing them. Once we've lifted all of our people off, we'll bombard the approaches from the city while the surviving guards and their families withdraw in the other direction. If anyone tries to hit them while we're still within range, we'll provide cover. That's the best deal they're going to get."

"Yes, sir. I'll pass that on and see what they say."

Five minutes later, as another flight of Syndic aircraft was torn apart in midair, and two more Alliance bombardments blew apart another surface particle-beam battery and a missile launch site preparing to fire, Carabali came back on. "They agree, sir. They say they're spreading the word for all of the guards to cease resistance and withdraw with their families toward the east side of the camp. They ask that we not engage them."

"Agreed, Colonel, unless they start shooting at us again."

"I'll pass the word for cease-fire, but we'll keep a strong force watching them, sir."

Over the next few minutes the movements of the Marines closing on the center of the camp changed, some speeding up to reach the center quicker and others veering off to form a defensive line between the center of the camp and the enemy symbols, which began appearing as the guards broke cover to withdraw toward the east. Geary zoomed in the view, seeing through the dust filling the air infrared signatures that indicated groups of humans appearing and joining the withdrawal. Switching views again gave him a series of windows showing what was being seen by Marines watching the Syndics pull out. Targeting solutions danced on the Marine HUDs as they caught sight of Syndic guards in light battle armor shepherding civilians with no protection at all through the streets of the camp. Weapons were aimed and ready, but the

Syndics behaved themselves, moving with haste, and the Marines held their fire.

He paused in his sweep through the Marine views as a sergeant's voice crackled. "Don't even think about it, Cintora."

"I was just practicing aiming," Cintora protested.

"Pull the trigger, and you'll be up on charges."

"Sarge, they messed up Tulira and Patal—"

"Lower your weapon *now*!"

Geary waited a moment longer, but Cintora had apparently realized he wasn't going to get away with anything and remained silent. If the sergeant hadn't been alert, or had been as angry with the Syndics as Cintora, it wasn't hard to imagine what would have happened.

Another urgent message drew Geary back to the big picture. "Our recce drones have spotted a third ground convoy en route the camp from the northwest, and what looks like infiltrators on foot closing from the southwest," Colonel Carabali reported. "Request both targets be taken under fire by the fleet."

Geary took a moment to look over the combat systems' firing solution, then hit approve and watched another barrage of kinetic projectiles hurled down toward the planet.

"Sir, the Free Heradao governing council is requesting a cease-fire."

"Free Heradao? Weren't they just the Heradao governing council before?"

"Uh, yes, sir. It's the same circuits they called on last time and the same transmission ID."

Geary glanced at Rione. "Any idea what the name change means?"

She looked frustrated. "Probably not a lot. They may have

merged with another group of rebels and picked up the 'free' from that, or they may have decided 'free' sounded better, or there may have been a turnover in their leadership. Or it could be something else. In any event, I wouldn't assume the name change has any identificance for us."

"You've talked to them, though. Are they worth talking to again?"

"No."

Desjani raised her eyebrows in surprise. "A short and straight answer from a politician," she muttered too low for Rione to hear. "The living stars have given us a miracle."

"Thank you, Captain Desjani," Geary said. "Madam Co-President, please inform the Free Heradao governing council that we will engage any threat against our ships or our personnel on the surface or any forces heading toward the POW camp. If they refrain from posing such threats, we will not strike at them."

"Sir, we've got another problem." Colonel Carabali looked unhappy, which was a clue that this was a major problem. "My screening forces on the west side of the camp are picking up signs that highly trained enemy forces in maximum-stealth gear are trying to infiltrate past my Marines. Detections are fleeting and small, but our best estimate is that we're facing perhaps a squad of Syndic Special Forces commandos."

"How much of a threat are they? Are they just scouts?" Geary asked.

"Their mission profile and some of the signs our gear has picked up indicates they may well be equipped with hupnums, sir."

"Hupnums?" It sounded like some whimsical creature in a fairy tale.

"Human Portable Nuclear Munitions," Carabali elaborated.

No wonder Carabali was unhappy. Geary checked the time line. "Colonel, it looks like you're getting close to being able to pull out. Even if those Syndic commandos manage to plant those things, they'll have to set the timers to give them time to get free of the blast zone. Why can't we get out of there well before the timers set off the nukes?"

Carabali shook her head. "Sir, I trained on Alliance hupnums, and everyone in my group, instructors included, believed that the timers on the hupnums were fake. We reasoned that any target worth sneaking in a nuke would be too valuable to risk failing a strike and perhaps having the nuke taken by the enemy during the time required for an individual to egress following planting the weapon."

Geary stared at her. "Are you saying you assumed the nuke would go off as soon as it was armed?"

"Or very soon afterward, yes, sir. I assume the Syndics would be even more inclined toward that logic, sir. We have to presume the hupnums will detonate immediately after they've been placed and armed."

That blew Geary's time line all to hell. "Recommendation, Colonel?"

"I've diverted two of the shuttles on their return trips long enough to pick up two Persian Donkeys. With those –"

"Persian Donkeys, Colonel?"

Carabali looked surprised that he didn't know the term. "Mark Twenty-Four personnel grouping simulators."

"Which do what?"

"They... each simulate a large group of personnel. Each Persian

Donkey uses a variety of active measures to create the illusion of many people. Seismic thumpers create ground vibrations appropriate to a crowd moving around, infrared bugs generate heat signatures all over the place, other bugs create audible noise, transmitters generate a level of message traffic and active sensor activity matching that of a military force around the site, and so on. For someone using remote nonvisual sensors, the Donkeys make it look like plenty of people are in a location."

He got it then. "You want to fool the Syndic commandos into thinking their targets are still present until it's too late for the Syndics to hit the real evacuation."

"Yes, sir," Carabali agreed. "But I need to keep a screening force in place, and by the time I get everyone else lifted, those commandos are going to be close. We can slow them down, but we can't stop them." An image appeared on Geary's display, showing the colonel's tactical planning screen. "I'll put the Donkeys here and here, with any line of sight to them blocked from the directions the Syndic commandos are coming in. I'll need to have platoons of Marines here, here, and here." Rough, bent arcs formed of individual Marine symbols flashed into existence. "Right after my last evac shuttle lifts, three shuttles will ground at these spots along the edge of the landing area closest to my people. At that point the last three platoons run like hell for the shuttles and boost out of there. The Donkeys will be set to self-destruct immediately afterward."

Geary studied the plan, nodding. "Does that leave enough time for the last shuttles to get clear if the Syndics realize what's happening and pop their nukes right then?"

"I don't know, sir. Probably not, but it's my best option."

"Wait a moment, Colonel." He spun toward Desjani and explained the situation. "What do you think? Is there anything we can do with enemy troops armed with nukes that close to our people's emergency evac?"

Desjani bent her head in thought for a long moment, then looked over at him. "There may be something we could try. I was only a junior officer, but as best I recall it worked at Calais Star System. A situation a lot like this, with the enemy coming right on the heels of the last shuttles out."

"What did you do?"

She twitched a humorless smile. "We dropped a saturation bombardment timed to cross paths with the evac shuttles and hit the surface just as the shuttles got enough altitude to clear the danger zone."

"You're kidding. Dropping that many rocks through the same planetary airspace that your shuttles are traversing? What did the shuttle pilots think of that plan?"

"They screamed bloody murder. The evacuees weren't thrilled, either. But we can do what we did then, download the bombardment pattern and planned trajectories of each projectile into the autopilots of the shuttles. In theory, the autopilots can weave a path between the rocks and make it up high enough before the rocks start hitting and blowing the surface sky-high."

He thought about it. He didn't like it. But... "You said it worked at Calais?"

"Yes, sir. Mostly it worked, anyway. Not every rock going through atmosphere sticks exactly to its preplanned trajectory. But at Calais we had a lot more shuttles lifting through the barrage than we'll be worried about here."

Mostly it worked. Geary called Carabali again. "Colonel, we've got an option to support your final lift." He outlined the concept Desjani had described. "It's up to you whether we try it."

It seemed that he'd finally managed to surprise Carabali. If that was surprise and not horror he was seeing. But the colonel exhaled and nodded. "If we don't try that, sir, odds are we'll lose all three birds and the Marines on them. At least this idea offers them all a much better chance. I'll notify the pilots of the last three shuttles of what's going to happen."

"Let me know if none of them want to volunteer so I can canvass the fleet for other pilots."

Carabali frowned slightly. "They already volunteered, sir. All three of those pilots are Marines. Please inform me when you have details of the bombardment, sir."

"Will do." Geary broke the connection with Carabali, leaned back, and took a deep breath. "All right, everybody. We're going with Captain Desjani's plan. We need the bombardment as finely timed as possible if those shuttles are going to have a chance."

"It's not exactly *my* plan," Desjani muttered, then swung into action. "Lieutenant Julesa, Lieutenant Yuon, Ensign Kaqui, pull up the Marine evac plan as most recently amended by Colonel Carabali and run a bombardment plan through the combat systems. We need something that will saturate the area the shuttles have left, and coordinated with the Marine time line so that the bombardment hits within five seconds of the shuttles clearing the danger zone."

"Captain," Lieutenant Yuon asked, "what if one or more of the shuttles develops a problem, or gets delayed otherwise?"

"Assume no delays. All three of the last birds have to lift exactly on time, or they'll die at the hands of the Syndics. I need that bombardment pattern five minutes ago."

The watch-standers leaped into action while Geary watched his display. On the portion given over to the ground battle, he could see the sudden appearances and disappearances of enemy symbols as traces of the Syndic commandos were picked up by Marine sensors. The Marines were firing on every detection, but apparently not getting hits against the extremely difficult targets moving through an environment full of things to hide behind. As the Syndic commandos snuck ever closer to the landing field, the Marines were slowly falling back themselves, trying to maintain a screen between the Syndics and the center of the camp.

On the field itself, the last liberated POWs were being bundled into shuttles, and Carabali was calling in her other Marines. The two Persian Donkeys were visible on the display, busily churning out indications of large groups of people still near the landing field.

A lot of things were going to have to work right. He hated depending on that.

"Strange, isn't it?" Desjani asked. "It's just like at Corvus, dealing with Syndic Special Forces commandos on a suicide mission."

"I guess it is sort of like that," Geary admitted.

"You didn't kill the ones at Corvus." She turned a questioning gaze on him. "But we're going to nail these."

"Right. At Corvus I wanted to underline the futility of the commandos' effort and deny them martyrdom. Here"— Geary waved at his display—"they're going to get their martyrdom, but they still won't accomplish their mission. We will accomplish our mission despite their best efforts, though, making their deaths meaningless. In any event, there's no other way to stop these commandos except by ensuring they get blown away."

"Captain!" Lieutenant Julesa called. "The bombardment plan is ready."

"Shoot it to me and Captain Geary."

Geary studied the result, fighting down qualms as he saw the trajectories of over a hundred kinetic bombardment rounds intersecting with those of the three shuttles, then saw the pattern hit just as the shuttles cleared the danger zone from the bombardment. "Well, Captain Desjani, let's hope this plan of yours works."

"You can call it my plan if it works," Desjani objected.

Geary hit the commands sending the plan to Colonel Carabali to pass on to her shuttles and transmitting it as an execute order to the ships tasked with being in the right positions at exactly the right time to launch the bombardments. Within moments, the battleship *Relentless* called back. "Sir, is this plan right?"

"It's right. We need it executed perfectly."

"That's putting it mildly, sir. The Marines are okay with this?"

"They're okay with it."

"Very well, sir. We'll put the rocks where they're supposed to go and make sure they hit at the right time."

"Thanks. *Reprisal*, any problems on your end?"

Reprisal's commanding officer answered about ten seconds later. "No, sir. We're loading the maneuvers and firing commands into *Reprisal*'s systems right now. We'll do our part."

Geary gazed bleakly at his display. Colonel Carabali was piling into one of the last shuttles on the POW camp's landing field along with the last Marines on the field. The three platoons holding off the Syndic commandos were still falling back as they tried to slow the commandos' infiltration toward the landing field. The momentary detections of the commandos showed them getting far too close to the landing field for comfort.

"Here come the last three shuttles," Desjani noted.

The operations watch called out right afterward. "Final evac shuttles landing in five, four, three, two, one, they're down."

All of the Marines in the last three platoons seemed to bolt as one for the shuttles. Geary wondered how long it would take the Syndic commandos to realize what was happening.

"*Relentless* and *Reprisal* are launching the covering bombardment," the combat-systems watch reported. Geary sat, watching the rocks head downward to where the three shuttles sat, the Marines just now reaching the shuttles and hurling themselves inside. On one side of the display, two time lines counted down, one for the shuttles to get off the ground and the other for the moment of impact for the bombardment. The two sets of numbers were far too close together for comfort.

Dauntless's bridge was as quiet as he'd ever heard it, quiet in that unnatural way when people waited to see the outcome of a life-or-death gamble.

"The shuttles have to lift within the next ten seconds," Desjani reported.

"Yeah. I see." He could also see a few final Marines sprinting toward their craft.

"Shuttle one is in the air, climbing at maximum," the operations watch reported. "We're seeing ground fire aimed at the shuttles. The Syndic commandos are breaking cover to engage the last shuttles. Shuttle defensive systems are firing back and engaging protective countermeasures. Shuttle three is in the air. Shuttle two reports a problem sealing the main compartment hatch." Geary felt his breathing freeze. "Shuttle two is lifting with the hatch open. Speed and protection will be compromised."

He could see the action, the tracks of enemy fire reaching for the shuttles as they tore skyward, counterfire from the shuttles racing downward to strike among the indications of Syndic commandos, who still remained almost invisible in their stealth gear. And, from above, just over a hundred bombardment projectiles seconds from passing through the same airspace as the shuttles.

It was strange how very long a second could be.

6

The tracks of shuttles and bombardment merged, then diverged, the shuttles clawing for altitude and the rocks hurtling down the final distance to the surface. Geary heard the shuttle pilots yelling over their command circuit. "One of those damned things almost took off my ear!"

"Severe turbulence! Trying to maintain control!"

"We lost the main hatch!" That was shuttle two. "Make sure those Marines are strapped in and their armor is sealed! That's all that's going to be between them and vacuum!"

Beneath the fleeing shuttles, the entire central section of the former POW camp blew skyward in a single huge blast as the impacts of all of the bombardment rocks merged. Debris and shrapnel shot upward, chasing after the escaping shuttles as if the planet itself were reaching to grab them and pull the shuttles back to the surface.

Then another explosion burst out of the destruction on one side of the camp, an even more massive blast mushrooming toward the heavens.

"One of the Syndic nukes detonated," the operations watch reported.

"Come on," Desjani urged the shuttles in a whisper as they raced upward with shock waves and debris still in hot pursuit.

"We're hit! Damage to starboard lift unit. Continuing on track, maximum velocity reduced twenty percent."

"Climbing clear of danger zone."

"Multiple strikes on our underside. Two penetrations. Shifting to backup on maneuvering controls."

Geary could never be sure at which moment the crisis passed, the instant in which the three shuttles outran the death of the POW camp and the Syndic commandos within it. But at some point there was no longer any doubt.

"All shuttles clear. *Colossus* is closing on shuttle two for an emergency docking. Shuttles one and three proceeding as assigned to *Spartan* and *Guardian*."

"Okay," Desjani said, grinning. "It was my plan."

"Right," Geary agreed, almost laughing with relief as he triggered his command circuit. "*Relentless* and *Reprisal*, excellent shooting. Every ship performed with distinction, and every Marine and shuttle in this fleet went above and beyond the call of duty. As soon as the final shuttle is recovered, the fleet will proceed toward the jump point for Padronis." He closed his eyes for a moment after finishing the transmission, breathing heavily. "And I thought fleet actions were tough."

Far beneath the fleet, the only movements within the remnants of the former POW camp were caused by debris falling back to the surface and the mushroom cloud still rising on one side. Desjani was smiling. "Those Syndics successfully carried out the suicide part of their mission, anyway."

Geary thought of what those commandos could have done to his Marines, his shuttles, and the thousands of Alliance prisoners who had been liberated, and nodded in agreement.

The next half hour felt like a major anticlimax as the shuttles found their assigned homes on different ships of the fleet. Far beneath the fleet, parts of Heradao's surface writhed as forces loyal to rebel factions and Syndic central authority clashed, but none of them tried to target the Alliance ships. "Do we need to provide cover for those withdrawing Syndic guards and their families?" Geary asked.

"There's no sign of pursuit, sir. It's likely most people on that planet think the guards went up with the camp."

"Good." After all the frantic activity, Geary felt fidgety waiting for the time when he could order the fleet into motion. While he waited, a postponed question popped back into his head. He bent a puzzled look at Desjani. "Why the hell do the Marines call their deception devices Persian Donkeys?"

Desjani replied with her own baffled expression. "I'm sure there's a reason. Lieutenant Casque, you don't have anything to do at the moment. See if the database can explain it."

"And who the hell named those things hupnums? It makes them sound cute."

This time Desjani just spread her hands helplessly. "I'm sure it was a committee. What did they call hupnums in, uh, the past?"

Geary wondered just what phrase Desjani had hastily avoided using to describe his time a century ago. "They called them PNWs. Portable Nuclear Weapons. Nice and simple."

"But every nuclear weapon is portable," Desjani objected. "Some may be carried by very large missiles or ships, but they're still portable."

He glared at her. "Did you ever work as an editor at your uncle's literary agency?"

"A few times. What does that have to with anything?"

"Do you *like* the term hupnums, Captain Desjani?"

"No! In the fleet we usually call them NAMs."

"NAMs?" Why couldn't the future come with a glossary explaining common terms? Though come to think of it, he had heard sailors using the term a few times.

"Yes." Desjani made an apologetic gesture. "Nuclear-Armed Marines. It's shorthand among the sailors for something that's a bad idea."

Geary fought to keep a straight face. "I guess some things never change. Do you think there was ever a time when Marines and sailors got along?"

"We get along fine if planetary forces try to mess with us," Desjani pointed out. "And when there's a mission to carry out."

"What about in bars?"

"That usually doesn't go so good. Unless there's planetary-forces types in the bars, too."

"Just like in the past," Geary agreed.

"Captain?" Lieutenant Casque called. "The database says those things are called Persian Donkeys because of some really ancient story. These people called Persians invaded some other place and got trapped by an enemy that was more mobile, so they had to get away at night without the enemy realizing they were going. The Persians had these things called donkeys that the enemy hadn't seen before, and these donkeys made a lot of noise, so the Persians left all the donkeys behind to fool the enemy into thinking all of the Persians were still there. I guess these donkeys were some kind of primitive deception device."

Lieutenant Yuon gave Casque a pained look. "Donkeys are animals."

"Oh. Captain, donkeys are—"

"Thank you. I know." Desjani seemed skeptical as she questioned Lieutenant Casque. "How old is this story? What does ancient mean?"

"Captain, the source is marked as 'ancient book— Earth' and that's as old as it gets. I guess the Marines read about it in that book."

"Excellent assumption, Lieutenant." Desjani made a who-knew gesture toward Geary. "There's your answer, sir. The Marines heard this ancient story. Maybe they study it as the first documented case of deception in warfare. No, that'd be that wooden horse thing I heard about once. Anyway, old story."

"Even older than I," Geary replied. "At least I'm pretty sure that must have happened before I joined the fleet." He'd never expected to be able to joke about how long ago that had been, but in the glow of relief after the ground engagement, such things didn't seem to hold as much anguish as they once did.

"Sir," the operations watch called, "all shuttles have been recovered."

"Excellent." Geary sent the orders accelerating the Alliance fleet toward a rendezvous with the repaired warships, auxiliaries, and escorts back in the region of the engagement with the Syndic flotilla. Once joined up again, the fleet would head for the jump point for Padronis. "Something just occurred to me. We knew how badly the Syndic fleet has been hurt lately, but how did the rebels in this star system know? They broke their leash almost as soon as we'd destroyed the Syndic flotilla here."

Rione answered, her voice thoughtful. "There's bound to have been rumors among the citizens of the Syndicate Worlds, but the only ones who would know the true extent of the fleet's losses would be senior personnel and CEOs. Which means some of the senior Syndics and CEOs are part of the forces that are trying to overthrow Syndic control of Heradao. The rot is just as bad as we suspected."

"Then this could be happening in a lot of places as news spreads," Geary said.

"Perhaps. But the Syndics still have considerable ability to try to retain control of individual star systems. Any collapse of the Syndicate Worlds will take a long time to work its way through all of the star systems."

"A long time? Too bad," Desjani murmured as she checked her display. "The shuttles bringing some of the liberated POWs to *Dauntless* are preparing to off-load."

Geary came to his feet. "Let's go welcome them."

"Yes," Rione agreed, "if the commanding officer of *Dauntless* doesn't object to my presence as well."

"Of course not, Madam Co-President," Desjani replied with a professionally detached tone of voice.

They arrived at the shuttle dock as the first bird dropped its main hatch, and the former prisoners began walking down the ramp. The liberated prisoners filed off the shuttle, gazing around with expressions of joy and disbelief. In the remnants of their old uniforms and cast-off, badly worn civilian clothes provided by the Syndics, they looked very much like the prisoners who had been liberated way back at Sutrah Star System. The entire scene, the emotions present in everyone, felt like that at Sutrah.

"I guess the thrill of liberating our own prisoners of war never goes away," Desjani murmured, somehow echoing Geary's own thoughts.

Just about then a voice called across the shuttle dock. "Vic? Vic Rione?" One of the newly liberated prisoners, tall and thin and wearing commander insignia on an old coat, was staring their way, his eyes widening with disbelief.

Victoria Rione was peering back at the man, her expression puzzled, then she gave a quick intake of breath. Recovering quickly, she called out a reply. "Kai! Kai Fensin!"

Rione stepped forward to meet Fensin as he left the line and walked quickly toward her. Some of the sailor escorts herding the former prisoners along to sick bay made abortive motions to stop Fensin but halted when Desjani made a quick gesture. "Vic?" Fensin asked in a wondering voice as he reached them. "When did you join the fleet? You haven't aged a day."

"Vic?" Desjani muttered too low for anyone but Geary to hear.

"Be nice," he muttered back to her before joining Rione.

Rione was shaking her head and looking embarrassed. "I feel much older, and I haven't joined the fleet, Kai. May I introduce the fleet commander, Captain Geary?"

"Geary." Commander Fensin smiled, his expression disbelieving. "They told us on the shuttles who was in command of the fleet. Who else could have brought it here to free us?" Looking suddenly aghast at himself, Fensin straightened to attention. "It's an honor, sir, a great honor."

"At ease, Commander," Geary ordered. "Relax. There'll be plenty of time for ceremony later."

"Yes, sir," Fensin agreed. "I served with another Geary once. Michael Geary. A grandnephew of yours. We were junior officers together on the *Vanquish*."

Geary felt his own smile slide away. Fensin caught it, looking anxious now. "I'm sorry. Did he die?"

"He may have," Geary answered, wondering how his voice sounded. "His ship was destroyed in the Syndic home system, covering this fleet's withdrawal."

"He pulled a Geary?" Fensin blurted, invoking the last stand for which Black Jack had become famous. "Of all people. I mean..." Fensin seemed simply horrified at his own verbal gaffes.

"I understand," Geary said. "He didn't think much of Black Jack after having to grow up in his shadow. But he seemed to understand me better at the end, when faced with the same situation." Time to change the subject to something that would hopefully be more comfortable. "How do you know Co-President Rione?"

"Co-president?" Fensin's stare shifted to Rione.

She nodded back to him. "Of the Callas Republic. And, uh, member of the Alliance Senate, of course, because of that. I went into politics to serve the Alliance after Paol..." Rione paused, blinking rapidly. "I'd been told he was dead, but recently learned he was still alive when taken prisoner. Do you know anything?"

Kai Fensin closed his eyes briefly. "I was on the same ship with Vic's husband," he explained to Geary. "Excuse me, I mean, Co-President Rione's—"

"I'm still Vic to you, Kai. Do you know anything?"

"We were separated soon after being captured," Fensin stated miserably. "Paol was severely injured. Somebody had told me he'd died on the ship, so I was surprised to see that he was still hanging on. Then the Syndics took the badly wounded away, supposedly for treatment, but..." He grimaced. "You know what happens to prisoners sometimes."

"They killed him?" Rione asked in a thin voice.

"I don't know. As my ancestors are my witness, Vic, I don't know. I've never heard anything else about him or the others taken with him." Fensin shrugged, his expression twisted with regret. "There were some others at the camp from our ship. I don't think any of them came to *Dauntless*, but we've talked a lot. There's not all that much to do but talk in the camps when the Syndics aren't making you dig ditches and break rocks. None of the others could say what had happened to Paol, either. I wish I could give you some last memory, some parting words, but everything was chaos and the Syndics were pulling us apart and he was barely conscious."

Rione managed a smile. "I know what his words would have been."

Fensin hesitated, his eyes going from Rione to Geary. "There was a lot of gossip on the shuttle, people trying to catch up. Somebody said something about a politician and the fleet commander."

"Captain Geary and I had a brief relationship," Rione said in a steady voice.

"It ended when she learned her husband might still be alive," Geary added. That wasn't strictly true, but close enough so that he felt justified in saying it.

Commander Fensin nodded, looking haggard now. "I wouldn't have blamed Vic, sir. Maybe before I went into that labor camp, back when I thought honor had a few simple rules to it. Now I know what it's like, thinking you'll never see someone again because the war has been going on forever and you can see the people dying in the labor camp who've been there almost all their lives and figure that will be you someday. There's a lot of people who were in that camp who found new partners, figuring they'd never again see their old ones. Married people who started caring for someone else, or who looked for someone else to care about them. There's going to be a lot of pain when they come home, I guess, one way or the other." He gazed at Rione. "I did it, too."

Rione gazed back, looking kinder than Geary had thought possible, as if meeting this man from her past had brought her back to a better time for her. "Did she come to this ship with you?"

"She's dead. Three months ago. The radiation on that world causes problems sometimes, and the Syndics don't waste money on expensive treatments for prisoners." Fensin's eyes appeared haunted now. "May the living stars forgive me, but I can't stop realizing how much simpler that made things. I don't know how my wife is now, whether she even knew I was alive, but now I don't face a choice. I haven't become a monster, Vic. But I can't stop that thought from coming."

"I understand," Rione replied, reaching for Commander Fensin's arm. "Let me help you to sick bay for your checkup with the others." She and Fensin moved off while Geary watched them go.

Desjani cleared her throat softly. "There but for the grace of our ancestors," she murmured.

"Yeah. It's a hell of a thing."

"It's nice to see that she can be human," Desjani added. "Vic, I mean."

He turned a slight frown on Desjani. "You know how she'll react if *you* call her that."

"I certainly do," Desjani replied. "But don't worry, sir. I'll save it for the right moment."

Geary took a few moments of his own to pray that he wouldn't be too close when that happened. "How many of these liberated prisoners will be able to augment your crew?"

"I don't know yet, sir. It's like after we pulled the others off Sutrah. They'll have to be interviewed and evaluated to see what skills they've got and how rusty they are. Then the personnel-management system will help the ships sort out who should go where."

"Can you—"

"I'll keep Commander Fensin aboard *Dauntless*, sir." Desjani gave him a hard look. "Hopefully that commander will keep the politician occupied and off our backs."

"You know, you are allowed to do nice things just to be nice even for her."

"Really?" Desjani, her expression unrevealing, looked toward the liberated prisoners again. "I need to welcome the others to *Dauntless*, sir."

"Do you mind if I welcome them to the fleet at the same time?"

"Of course not, sir." She gave him a rueful look. "I know how little you like their reactions to seeing you."

"Well, yeah, but it's still my job to greet them."

It felt odd, moving among the liberated prisoners, some of them elderly after decades in the Syndic labor camp, to know that all of them were born long after him. He'd gotten over that with the crew of *Dauntless*, able to forget that their lives had begun many years after his had supposedly ended. But the prisoners brought it home again, that even the oldest of them had come into a universe in which Black Jack Geary was a figure of legend.

But then an enlisted sailor with plenty of years behind her spoke to him. "I knew someone from off the *Merlon*, sir. When I was just a child."

Geary felt a curious hollowness inside as he paused to listen. "Off *Merlon*?"

"Yes, sir. Jasmin Holaran. She was, uh..."

"Assigned to hell-lance battery one alpha."

"Yes, sir!" The woman beamed. "She'd retired in my neighborhood. We'd go listen to her tell stories. She always told us you were everything the legends said, sir."

"Did she?" He could recall Holaran's face, remember having to discipline the young sailor after a rowdy time on planetary leave, see the promotion ceremony in which she'd advanced in rate, and another moment when he'd praised the hell-lance battery of which Holaran was a part for racking up a great score in fleet readiness testing. She'd been a capable sailor and occasional hell-raiser, no more and no less, the sort of so-called "average" performer who got the job done and kept ships going on a day-to-day basis.

Battery one alpha had been knocked out fairly early in the fight against the Syndics, but Geary hadn't had a chance during the battle to learn which of that battery's crew had lived through the loss of their weapons. Holaran had survived, then, and made it off *Merlon*. Served through the subsequent years of war and survived that, too, where so many others hadn't. Retired back to her home world, to tell stories about him to curious children. And died of old age while he still drifted in survival sleep.

"Sir." Desjani was standing next to him, her face calm but her eyes worried. "Is everything all right, sir?"

Wondering how long he'd been standing there without speaking, Geary still took another moment to answer as feelings rushed through him. "Yes. Thank you, Captain Desjani." He focused back on the former prisoner. "And thank you for telling me about Jasmin Holaran. She was a fine sailor."

"She told us you saved her life, sir. Her and a lot of others," the older woman added anxiously. "Thank the living stars for Geary, she'd say. If not for his sacrifice, I would have died at Grendel and missed so much. Her husband was dead by then, of course, and her own children in the fleet."

"Her husband?" He was certain Holaran hadn't been married while on *Merlon*.

Because of what he'd done, she'd lived, had a long life, a husband, and children.

"Sir?" Desjani again, her voice a little more urgent.

Apparently he'd been standing silently again as he thought about everything. "It's all right." He took a deep breath, feeling the lifting of a burden he hadn't been aware of carrying. "I made a difference," he murmured too low for anyone but Desjani to hear.

"Of course you did."

"It's a pleasure to meet you," Geary assured the former prisoner. "To meet someone who knew one of my old crew." He meant it, he realized with surprise. A moment he had dreaded had brought him release from some of the pain he carried because of the past he'd lost. "I'll never forget them, and now you've reconnected me to one of them."

The woman beamed with pleasure. "It's the least I can do, sir."

"It's a very big thing," he corrected the former prisoner. "To me. My thanks." Geary nodded to Desjani. "It's all right," he repeated to her.

"It is, isn't it?" Desjani smiled. "Liberating POW camps seems to raise a lot of ghosts, doesn't it?"

"Raise them and maybe bring us all some peace when we look them in the eye." With some more words of gratitude to the older woman, he moved on to speak to others, a warmth having replaced the hollowness he'd felt for a moment.

The warmth didn't last too long. He and Desjani were leaving the shuttle dock when an urgent call came down.

"Captain Geary?" the operations watch called, her image small on his comm pad. "There seems to be some problem with the former prisoners of war."

So much for moments of relaxation. "What is it?"

"The most senior officers from the camp are demanding to be brought to *Dauntless* and kept in protective custody." From what he could make out of the lieutenant's expression, even she didn't believe what she was saying.

Geary just looked at his comm pad for a moment. "They're asking me to arrest them?"

"Yes, sir. Would you like to speak to them, sir?"

Not particularly. But he tapped the nearest large comm panel on the bulkhead and gestured to Desjani. "Listen in on this, please."

The panel lit up with a much bigger image. He saw two women and a man, one of the women and the man wearing fleet captain insignia on the worn civilian clothing the Syndics had provided and the other woman bearing a Marine colonel's rank. All three of them looked elderly, leaving Geary wondering how long they'd been prisoners. "I'm Captain Geary. What can I do for you?"

They took a moment to reply, a moment spent staring at him in the way Geary had come to expect but never expected to like. Finally, the female captain spoke. "We request that we be placed in protective custody as soon as possible, Captain Geary."

"Why? We just liberated you from one prison. Why do you want to go into cells on fleet ships?"

"We have enemies among the former prisoners," the male captain stated. "We were in charge of the prisoners because of our rank and seniority. Some of the former prisoners disagreed with the decisions we've made over the last few decades."

Geary glanced over at Desjani, who was frowning at the three officers. "I'm Captain Desjani, commanding officer of *Dauntless*. Which decisions generated such problems that you want to be transferred to custody on my ship?"

The prisoners looked at each other before replying, then the female colonel answered. "Command decisions. We were forced to take into account the consequences of every decision and every action by the prisoners."

Even Geary could tell that they were avoiding giving specifics. Desjani leaned close to him. "Do as they want. Arrest them. We want these three under our control while we find out what's going on."

Geary nodded to her, but making the gesture seemed to be aimed at the three former prisoners. "Very well. We need to look into this, but until then I'll grant your request." He checked the data next to their images. "All three of you are on *Leviathan*? I'll order Captain Tulev to confine you to quarters."

"Sir, we'd be more comfortable under your direct control."

He let his expression harden. "Captain Tulev is a reliable and trustworthy officer of the fleet. You couldn't be in better hands."

The three former prisoners exchanged glances. "We need guards, Captain Geary."

Stranger and stranger. "Captain Tulev will be told to place Marine guards outside your quarters. Is there anything else you can tell me?"

The female captain hesitated. "We're preparing a full, official report of our actions."

"Thank you. I look forward to seeing it. Geary, out." He broke the connection, then called Tulev. "Captain, there's something weird going on."

Tulev listened, his face betraying no emotion. "I will have the sentries placed. Captain Geary, I've already been questioned by some of the other liberated prisoners, demanding to know where those three senior officers are located."

"Demanding?"

"Yes. I've already chosen to keep those three isolated while trying to discover the reasons for the hostility I've seen toward them."

Desjani broke in again. "Have any of those demanding to know where the senior former prisoners are located expressed any specific grounds for their questions?"

"No. They're concealing their motives from me. All of them are officers, though. But I will find out what is behind all of this. Now, if you will excuse me, I must get the Marine guards in place."

After Tulev had broken his connection, Geary looked toward Desjani. "Any ideas what might be behind this?"

Desjani made a face. "A few. They seem to be afraid for their lives, which implies something far more serious than disagreements over the wisdom of decisions."

"Then why aren't the other prisoners telling us what happened instead of hiding their problems with those three? They were all down in that camp together. Why wouldn't the other prisoners have been able—" Geary stopped and called Colonel Carabali. "Colonel, did you meet the three senior Alliance officers at that POW camp?"

Carabali, who looked drained from the recent action, her battle fatigues streaked with sweat and creased where the battle armor had pressed against them, straightened herself as she answered. "Two captains and a colonel? Yes. They came out to meet us as we landed. I think they evac'd on the first shuttle up. I don't recall seeing them after that. Some of the other former POWs were looking for them." Carabali paused. "I did see their quarters. Separate from the rest. It looked like a bunker. A Syndic guard post in front of it, though abandoned when we touched down. Odd.

But I really didn't have the opportunity to deal with those things on the surface, sir."

"Understood, Colonel. Thank you." Geary bent his head, trying to think. "How do we get answers, Tanya? Before something happens?"

She'd been concentrating, and now smiled briefly. "Perhaps you and I should have a private talk with Commander Fensin."

"Fensin?" He remembered the look and the bearing of that officer. Eager, professional, and a tendency to speak his thoughts impulsively. "That might work if we have Rione along to help soften him up."

"Must we? Oh, you're probably right. She's a lever we can use if he tries to clam up."

"You sound like you already know what's going on," Geary suggested.

"No, sir. I fear I know what's going on, and if Commander Fensin hesitates to speak, I may be able to prod him into admitting it." She tapped her comm pad. "Bridge, locate Co-President Rione and Commander Fensin. They should be together, probably in sick bay for his medical screen. Captain Geary and I need to see them in the fleet conference room immediately."

The watch-stander who answered spoke cautiously. "We're supposed to order Co-President Rione to the conference room, Captain?"

Desjani gave Geary a sour look as she replied. "No. Inform her that Captain Geary urgently requests her presence there along with Commander Fensin. That should satisfy diplomatic niceties."

* * *

Commander Fensin was smiling as he took a seat in the conference room while Desjani sealed the hatch. Rione sat beside him, impassive but watching Desjani in particular very closely.

Geary didn't waste time. "Commander Fensin, what's the story with the three senior Alliance officers among the prisoners?"

The smile vanished, and a variety of emotions rippled across Fensin's face before he managed to control himself. "Story?"

"We know there are problems. Why would they be afraid of the other former prisoners?"

"I'm not certain I understand."

Desjani spoke. "Perhaps this word will be easy to understand. 'Treason'?"

Fensin stopped moving. After a moment, his eyes went to Desjani. "How'd you find out?"

"I'm the commanding officer of a battle cruiser," she replied. "What exactly did they do?"

"I took an oath—"

"You took an earlier oath to the Alliance, Commander," Desjani said. "As your superior officer, I want a full report."

She'd taken control of the interrogation, Geary realized, but Desjani was getting answers, so he didn't protest.

Rione did. "I would like an explanation for this. Commander Fensin has not even been given the opportunity to complete his medical screening yet."

Geary replied. "I believe you'll get your explanation when Commander Fensin answers Captain Desjani."

Fensin had been staring at Desjani and now slumped back, rubbing his face with both hands. "I never liked it anyway. If we somehow ever get out, everybody stay quiet until we get them. As if we were a criminal mob rather than members of the Alliance military. But as the years went by one by one endlessly, it seemed to make sense. We'd never be rescued, never be freed. We'd have to do what needed to be done if justice was ever to be served. And the rules didn't change when we were rescued. We'd agreed to do it when we could."

Rione reached and grasped Fensin's other hand. "What happened?"

"What didn't." Fensin stared toward the far bulkhead, his eyes looking into the past. "They betrayed us, Vic. Those three."

"How?" Geary demanded.

"There was a plan. Hijack one of the Syndic supply shuttles but keep it quiet. Get to the spaceport and grab a ship. Only twenty prisoners might make it out, but they could have taken a lot of information back to Alliance space. Who was in the camp, what we knew of the situation behind the border in Syndic space, that kind of thing." Fensin shook his head. "Crazy, I guess. Only one chance in a million it might work. But against a lifetime as a prisoner of war, some people thought those odds were good enough. The three senior officers in the camp told us not to, but we pointed out the fleet's standing orders for prisoners to resist where feasible. So they told the Syndics. The only way to stop the plan, they said. Because the retaliation against the remaining prisoners would be too severe, they said. Because they'd agreed to keep us in line for the Syndics in exchange for certain privileges for us. Privileges! Enough food, some medical care, the sort of things the Syndics were obligated by simple humanity to provide anyway."

Fensin closed his eyes. "When the Syndics found out about the plan, they ran us through interrogations until they'd identified ten of the prisoners who were going to hijack the shuttle. Then they shot them."

"Was this an isolated incident?" Geary asked. "Or a pattern of behavior?"

"A pattern, sir. I could talk all day. They did what the Syndics wanted and told us it was for us. Keep quiet, behave, and it would benefit us. Resist, and we'd get hammered by the Syndics."

Desjani looked like she wanted to spit. "Those three focused on one aspect of their mission, the welfare of their fellow prisoners. They forgot every other aspect of their responsibilities."

Fensin nodded. "That's right, Captain. Sometimes I could almost understand. Among them they'd been prisoners of war for a combined total of more than a century."

"A century isn't long enough to forget important things," Desjani replied, looking at Geary.

He rapped the table to draw Fensin's attention, uncomfortable with Desjani's observation despite (or perhaps because of) the truth in it. "What's the objective of this conspiracy of silence? Why not tell us immediately what those three did?"

"We wanted to kill them ourselves," Fensin answered in a matter-of-fact way. "We held emergency courts-martial, in secret of necessity, and reached verdicts of treason in all three cases. The penalty for treason in war time is death. We wanted to make sure those sentences were carried out before any of those three managed to lawyer their way into being formally charged and tried on lesser offenses. And, in truth, we wanted revenge for ourselves, for those who died." He looked around at the others. "You can't know how it feels. I... Do we have access to imagery of the camp? Before you pulled us out?"

"Certainly." Desjani entered some commands. Above the table appeared an overhead view of the POW camp on Heradao as it had looked before being smashed to bits during the fight to liberate the prisoners.

Commander Fensin, working the controls with the clumsiness of someone who'd not been allowed to use the like for years, zoomed the image in on one side of the camp. As the picture zoomed closer, Geary could see a large open field, and that the field was partially filled with neat rows of markers. "A cemetery."

"Yes," Fensin agreed. "That POW camp had been in existence for about eighty years. A generation of prisoners had aged and died there. There weren't a lot of real elderly because of the harsh conditions and the limitations on medical care." His eyes rested on the imagery of the grave markers. "All of the rest of us believed that eventually we'd end up in that field as well. There weren't any prisoner exchanges, and why should we expect the war to ever end? After five or ten or twenty years, even the strongest beliefs faded into resignation. We'd never see our families again, we'd never go home again. All we had left was each other, and what dignity we could retain as members of the Alliance military."

He focused on Rione, as if she were the one he most wanted to convince. "They betrayed that. They betrayed us. Those things were all we had left, and they betrayed those things. Of course we wanted to kill them."

They sat in silence for a few moments, then Desjani gestured toward the image still hovering before them. "Did the Marines get records of those graves while they were on the ground? The names of those who rest there?"

"I doubt it." Fensin tapped his head with one finger. "They didn't have to. Every one of us had names to remember. I was one of those who had to remember all of the dead whose last names began with F. The list of the honored dead is in our memories. We couldn't take them home because they've already gone to join their ancestors, but we will take their names to their families."

For a moment Geary imagined that he could see them, the prisoners going painstakingly over the names of those who had died, checking their lists against each other, committing the names to the only form of record they had. Year by year, as the lists grew longer, never knowing if anyone in the Alliance would ever hear those lists, but keeping them in their memories just the same. It was all too easy to sense how the prisoners had felt in that POW camp, which they had every reason to believe would be their jail until they died. All too easy to understand their need for such rituals and their sense of betrayal. "All right." Geary looked a question a Rione.

She looked down, then nodded. "I believe him."

"So do I," Desjani added without hesitation.

Geary tapped the comm controls. "Captain Tulev, get those three senior former prisoners onto a shuttle with Marine guards. Take them to..." He pondered his options. He needed a ship without former POWs from Heradao on board, but every warship had those.

Every warship.

"*Titan*. Take them to *Titan* with orders that they be confined under guard until further notice. All three are under arrest."

Tulev nodded as if unsurprised. "The charges? We are obligated to provide them to those under arrest."

"Treason and dereliction of duty in the face of the enemy. They told me they were preparing a report on their actions. Make sure they have the means to produce that report. I want to see it." That wasn't strictly true. The last thing he wanted to do was read through that document if what Commander Fensin had said was accurate. But he had an obligation to see what the three officers said in their own defense.

Once Tulev had signed off, Geary faced Fensin again. "Thank you, Commander. I think I can promise you that if what you told us is confirmed by your fellow former prisoners, then formal courts-martial back in Alliance territory will reach the same conclusions you did."

"Do we have to wait?" Fensin asked with shocking calmness. "You could order them shot right now."

"That's not how I do business, Commander. If your statements are true, those three will condemn themselves with their own report, then no one will doubt the necessity of carrying out justice."

"But Captain Gazin is so old," Fensin argued. "She may not live until we reach Alliance space, and she'd escape the fate she deserves."

Desjani answered him in her command voice. "If she dies, then the living stars will render judgment and justice, Commander. No one can escape that. You're an officer in the Alliance fleet, Commander Fensin. You held to that as a prisoner. Don't forget it now that you're back with us."

Rione's expression hardened, but Fensin just stared at Desjani again for a moment, then nodded. "Yes, Captain. Forgive me."

"There's nothing to forgive," Desjani assured him. "You've been through hell, and you did your duty by telling us the truth. Continue to do your duty, Commander. You were always part of the fleet, but now you are with it once more."

"Yes, Captain," Fensin repeated, sitting straighter.

Rione looked to Geary. "If there's nothing else, I'd like to spend some time with Commander Fensin, then get his medical screening accomplished."

"Of course." Geary and Desjani stood together and left. He looked back as the hatch closed and saw Rione still holding Fensin's hand, no words passing between them. "Damn," he muttered to Desjani.

"Damn," she agreed. "Are you sure we shouldn't shoot them now?"

So Desjani had been tempted, too, but hadn't argued with him in front of the others to avoid appearing to undermine his own position. "Sure? No. But it has to be done right. There can't be any perception of mob justice. Good job getting Fensin to talk. How did you know to prod Fensin with a question about treason?"

She made a face. "Some of the conversations I had with Lieutenant Riva. He talked a few times about things like that. I didn't really understand before, but I remembered how he'd get very angry when talking about anyone who he thought had been too compliant with the Syndics. Something about this made me recall that." Desjani looked down the passageway, and added something in a bland voice. "It's not like I think of Riva. Not at all, usually."

"I see." To Geary's surprise, he realized he had felt a twinge of jealousy. He had to change the subject. "I wonder if I might not have ended up going down that same misguided road that those three did if I'd been captured."

Desjani frowned at him. "No. You wouldn't have. You care about the personnel under your command, but you also know the risks they have to run. You've always been able to balance those things."

"I care about them enough to send them to their deaths," Geary replied, hearing some bitterness creep into his tone.

"That's exactly right. Too much callousness, and their lives are wasted. Too much concern, and they die anyway, with no result. I don't pretend to understand why things are that way, but you know they are."

"Yeah." He felt the momentary depression lifting and smiled at her. "Thanks for being here, Tanya."

"It's not like I could be anywhere else." Desjani smiled back, then her face went formal, and she saluted. "I need to see to my ship, sir."

"By all means." He returned the salute, then watched her walk away.

She had a ship to see to and he had to call *Titan* and let Commander Lommand know that a particularly unwelcome cargo would be arriving on his ship soon. The burdens of command varied, but burdens they always were.

By the next morning he felt better. The third planet of Heradao was comfortably distant, the fleet had finished joining up with the units left behind in the area of the space battle, and the entire Alliance force was headed for the jump point for Padronis. Even the old Syndic ration bar he chose for breakfast didn't seem to taste as bad as usual.

At about that point, the comm unit in his stateroom buzzed. "Sir, you have an urgent request for communications from Commander Vigory."

"Commander Vigory?" Geary tried to match the name to a ship or a face, failed, and checked the fleet database. Another former POW from Heradao. No wonder his name hadn't been familiar. Vigory was on *Spartan*, and according to the summary in the database, he'd had a fairly routine career before being captured by the Syndics. "All right. Put him through."

Thin and intense, Commander Vigory resembled other Alliance personnel liberated from Heradao. "Captain Geary," he began in a stiff voice, "I wished to pay a call and render proper respects to the fleet commander."

"Thank you, Commander."

"I also wished to inform you that I am still awaiting a command assignment."

Still awaiting? Geary's eyes went to the time. It had been less than a day since the fleet left orbit about Heradao's third planet. Then his mind fastened on the rest of Vigory's statement. "Command assignment?"

"Yes, sir." Vigory's eyes were demanding as he gazed at Geary. "A review of fleet records indicates numerous ships in this fleet suitable for an officer of my rank and seniority are currently commanded by officers junior to me."

"You expect me to relieve some existing commanding officer so that you can have his or her ship?"

The question seemed to startle Commander Vigory. "Of course, sir."

Geary fought down an impulse to cut off Vigory at the knees and tried to speak in a reasonable but firm tone. "How would you feel if you lost your command under those circumstances, Commander?"

"That scarcely matters, sir. This is a question of honor and proper deference to my rank and position. I have no doubt that any ship in this fleet would benefit from my experience and ability to command."

No, Vigory probably had never had a doubt in his life, Geary thought as he looked at the man. According to the records available, Vigory had been taken prisoner about five years ago, meaning that he was a product of a fleet in which individual honor meant everything and ships fought without regard for sound tactics. Maybe he was a decent officer despite that, but at this point, retraining a ship's commanding officer would be just one more thing to worry about, besides being grossly unfair to some other officer.

"Commander, I'll lay this out as clearly as I can. Every commanding officer in this fleet has fought for me all the way from the Syndic home star system, rendering brave and honorable service in numerous engagements with the enemy." That was an exaggeration in a few cases, but Vigory didn't seem the sort to grasp distinctions. "I will not relieve any of my current commanding officers without cause based on their performance. This fleet is returning to Alliance space, and once there you can request a command assignment on a new-construction warship or a warship whose commanding officer is rotating to a new assignment."

Vigory seemed to have trouble understanding. "Sir, I expect very quickly to receive a command assignment in this fleet suitable to my rank and seniority."

"Then I regret to inform you that your expectations are

misplaced." Geary tried not to get angry but could hear his voice getting sharper. "You will serve as needed by the Alliance, just like every officer in this fleet."

"But... I..."

"Thank you, Commander Vigory. I appreciate your willingness to serve as your duty to the Alliance requires."

The conversation over, Geary leaned back and covered his eyes with one hand. A moment later the alert on the hatch to his stateroom chimed. *Great. This morning is going downhill fast.* He authorized entry, sitting up straighter as Victoria Rione entered. "Captain Geary."

"Madam Co-President." They'd had plenty of physical intimacies in this very room, but that was over and done, and neither would presume on their earlier relationship.

"I hope I'm not interrupting anything," Rione continued.

"I was just trying to remember why I wanted to rescue the Alliance POWs on Heradao," Geary confessed.

She flicked a smile at him. "Because you have an annoying habit of insisting on doing what's right even when common sense might dictate acting otherwise."

"Thank you. I think. What brings you here?"

"The Alliance POWs liberated from Heradao."

Geary didn't quite stifle a groan. "Now what?"

"This may be good news, or perhaps useful." Rione inclined her head toward another part of the ship. "Sometime after you left us yesterday, Commander Fensin confessed to me that the best thing he could have been told was what your captain said to him, reminding him of his responsibilities as an officer of the Alliance and ordering him to live up to those responsibilities." She paused before continuing. "From what Kai Fensin said, he and the other POWs on Heradao long lacked a firm hand they respected to give them purpose. He thought all of them would benefit from treatment such as your captain gave him."

Geary refrained from pointing out that his "captain" had a name, and that Desjani wasn't "his" in any case. "That makes a great deal of sense. They're not used to having senior officers they respect or to whose orders they'd listen."

"Kai suggested you might want to inform others in the fleet of this, so they'd be able to treat the other former prisoners accordingly. In that respect, they're not like the ones we liberated from Sutrah."

"Thank you," Geary repeated. "I think he's right."

"Yes, and so was your captain. My instincts to protect Commander Fensin were wrong."

"Don't beat yourself up about that. Desjani and Fensin are both fleet." Rione just nodded silently. "How are you doing?"

She gave him a searching glance. "Why do you ask?"

"You seem to have been very happy to find Commander Fensin."

Rione's eyes flashed. "If you're implying—"

"No!" Geary raised both palms in apology. "That's not what I meant. It just seems that meeting him was a good thing for you."

She subsided as quickly as her anger had flared. "Yes. He reminds me of many things. Of the life I once had."

"I could tell." It was best not to tell Rione that Desjani had been able to see it as well.

"Could you?" Rione bent her head for a moment. "I sometimes wonder what will happen if my husband lives and we are united again. In the years since he left, I have changed in many ways, become harder and stronger and... not the woman he left."

"I saw that woman. When you were with Kai Fensin."

"You did?" Rione sighed. "Maybe there's hope for me, then. Maybe she's not dead after all."

"She's not, Victoria."

Rione raised her gaze and looked at him with a twisted smile. "That's one of the few circumstances under which you can still call me that, John Geary. Thank you. I've said what I needed to say." She walked to the hatch but paused in it before leaving, her back to him. "Please thank your captain on my behalf for her words to Commander Fensin. I'm grateful." Then she was gone and the hatch was sliding shut.

He drafted up a message telling the fleet's ship captains to be firm with the former POWs from Heradao and to get them assigned duties as soon as possible. After sending it, Geary settled back and stared at the star display again.

Roughly two more days until the fleet reached the jump point for Padronis. That star should be quiet, with no known Syndic presence. For that matter, Atalia, the next and last Syndic star system they had to transit, should be quiet, too, despite its human population. If Alliance intelligence was anywhere near right then the Syndics had used up everything they had. No identificant number of warships could be available to contest the rest of the fleet's journey home.

Could he finally relax?

Five minutes later, Lieutenant Iger called from the intelligence section with a very urgent summons.

7

Calls from Lieutenant Iger in the intelligence section were usually interesting and sometimes very surprising. Never *pleasantly* surprising in Geary's experience, but the unpleasant news had often proven to be critically important.

Since Iger looked unhappy when Geary arrived, he assumed this would be one of those unpleasant news times. "Tell me the civil war in this star system isn't going to cause us any more problems, Lieutenant."

"Uh, yes, sir. The civil war here shouldn't cause us any more trouble, sir. This is an entirely different problem."

"Oh. Wonderful. Big problem?"

"Yes, sir. Real big."

Geary rubbed the back of his neck, feeling a headache coming on. "All right. Lay it out."

"We've been analyzing Syndic communications in this star system, Captain Geary," Iger reported. "That is, the messages that were already on the fly when we arrived here. It's standard procedure, trying to identify traffic patterns and important messages so we can try to break them out and decipher as much of them as we can. The first thing we noticed is that there's been a much-higher-than-usual concentration of highest-priority messages sent in this star system. Again, that's before central authority collapsed."

Geary nodded. Light-speed limitations were usually a problem, but not if you were trying to intercept messages sent days or hours ago, before anyone knew the enemy would be arriving in a particular star system. Those messages were still heading outward at the speed of light if you could find them. "Any idea what they're about? The Syndics thought we were coming here, so that might account for them."

"No, sir, not all of them. We've been able to do some partial breaking of the high-priority messages we've intercepted." Iger turned and tapped controls, bringing up a series of lines of information. "These are pulled from voice transmissions and various forms of text messaging. Those kind of informal communications are usually the most useful because people say things without thinking. There are several references in these to something we've never seen before. Right here, and here, and in this one."

Geary read the indicated lines, frowning. "Reserve flotilla? You haven't heard the Syndics use that phrase before?"

"No, sir. A search of intelligence databases turned up only three references to the term in reporting about the Syndics over the last few decades. No actual data exists, just identification of the use of the term 'reserve flotilla' by the Syndics without any means of determining what it meant." Iger pointed to another line. "This was a requisition for supplies. We've been able to break a fair amount of this message because we know how the Syndics format those requisitions and so knew what certain sections had to mean. These parts are segments of the overall requirement, then here's some of the portion of that requirement that Heradao was supposed to provide. One of the things about the Syndics is they use very rigid logistics. If you want to provide food for a D-Class battle cruiser for sixty days, you order X of this and Y of that and so on."

"That looks like an awful lot of Xs and Ys," Geary commented as he read the intercepted requisition.

"Yes, sir." Iger blew out a long breath. "Assuming it's a standard sixty-day supply, which the Syndics tend to adhere to, and a standard mix of units, this requisition would cover a force estimated to include fifteen to twenty battleships, fifteen to twenty battle cruisers, and somewhere between one hundred and two hundred heavy cruisers, light cruisers, and Hunter-Killers."

Geary felt a lot of reactions, some of them very negative. How could a Syndic force of that size still exist? His fleet had fought heroically and taken serious losses, but the path home had finally seemed clear. Right up until that moment. He tried to focus on the most constructive questions. "This definitely isn't related to the force we just destroyed?"

"No, sir. Definitely not. It was being sent out of the star system."

"You're estimating that a Syndic force of that size exists right now and is in a star system not too far from here?"

"Yes, sir." Give Iger full credit, he didn't try to weasel around when it came to bad news.

"How? How did the Syndics have a force of that size that our intelligence resources weren't aware of before this?"

Iger pointed again. "We can only guess, sir, but I think it's a good guess. Some of the message traffic we believe is related to this reserve flotilla mentions two Syndic star systems. Surt and Embla."

"Surt? Embla?" The names were vaguely familiar, though Geary couldn't remember why. "I can't recall where those are."

"That's because they're a long ways from Alliance space," Iger advised, moving to the star display nearby. "Here. On the Syndic border farthest from the Alliance."

It suddenly all made sense. "A reserve flotilla. Held on the Syndic border facing the aliens as insurance in case the aliens attacked the Syndics."

"Yes, sir," Iger agreed. "That seems like the most reasonable interpretation. A force kept so far from us that the Alliance couldn't pick up indications of it and never knew of its existence. But now the Syndics are so worried about our getting home with a Syndic hypernet key that they pulled that reserve flotilla out of position to try to stop us."

"Damn. We didn't need that."

"No, sir."

"Any idea where they are now?" Geary asked, eyeing the star display.

"Not too far from here," Iger suggested. "A star system within one or two jumps. That's our best guess. Or they were there fairly recently."

"Kalixa? It was a possible objective for us from Dilawa. They could have defended the hypernet gate there, and the gate would allow them to shift position quickly if we ended up not going to Kalixa."

Iger nodded. "That's as good a guess as any, sir. But the picket ships from here will be at Kalixa soon to tell them we went to Heradao, so they'll probably shift to a star system blocking our way home from here."

One more big battle left to fight, then, with a possibly veteran force that was fully supplied with fuel cells and expendable weaponry. His anger at this turn of fate shifted as Geary thought about what might have happened if the Alliance fleet had run into the Syndic reserve flotilla without warning that it even existed. "Lieutenant Iger, you and your people have done an outstanding job. This is critically important information. Well done."

Iger beamed. "Thank you, sir. I'll make certain everyone in intelligence knows you said that." But then the intelligence officer looked uneasy. "Sir, I know our first priority is worrying about the consequences of this for us, but if the Syndics have been maintaining for who knows how long a major force along their border with what ever those aliens are, they must have had good reason to be wary of what the aliens might do. What if the aliens realize the reserve flotilla is gone from the border?"

"Good point, Lieutenant, but I'm sure they already know." Geary indicated the symbols for hypernet gates. "If those aliens can redirect ships within a hypernet, that means they can tell when ships are using that hypernet, and the only way that reserve flotilla could have come that far in any reasonable amount of time is by using the Syndic hypernet."

"Then they know they have a window of opportunity." Iger bit his lip. "And if we destroy this reserve flotilla, which we'll have to do if we encounter it, then that window will be as big as a supernova."

Geary studied the Syndicate Worlds' territory portrayed on the star display, imagining what could happen if the Syndic leaders lost their grip on dissident star systems, if their fleet was temporarily too weak to defend Syndic space, if the aliens chose to attack at that point. From what Geary knew of history, one of the truisms of empires was that they were only as strong as their ability to keep their own populace in line. If they lost that, empires tended to fall apart very rapidly, and the Syndicate Worlds were in many ways an empire in all but name.

He needed to destroy this Syndic reserve flotilla in order to get his own fleet home. But by doing that he might be triggering events in which many Syndic-controlled star systems ended up like Heradao.

"Sir?" Iger asked, interrupting Geary's train of thought. "Do we have any idea what the intentions of the aliens are?"

"No, Lieutenant. Just guesses based on far too few facts. Just as important as intentions, we have no idea what their capabilities may be. We still know practically nothing about these aliens. Lieutenant Iger, if we run into that reserve flotilla we need to capture as many senior Syndic officers from it as possible and find out what they know. Surely they would have been briefed on what ever the Syndics have managed to learn about the aliens."

"Most likely, sir," Iger agreed, then looked aggravated. "Although you'd be surprised how many times people get totally focused on keeping a secret and try to keep important information like that from those who need it the most for fear of its being compromised."

"That still happens? Well, hell, of course it does. It was

probably happening back when those original Persian donkeys were making noise."

Time for another fleet conference. He didn't hate them nearly as much as he used to, but was still acutely aware that some of the officers among those whose images were shown around the virtual table were actively plotting against him and ships of the fleet itself. Most of the commanding officers of the fleet's ships seemed cheerful though, after the latest victory and knowing how close they were to home.

Unfortunately, it was also time to break the bad news. "I've asked Lieutenant Iger from intelligence to be present so he can brief everyone on something he and I have already discussed." Waving toward Iger, Geary sat down. Since he already knew the content of Iger's briefing, he spent the time watching the reactions to the news.

Cheerfulness faded into disbelief, followed by a general sense of anger.

Captain Armus put the feelings into words. "How could our intelligence be so wrong?"

Geary answered. "As Lieutenant Iger explained, this reserve flotilla has been kept so far from Alliance space that there were no indicators of its existence that we could detect."

"Why?" *Daring*'s commanding officer asked. "That's a lot of ships, and I know the Syndics could have used them at different times in the past. Why leave them sitting on the border of Syndic space farthest from the Alliance?"

"We can only speculate as to the reasons," Geary replied. Strictly speaking, he was being truthful. Everything known about the aliens on that side of Syndic space was speculation. "But they did do it, and now it seems they've brought that flotilla here."

"Where are they?" *Dragon*'s commanding officer questioned Iger.

"We believe they're somewhere within a jump or two of Heradao."

Geary pulled up the star display for the region. "When we arrived in Heradao, Captain Desjani and I wondered why the Syndic flotilla here had left a clear path open for Kalixa. It may well be that the reserve flotilla was waiting for us at Kalixa. If we'd gone that way, the Syndic flotilla here would have followed and we would have been trapped between two powerful enemy forces."

"Typical Syndic trick," Captain Badaya complained. "How long will they wait at Kalixa to see if we show up?"

Desjani pointed to the display. "A Syndic HuK stationed at the jump point to Kalixa jumped that way after we'd defeated the flotilla here. There's another near that jump point that's waiting to see which we way we go, and, of course, there are two HuKs hanging around the jump point for Padronis."

Badaya studied the display, then nodded. "Atalia. They'll know when we jump for Padronis, they'll know we can't reach Kalixa from Padronis, so they'll head for Atalia and try to stop us there since they know we have to go that way."

"That's a very good estimate," Geary agreed. "It's what Lieutenant Iger and I came up with, too."

"We seem to be glossing over some major failures," Captain Kila said in a mild tone at odds with her words. "Somebody just *misplaced* a Syndic flotilla comprised in part of twenty battleships and twenty battle cruisers?" Lieutenant Iger, visibly uncomfortable, started to answer her. "No, *Lieutenant.* I'm not interested in hearing excuses. If you were a line officer you'd be relieved for cause and—"

"Captain Kila." Something in Geary's voice made even Kila stop speaking. "Lieutenant Iger works for me, not you. If not for the efforts of him and his subordinates, we wouldn't even know this flotilla existed."

Kila turned a hard look on Geary. "Just for the record, then, Captain Geary, you don't believe in holding people accountable for their failures?"

Something inside Geary snapped. "If I did, Captain Kila, I would hold you accountable for the loss of the battle cruiser *Opportune.*"

Dead silence fell.

Out of the corner of his eye, Geary could see Desjani giving him a warning look. He knew what she'd be saying out loud if she could. *You can't condemn an officer in this fleet for being too aggressive. None of your officers will accept that, not even now.*

Kila seemed to be searching for just the right reply.

Captain Caligo spoke up before Kila could. "We need to focus on the future, not the past. The Syndics are the enemy, not our fellow officers."

The words were unexceptional, but perhaps because of that the tension eased.

"Caligo's right. It doesn't matter where the Syndics came from," *Warspite*'s captain declared. "We're going to meet them at Atalia. That's all I care about."

Geary took a deep breath. "Right. We'll go into a final battle formation just before jumping for Atalia from Padronis. The worst case for us will be a fight right off the jump exit, but the Syndics seem to have abandoned that tactic. Once we have time to evaluate their position and formation, we'll move in and hurt them."

"We're going to be very low on fuel cells," Tulev observed. "The loss of *Goblin* couldn't be helped, but it made things worse."

"I know. That just means we have to win despite the logistics situation." As plans went, that was inspiring but totally useless. He couldn't think of anything else to say, though.

"We're better than they are," Desjani interjected calmly. "We can fight smarter and harder." Officers were perking up around the table at her words. Badaya gave Desjani an approving look that Desjani didn't seem to notice. Kila gave her an equally scornful look, but Desjani ignored that as well. "We'll win again, because we also have a combat leader the Syndics cannot match."

That went over very well. Even Tulev quirked a small smile. "I cannot argue with Captain Desjani on that last. I have full confidence in Captain Geary, based on his record against the enemy."

"Thank you," Geary said. "Now, you all know what we'll face. We'll deal with this Syndic flotilla just as we have the other enemy flotillas we've encountered. I consider the chances of that reserve flotilla being at Padronis to be very small, but we'll also be ready when we arrive there just in case. I'll see you all again at Padronis."

When the virtual presences had all vanished, and Lieutenant Iger had hastened out of the room with ill-concealed relief, Geary turned to Desjani with an apologetic shrug. "Sorry. I know I lost it with Kila."

"It's what she wanted," Desjani pointed out. "She's an enemy, sir, and you need to follow the same rules with her that you do with the

Syndics. Don't let her lure you into an ambush."

"Okay. I got it. Next time I start to say something stupid, give me a good swift kick."

Desjani raised both eyebrows. "That would certainly earn me some interesting glances. Lately, I'm already getting too many of those as it is every time I open my mouth."

"Uh, yeah. Maybe instead you should just discreetly give me your don't-go-there look."

"I have a don't-go-there look?"

"Hell, yes. Don't pretend you don't know what I'm talking about."

"I haven't any idea." Desjani headed for the hatch. "Just be careful what you say around Kila. She's waiting to pounce."

"One more thing." Desjani paused, waiting for Geary to continue. "Co-President Rione asked me to thank you for the way you handled Commander Fensin. It did him a lot of good."

Desjani shrugged. "I did my job, sir. I'm pleased I was able to render assistance to Commander Fensin."

"Is there any response you want to give Co-President Rione?" Geary pressed, hoping for some thaw between the two women.

"No, sir. I wouldn't want you to feel obligated to speak with her on my account."

He watched her go, knowing full well that the bad blood between Desjani and Rione was partly his fault but having no idea how to win that particular engagement.

There was one last thing that had to be done before the fleet left Heradao. It had happened in every star system in which the fleet had fought, but that didn't make the event any easier. Geary had put on a dress uniform and stood stiffly in the shuttle dock before a ceremonial guard of Marines and sailors similarly attired in their most formal uniforms. Black bands with a broad strip of gold trim on either end adorned every left arm.

Geary cleared his throat and tried to speak evenly. "Every victory comes at a price. Many of our comrades have died in this star system, fighting for their homes and families, for what they believed in, for the friends who fought beside them. Now we must bid farewell to the remains of those who fell in honorable battle. May all honor be given to their memories, and may all comfort be given to those they leave behind. Their spirits have already gone to join their ancestors, and now their bodies will be consigned to one of the beacons the living stars have given to us. Our prayers and our thanks go with them."

Captain Desjani stepped forward, her face stern, and pivoted to face the Marines. "Ready." The Marines brought their weapons up. "Fire." The weapons, set to the lowest discharge levels, winked bright lights off the overhead. "Fire." More lights. "Fire."

Desjani stepped back.

Geary turned to face her. "Launch the remains of the honored dead on their final journey."

Desjani saluted, pivoted again to give the order and transmit the same command to every ship in the fleet that had suffered losses.

The Alliance fleet launched its dead, hundreds of capsules holding bodies, a flotilla of the departed aimed for the star Heradao.

Geary heard Desjani praying softly and similar sounds from others around him. He waited a respectful interval, breathing a few words to his own ancestors on behalf of those who were gone, then called out a last command. "Dismissed."

Marines and sailors marched out slowly, along with most of the others who had been present. Geary stood silently, his eyes on a large display screen showing the multitude of body capsules sailing away from the fleet.

Desjani came to stand beside him. "It's always the hardest part," she commented. "Saying good-bye."

"Yeah. I wish we could have taken them home for burials on their home worlds."

She shook her head. "It's not practical. We'd have to wrap garlands of the dead around the outer hulls of our ships. There wouldn't be anything dignified about that. This way they get the most honorable burial possible, consigned to the embrace of a star."

"Burials in space were rare in my time," Geary said. "But then, we didn't have so many dead to deal with."

"It's the best possible resting place," Desjani insisted. She placed one hand on her heart. "Everything that makes us came from the stars. Now these dead are returning to a star, and someday it will cast the elements within them outward just as stars have done since the beginning, and in time those elements will combine to form new stars, new worlds, new lives. 'From the stars we came, and to the stars we return,' " she quoted. "This is a good fate, the last honor we can render those who died alongside us."

"You're right." Even the most militant agnostic couldn't argue the literal truth of what Desjani had said, and though Geary found the sheer scale of the time involved to be unnerving, he also felt the comfort of being part of an eternal cycle symbolized by the gold strips on either side of the black mourning band he wore. Light, dark, light. The dark was just an interval.

"And you must never forget," Desjani added, "that if not for you, every man and woman in this fleet would either already be dead, or would be in a Syndic labor camp with nothing to look forward to for the rest of their lives except their eventual deaths far from all they loved."

"I didn't do it alone. It couldn't have happened without the efforts and courage of every one of those men and women. But thank you. You give me strength when I need it the most."

"You're welcome." Her hand rested very briefly on his arm near the mourning band, then Desjani left without another word.

He stayed there a little longer, watching the capsules recede on their journey to the star.

Several hours later, the Alliance fleet jumped for Padronis, the cities and planets of Heradao still convulsing in civil war in the fleet's wake.

Another star system abandoned by humanity, Padronis held nothing the Alliance fleet could use. Geary shook his head as he took in the assessments of the fleet's sensors on what the Syndics had left behind at one small rescue station when they abandoned this star. There couldn't be anything there for which it would be worth slowing down any of his ships.

Not that they'd expected anything else. Padronis was a white dwarf star, glittering alone in the emptiness of space, unaccompanied by the array of planets and asteroids that usually orbited stars. Like other white dwarf stars, every once in a while Padronis would accumulate too much helium in its outer shell and go nova, ejecting the outer shell and brightening a great deal for a short time. These occasional novas hadn't been beneficial for anything once near Padronis. Any worlds or rocks had all been long since smashed and hurled into the darkness between stars, leaving only the relatively recent and now-abandoned Syndic facility orbiting Padronis. Someday, Padronis would go nova again, and that facility would be blown away as well, but the fleet's sensors had analyzed the star's outer shell and concluded that the date of that event was still comfortably distant in the future.

"Imagine having to be the crew on that thing," Geary remarked to Desjani, indicating the abandoned Syndic facility on his display. "They needed an emergency station here when lots of ships had to pass through using jump drives, but those on it must have felt murderously isolated. This is as close to nothing as any star system can be."

She grimaced and nodded. "The only thing worse would be getting stuck in a black-hole system, though no one but science geeks would be likely to do that. I'll lay you odds they crewed the station here using criminals. Go to a labor camp for years or go to Padronis. I wonder how many chose the labor camp."

"I think I would've." Geary was about to add something else when his display flickered, then vanished completely as the lights on *Dauntless*'s bridge dimmed.

"What happened?" Desjani demanded of her bridge crew, punching her own nonresponsive controls to try to get status reports.

"Emergency system shutdown," a watch-stander reported, his voice startled. "As far as I can tell just about everything on the ship has gone off-line except for the emergency backups."

"*Why?*"

"Cause unknown, Captain. I— Wait. Engineering is using the sound-powered comm system to update us. They say the power core did an emergency crash. They're running evaluations on everything before bringing it back online."

Desjani clenched her fists. "What could have caused the emergency crash?"

The engineering watch-stander looked pale under the dimmer emergency lighting. "Unknown as yet. Thank the living stars the core managed to shut itself down, Captain. Anything that would trigger an emergency crash would be as serious as it gets."

Geary spoke into the silence that followed that report. "We just narrowly avoided a power-core failure?"

"Looks like it. A catastrophic power-core failure." Desjani's face was grim as she turned to her watch-standers. "I want full status reports from all departments as soon as possible and an estimated time from engineering to restart the core whenever they can provide one."

"Do we have any communications with the rest of the fleet?" Geary asked.

"Emergency systems are online, sir. Voice only, no data net."

"Notify the rest of the fleet what happened to us."

"Yes, sir." The communications watch paused, then drew in a shocked breath. "Sir, we have a message from *Daring* reporting that *Lorica* suffered a power-core failure at the same time as our system shutdown. *Lorica* was totally destroyed. No signs of survivors."

One such failure in routine circumstances would be a rare but-not-impossible event. Two at the exact same time could only mean sabotage. Whoever had been planting worms in the fleet's systems had struck again.

"Bastards," Desjani breathed, her jaw muscles standing out. Raising her voice, she spoke with what Geary thought was amazing control. "Inform engineering that the likely cause of the emergency crash of the power core was a worm in the operating systems."

All of the watch-standers stared back at her, their expressions horrified, then the engineering watch hastily nodded. "Yes, Captain."

"Captain Geary," the operations watch-stander called. "*Daring* is asking what instructions to relay to the rest of the fleet. Should they maintain station on *Dauntless* even if she drifts off course and speed?"

That had the virtue of being a relatively simple decision. Maneuvering one ship back into position would cost a lot less in fuel than having the entire fleet trying to match anything *Dauntless* did while her own propulsion and maneuvering systems were shut down. "Tell *Daring* to assume role as fleet guide until *Dauntless* gets power back."

It was less than twenty minutes before *Dauntless*'s systems-security officer called the bridge, but it felt like the longest twenty minutes of Geary's life. It was easy to overlook how accustomed he was to being able to scan a display and see everything he needed to see, easy until that display was gone and nothing could be seen in front of his fleet command seat but the part of *Dauntless*'s bridge visible from that angle. There weren't any physical windows, of course, not here deep within *Dauntless*'s hull, and not on the outer hull, either. That arrangement made a great deal of sense in terms of maintaining hull strength and integrity, but at times like this even a single small window would have been a welcome connection to the rest of the fleet.

"We found it, Captain Desjani," the systems officer reported, his voice sounding oddly distant across the voice-powered emergency circuit. "The worm tried to induce core overload failure, but our safety backups managed to crash the core first."

"Do you have any idea why *Lorica*'s safety backups didn't manage to save her?" Desjani asked.

"I can only guess, Captain. Operating systems are hugely complex, so every ship's operating systems are subtly different even when they're supposed to be identical. *Lorica*'s safety backups may have been just enough dissimilar to add up to a critical difference. Or maybe the attempted overload instructions came during the right portion of the millisecond when our backups were watching for something like that, but not when *Lorica*'s were. I don't want to imply carelessness by the dead, but it's possible that *Lorica*'s systems people hadn't tweaked their safety backups recently enough. There's just no telling, and we'll probably never know since I assume there's not enough left of *Lorica* to tell us anything."

Desjani closed her eyes momentarily, her lips moving in a brief prayer. Geary understood how she felt. *Dauntless*'s survival had been a near thing. "Are you certain," she demanded of her officer, "that there's nothing else lurking in the systems?"

"We've found nothing else, Captain."

"That's not what I asked."

"Yes, Captain! I mean, no, Captain! If there were any other worms, we'd have found them. I'd bet my life on it."

Desjani's lips curled upward at the edges in a humorless smile. "That's exactly what you're doing. Make certain that worm is completely eliminated and keep looking for other threats in our systems. Notify me when you and the chief engineer feel comfortable with restarting the power core."

"Yes, Captain. Estimated time is another fifteen minutes."

She slumped back in her command seat, then looked around the bridge. "At ease, everyone. It'll be another fifteen minutes. Be ready to hit the deck running when the power comes back on."

Geary stared at the nearest bulkhead, lacking the welcome distractions of dealing with the immediate problems Desjani and her crew had to address. "We have to find the people responsible for this," he finally muttered to Desjani out of frustration. "This time they've succeeded in destroying one of our ships."

"But why *Lorica*?" Desjani asked in a very quiet voice. "Do you have any idea?"

"Yeah." Commander Gaes, *Lorica*'s commanding officer, had been the one to warn him about the first worm in the fleet. She'd known something, and apparently that something had been too much for whoever was behind the worms.

Desjani nodded, watching Geary. "Gaes went with Falco, but since *Lorica* rejoined the fleet, she's been a supporter of yours. Her contacts with dissident officers must have been useful to you."

"They were. Apparently I wasn't the only one to think so."

"We'll get the ones responsible for this, Captain Geary," Desjani promised. "Someone will know who did it and they'll surely talk now."

He wasn't so certain of that. Worms designed to directly destroy Alliance ships would have aroused protests if knowledge of them had been spread to more than a very few people, and those few people were now aware that exposing themselves would guarantee firing squads.

They waited silently after that. With everything except emergency systems down, the few working lights dim, the bridge began to feel claustrophobic. Geary wondered if the temperature was getting as warm as his imagination insisted, whether the air was becoming fouler. He knew emergency backups would power essential functions for much longer than it had been since the core crashed, though, so Geary made an effort to relax and look unconcerned.

"Power-core systems have been scrubbed," the welcome report finally arrived. "The worm responsible for the shutdown is confirmed gone. Request permission for restart of power core."

"Do it," Desjani snapped. A few minutes later the lights on the bridge brightened, and the vent fans hummed a little stronger. Less than a minute after that, the displays reappeared floating in front of everyone. "Get us back where we belong," she ordered the maneuvering watch. "We probably drifted a little out of position relative to the other ships. Take station on *Daring* and we'll reassume guide duties for the fleet."

The reappearance of his displays helped a lot. Geary had been fighting down an irrational worry that more ships had been lost, and he just hadn't been told. Now he could confirm that only *Lorica* was gone. As if that was good news. Checking the reports from the ships closest to *Lorica* when she'd exploded, Geary grimaced. "No survivors."

"If there had been survivors, they would have had to have ejected their escape pods prior to the core overload," Desjani pointed out.

"They wouldn't have survived for long after that once the rest of the fleet realized what that implied."

She was right, of course, but that didn't help much. Taking a deep breath, Geary called up a communications window and broadcast to the fleet. "This is Captain Geary. *Dauntless* and everyone on her are safe. We're investigating the cause of the core overload on *Lorica* and the core crash on *Dauntless*. Anyone with any information regarding either incident please forward it to me immediately."

Investigating. A big word for something unlikely to produce any results. If the ones responsible for this worm were as diligent as they'd been with earlier worms, there'd be absolutely no identifiers that could be used to trace the worm back to its origin. Knowing that, Geary had to restrain himself from walking to the nearest bulkhead and punching it in aggravation.

Instead, he brought up his message queue, not expecting to see the answers he needed but still looking for distractions. Geary frowned as he noticed all of the highpriority messages already blinking in his queue. They must have all been put into the fleet net while *Dauntless*'s systems were down, meaning they wouldn't be answers to his request for information. It would take forever to get through all of them, and most were probably just variations on "what happened" and "are you all right?"

Then he stopped and stared.

One of the messages was tagged as being from *Lorica*.

"Captain Desjani, can you confirm the time of *Lorica*'s destruction for me?" Geary asked.

She gave him a puzzled glance, clearly wondering why that information was important at the moment. "Our own power core did its emergency crash at 1412. According to system records we received from the rest of the fleet, *Lorica* blew up at... two point seven seconds past 1412."

Geary checked the message again. "I have a message in my queue from *Lorica* with a transmission time of 1415."

"Sir?" Desjani stepped over beside him, leaned over Geary's shoulder to view his display, then tapped some controls next to his hand. "The fleet communications net sees the message as having been received for transmission after 1414. It was sent on the next full minute." She straightened and glared at her communications watch. "How could the communications system see a message as having been received from *Lorica* well after that ship was destroyed?"

"It wouldn't have, Captain. Even if it was delayed in delivery, the system would log when it was actually sent." The watch-stander looked briefly baffled, then nodded as understanding came. "The message had to have been parked and hidden in the system. People aren't supposed to do that, but there are several ways to manage it. *Lorica*, or somebody on *Lorica*, sent that message out at some earlier time into the comm-system net but had it concealed under a protocol that wouldn't make it visible to the system until something happened, like a certain time arrived."

Geary shook his head. "Why would *Lorica* have done that?" He could think of a number of reasons why someone who had screwed up would want a message time to be different from when it was actually sent, but couldn't understand what might have prompted someone on *Lorica* to set that up. Calling up the message, Geary scanned it. It wasn't actually a message, but a big dump of code. "Captain Desjani, who can tell me what this is?"

She eyed it, then tapped some more controls. "With your permission I'll get an assessment from my systems-security officer before we send this anywhere else, sir. We don't know what might be in it."

He felt a momentary surge of fear and anger at himself. "This could be the worm that almost destroyed us?"

"Not sent that way," Desjani replied with a shake of her head. "The filters and firewalls in this part of the comm. system don't let anything active through. Trying to send the worm this way would be like shooting a picture of a missile at us instead of the actual missile. If that's what this is. My systems people should be able to tell."

The response came fairly quickly, the face of Desjani's systems-security officer appearing in small windows on both her and Geary's displays. The lieutenant commander seemed stunned. "Sir, Captain, I mean, uh... that message from *Lorica*. It's the coding for the first worm, the one that would've messed with every ships' jump drives."

"That worm came from *Lorica*?" Geary felt a deep sense of disappointment. He'd trusted Commander Gaes, given her a second chance, and yet—

"No, sir. The message is a copy of the first worm, with the system-tracking information and originating ship's identity still on it. I have no idea how *Lorica* got a copy of that." D*auntless*'s systems-security officer swallowed nervously. "According to what's in *Lorica*'s transmission, that worm originally came from *Inspire*, sir."

8

Geary felt a coldness spreading through him. "You're certain? There's no doubt?"

"Not if that message is real, sir. It could've been faked, of course, though it'd be very hard to construct a false system-tracking record that authentic-looking. But to me it looks like someone on *Lorica* discovered where that worm came from and had a message containing the information planted in the comm system under a dead man release, so if the cruiser registered as destroyed, the message was sent."

So Commander Gaes had known who was responsible but had kept that information close for reasons that would never be known now. But she had also made certain that if she was silenced, then the truth would come out.

Desjani's face was flushed with rage. "This is good enough cause to get Kila into an interrogation room and see what she really knows about it."

"Yeah," Geary agreed, thinking of the dead on *Lorica* and already mentally phrasing his orders to a firing squad for Captain Kila, but as he reached for his controls to order the Marines on *Inspire* to act, another hand came down on his, and Victoria Rione's voice spoke intensely.

"Wait. You want to make certain you get her."

Geary rounded on Rione, wondering when she'd arrived on the bridge and gotten close enough to overhear his and Desjani's conversation. But before he could speak, Desjani did.

"If we want to be certain we get her, then we do it as fast as possible!" Desjani whispered vehemently. "That woman tried to destroy my ship!"

"I know what she tried to do!" Rione whispered back angrily. "Listen to me! Kila has done a magnificent job of covering her tracks. Her actions clearly include contingency plans for eliminating evidence and potential witnesses against her, as we saw in Lakota when the shuttle carrying those two officers was destroyed. If we don't lay a careful trap, she might already have some plan in place for dealing with something like this."

Geary fought down his own desire for instant vengeance, recognizing the truth in Rione's advice. "What do you suggest? We can't let her keep operating."

"No." Rione paused in thought. "One hour. That's enough time to set up our own trap. Call a fleet conference in one hour. Kila will believe that means you still have no idea who's responsible for what happened to *Lorica* and almost happened to *Dauntless*. She'll be expecting another in effective appeal for anyone who knows anything to come forward. If we can keep her in ignorance of this evidence until then, we can prepare a trap she won't be able to avoid."

Desjani glared at Rione, but Geary could see her thinking. Then Desjani nodded abruptly. "That's good advice. I'd take it, sir."

Rione glowered back at Desjani. "Thank you so much for the vote of confidence."

"Both of you try to remember who the enemy is," Geary ground out, trying to control his own emotions. The watchstanders on the bridge had already surely noticed something unusual going on between him, their captain, and Rione. He had to divert the gossip about that away from the message he had asked about earlier. "All right, Madam Co-President. Design your trap and tell me what you need. But first give another good long glare at Captain Desjani and stalk off the bridge as if you two had been arguing again."

"We have been arguing. Even *you* should have noticed that." Rione smiled coldly at Geary, then shifted her gaze to Desjani and stepped slightly away. "Pardon me for wanting to be involved in your decisions," she stated in a low voice that could still surely be heard by the watch-standers. "I thought I should be aware of what caused the loss of power on this ship."

Desjani smiled at Rione in a forcibly polite way. "When I find out more, I will ensure you are told. Thank you, Madam Co-President."

Rione stalked off the bridge, and Geary stood up, not having to fake a renewed gust of frustration. He wanted Kila in a cell right now, he wanted Kila in front of a firing squad right now, but he couldn't rush into it. Rione had been right about the need to plan an ambush. They had to make certain that Kila didn't have any more opportunities to destroy potential evidence or kill potential witnesses against her. He spoke clearly for the benefit of the watchstanders who might be listening. "Captain Desjani, let me know the instant anyone finds out anything more about what caused the loss of *Lorica* and the problem on *Dauntless*."

"My systems-security officer is working the issue, sir," Desjani replied, her voice quivering with suppressed anger. That's exactly how her crew would expect their captain to feel about an attempt to destroy their ship, though. And if they wondered what else might have her angry, the widely known bad blood between their captain and Victoria Rione would surely explain the rest of their captain's ill humor at the moment.

Geary sent the message calling a fleet commanding officers conference in one hour, then left the bridge, noticing the watchstanders all doing their best to avoid attracting the attention of Captain Desjani where she sat scowling at her display. He paused for just a moment, recalling his own days as a junior officer, when reading the captain's temper and steering as wide of that individual as necessary on bad days formed an important part of the standard routine no matter the ship or the captain.

In the days when Geary had been a junior officer, the idea of open dissent against fleet commander would have been thought insubordinate. A fleet captain conspiring against that commander to the extent of destroying Alliance warships would have been simply unthinkable. So much had been altered in the last century, driven by the stresses of an apparently unending war. But steering clear of a captain in a foul mood hadn't changed in the hundred years he'd been in survival sleep. It probably hadn't changed in a thousand years or more. No matter how much was different from the past, some traditions and practices withstood the stresses of time and events.

Not all of those traditions and practices were necessarily good or wise, but he still found the thought comforting.

One hour later he was in the conference room again, the atmosphere in the compartment as tense as it had ever been. Geary stood at the head of the table, trying not to look toward where Captain Kila's image would appear, as the images of the fleet's ship commanders popped into place, and the table and room appeared to expand to accommodate them.

Desjani entered the room, the only one besides Geary who was physically present, and took her seat next to him. She caught his eye and nodded, then fixed her gaze on the table surface. He could sense the tension in Desjani, like that of a great cat ready to spring but holding herself back by force of will. It was the same impression Desjani gave when preparing for a firing run against a Syndic warship, but this time her target was one of the Alliance fleet's own officers.

To Geary's surprise and gratitude, the image of Captain Duellos showed up next to that of Captain Cresida. Duellos's uniform had been cleaned and patched up. Aside from the slight stiffness of his movements, it would have been hard to tell how much he had been through lately.

The image of Co-President Rione appeared among the captains of the fleet's ships from the Callas Republic and the Rift Federation. She also looked directly at Geary and nodded, though in her case the gesture also conveyed the message that the ambush was ready to spring. Rione's eyes held a warning reminder, too. *You're a lousy actor and very bad at lying, Captain Geary,* Rione had told him less than half an hour ago. *You'll be angry, but try to make that anger look like it's directed at someone whose identity you don't know. Don't say anything about the first worm or speculations about where the worms have come from until you get the signals that the trap is ready. If you don't talk about what we know, then you won't be lying, and you won't sound like you're lying.*

There were worse flaws to have than an inability to lie well, he thought as he waited for everyone's image to arrive at the conference. At least as long as he had Rione along to help him past places where he might otherwise have to lie. Geary imagined how the fleet's officers would simply nod knowingly if they ever found out he needed a politician to provide advice on avoiding the truth.

Colonel Carabali appeared as unruffled as ever, but she also took a moment to nod to Geary in apparent greeting, actually confirming that her Marines were ready.

The last officers arrived, most of them relatively junior commanding officers from the smallest and therefore most distant warships who had slightly misjudged the time delay for transmissions at the speed of light to cross between their ships and *Dauntless*. Now everyone sat silently as Geary stood up and began speaking in as controlled a voice as he could manage. "One of our heavy cruisers, *Lorica*, has been destroyed and her crew murdered by individuals whose political goals are more important to them than the lives of our fleet's personnel." Rione had suggested those exact words, linking the ones responsible for the loss of *Lorica* to the sort of politics the fleet scorned. "*Dauntless* narrowly avoided destruction as well."

Captain Badaya slammed his palm onto the table before him, the meeting software obligingly adding the sound of the gesture as if Badaya had physically hit the table on *Dauntless*. "Backstabbing bastards! How can anyone in this fleet with any knowledge of those responsible for this hold back?"

"I don't know," Geary replied, letting his eyes search the faces of every officer. He noticed that Kila looked around as well, with a perfectly calculated expression of righteous anger, a move that, Geary realized, kept her from having to meet his gaze. "This is the last chance for anyone here who knows anything. Tell us what you know, or you'll face the same punishment as those who did it."

No one answered.

"I know there are those who disagree with my decisions as commander of this fleet," Geary added. "Dissent is one thing. Murder and the destruction of Alliance warships is another. I believe I've given everyone adequate grounds to be certain that I will keep my word. Those who destroyed *Lorica* also surely destroyed the shuttle carrying Captain Casia and Commander Yin in Lakota Star System. Those officers were murdered, too, to keep them quiet. Anyone who knows anything about this should realize that their lives are in the hands of someone who will kill rather than risk exposure. You will be protected if you come forward now."

More silence, longer this time.

Duellos looked like he was tasting something foul. "I increasingly suspect that whoever is behind all of this is operating under a cloak of anonymity. I cannot believe that if their identities were known to many of those who once supported them, that they would not be revealed now."

"If someone could find a thread leading to them," Captain Tulev objected, "then they could trace that thread back given time and determination no matter how many precautions had been taken."

"Maybe that's why Commander Gaes died on *Lorica*," Captain Cresida interjected. "She went with Falco, so at one time she was tied in with those opposed to Captain Geary's command of this fleet. She'd also acquitted herself loyally since that time, though. Maybe she used the contacts she knew of to find the ones behind all of this." Cresida hadn't been told that, but she was shrewd enough to connect the dots once *Lorica* was targeted for destruction.

Daring's commanding officer shook his head. "It's all speculation. We need hard data. We need evidence!"

"Do we?" Cresida asked. "The truth would come out in an interrogation room. I hereby volunteer to be questioned in an interrogation room about my knowledge of the worms that have been used against this fleet, and I urge all of my fellow commanding officers to do so as well."

Captain Armus of *Colossus* frowned. "That's a very big step to take. You're indirectly questioning the honor of every officer in the fleet. If we agree to being interrogated, we move the line of what's permissible against our fellow officers, even those who aren't even remotely suspected of a crime. We move that line very, very far."

A lot of the officers present nodded in agreement. Even Geary found himself reflexively rejecting Cresida's idea. By establishing a precedent for broad interrogations of any officer, whether that individual was suspected of crimes or not, the cure might be worse than the illness represented by someone like Captain Kila.

But if he hadn't received that message from *Lorica*, would he feel the same way? Or, driven by anger and frustration, would he have reluctantly agreed with Cresida and perhaps fatally undermined a critical component of the fleet? He'd been appalled by the compromises made in the principles of the Alliance over the hundred years of war, but moments like this helped Geary see how easy it was to make such compromises, to abandon important principles "just this once because it was important."

"Co-President Rione volunteered to be interrogated when she was under suspicion," one of the Callas Republic captains reminded everyone.

"A politician can scarcely be considered to have a conception of honor equal to that of a fleet officer." Armus blurted out the statement, then reddened as he realized he'd said it in Rione's presence.

"Given her position as an Alliance senator," Duellos pointed out, "it was a comparable act."

"And," Captain Desjani stated in a deceptively dispassionate tone, "since many here believe politicians have much more to fear in the way of wrongdoing being revealed in such interrogations, Co-President Rione's offer was arguably of even greater identificance than if a fleet officer made such an agreement."

"Thank you, Captain Desjani," Rione replied in a voice that could have cut through hull armor.

Geary had been stalling while Kila was occupied with the meeting, letting the debate ramble to kill time. Now Colonel Carabali looked aside at something visible to her, then nodded again to Geary. The trap was set.

Geary rapped his knuckles on the table to get everyone's attention. "We need not question the honor of every officer in this fleet, nor do we need to subject officers to blanket questioning in ways that would harm the structure and discipline of the fleet." He had their attention, all of the other officers watching him and clearly wondering what he would say next. Even Desjani managed to do a decent job of looking puzzled. "Instead, we'll let the dead speak."

Varying expressions of shock and surprise appeared on every face as Geary tapped the table with one fingertip.

"*Lorica*'s commanding officer was able to transmit something important just before her ship's destruction, something she'd found. Her ship was probably targeted because the plotters suspected that Commander Gaes had learned too much, just as Captain Cresida speculated." He couldn't be certain of that, couldn't know for how long Gaes had been aware of the identity of the ship from which the original worm came. Gaes had known about the original worm, she'd warned Geary of it, but if she'd known who was behind it, she hadn't told him then. Gaes had died in the line of duty, though, and had given him the information he desperately needed, so in Geary's eyes she deserved to be given every benefit of the doubt.

Geary entered a command. The message from *Lorica* appeared, floating above the table, the meeting software making it appear to face everyone. "You'll recall the first worm placed in this fleet's operating systems, the one that would have disabled most of the jump drives, except for a few ships like *Dauntless*, which would have been doomed to remain in jump space forever." He indicated the message. "This identifies the one thing we lacked, the information revealing from which ship that worm originated." Everyone was staring at him as Geary shifted his gaze and focused on Kila.

"Captain Kila, that worm originated from *Inspire*."

Kila appeared taken aback at the news. "Are you certain?"

"Yes, Captain Kila. Would you care to explain how your ship is the source of treasonous and malicious software aimed at your comrades in this fleet?"

"I don't care for what you're implying, Captain Geary!" Kila snapped back at him.

"We should immediately send orders to *Inspire* to arrest those who could have been involved," Badaya urged. "Do it now, before they hear about this."

Kila turned on Badaya. "This message hasn't even been authenticated yet. Did it actually come from *Lorica*? If it did, is it real or fabricated? I assure every officer here that if I had known anything about such a thing, I would have personally ensured that those responsible were brought to justice! As for your suggestion, Captain Badaya, I am fully capable of ordering the arrest of those officers and ensuring that anything they know is revealed."

If he hadn't been tipped off by Rione to watch for it, Geary wouldn't have noticed how one of Kila's hands slipped out of sight during her impassioned denial. That hand could easily be manipulating controls outside the view of the conferencing software. "The message can be examined by anyone seeking to establish its authenticity," he replied, trying to keep his voice calm even though he wanted to yell back at Kila. "Every communications and security officer who has looked at it thus far has identified its original source as *Inspire*. You were unaware that the worm originated from *Inspire*?"

"Of course I was!" Kila glared around, her gaze fixing on

Duellos. "You set this up, didn't you? The long-ago scorned lover finally finding his revenge!"

Duellos had no trouble looking innocent as he shook his head, since he hadn't been advised beforehand of the message, but his dislike of Kila was still apparent. "I would think that a commanding officer would be less concerned about herself and more concerned about discovering the source of that worm aboard her ship."

"Whoever is responsible will be brought to account!" Kila stood. "I need to be supervising the search on *Inspire* for whoever did this, before they learn about this information, assuming," she added quickly, "that the message supposedly from *Lorica* is authentic."

Geary looked at Colonel Carabali again as the Marine listened to something not audible to the meeting, then the Marine commander nodded a final time, and Geary smiled grimly at Kila. "We should start with your ship's systems-security officer, don't you think, Captain Kila? And the communications officer and the executive officer?"

"Of course!" Kila said. "If you let me start my investigation, I will ensure they aren't alerted about this possible evidence in time for them to—"

"The investigation has already started." Geary broke in. "Colonel Carabali, can you bring everyone up to date?"

Carabali avoided looking at Kila, her own face set in rigidly professional lines as she spoke in a flat voice. "On instructions from Captain Geary, my Marines assigned to *Inspire* waited until this meeting began, then covertly took into protective custody the executive officer, communications officer, and systems-security officer on *Inspire*."

The images of the fleet's commanding officers were now staring either at Carabali or Geary or Kila. Geary hoped he wasn't looking triumphant. Kila's face revealed nothing but seemed to have become unnaturally stiff.

"The officers taken into custody," Carabali continued, "were placed inside a maximum-isolation security cell while they were checked for anything dangerous to themselves or *Inspire*. Maximum-isolation cells include complete coverage based on an ancient device called a Faraday cage, which blocks any incoming or outgoing radiation. Communication is maintained using physical messages passed through a series of shielded locks." Colonel Carabali paused for a moment, then looked straight at Kila. "Approximately three minutes ago, examinations of the systems-security officer and the communications officer on *Inspire* revealed the presence of INBNDs. As of one minute ago, sensors on the outside of the security cells detected and grounded out a series of signals used for high-security, coded transmissions. The signals must have been generated inside *Inspire*'s hull."

Captain Tulev spoke into the momentary silence that followed. "INBNDs?"

"Injected nano-based neural disruptors," Carabali explained, "which are commonly known as 'brain barbecues' for their effect on the nervous system once triggered. They can be injected into an individual without that person's knowledge if the individual is distracted. The intercepted signals appear to have been intended to trigger the brain barbecues."

This time the silence was longer. "Someone just tried to kill those three officers?" Captain Badaya finally asked incredulously.

"The systems-security officer and the communications officer, definitely. We're still examining *Inspire*'s executive officer to see if INBNDs are present in his body." Carabali's eyes didn't leave Kila. "As I said, the intercepted signals originated on *Inspire*."

Desjani had her own gaze locked on Kila as if she were a hell-lance battery ready to fire. "How strange that someone tried to kill those officers right after those in this meeting were told of the worm that originated from *Inspire*. Who on *Inspire* would have known that those officers were going to be questioned?"

Duellos nodded, his own expression as hard as the armor on a battleship. "It will certainly be interesting to see whom those officers implicate once they are informed that someone tried to kill them. To keep them silent? To make it appear that they were the only guilty ones? We would have been left with two or three dead officers and perhaps some convincing evidence that they committed suicide after learning they were suspects."

Kila's single-minded devotion to promotion had left her few friends and admirers among her peers or juniors, and Geary could see every other commanding officer in the fleet watching Kila with an appalled or angry expression. Even Caligo seemed stunned.

"Captain Kila," Geary stated with what he felt was admirable restraint, "in light of recent events and the evidence available to the fleet, you are hereby relieved of command while the situation on *Inspire* is investigated. Colonel Carabali, please send some of your Marines to escort Captain Kila to a shuttle for transfer to *Illustrious*."

Kila looked around the table contemptuously, then raised one arm in a dramatic gesture before lowering it to tap something on the control panel before her on *Inspire*. "Never mind, Colonel. Your

Marines won't be able to enter my stateroom. The Alliance is going to lose this war because it's weak, because its fleet officers are *weak*. None of you are fit to command this fleet, especially you, *Captain* Geary. You care more for the lives of Syndics than you do for the lives of Alliance citizens!"

Badaya spoke in a voice so deep he seemed to be speaking from his gut. "You murderous bitch. How dare you claim to care for the lives of Alliance citizens when you murdered the crew of *Lorica* and tried to murder the crews of *Illustrious*, *Dauntless*, and *Furious*!"

Kila bared her teeth at Badaya. "We are all sworn to die for the sake of the Alliance, and the unfortunate sacrifice of those crews would have been for the highest cause. It would have been no different than if they died in combat against those who would weaken and destroy the Alliance. If we want to swap accusations of treason, I'm ready. What has Geary promised you after he takes over the Alliance? You call yourselves loyal? You're pathetic and corrupt, selling yourselves out for someone who wants power but won't do what's necessary to save the Alliance."

Duellos answered, his voice as cold as Geary had ever heard it. "The Alliance has been doing what some people claimed to be 'necessary' for the last hundred years and is no closer to winning the war."

"Because of half measures and hesitation!" Kila declared. "Always pulling back from what necessity demanded. The enemy deserves no mercy. None. They deserve death, and only when they realized that we were willing to kill every one of them would they have given in."

"And if the enemy didn't give in?"

Kila swept one hand in a dismissive gesture. "Then they'd all be killed, and the war would end that way."

Tulev spoke, his voice flat. "I have as much right as any to comment on that. I don't know what the Syndics deserve, but their killing of the Alliance's people has never served to persuade us to surrender. Even if your proposal weren't physically beyond the capabilities of even the Alliance, it would be fundamentally flawed in its belief that humans would bow before mass murder of their own."

"Your spirit died at Elyzia," Kila replied, causing a rare display of emotion by Tulev as his face reddened. "I don't fear to speak the truth about such things. But none of you want the truth, none of you want to face your own shortcomings. You could have had a leader who would have done what needed to be done, but you'd rather die by stages, pathetic shadows of what fleet officers used to be."

Geary shook his head. "Fleet officers never believed in killing their own to satisfy their ambitions."

Kila's snarl turned smug. "My ambitions? Do you think I was delusional enough to think a herd of sheep like this would accept me in command? Your pitiful egos couldn't have accepted that. I had someone who would listen, who'd be accepted by all of you, even though he now lacks the courage to stand beside me." She turned and looked directly at Captain Caligo, who stared back. "Weren't you going to tell them? Staying in the background isn't going to work this time. I have no intention of falling on my sword to protect you while you try to hide your own involvement."

Caligo shook his head violently. "I don't know what—"

"We agreed that we were willing to die for the Alliance, remember?" Kila goaded him. "I saw your face just now, saw that you were ready to blend in again, being what ever those around you wanted to see. What do you think they see now?"

Caligo had gone very pale. "You're lying. There's no proof for any of this."

"Do you think I was stupid enough to trust you?" Kila stood at attention, her contemptuous gaze sweeping across every officer there, then reached down and tapped a sequence of commands. "You wanted evidence, *Captain* Geary? I just transmitted enough to make it clear that Caligo agreed to everything." Her eyes were fixed on Geary now. "My enemies have always wanted to drag me down out of envy, but if you were really Black Jack, I could have supported you! I could have stood with a real man, but that man died in survival sleep and left you, an empty shell. All you deserve is that dishonorable politician and that simpleminded captain. I only hope one or both of them wake up and stick a knife in you someday. It's the only thing you're worthy of."

Duellos shook his head, looking regretful but unyielding. "You're so certain of what everyone else deserves, but you're a poor judge of that. You made your enemies, Sandra, your ambition blinded you, and now you will face the firing squad you deserve."

"You have no right to judge me."

Captain Armus answered. "The crew of *Lorica* has that right, don't they, Kila? Soon enough you'll be facing them. If I were you, I'd be preparing to beg forgiveness. None of them survived to see you die, but we will witness that moment for them."

Kila glared at him, staying at attention. "I won't give any of you the satisfaction of watching me die. I'll see you all in hell, which is where you've chosen to be led." She slammed her hand down on her controls back on *Inspire*, and her image vanished.

"Colonel?" Geary demanded.

Carabali was listening to a report, then frowned. "My Marines can't override the lock on Captain Kila's stateroom. They've sent for—" Carabali paused, looking to one side and nodding to someone, then faced Geary again.

"My Marines report an explosion inside Captain Kila's stateroom. It appears to have been equivalent to two standard room-clearing charges."

"What are the chances anyone in the room with that is still alive?"

"Zero."

The conference room was silent, everyone staring at the spot that Captain Kila's image had once occupied. The quiet was finally broken by a high-priority message alert. "Was this cleared by the security screens?" Geary asked.

Desjani spoke rapidly into her data unit, then nodded. "It's clean."

He opened it, seeing a mass of files and archived e-mails. Selecting a few at random, he read them, seeing hatred and contempt for him, and much else as well. "This is the evidence that Captain Kila sent before killing herself," he informed the other officers. He popped one of the old e-mails onto the display over the table so everyone could read it.

Tulev was the first to comment. "From Captain Caligo, reaffirming his commitment to follow instructions from Captain Kila in return for her backing as commander of the fleet. Can we be certain of the authenticity of this document and the others provided by Captain Kila?"

Badaya was glaring at Caligo. "They certainly constitute adequate grounds for interrogation. If Captain Caligo is innocent of involvement in the attempts to destroy Alliance warships and the destruction of *Lorica*, I'm sure he won't object to the chance to clear himself."

Caligo swallowed and spoke. "As my fellow officers, you surely adhere to the principles in which the fleet believes."

"Was that a yes or a no?" Duellos asked.

"Every officer has a right to have his full record considered and his honor not questioned without reason..." Caligo's voice trailed off as even he realized that some powerful reasons existed.

Desjani leaned forward, her expression as stern as Geary had ever seen it. "There is exactly one thing that might grant you an honorable death instead of that of a traitor and a coward. Tell us everything you know and everyone who was involved in this. We'll get that anyway, even if you have to be read the names of every person in this fleet so we can see your reactions in the interrogation chamber. But it will save time and possibly ships if you talk now." She looked around the table. "Kila may have tried to activate another worm. Until we know everything, we have to assume the threat isn't over."

This time the looks bent toward Caligo were frightened and dangerous. He quailed before them and shook his head. "I don't know. I swear."

"Do you know which parts of the fleet net Kila was using to send out the worms? Do you know any identifiers? Who wrote them?"

"Y-yes."

Colonel Carabali listened to another report. "My Marines have blown the hatch on Captain Kila's stateroom and entered. They confirm that she's dead. They're doing a sweep for physical booby traps and recommend that fleet software experts do a careful search for any triggers in that stateroom that might activate destructive worms."

"Is there anyone on *Inspire* we can trust to do that?" Geary asked the officers around the table.

"Send in a team from *Valiant*," Cresida suggested. "They're probably the sharpest software geeks in the fleet."

Commander Landis, *Valiant*'s commanding officer, smiled tightly. "My software-security team is good. I'll have them shuttled over to *Inspire*. I'd recommend every system on *Inspire* be scrubbed. That will take a while."

"Can you get it done before we jump for Atalia?" Geary asked.

"Yes, sir. One way or the other, we'll have *Inspire* certified clean before the next jump."

"Thank you, Commander Landis. Get going on that immediately." Geary faced Captain Caligo, who was now sitting perfectly still, like a rabbit caught in the open and trying to avoid attracting attention. It seemed pretty clear that he wouldn't commit a spectacular act of suicide like Kila had. "Captain Caligo, you are hereby relieved of command effective immediately. You'll be taken into custody and transported to *Illustrious*. I expect you to provide us with all of the information you've promised to deliver, and I expect to start seeing that before you reach *Illustrious*."

Caligo didn't respond, just sat staring at the table.

"Captain Caligo, do you understand?" Geary asked in his harshest voice.

"Yes, sir." Caligo bent his head and began speaking quietly into a recorder in his stateroom. He was still at it when the Marines assigned to *Brilliant* arrived and removed him from the meeting software.

Afterward, everyone sat, seemingly stunned. To Geary's surprise, it was Captain Armus who broke the silence, speaking gruffly. "Captain Geary, I've not hesitated to speak up when I disagreed with you. But now I apologize for anything I have said or done that may have encouraged Kila and Caligo to believe their actions were justified."

"Thank you, Captain Armus. I haven't always been happy with your dissents, but I recognize the need for them and appreciate your willingness to speak your mind. I do not hold you at fault in any way for the actions of Kila and Caligo." Geary looked around the table, easily able to see how badly rattled his commanding officers had been by what had taken place. "A terrible thing has happened. Two of our officers have broken faith with the rest of us. There may be more, but we have the leads we need to unravel the rest of the plot if need be. My confidence in everyone still here is unshaken. I have said before and I will say again now that no one has ever been privileged to have a finer group of officers serving under him, and no one has ever been so honored as to command such a fleet as I have. I thank you for your service and your loyalty and your sacrifice. I will do all I can to live up to the honor that has been given me to serve as your commander."

He wasn't sure how they'd react, but one by one, then in a rush, every officer stood to attention and wordlessly saluted him.

Geary returned the salutes, feeling overwhelmed. "Thank you. The investigation will continue, but let's put this ugliness behind us and prepare for battle at Atalia."

They cheered then, after which the virtual presences vanished slower than usual as images crowded forward to bid individual farewells to Geary. Finally, he was alone in the room except for the real presence of Desjani and the remaining image of Rione.

Desjani saluted as well, an unmistakable look of pride on her face as she gazed at Geary.

"What?" he asked.

"I'll explain it to you someday," she replied with a smile.

"By your leave, sir."

"Certainly, Captain Desjani."

After she'd left, Rione's image sat silent, her face in her hands.

"Are you all right?" Geary asked.

"I underestimated you," she replied in a low voice.

"I don't understand."

Rione lowered her hands and looked at him. "You're even more dangerous than I thought. They're yours. You must have seen that. And even I found myself wondering what I would do if you announced you would become the leader of the Alliance."

"Don't be ridiculous. You know exactly what you'd do."

"I suppose." Rione stood up. "You need to talk to Badaya. Soon. Otherwise, the momentum to make you a dictator may become unstoppable."

"I'll talk to him before we leave Padronis."

"Good. There are very few people in human history who have rejected the kind of power you could have, John Geary."

"I've rejected it," he insisted, "because I'm not qualified to wield it."

"And that belief of yours, ironically, is what would enable us to trust you with that power." She leaned closer. "Hold to your oath, Captain Geary. Only your example and forbearance can save the Alliance." Then her image vanished as well.

On his way back to his stateroom, Geary realized that he had two more decisions to make and not much time to make them. Reaching his stateroom, he immediately called the bridge. "Captain Desjani, please get ahold of Captain Duellos and have him call me as soon as possible."

Sitting down, Geary tried to absorb all that had happened. It was hard to believe that dangerous opposition to him within the fleet had finally been brought to an end.

His hatch alert chimed and Geary gave the hatch an irritated look. *Can't I have five minutes to deal with this?* But he didn't know how important this visitor might be. "Please enter."

Co-President Rione stepped inside his stateroom, then made a questioning gesture around her. Understanding what that meant, Geary activated the stateroom's highest-security seals. "What is it?"

"I want you to know that my agents within the fleet have detected no signs of any other opposition. They've been watching as the news about Kila spreads. There are no signs of other worms, no signs of anyone expressing any support for her or Caligo, no missteps that might indicate hidden sympathies for them."

"That's good to know." Could he finally dispense with such things and no longer worry about someone having to monitor his own officers for indications they might pose a danger to the fleet? "I'll feel a lot better, though, as soon as *Valiant*'s geeks finish sweeping *Inspire*'s gear."

"Of course."

An insistent buzzing told Geary that someone was trying to contact him using command priority. "Excuse me, Madam Co-President, but I probably need to take this." He accepted the message, and Captain Desjani appeared on the comm panel.

"That's perfectly all right," Rione replied. "I've told you what I needed to say, and I didn't mean to intrude on your rendezvous with your special friend."

Geary was still searching for the right, unheated reply when Rione left.

Desjani's image was glaring from the comm screen. "Sir, I swear that I am *this* far from hurting that woman," she hissed, holding her thumb and forefinger less than a centimeter apart.

"That would be a violation of Alliance law and fleet regulations," Geary replied wearily.

"Only if they prove I did it knowingly. I could beat the hell out of her in some really dark place and say I didn't know who she was."

At the moment, the idea did sound tempting. Geary tried to shake it out of his head. "No. We need her."

"Do I get to beat her up when we don't need her anymore?" Desjani asked. *"Please?"*

More temptation. "I can't promise you that. Even though at times like this I'd like to. What's up?"

"Captain Duellos is ready to speak with you. You had a security hold on incoming transmissions, so he couldn't get through," Desjani added in accusing tones.

"Sorry. I'll lift the hold. Thanks."

"My pleasure, sir," she responded pointedly. before her image vanished.

Geary sighed and waited for Duellos to appear. A moment later the other captain did, his virtual image seeming to stand in the stateroom with Geary. "You wanted to speak with me, Captain Geary?" Duellos asked.

"Yes, but first please take a seat." Duellos nodded gratefully and sat down in a seat on *Furious*, the image in Geary's stateroom mimicking the gesture on one of Geary's seats.

"I need to know how well you're doing. You seemed fine during the confrontation with Kila, but are you really in good shape inside?"

Duellos cocked an eyebrow at him. "I'm doing as well as can be expected for a captain without a ship."

"Do you want another ship?" Geary asked bluntly. "I've got a couple of battle cruisers that suddenly need captains."

"*Brilliant* and *Inspire*?" Duellos drew in a long breath. "Which one?"

"Which one can you handle? I don't think *Brilliant* has any special problems aside from the shock the crew must be feeling."

Duellos bared his teeth in a humorless grin. "But you need me on *Inspire*."

"That's true." Geary sat down opposite Duellos. "I need the best I've got on *Inspire*, and that's you. I have no idea how badly Kila messed up that ship, but it might be a real snake pit. The former commanding officer is dead, the former executive officer, systems-security officer, and communications officer are all under arrest, and the remaining officers are all going to have to be investigated."

"A real opportunity to excel," Duellos murmured with more than a trace of sarcasm. "Many of my officers got off *Courageous*, so if I was authorized to bring some of them along..."

"Granted. Take as many of *Courageous*'s old crew as you want.

Inspire took some serious personnel losses while Kila was making glorious charges against the enemy and needs the replacements."

Duellos thought for a few moments while Geary waited, then finally nodded. "*Inspire*'s crew will be needing a lot of rebuilding. I'll do my best."

"Thank you. I couldn't ask for more, or a better officer for the job. *Inspire* herself needs a lot of rebuilding, too. She's pretty badly shot up."

"Having to focus the crew on repairing the ship may help repair their own morale." Duellos quirked a small smile. "At times like this, seeing something tangible accomplished can make a big difference. I assume you want me on *Inspire* an hour ago?"

"Yes," Geary agreed, "but take the time you need to choose which personnel from *Courageous* you're taking with you. Like I said, you can have all of them if you want. I'll position *Inspire* near the auxiliaries so they can provide repair support and services easily."

"Another ship and right back near the auxiliaries? I may get a reputation as a bad-luck captain out of this." Duellos smiled slightly again. "Thank you for not asking me to take *Orion*."

"I don't know what the hell I'm going to do with *Orion*."

"Put Numos back in command," Duellos suggested. "He'll cause *Orion* to be destroyed in the next engagement for certain."

"If her crew doesn't start performing, I may do just that." Geary looked upward as if addressing the living stars. "I'm joking." Lowering his gaze to Duellos again, he indicated the fleet status display. "The First Battle Cruiser Division is down to one ship, *Formidable*, and the Seventh only has *Brilliant* and *Inspire*. I was thinking of folding them into a single division, a reconstituted

First Division containing all three ships."

Duellos shook his head, looking haggard for a moment. "Combining two battle cruiser divisions and getting only three ships in the result. I think that's a good idea, but it also indicates how badly torn up this fleet has been." He paused, then nodded firmly. "Yes. A good idea. *Formidable* won't be lonely, and *Inspire* and *Brilliant* will have a fine ship as a division mate and a symbolic new start. Who do you plan to give *Brilliant*?"

"Beats the hell out of me. Captain Baccade off *Intrepid* was pretty badly hurt along with her ship. She's in no shape to take another command yet."

"I understand Commander Vigory is eager for a ship," Duellos commented blandly.

Geary shot him an annoyed look. "He told me that within a day of being liberated from the POW camp. I'm not impressed by his record, and I don't have time to teach a new commanding officer how I fight."

"Just thought I'd mention it since he's devoting a great deal of time to complaining about your decisions. That one regarding him and many others." Duellos smiled wryly. "I was watching him to see if he'd be contacted by the conspirators against you and lead us to them. But events here in Padronis took place before anyone working for Kila or Caligo could contact him."

"Not everyone opposed to me is a traitor," Geary grumbled. "I'll make sure he's being kept busy, but I'm not going to give Vigory *Brilliant* or any other ship. I think he's just too assertive on his own behalf. Self-confidence is important, but not when it tramples on discretion."

"As recently demonstrated to us in as graphic a way as possible." Duellos seemed to think for a moment. "We lost *Tarian* at Heradao. Her former commanding officer, Jame Yunis, has a fine reputation."

Geary pulled up Yunis's records and skimmed them. "He does look good. You think he's up to it?"

"Yes."

"Okay. I'll give him a good look and make a decision before we jump for Atalia." Geary exhaled slowly. "Would you mind hanging around a couple of more minutes while I call Captain Desjani down here and we go over something with you? I'd like your impressions because I'm only going to get one chance to get it right. I will have to ask that you never divulge it, though."

Duellos watched him for a long moment. "I can't agree to anything that would violate my oath, you understand."

"This won't. I swear."

Desjani only required a few minutes to join them. Geary went over his planned pitch, then waited. Once again, Duellos spent a while thinking, then nodded. "I can't think of any way to improve that, but you're walking a tightrope, you know."

"One of many," Geary agreed.

"If you're going to speak with Badaya now, I'll be happy to wait a few moments to make it appear as if I am, uh, 'backing' what you're not really doing."

Desjani nodded. "That'd be a good idea. Duellos is widely regarded as a special confidant of yours. His presence when Badaya arrives would please Badaya."

"As would yours," Duellos pointed out.

She gritted her teeth. "Do I have to? He's going to say something.

I know he will. And I'll have to pretend I didn't hear it."

"Just for a few minutes, Tanya," Duellos suggested. "Then we can leave and let Badaya have his special talk with Black Jack."

"Roberto, you know that Captain Geary and I haven't—"

Duellos held up both hands to forestall her. "Of course I do. All of your friends know that, Tanya. You wouldn't do such a thing with your commanding officer, no matter what." Desjani looked away, her gaze on the deck. "I imagine having to deal with the rumors is no fun at all."

"Many things are difficult to deal with," Desjani muttered. "I'll manage."

Duellos gazed at Geary as he answered her. "I'm certain you will, Tanya. All right, then. Let's summon Badaya and get this over with. What happens if you can't convince him?"

"I don't know. I might have to bring the whole thing out in the open, make a public speech to the entire fleet declaring that I will not support a coup against the Alliance government, but I'm afraid some people would just read my bringing up the subject of a coup as implying I'm actually trying to sound out backing for one."

"That's exactly how those favoring a coup would see it," Duellos agreed. "Let's hope you can divert Badaya and the many who believe like him onto a course that we can all live with. Otherwise, the victory of bringing the fleet home may turn into the greatest defeat the Alliance has ever suffered."

9

As Duellos had guessed, Badaya seemed very pleased to be summoned to a conference featuring himself, Geary, Duellos, and Desjani. "You're getting *Inspire*, Duellos? Excellent. Too bad you'll have to share *Inspire* with Kila's remains for a little while longer."

"I thought we'd dispose of Kila's remains here," Geary commented. "Why wait until Atalia?"

Badaya gave Geary a surprised look. "You're not familiar with fleet regulations regarding the disposition of the bodies of traitors?"

"No. I assumed Kila would have an unceremonious burial in space."

"She doesn't deserve an honorable burial," Desjani interrupted.

"More to the point," Badaya said, "regulations deny that option for Kila. They state that the remains of traitors are to be disposed of in jump space. No exceptions, no alternatives."

Geary stared at him, then at Desjani and Duellos, both of whom nodded back solemnly. "I'll admit I'm surprised. That's the harshest possible treatment, consigning someone to jump space for eternity. How did a measure that extreme get approved?"

Duellos ran one hand across the table before him, speaking with unusual somberness. "The answer to that lies in some very unpleasant history that you had the good fortune to sleep through, Captain Geary. About fifty years ago, wasn't it?" Desjani and Badaya nodded. "I'll spare you the details, but suffice to say that if a harsher punishment had been possible, it would have been approved."

"Then you're saying I'm probably the only person in this fleet who'd be surprised to learn about consigning the bodies of traitors to jump space?"

"Most likely."

Geary sat down, looking at his hands clasped on his knees before him. "I guess this is one of those places where I'm old-fashioned. I fully accept that we have the right to judge people like Kila and impose our punishments upon them, but burying her remains in jump space... isn't that sort of eternal punishment supposed to be the province of powers greater than us?"

After a moment, Desjani answered. "I'm not an expert at such things, but the burial in jump space is a symbolic gesture by humanity. It's not the last word because we don't get the last word. Just because we can't find something lost in jump space doesn't mean the living stars can't do so. If they want her, they'll get her."

"You don't see it as eternal?" Geary asked, genuinely surprised by Desjani's reasoning but unable to think of an argument against it.

"Nothing humans do is eternal. Nothing we do binds the decisions of powers greater than us. The final judgment always rests with them." Desjani gestured outward. "I know what fate I think Kila deserves, but in the end it's not my call, or yours. The gesture of burial in jump space expresses our feelings about her crime, and that is as far as it goes, speaking in terms of eternity."

"I see." He thought of the dead on *Lorica*, sailors struck down without warning by someone they trusted to fight alongside them. He thought of the crews of *Dauntless* and *Illustrious* and *Furious*, all of whom would have died if the first worm planted by Kila hadn't been discovered. "All right. I understand the appropriateness of the gesture. Kila's remains will be consigned to jump space on the way to Atalia."

Duellos made a face. "They'll be disturbing the sleep in any number of the crew until then, I have no doubt."

"Are you willing to carry out the punishment, or would you prefer I ask some other captain to volunteer?" Geary asked Duellos.

He spent a few moments thinking, his eyes turned aside, then nodded. "If not me, then who? I won't curse her as her body leaves. I'll regret what she could have been."

Badaya laughed harshly. "You're a better man than I am, then. I know courtesy bids us not to speak ill of the dead, but that rule is going to be sorely tried when it comes to Kila."

This time Geary nodded. "I understand. I'm not exactly thrilled with her myself. Now, what about Caligo? I appreciate you taking him aboard *Illustrious*. Is he cooperating as he promised?"

The unforgiving humor vanished, Badaya's face now reflecting distaste. "Cooperating? He's babbling. In my opinion, Caligo is saying anything he thinks we want to hear, and he's going to keep talking as long as he thinks it will help keep him alive. The interrogation gear is having a lot of trouble evaluating him because Caligo seems to have the ability to convince himself that what ever he's saying at the moment is true."

Duellos shook his head. "Meaning we can't trust it?"

"No, not in my opinion. There may be truth in his statements, maybe a lot of truth, but we need to double-check everything he's saying and find out if there's any proof to support it."

Geary drummed his fingers on the table. "How long will that take?"

"I don't know." Badaya made a motion as if he wanted to slap Caligo right then and there. "But I doubt we can check it all out before we return to Alliance space. I don't say that lightly. I want the little bastard dead. But if we execute him before we investigate some of his allegations, it could permanently tar individuals who might be innocent. It's bad enough what he and Kila did. Compounding the damage with injustice would make us their accomplices. In my opinion."

"I agree," Duellos said. "We don't always see eye to eye, Captain Badaya, but I believe you're absolutely right about that."

"You should order psych evals of Caligo, too," Desjani insisted. "You can do that, Captain Geary, whether Caligo approves or not."

Badaya scowled at her. "Are you trying to give Caligo a medical defense against his actions?"

"No," Desjani replied coldly. "We've all seen him. That defense wouldn't fly. But I think it might be important to try to understand how anyone could go so far off course. Destroying Alliance warships and killing their crews. There are plenty of ambitious officers in the fleet, and some who would do *almost* anything to earn promotion and authority, but Caligo was willing to do *anything*. If something in particular led him to make such decisions, something beyond the desire for power, I think it's worth finding out."

"Hmmm." Badaya shrugged as if he found the topic distasteful. "I wouldn't be surprised if the answer to that is in what Kila offered him. And I'm not just speaking of the power of being her figurehead. There's plenty of stories about Kila, some of them extremely lurid. More than one man has been led astray from duty and honor by his appetites." He made an apologetic gesture to Desjani. "Needless to say, no one here would fall into Kila's category."

Desjani, her face like stone, acted as if she hadn't heard a word Badaya said, but her eyes briefly accused Duellos, who gave a contrite look back.

Captain Duellos sighed into the awkward silence. "I wish that the Syndics had spared us the trouble of finding her out. When I think of how many battles Kila survived, and for what? To betray those who guarded her flanks. Now I feel stained by her dishonor, shamed that any officer could do such a thing."

"Her actions don't reflect on you," Geary replied. "Or on anyone but her."

"So you say, and I appreciate it." Duellos gazed soberly into the distance. "I need to have a talk with my ancestors."

"That's never a bad idea," Badaya agreed.

Geary gestured toward Desjani and Duellos. "All right. I need to have a private talk with Captain Badaya now. Would you two mind?"

Duellos and Desjani left, both playing their roles well, as if both were part of the sort of conspiracy that Badaya expected.

Geary stood up, feeling a bit nervous. Rione had been right when she accused him of being a lousy liar, but he had to act out this role as well as he could. He walked back and forth for a moment to work out his nerves, then faced Badaya. "Captain, I wanted to talk with you regarding what actions should be taken when the fleet returns to Alliance space."

"Of course." Badaya stood up as well, his tension betraying eagerness. "You're ready to agree? The Alliance needs you."

Geary didn't look at him, bowing his head for a moment. "Captain Badaya, I hope you appreciate how very difficult even speaking of such a thing is for me. I come from a time when the idea of the fleet's acting against the government would have been unthinkable."

Captain Badaya grimaced, then shook his head, the movement slow and ponderous as if a heavy weight were resting on it. "Don't think I've made the offer lightly, Captain Geary. Not me, and not any other officer. It's not an easy thing to decide, even for those of us who've endured the consequences of our government's incompetence and corruption."

"I appreciate that." Geary sat down again and gestured for Badaya to do the same. "I'm just having trouble grasping why you all came to the decision you reached."

"Why?" Badaya sat heavily, hunched over a bit and frowning toward his hands where they rested between his knees. "Sometimes the options all seem worse. You know that. We've all taken an oath to the Alliance, but what does defending the Alliance mean? Does it mean letting politicians continue to let their greed and ambition destroy the Alliance?"

"There's more than one way to destroy the Alliance," Geary stated carefully.

Badaya's answering grin was tight and humorless. "True. You haven't experienced it, though. Not enough backing when it matters, too much interference in command decisions, waste, profiteering, starving us of what we need to win, then blaming us when it goes to hell." He looked at Geary, his gaze measuring. "They used you against us, you know. The legend of the great Black Jack Geary, who'd never go against the political leadership, never question their demands however unreasonable, never fail to salute and charge off to die. That's one of the biggest reasons a lot of us were worried about you."

He hadn't seen things in that light before, but it made sense that officers would have distrusted him on those grounds, if they thought he was a puppet of politicians they distrusted in turn. "What made you decide you could trust me? I haven't spoken against the government."

"No, but you demonstrated very clearly your loyalty to your fellow officers and the fleet," Badaya pointed out. "You won battles and kept our losses down. You're a fighter, and only a blind fool couldn't see how dedicated you were to those who fought alongside you." The other captain looked down again, grimacing. "Honor says we should abide by our oath to the Alliance, but what does that mean? Does it mean letting our fellows die?"

"If an officer doesn't want to execute orders—" Geary began.

"He or she can resign," Badaya finished. "Certainly. Walk away and leave his or her fellows to fight on without them, to fight and die following orders one personally thinks are foolish. Where's the honor in that? We can't leave our comrades in arms. Yet we can't let them keep dying for nothing, and we can't let the Alliance be destroyed by politicians who care nothing for those who die. You see? It's a hard road, yet it leads to one option, to honor our oaths to the Alliance and our loyalty to our comrades by backing a leader who will do what's right."

Geary shook his own head. "What makes you so certain that I'll know what's right?"

"I told you. I've watched you. So has everyone else. Why do you think Kila and Caligo shifted from trying to discredit you to trying to kill you? Because they knew that after enough experience with you, this fleet wouldn't allow you to be deposed." Badaya laughed. "By my ancestors, if I tried to act against you now, my own crew would revolt. I'm not saying you couldn't lose the loyalty you've acquired, but it would take some serious misjudgments, and as long as you listen to Tanya Desjani, you won't have to worry about that."

He hadn't wanted Tanya brought up again even in passing. Time to get the subject back on track. "Captain Badaya," Geary said slowly, "I've been seriously considering options once we reach Alliance space, and something disquieting has occurred to me." Badaya gave him a keen look but remained silent.

Geary activated the star display on the table between them, setting it to display a vast reach of the Alliance and Syndic space as well. "It seems so easy, so certain. We return, I assume what ever authority is needed, and the politicians are put in their proper place." Badaya nodded. "And yet I found that I kept thinking about the attack this fleet launched on the Syndic home star system."

Badaya frowned this time. "I don't understand the connection."

Leaning closer to the star display, Geary indicated the representation of the Syndic home star system. "Apparently a sure thing, but it was a trap. Why did I keep thinking of that when I thought about our return to Alliance space? I haven't been sure, but I think I'm beginning to understand what's bothering me."

"If you're thinking they're similar," Badaya objected, "they aren't. This fleet outguns anything in Alliance space by a wide margin. The politicians couldn't defeat it, even if they were insane enough to order it attacked."

"It's not that," Geary said as he carefully chose his words to match those he'd gone over with Desjani and Duellos. "I think that it's a question of not playing by the rules our enemies want us to follow."

Badaya cocked his head, regarding Geary. "Meaning? You've been adamant about following rules, about abiding by the policies and beliefs of our ancestors."

"Yes. *Our* rules." Geary walked to the display and pointed randomly at Syndic star systems. "The Syndics want us to play by *their* rules. Things like bombarding civilians and killing prisoners. Because if we do that, it's to the Syndic leaders' advantage. Their own populace won't revolt against their leaders as long as they're scared of us."

Badaya nodded. "I've seen the intelligence reports of what we've learned from being deep inside Syndic space. By matching Syndic atrocities, we worked against ourselves. I won't deny that. What does that have to do with our return to Alliance space?"

"I'm wondering if our opponents in Alliance space *want* me to seize power."

Badaya leaned back, his eyes narrowing in thought as he gazed at Geary. "Why would they want that? They don't even know you are with this fleet yet."

"They don't necessarily want me," Geary explained, "but they must have known about Admiral Bloch and his ambitions."

"I didn't know you were aware of Bloch's goals. You've obviously done your homework on this." Badaya rubbed his chin, looking away from Geary as he thought. "He thought winning at the Syndic home star system would give him the stature to try to seize power. Whether he could have actually had the backing within the fleet to do that is another question, but it wasn't beyond the realm of possibility. I believe our political leaders are corrupt, but I don't think all of them are stupid, so some of them must have known of Bloch's ambitions and the potential for him to achieve them. Yet they let Bloch lead this fleet anyway. I hadn't put that together before." He centered his gaze on Geary again. "Why?"

Geary tapped the table lightly to emphasize his words. "I've been doing some research. Historically, corruption is a problem in every form of government, but it's far worse in dictatorships than it is in elected governments. That's because dictatorships don't have formal limits on the powers of officials and don't have a free press or open government that exposes corruption."

Badaya frowned again. "You wouldn't be a dictator."

"I wouldn't be elected," Geary pointed out. "No matter my intentions, I'd have to rule as a dictator. Now, what form of government would corrupt politicians favor the most?"

The frown deepened. "They want you to take over so they can operate their corruption freely? Why would they think you or even Admiral Bloch would allow that?"

"Because I'm not a politician." Geary nodded toward the representation of Alliance space. "What ever Bloch thought of his political skills, I think he was probably outclassed by those who have politics as a profession. A military officer in power could be manipulated by corrupt politicians, manipulated in ways that would enhance the power and the wealth of those politicians far more than could be managed in an open, democratic system."

Badaya sat silent for a long time, then nodded as well. "I see your point. A fleet officer wouldn't know how to play their games any more than the politicians could command a fleet action. The politicians want a puppet they could pull the strings on and hide behind, just like Kila wanted to use Caligo. Is that what helped you see this? It wouldn't matter who the officer was who seized power. Hell, the politicians would probably be thrilled that it was you because of what they could get away with by claiming it was what Black Jack wanted." He nodded again. "Playing by their rules. I see what you mean. They want a fleet officer to try being a politician because they can run rings around us with words that don't mean what they seem to mean. But what do we do? Just let them keep running the Alliance into the ground?"

"There's a middle ground." He didn't like saying this, let alone admitting it. But what he was about to say was true. "I have the potential to take over. I could really overthrow the government." The words felt sour in Geary's mouth as he spoke of something contrary to his oath and his beliefs. "The politicians know that. The decent ones, the ones who can be brought around, will know they have to listen to me."

Badaya smiled. "They'll be afraid not to do as you say, afraid enough for you to get things done. And the corrupt ones will cooperate with you because they'll want to curry your favor for when you do take over." He held up one hand, palm out, as Geary started to speak. "I understand you don't want to give them that opportunity. But if they're anything like we believe, it won't even occur to them that you could resist the temptation."

He hadn't thought of that, but Badaya's suggestion made sense. Geary nodded. "I remain a threat, someone they have to listen to, yet the strengths of the Alliance government, of our demo cratic principles and individual rights, also remain intact."

"Clever." Badaya's smile grew. "You out thought them, didn't you? Just like you've out thought the Syndics. I made the same mistake a lot of other people did, assuming that the politicians weren't just as capable of manipulating us as they were of enriching themselves. Is that why you had that affair with Rione? To learn all you could about them?"

It took Geary a moment to calm himself enough to trust his response. Badaya was honorable enough by today's standards, and a decent officer, but to call him undiplomatic was an understatement. "I learned a number of important things from Co-President Rione," he finally said, a true statement Badaya could interpret any way he wanted. "But," he added while fixing Badaya with a sharp look, "Rione can be trusted."

"You'd know," Badaya agreed with an amused expression. "After all, you have seen parts of her none of the rest of us have." He chuckled at the clumsy joke while Geary hoped he wasn't flushing with discomfort. "Now, I take it you want your supporters in the fleet to know what you intend?"

"That's right." Geary kept his voice level. "It's important that everyone understand what is going on." Or rather, what he wanted them to think was going on. *I will not dictate to my political leadership. I just pray the military and political superiors I deal with will listen to me or at least not obviously dismiss me.* "The last thing we want is for my hand to be forced by officers who think they're doing me or the Alliance a favor but will actually be playing into the hands of the most corrupt politicians."

"I think I can guarantee you that won't happen now." Badaya smiled admiringly as he stood up. "All of those times you denied wanting enough power to change things you were studying the situation and planning options, weren't you? I should have guessed. A good commander doesn't play by the enemy's rules. I'm going to remember that."

Geary slumped down after Badaya's image vanished, rubbing his eyes with one hand and feeling dishonest, manipulative, and even a bit dishonorable. He hadn't directly lied to Badaya, but he'd certainly misled the man as thoroughly as any politician could have done.

After a while he called Rione to his stateroom. She came in, evaluated his attitude, then smiled approvingly. "You did it. Badaya bought it?"

"Yes. I think so."

"Good. And you're unhappy."

"I don't like lying to people," Geary told her coldly. "Maybe that's why I'm so bad at it. I don't like knowing I can be good enough at it to deceive even someone like Badaya."

Rione walked slowly to one side. "Lying? What lie did you tell?"

"You know perfectly well——"

"What I *know*, Captain Geary, is that what you told Badaya is, as near as we can determine, truthful. Now try to get this through your thick head. Captain Badaya didn't 'buy' anything. Do you believe that a military dictatorship would be a disaster for the Alliance? Yes? Then what did you lie about? I admit comparing it to the Syndic ambush hadn't occurred to me, but once you and your captain came up with that, I thought it was brilliant."

He set his jaw and glared at Rione. "Stop calling her that. Nobody owns Desjani, especially not me."

"Fine, if you care to believe that." Rione matched his glare. "You need to remember that you're doing nothing for personal gain. You don't want wealth or power. So why the hell should you feel guilty about forestalling a military coup against the government of the Alliance?"

"Because no Alliance officer should have even thought of such a thing!" Geary yelled, the shame and anger bursting from him. "I never should have received such an offer and when I did my immediate refusal should have been the end of it!"

Rione watched him for a moment, then looked away herself, her face shadowed by emotion. "We're not the people our ancestors were, John Geary. We'll always let you down when you compare us to those you knew a century ago."

Her unexpected and very unusual candor extinguished Geary's rage. "It's not your fault that you were all born into a war that was already ancient. It's not your fault that you inherited the pain and distortions caused by decades of war. I can't pretend that I'm better than you because I was spared that."

"But you are better than us," Rione insisted with bitterness in her voice. "You're what we should have been, what our parents and our grandparents should have held on to, the belief that ideals must be honored. Do you think I can't see that? If we had done our jobs as the situation demanded of us, then none of this would have happened. And, yes, I very much include the Alliance's political leadership in that."

"You inherited the war," Geary repeated. "I can't pretend to understand everything that happened in the last century, but there seems plenty of blame to go around and more than a few things that nobody could have helped."

"I don't believe in making excuses for failures, Captain Geary. Not mine and not anyone else's. Just remember that the people you trust approve of what you did just now. If you don't trust yourself, trust them." She turned without another word and left.

Six hours to the jump for Atalia. As much as Geary feared finding the Syndic reserve flotilla there, he also had a growing restlessness, a desire to see this to the end. One way or the other, the Alliance fleet's long retreat would be over soon.

"Captain Geary." Colonel Carabali's expression revealed nothing. "Request permission for a private meeting prior to the jump for Atalia."

"Of course, Colonel. I have no scheduled commitments for a couple of hours, so we can have that meeting whenever you're ready."

"Now would be fine with me, sir."

"Okay." Geary authorized Carabali's image to appear in his stateroom, then waved her virtual presence to a seat. The colonel walked over to it and sat, her back straight, rigidly formal. "What's this meeting about?"

"Consider it a reconnaissance mission, sir." Colonel Carabali gave Geary a penetrating look. "What do you intend doing when this fleet reaches Alliance space, Captain Geary? I've heard various reports and wish to know the truth for certain."

The loyalty of the Marines to the Alliance was legendary, but given all of the other changes he'd seen, Geary had been wondering for some time how the Marines now felt about political authorities in the Alliance and how they felt about the offers to Geary to become a dictator when the fleet made it back to Alliance space. But he'd never come up with a way to ask those questions without making it appear that he was sounding out the Marines for support, which was the last thing he wanted. Now Geary sat down opposite the colonel, holding his eyes on hers. "I intend following what ever orders are given to me. I will have suggestions and a proposal for an operation, but I have no way of knowing how those will be taken. Is that what you need to know?"

"For the most part." Carabali studied Geary for a moment. "I won't insult your intelligence by pretending both of us don't know that you're not just any fleet officer. You can choose to obey what ever orders are given you, but you do have other options."

"And you want to know if I intend exercising those options?"

Carabali nodded, her face still impassive.

Geary shook his head. "No, Colonel, I do not intend exercising any options that would conflict with my oath to the Alliance. Is that clear enough?"

"From you, yes." Carabali paused again. "There are some close-hold messages being passed around the fleet that indicate you intend doing more than just following orders."

"People hear what they want to hear, Colonel. As long as it keeps them from actions that would be harmful to the Alliance, I'm okay with that."

" 'Harmful to the Alliance' meaning?" Carabali pressed.

Geary sat back and shook his head. "The Alliance's greatest strength has never been its star systems or population or fleet. It's the principles we believe in and practice. I don't think the Syndics could ever hurt us as badly as we could hurt ourselves. I won't stage a coup, Colonel, and I'll do everything I can to keep one from being staged in my name." He didn't fear word of that getting back to any of his most misguided supporters. It was what he'd told Badaya, after all.

She studied him, then nodded. "Will you attempt to remain in command of this fleet?"

"Yes."

"Even though you only took command in the Syndic home star system because you had to do so?"

"Yes." Geary let a small smile show. "I didn't know it was that obvious."

"It wasn't." Carabali let her own tiny smile flicker on and off again. "I'm used to trying to figure out what's beneath the surface of fleet officers. The lives of my Marines often depend on that." Her expression went wooden once more. "Do you think you can end this war?"

He started to reply, then shot Carabali a questioning look. "You said 'end,' not 'win.' "

"I asked the question I meant to ask, sir."

"I need to be certain of that." Geary leaned forward slightly, searching her expression but seeing nothing but the professional mask. "There's a lot I'm still learning about what this war has done, about how the fleet and the Alliance feel about it."

Carabali raised one hand to her chin and rubbed it for a moment as if contemplating the question. "I'll fight as long as I have to fight to protect the Alliance. Beyond that... I'm tired of making decisions about who lives and who dies, Captain Geary. A little of that goes a long way."

"I know. Believe me."

"Yes, you do, but not in the same manner. The fleet offers certain luxuries that ground fighting doesn't, and your own personal history is different from ours. You grew up at peace, and you spent your fleet career at peace until Grendel." Carabali looked away, her eyes seeming to focus on something far away. "May I tell you some history? There was a lieutenant who'd grown up with the war and joined to follow in the footsteps of her grandmother and her father. On one of her first ground-combat missions she and her Marine platoon were cut off from the rest of their unit. The atmosphere around them was toxic with Syndic defensive chem agents. The power on their battle armor was running low, and if it went too low for life support, the lieutenant and her platoon would die."

Geary watched the colonel's face, which still revealed little. "An ugly situation no matter how experienced an officer."

"Yes. I didn't mention that the lieutenant's platoon had captured a breached Syndic bunker along with a number of Syndic self-defense-force personnel. The Syndics all had suits with plenty of power reserves, and the lieutenant's leading noncommissioned officer informed her that it would be possible to jury-rig a means of draining the Syndic suits to recharge our own power cells."

The colonel paused again while Geary put himself there and tried not to shudder. "But if the Syndic suits were drained, the prisoners would die."

"Or they'd have to be killed to keep them from attacking the Marines once they realized they were going to die," Carabali agreed. "The lieutenant knew there was only one decision possible, but she also knew it would be a decision that would haunt her forever."

"What did the lieutenant do?"

"The lieutenant hesitated," Carabali stated in a voice as collected as if she were providing a routine report, "and her leading noncommissioned officer, as ruthless a bastard as any sergeant has ever been, suggested that the lieutenant leave the bunker for a little while to see if she could reestablish communications with the rest of the Alliance forces from the outside. The lieutenant grasped at the suggestion, knowing what she was really agreeing to, and left the bunker, standing outside until the sergeant appeared with enough charged power cells to keep her battle armor going. The entire platoon, it seemed, had enough power to try to regain Alliance lines. The lieutenant led the way, and she and her platoon made it back that evening. No one asked how the platoon's power supplies had held out so long. The lieutenant received a medal for saving her entire platoon under such difficult circumstances."

Without even thinking, Geary's eyes went to the left breast of Carabali's uniform, searching for the combat-award ribbon that might mark the event.

But the colonel kept speaking, her voice flat. "The lieutenant never wears that medal or its ribbon."

"Did the lieutenant ever go back into the bunker?"

"The lieutenant didn't have to. The lieutenant knew what was inside." Carabali nodded toward the star display. "Somewhere, right now, another Alliance lieutenant is facing that same kind of decision, Captain Geary. Somewhere, a damned Syndic officer is making a similar decision, because it's the only decision to be made. Too many of those decisions have already been made."

"I understand."

"What decision will you make, sir?" Carabali looked back at him. "Can you end this war on acceptable terms?"

"I don't know." It was Geary's turn to point to the stars. "What I propose depends in part on what happens between here and Alliance space, but at this point... Colonel, I'll have to ask that you not repeat this outside this meeting."

"Of course, sir."

"At this point it appears I may have to propose seriously hazarding this fleet again, right after I get it to safety. I'm not sure how that will sit with the leaders of the Alliance, or with the personnel in this fleet for that matter."

Carabali frowned slightly. "If that proposal were made by another officer, it wouldn't sit well. But you have built up a tremendous reserve of trust, sir."

"Even though we've lost a lot of ships?"

"Your concept of a lot still differs from that of people who have grown up in this war, sir." Carabali reached one finger up to touch her rank insignia. "These were my grandmother's, and then my father's. Both of them died in combat before they were able personally to hand down these insignia to one of their children. I had hoped to break that family curse, but, Captain Geary," the colonel stated with her eyes locked on his, "if my death in combat were to ensure my children didn't have to wear these because the war had ended in a way the people of the Alliance could live with, then I would willingly make that sacrifice. That's the crux of the matter here, sir. We've been willing to die for a long time, but that willingness has been colored by despair that our sacrifices will accomplish little. We trust you to make our deaths count, if it comes to that."

Geary nodded, feeling a heaviness filling him. "I promise to do my best."

"You always have, sir. And if you hold to your promise not to violate your oath to the Alliance, the Marines in this fleet will do their best by you as well."

This time Geary frowned, thinking through the words. "That's an uncharacteristically ambiguous statement, Colonel."

"Then I'll state clearly that if you give orders to act against the Alliance government, I and my officers will do all we can to ensure the Marines do not obey such orders."

"That won't be a problem because I won't give such orders."

"Then we understand each other." Carabali looked away for a moment, her eyes hooded in thought. "But if we receive orders to arrest you... that's when it gets hard. It should be simple. Obey lawful orders. But it won't be if you haven't violated your own oath. A long time ago a wise man said that everything in war is simple, but all of the simple things are complicated. Like this. Is it lawful to arrest an officer, one with an unblemished record, because of what he *might* do? Military and civilian lawyers could argue that point for a long time. As you said, the Alliance is about the principles we hold dear, and one of those has always been the rights of our people."

"That's true, Colonel." Geary stood up. "I swear that I will do everything I can to avoid such a conflict between orders and principles. We're on the same side and, frankly, I like it that way."

"Me, too, sir." Carabali rose as well. "You're not bad for a space squid."

"Thank you, Colonel. You're not half-bad yourself." Carabali flicked another smile, then came to attention and saluted. As she moved to break the connection, Geary spoke again. "Colonel. There's no other decision that lieutenant could have made."

Carabali nodded back to him. "The lieutenant has always known that, sir, but she's also always hated the decision she had to make. By your leave, sir." The Marine colonel saluted again, then her image vanished.

Geary sat down again slowly. He felt like he was juggling a hundred balls at once, and if he dropped one then the Alliance would shatter.

He went up to the bridge an hour before the jump for Atalia. The Alliance fleet was arranged into a battle formation consisting of a main body and a supporting formation to either side, ready in case the Syndic reserve flotilla was waiting to fight right outside the jump exit. Geary reviewed the fleet, reviewed its logistics status, wincing at the low levels of fuel cells and expendable weaponry, then called his ship captains. "Be ready for anything when we leave jump. If the Syndics are right there within range, all ships are to engage targets of opportunity with every available weapon. More likely they'll be at least a short distance from the jump point, and we'll be able to maneuver into a favorable position before attacking. We'll see you at Atalia, and after that Varandal."

"Fifteen minutes to jump," the operations watch reported.

Rione came out of the observer's seat and leaned on the back of Geary's seat. "Should I bother asking why a fleet in this condition is planning on attacking at Atalia rather than running for the jump exit for Varandal?"

"Because the Syndics will surely be prepared for our trying to run past them," Geary replied. "Make no mistake, if the opportunity permits I'm going to head for that jump point. But I don't expect the Syndics to give us a free shot at it."

"They won't stop us," Desjani stated calmly.

Rione eyed her for a moment before answering. "I believe you." Then she returned to her seat while Desjani frowned, clearly trying to find some hidden meaning in the response and failing.

Geary watched the seconds count down as the fleet approached the jump point, then he sent the order. "All ships, jump for Atalia."

In three and three-quarter days, they'd find out what waited for them at the last Syndic star system they had to cross on the way home.

Jump space had plenty of negatives. There was the itching sensation, which grew worse the longer you were in jump space, a feeling most people described as feeling like your own skin didn't fit right anymore. There was the growing sense of unseen presences lurking just out of sight. Always, no matter how short the journey, there was the endless gray nothing, a universe lit by no stars.

There were the strange lights of jump space, which flared according to no known pattern and for no known reason. With no way having been discovered to explore jump space, the lights remained a mystery. Looking at them now, Geary couldn't forget that legend held that his spirit had been one of those lights during all the long years his body rested frozen in survival sleep.

However, jump space did have the singular virtue of being bland and unsurprising. Isolated within the strange confines of jump space, ships could barely communicate by the simplest of messages, and nothing could be seen of the normal universe. Compared to the sometimes unceasing events of normal space, Geary found himself at times treasuring the relative peace that isolation offered.

But no one could stay in jump space forever. Sooner or later, the real universe would have to be faced.

"We'll be arriving in Atalia in two hours." Desjani stood before him in his stateroom, the star display between them. "It'll be a tough fight."

"I just hope that reserve flotilla is smaller than Lieutenant Iger estimated and that they're not lined up in front of the jump exit to hit us all at once with everything they've got." Geary stood up and activated the display, calling up an image of how his ships would look if anyone could actually see them all in jump space. Ranks of capital ships, flocks of cruisers and destroyers, the bulks of the surviving auxiliaries nestled near the center.

His fleet. He shouldn't think that, but he did. He'd brought it this far, and the living stars willing, he'd take it all the way home. But what would happen then?

"What are you thinking?" Desjani asked.

"I'm wishing I didn't have to do what I know I have to do."

"Turn over command of the fleet at Varandal? I don't think that's going to happen, sir."

"I'm just a captain. A very, very, very senior captain, but just a captain."

"You're Captain Geary. *The* Captain Geary. That's different."

He exhaled slowly. "But if I do retain command of the fleet..."

Desjani raised a questioning eyebrow. "You've figured out what to do next?"

"I've been thinking. There's only one thing we *can* do next if we make it home. If we give the Syndics enough time, they'll recover from the blows we've dealt them. We destroyed the Syndic shipyards at Sancere, but those were far from the only shipyards the Syndics have turning out warships. Every day brings them closer to replacing their losses. That means we'll have to hit them again as soon as possible, when they're off-balance, hit them as hard as we can." He grimaced. "Their leaders, I mean. The foundation of their power, the fleet that allowed them to attack us and coerce their own people, will hopefully be gone for a while after Atalia. We can't defeat the Syndics star system by star system because there's just too damn many star systems, but there'll never be a better time to lop off the heads of the Syndicate Worlds."

Desjani smiled grimly. "We have to go back?" She reached over and tapped the controls, the images of the fleet's ships being replaced with a representation of the stars in a very large area of space. One of those stars, distant from Varandal, glowed brighter than the others, highlighted by the display. "Back to the Syndic home star system. But this time it'll be different."

"Yeah. Once the fleet is resupplied, and we've replaced what losses we can." He shrugged. "That's what I'll recommend. Even though it's the last thing I want to do."

She gave him a look that for an instant told him that Tanya knew full well what he wanted but that neither of them could follow that road yet. Then it was gone, and Captain Desjani was nodding to him. "Then we can deal with the aliens."

"Then we can try to figure out how to deal with them. If they haven't directly attacked us already. If we make it home. If I remain in command of the fleet. There's a lot of uncertainties. It's kind of crazy, isn't it? We've narrowly escaped destruction time after time getting out of the trap the Syndics laid for this fleet, but I'm going to suggest we go back there."

Desjani smiled again. "If your craziness is caused by something infectious, I hope you bite every admiral we encounter."

He couldn't help a laugh. "We're getting a bit ahead of things. We're still one jump and a Syndic reserve flotilla away from Alliance space."

"Then, Captain Geary, let's get ready to kick some Syndic butt so we can make that jump."

"Sounds like a good idea, Captain Desjani. Let's get up to the bridge."

Two hours later he waited as the seconds ticked down toward the moment when the Alliance fleet would leave jump space. Waited to find out if his worst fears would come true, if volleys of missiles and grapeshot would slam into the Alliance fleet almost as soon as it appeared at Atalia. If that happened, a smaller-scale version of the ambush in the Syndic home system that had led to his gaining command of what was left of the Alliance fleet, he'd be lucky to get through the first moments with half of his ships still in one piece.

"Stand by for exit from jump space," the operations watch-stander called.

"Weapons ready," Desjani ordered. "Set them to fire on auto the instant they identify targets within their engagement envelopes."

The same orders were being given on every ship in the fleet. Geary sat, tense, wondering if the next few seconds would hurl the Alliance fleet into its most desperate fight since they had left the Syndic home star system.

"Exiting jump space in five, four, three, two, one. Exiting now." The stars reappeared.

Dauntless yawed down and over as the fleet's warships began a preplanned evasive maneuver. It took a moment for Geary to get his mind around what he was seeing as the fleet's sensors rapidly updated the display before him.

The first thing that registered clearly was that no weapons were firing. Then he saw that there were no Syndic warships near the jump exit. He breathed a prayer of thanks, then pulled out the scale on his display to see where the enemy was within the star system.

Being a border system, Atalia had been the scene of many clashes between the Syndicate Worlds and the Alliance. Most of the wreckage from those clashes had been allowed to extend slowly through the empty spaces of the star system. The remains of Syndic and Alliance warships had been accumulating in this star system for almost a hundred years.

But scattered along a ragged arc stretching between the seventh planet of the Atalia Star System and the jump point for Varandal lay spreading fields of debris that were still fairly compact, some flocks of escape pods, and a small number of damaged Syndic warships. "The aftermath of a battle?" Geary asked.

"One that's still going on," Desjani corrected.

10

Pulling his display out farther, he saw them. Almost four light-hours away, Alliance and Syndic warships were clashing. The jump point for Varandal was about as far from Atalia's star as the jump exit at which the Alliance fleet had arrived, but partway around the curve of the outer boundaries of the star system. Geary stared at his display as the fleet's sensors added details. He almost winced as a cluster of Alliance ships vanished, then realized that they had not been destroyed but had jumped out of the system.

More Alliance warships vanished, leaving him wondering how many had been here. One remained, however, a single battleship staggering toward the jump point as overwhelming numbers of Syndic warships made firing passes.

"The system identifies that battleship as the *Intractable*," Desjani reported. "She was one of the battleships left behind to guard Alliance space when this fleet went to the Syndic home star system." She hesitated before continuing. "When we left, *Intractable* was part of the same battleship division as *Dreadnaught*."

Dreadnaught, the ship commanded by Jane Geary, his grandniece. Had *Dreadnaught* already jumped for Varandal, or were pieces of that Alliance battleship drifting through this star system?

In time, the fleet's sensors could analyze the most recent debris and make guesses as to how many warships had died here in the latest engagements. For the moment, Geary could only watch images almost four hours old, knowing that there was nothing he could do to save *Intractable* as she covered the withdrawal of the rest of the Alliance force with her.

"It won't be much longer," Desjani muttered, watching the same images as Geary. "*Intractable* was the only Alliance warship left near the jump point. Everybody else had already gotten away."

"Is there any chance that she made it to the jump point?"

"Not unless the Syndics decided to stop shooting."

Rione was leaning forward, her voice urgent. "We have to do something. Distract the Syndics. Something!"

"Madam Co-President," Geary replied heavily, "the Syndics won't even see this fleet for almost four hours. *Intractable* was almost certainly destroyed nearly that long ago. We're just seeing it now."

"Damn," Rione whispered.

On the four-hours-old images, *Intractable* seemed to have lost maneuvering control, sliding sideways and over as Syndic hits pushed the Alliance battleship off course. "Her crew's leaving," Desjani said, as escape pods began flinging themselves away from the stricken battleship. "There still seem to be a few weapons working, though."

Four hours ago, a volley of Syndic missiles had been fired, curving in to slam into *Intractable* and shatter the massive warship, by then almost defenseless. *Intractable*'s hull had broken, the forward portion spinning away while the after portion came apart into smaller pieces. Geary closed his eyes for a moment, then opened them to see the remnants of the battleship tumbling in different directions, no sign of life remaining on them. *May your ancestors welcome you and the living stars warm your spirits.*

"We'll avenge them," Desjani almost snarled.

"Yeah. We will. We've obviously found the reserve flotilla." Geary began working up the intercept, assuming the Syndics would turn back toward this jump point. "How long until the fleet's sensors give us a picture of what happened here?"

"It should be pretty quick now." On the heels of her words, system estimates began popping up. Desjani's jaw tightened as she viewed her displays, where the fleet's sensors and evaluation systems were showing their analysis of the latest wreckage. "The most recent debris correlates to two or three Alliance battle cruisers. Somewhere between nine and thirteen destroyers. One or two light cruisers. Four to six heavy cruisers. And two battleships, counting *Intractable*." She let out a long breath. "*Intractable* held off the Syndics so the rest could get away, but there's no way for the sensors to tell us how much that was."

"At least it wasn't one-sided." Geary watched new estimates appear. "It looks like they cost the Syndics one or two battle cruisers, a battleship, somewhere between ten and twenty HuKs, six or seven heavy cruisers, and eight to eleven light cruisers. Plus what was too damaged to pursue them through the jump." A badly damaged Syndic battle cruiser, three heavy cruisers, and one light cruiser were spread out along the path of the battle, all of them limping on courses toward the second planet in the star system. Near the jump exit, another battle cruiser mauled by *Intractable*'s last stand looked like it was turning toward the inner system, too.

The fleet's sensors were peering four light-hours across the edge of the star system, looking through the debris of battle to evaluate the size of the Syndic force, and those results finally appeared as well. "Sixteen battleships, fourteen battle cruisers, twenty heavy cruisers, forty-five light cruisers, one hundred ten Hunter-Killers." He'd been hoping that Lieutenant Iger's estimates were way too high. In fact, they seemed to have been all too accurate. "That's what's still operational in the reserve flotilla."

"We can take them," Desjani insisted.

"We're going to have to. But I can't finish plotting an intercept until they turn around and settle on new vectors."

He waited impatiently, the Alliance fleet eating up the distance to the jump point but close to two days' travel away, until Desjani suddenly gasped. "They're not turning around. They're re-forming. They're going to jump after the Alliance ships that escaped."

"Jump to Varandal?" The only thing worse than fighting the reserve flotilla here might be having to fight it at Varandal if the Syndics were able to inflict enough damage at that star system before the Alliance fleet could catch up to them.

"Still almost four light-hours distant." Desjani slammed a fist against the arm of her seat. "They're going to jump before they even know we're here."

"Maybe that'll let us surprise them at Varandal." His eyes went to the estimates of Alliance losses here. *Two battleships. Had the other one been* Dreadnaught? Was his grandniece Jane Geary dead, just when Geary had gotten heartbreakingly close to home, or was she in one of the escape pods littering this system?

More symbols were proliferating on the displays, revealing the escape pods within Atalia Star System. There were a lot of Alliance escape pods from the warships destroyed here. Geary settled back, his eyes going from the Syndic reserve flotilla where it was re-forming in preparation for jumping to Varandal, to the badly damaged Syndic war ships limping toward safety and also still unaware of the arrival of the Alliance fleet here, to the flocks of Alliance escape pods, to the status display showing how much fuelcell reserves remained on the fleet's warships.

"I need advice, Tanya." She focused on him. "We can easily swing our courses past those damaged Syndics and take them out on our way to the jump point. However, the Alliance sailors in those escape pods will be counting on us to pick them up, but that will require slowing the fleet's ships a lot for the pickup. That'll cost fuel cells we don't have to spare, and delay the time until we reach the jump point for Varandal."

Desjani drummed her fingers on the arm of her seat for a moment, then turned to her engineering watch. "If those escape pods turn onto the same vectors as this fleet and burn all of their remaining fuel, what velocity can they reach?"

The engineer quickly ran figures. "Captain, working back to how long they've probably been in space and how much the pods must have burned during their launches, then they could probably get up to point zero one light if they reactivated the escape-launch burn sequence. But they'd have nothing left afterward."

"That helps some, but not enough. The fleet would still have to brake quite a bit." Desjani shook her head. "Even if we could afford the fuel-cell consumption, it would still delay us a lot. And most of our ships have as much personnel on board as they can handle as it is. Getting them overcrowded could be ugly if those ships need to be evacuated in the fighting at Varandal, and there aren't enough escape pods available. What we need is two fleets." Her eyes went to the display as alerts pulsed. "The Syndic reserve flotilla jumped for Varandal three hours and forty-one minutes ago."

"Too bad we didn't get here over three hours earlier. If they'd seen us before they jumped, they might have hung around and simplified things for us." Geary ran his eyes across the fleet status display. "Two fleets. Maybe that's what I'll have to do. Break off some of the ships to pick up the escape pods and follow after the rest."

"Who can we spare?"

"No one. But we have ships that will have trouble keeping up anyway." The choices seemed simple, but it wasn't just a matter of physics. He called *Illustrious*. "Captain Badaya, I have a request to make of you."

Six seconds later Badaya's answer came in. He looked weary, but that was to be expected since Badaya had probably been pushing himself and his crew around the clock to get the damage to *Illustrious* repaired before the likelihood of battle. There was only so much that *Illustrious*'s crew could do, though. "What do you need, Captain Geary?"

"I need those Alliance escape pods recovered, but I can't afford to slow the entire fleet to do that. On its way to the jump point for Varandal the fleet can eliminate the remaining Syndic warship presence in this star system, but whoever slows down to pick up those escape pods will still need enough firepower to protect them if something unexpected happens."

Six seconds later Captain Badaya nodded. "Who were you thinking of, Captain Geary?"

"The three auxiliaries. *Orion. Incredible. Resolution.* The most badly damaged escorts. And because those ships will need a reliable and capable commander, *Illustrious.*"

Badaya eventually nodded again. "We've done a lot to patch up *Illustrious*, but she's still going to be at a disadvantage during a fleet engagement. I understand your logic. But it's a very hard thing to think of missing the fight in Varandal."

"I understand." Badaya had his faults, but he'd earned the right to have his pride and honor given full consideration. "That's why I'm asking you to accept the assignment. If any Syndics pop out of the jump point for Varandal before you get to it, you'll have to fight your way through them. I need somebody in command of the force who can be counted upon to do that, and I'm giving you two battleships and two battle cruisers to do it." He didn't bother adding what he and Badaya both knew, that all four battered ships didn't add up to the combat capability of a single, undamaged battleship.

"Not much chance of Syndics making it back here before we leave," Badaya observed, "though it's not impossible. But if you maul the Syndics who've jumped to Varandal, some of them may be heading for the jump point back to here when we arrive at Varandal. We'll be well positioned to block them and wipe them out."

"That's true."

"It's an honorable assignment," Badaya concluded. "We won't

leave any Alliance sailors behind here, *Illustrious* won't slow down any of our fellow battle cruisers, and we'll be far enough behind the rest of you to intercept Syndics trying to flee Varandal. Thank you for your confidence, Captain Geary."

"You've earned it, Captain Badaya." Which was true enough. Aside from the dictator thing, he wasn't a bad commanding officer. Badaya tended to be too reactive rather than coming up with new ideas before the enemy did, but give him orders and he'd execute them or die trying. Moreover, he believed in Geary, believed in him enough to accept an assignment that Badaya probably would have refused if given it six months ago.

"Thank you, Captain Geary," Badaya repeated. "That other matter we discussed, about options once the fleet reaches Varandal. Everyone who needs to know is aware of your wishes in the matter and all have promised to abide by them. Even if *Illustrious* doesn't make it to Varandal, your flank is covered."

"That's good to know, Captain Badaya." Geary breathed a prayer of thanks that for once Badaya had phrased something carefully and discreetly. He'd learned several times that supposedly private communications were usually anything but that. "I'll prepare the orders for the ships accompanying *Illustrious*. We'll see you all at Varandal."

"*Orion*'s not going to be happy," Desjani observed as she double-checked Geary's plans.

"*Orion* doesn't deserve to be happy. Once we're back in Alliance space, I'm going to recommend breaking up her crew and getting mostly new personnel on board. Nothing else has worked to rebuild that crew."

"Maybe watching Numos get shot by a firing squad after his court-martial will help motivate them," Desjani said cheerfully.

"It might." His frustration with the slow pace of repairs by *Orion*'s crew had grown great enough that even he spent a moment enjoying the idea. "Then again, ever since they saw *Majestic* blown apart at Lakota, *Orion*'s crew has made creditable progress on fixing up their armor and weapons."

"But not their propulsion," Desjani noted dryly. "Maybe you should drop a hint that while they can protect themselves better now, they still can't run away."

"I'll pretend I didn't hear that, Captain Desjani." Instead of being abashed, she just grinned as he continued. "I don't think *Resolution* and *Incredible* will complain much, though."

"You wouldn't want to try separating those two ships," Desjani replied. "They've apparently mated for life after bonding at Heradao."

"Why are you in such a good mood, Captain Desjani?"

"Because the Syndic reserve flotilla has jumped to Varandal, Captain Geary, and will now be trapped between the Alliance forces that fled here and this fleet, as well as facing all of the defenses Varandal has to offer." Desjani smiled like a wolf. "They're meat."

"That may be, but they're meat with teeth."

Despite the huge virtual size of the conference-room table, Geary couldn't help noticing that it was smaller than it had been for earlier meetings. There were fewer ships and, therefore, fewer commanding officers left in the fleet. But at least after the events in Padronis. the poison seemed to have finally been drawn from the fleet, and any debate here would be open and genuine. "I'm sure you're all familiar with the situation. The Syndic reserve flotilla jumped for Varandal before they knew we'd arrived at Atalia. They're pursuing an Alliance force whose size remains uncertain and will undoubtedly try to reduce the Alliance facilities at Varandal as well as destroy the rest of the Alliance warships there. We have to get to Varandal in time to assist our comrades there on warships and the planets and orbital facilities."

He gestured toward the display hovering over the table. "The main body of the fleet will proceed to the jump point for Varandal as fast as our fuel-cell situation will allow, taking a course that will allow us to sweep up the damaged Syndic warships remaining in this star system. A formation made up of *Illustrious*, *Incredible*, *Resolution*, *Orion*, *Titan*, *Jinn*, *Witch*, and the most badly damaged cruisers and destroyers will slow down enough to recover the Alliance escape pods in this star system, then follow the rest of us to Varandal."

Every eye went to Captain Badaya, doubtless expecting him to explode with disagreement, but Badaya just nodded, his expression set. "*Illustrious* is honored to be given responsibility for this critical task. Make sure the rest of you leave some Syndics for us at Varandal."

"Be careful what you ask for," Commander Parr from *Incredible* cautioned. "But we'll be happy to fight alongside the other ships with us."

Duellos looked as tired as Badaya. "The odds don't look to be good at Varandal, and I see your projected movement will bring us to Varandal with less than twenty percent fuel-cell reserves."

"That's right." Geary tried to say it casually, as if it were routine to go into battle against superior numbers with fuelcell reserves so low that the real risk existed of warships running out of power during the engagement at Varandal. "There's nothing we can do about the fuel-cell situation. The remaining auxiliaries are using their shuttles to distribute the fuel cells they manufactured during the last jump, and after that we'll have to count on refueling after we deal with the Syndics at Varandal. We'll have a better idea of the odds we face at Varandal once the Alliance escape pods can provide us with a listing of the warships that were with the Alliance force that came here. So far all we can do is estimate how many Alliance warships were lost here."

Everybody checked the time. "The nearest pods should have seen us by now," Captain Armus grumped. "We'll have to wait another half hour before any message from them can reach us."

"Unfortunately, yes. But it's still over a day before we reach the jump point for Varandal. We have time. Too much time, but there's nothing we can do about that."

Nothing but sit on the bridge of *Dauntless*, bulleting through space at point one two light speed, waiting to hear what the Alliance personnel in the escape pods could tell the fleet.

The first voice coming over the circuit from an escape pod was so distorted by mingled joy, disbelief, and stress that it was a little hard to understand. "This is Lieutenant Reynardin. I believe I'm the senior surviving officer off of the battle cruiser *Avenger*. You can't imagine how good it is to see the Alliance fleet here. The Syndics were claiming that you'd been destroyed, but everyone said it couldn't be true. Not our fleet. Bless our ancestors and the living stars..."

Geary tried to fight down a wave of annoyance as the lieutenant jabbered on. Desjani was drumming her fingers on the arm of her command chair, her own impatience obvious. It wasn't too hard to imagine what Desjani would be saying to Lieutenant Reynardin right now if he was within shouting distance.

Rione must have read the same emotions on Geary and Desjani. "Lieutenant Reynardin has lost his ship and many of his friends and shipmates. He's surely suffering from shock."

"He's a fleet officer," Desjani replied, biting off each word. "Maybe when he gets the message from Captain Geary asking for information, he'll actually tell us something useful."

They could tell when that had happened a few minutes later, because Lieutenant Reynardin suddenly fell silent. When he spoke again, the lieutenant sounded half in tears. "Captain Geary. Sir. An honor... I... your orders. Yes, sir. What happened. We launched a spoiling attack. It was Admiral Tagos's idea, to keep the Syndics off-balance."

"Tagos?" Desjani muttered, then shook her head at Geary. "How the hell did she make admiral?"

"Admiral Tagos was on *Auspicious*," Reynardin continued. "I didn't see everything that hit *Auspicious*, but her power core blew, and I'm certain there weren't any survivors."

Geary nodded wearily, imagining from what he'd seen when he took command of the fleet that Tagos had been promoted because of political skills and "fighting spirit," then demonstrated both by rushing into a hopeless battle.

"*Avenger* and *Auspicious*. That accounts for two Alliance battle cruisers," Desjani noted as Reynardin rattled on in a shock-fueled stream of consciousness. "Maybe somebody else on his escape pod will take over the comm panel."

"Let's hope so." With the nearest escape pods still over two light-hours away, any attempt to try to get Lieutenant Reynardin to focus on the questions he'd been asked would be a very long and tedious process.

"It was pretty terrible," Reynardin continued. "Just... everything."

"Somebody please shoot him," Desjani ground out.

"He's in shock," Rione protested again.

The argument was cut off by the communications watch. "Captain, we've got another escape pod calling in."

"Put it on!" Desjani ordered in the tones of someone who'd just been delivered from torment.

This officer immediately sounded like a steadier individual. "Ensign Hochin here, sir. Hell-lance battery officer on *Peerless*. I'm afraid I can only tell you the status of the Alliance forces here up to the point that we evacuated *Peerless*."

"That's something, anyway." Desjani glanced at Geary. "*Peerless* was another battleship in the same division as *Dreadnaught*."

Which meant *Dreadnaught* either hadn't come along, or more likely had been able to escape back to Varandal. Geary felt a wave of comfort at the knowledge that his grandniece's ship hadn't been lost here, and guilt at his relief because it meant another ship had suffered that fate.

"We had five battle cruisers," Ensign Hochin was saying. "I know we lost *Avenger*. Six battleships. As far as I know only *Peerless* was destroyed."

"Oh, damn," Desjani cursed. "I should have realized. The closest escape pods to us are from the Alliance ships destroyed earliest. The sensors on the pods are rudimentary, so they won't have much idea of what happened after their ships were lost. To get a decent picture of how many Alliance ships made it back to the jump exit, we'll have to wait until we hear from the escape pods off *Intractable*."

"Another hour?" Geary guessed.

"At least."

But Hochin was still talking. "I expect you'll plan on wiping out the Syndics left here, but some pods off *Mantle* passed on word to us that one of the Syndic heavy cruisers picked up some of our personnel in escape pods from *Peerless*. They think it was between forty and sixty of our people, but it could have been less."

"Damn." Geary checked the positions of the Syndic heavy cruisers on the display. "Which one?"

"As best we can determine from the location of *Mantle*'s escape pods and their description of the course of the Syndic cruiser," Hochin continued as if he had not heard Geary, "it should be located in an area about one and a half light-hours from the star Atalia, slightly above the plane of the system, pretty close to a line between the jump point from Kalixa and the star. *Mantle*'s people said the Syndic cruiser had heavy damage forward."

"This one!" the combat-systems watch cried out triumphantly. "We had to work his course back, but it has to be this one."

"Is it damaged forward?" Desjani asked.

"Yes, Captain. A lot."

"Excellent." Desjani nodded to Geary. "That's one ensign who deserves a field promotion to lieutenant."

"Remind me about that." The heavy cruiser in question had

been badly torn up forward, but apparently retained most of its propulsion capabilities. Since seeing the Alliance fleet, it had accelerated to point zero six light speed. "Can we intercept him?"

"Not the *Illustrious* formation, sir," the operations watch reported with considerably less happiness. "After slowing to pick up these other pods, they won't be able to accelerate fast enough to catch that cruiser."

"What about us?" Geary asked.

The operations watch ran courses and speeds, then made a dissatisfied gesture. "The Eighth Light Cruiser Squadron on the edge of our formation farthest to starboard could manage an intercept with the least accelerating and braking, sir. The Twenty-third Destroyer Squadron could accompany them."

Geary checked the weapons on those ships against what the Syndic heavy cruiser was assessed to have left. "That should be enough firepower, but this isn't just about taking out that cruiser. We need to get the POWs off, and light cruisers and destroyers don't carry Marines."

"Ask them to surrender," Rione urged.

"That hasn't been a wildly successful option in the past, Madam Co-President."

"Maybe this time will be different. What does it cost you to demand their surrender? Or at least the surrender of the Alliance personnel that they have captured?"

"Not a lot," Geary admitted.

"You could make a deal," Rione suggested. "Offer to trade them the continued existence of that heavy cruiser for releasing our people."

Geary could feel the attitudes of the fleet personnel around him stiffening at the suggestion. Only Desjani spoke, though, and that as if to herself rather than addressing Rione. "Standing orders require all feasible efforts to destroy the enemy and prohibit allowing Syndic forces to escape as long as they retain any combat capability."

As fleet commander, he could override those standing orders, but in this case that didn't seem like the right thing to do. What else did he have to bargain with, though?

Rione looked around in frustration. "Make a deal, Captain Geary! If you won't agree to them keeping their ship, then you still have the lives of Syndic crew in your hands!"

He blew out an exasperated breath. "Syndic commanders haven't proven to care very much about the lives of their crews."

"Some of them have! You've made comments about them, about how the crews abandoned ship too early. Why did their commanders do that if they didn't care about their crews?"

That was a point. Those cases could have represented panic, but they also could have been the result of captains' concern for the fate of their personnel. "And maybe if that Syndic captain isn't that worried about the crew, they'll be worried about their own life. It's worth a try." He recorded a demand and sent it off, sent orders to the Eighth Light Cruiser and Twenty-third Destroyer Squadrons to accelerate a bit more and alter course to intercept the Syndic heavy cruiser, then settled back again to wait with growing restlessness.

"Captain?" the combat-systems watch reported. "There is something odd about the damage to that Syndic heavy cruiser, the one who picked up some of the escape pods from *Peerless*."

Desjani glanced back at the watch-stander. "Define 'odd.'"

"We focused sensors on it, and analysis of the damage indicates it was caused not by multiple impacts but by a single massive blow."

"One hit?" Desjani frowned in thought. "What could have done that?"

"Unknown, Captain. No single weapon in the Alliance inventory could inflict that kind of hit."

Desjani frowned deeper. "What about a collision?"

The watch-stander ran some figures. "In theory, Captain, that's possible, but the odds of a head-on collision being strong enough to inflict that much damage and not a lot more are very, very small. What ever hit that cruiser hit it right on the bow, and not a lot tends to survive head-on strikes. It seems to have hit the entire bow, too, so it wasn't something small."

"Hmmm. That's very strange. But in the absence of any evidence of another cause, we'll have to assume a collision is what did it. Let me know if any other details show up to explain the damage." Desjani looked back at Geary as if aware of something he hadn't said out loud. "Sir?"

"Why'd they jump to Varandal?" he asked her.

"The Syndic reserve flotilla? To destroy what was left of the Alliance force that attacked here."

"But their orders must have been to stop *us* before we reached Varandal. Syndics don't improvise on their orders." Geary glared at the display as if an answer was hidden there. "Why didn't they stay here to hit us when we arrived?"

Desjani frowned. "They must have been ordered to go to Varandal. The Alliance warships that came here ran into the reserve flotilla on its way to the jump point for Varandal." She tapped some commands and studied the results. "That matches the debris trail. The reserve flotilla wasn't going to wait here for us. They must have planned on jumping before we got here, reducing Varandal's defenses, then hitting us when we arrived home with our guard down and our fuel and weapons at the lowest possible state."

That made sense, though something about the situation still bothered him. "It would have been easier to do all of that here at Atalia." No one else offered suggestions, so Geary leaned back and thought, his ideas going nowhere this time.

He hadn't realized how much time had passed until the communications watch called him. "Captain Geary, sir. The commanding officer of that Syndic heavy cruiser is offering to surrender her prisoners in exchange for your agreement not to attack the escape pods from her ship."

Desjani's reaction was quick. "It's a trap. Or a trick."

"Could be," Geary agreed as he accepted the message.

An image of the captain of the Syndic heavy cruiser appeared. She looked defiant but her eyes had a glazed look, as if she were suffering from shock, too. "My ship cannot defend itself against your attack. I am willing to surrender my prisoners in exchange for your agreement for safe passage for my crew. I will remain aboard my ship as a hostage along with the prisoners after my crew evacuates and put up no resistance to what ever boarding parties you send in to take off the prisoners, but if any attempt is made to capture my ship or penetrate beyond the prisoner holding area, I will destroy my ship. Those are my conditions. If you do not accept them, then I will fight to the death of my ship and all who are on it."

"You won't get a better offer," Rione pointed out.

"Or a more dangerous one," Desjani countered. "She can wait until our ships close to take off the prisoners, then overload her power core."

It wasn't an easy decision. Syndics hadn't exactly proven themselves trustworthy in previous dealings. "There's something about this one," Geary commented. "Look at her eyes. She's seriously rattled by something."

Desjani's own eyes narrowed as she studied the Syndic commander. "They won here. It is odd to see her looking so dazed. Maybe she got hurt during the battle."

"Maybe." Everyone was waiting. Only he could decide this one. Again. He remembered Colonel Carabali's comment about making decisions about who lives and who dies. He didn't want to have to do that again, but he had to. "All right. I'm going to agree to her terms. It's the only possible way to save the prisoners on her ship unless we abandon them and let the cruiser get away."

Desjani kept her face impassive, her fingers running across her display. "Recommend you use *Rifle* and *Culverin* from the destroyers heading to intercept the heavy cruiser. They'll have to swing very close, match vectors, then put lines across and manually transfer the prisoners. Send the rest of the squadron to watch over the Syndic escape pods as a threat."

Geary nodded approvingly. "What about the light cruisers?"

"Have them dance around the heavy cruiser," Desjani advised. "Create the impression they might get a lot closer, and if the Syndics are planning to blow the heavy cruiser, that might make them wait in hopes of bagging some of our light cruisers."

"All right."

Close to two hours later, *Rifle* and *Culverin* sidled up to the Syndic heavy cruiser, carefully matching their speed and direction exactly to that of the enemy warship. When they were done, the three warships were still hurtling at tremendous velocity through space, but relative to each other they were all motionless, as if the three ships were hanging unmoving in the vastness of space. A short distance from the Syndic heavy cruiser, *Rifle*, and *Culverin*, a small cluster of Syndic escape pods marked the escaping crew of the cruiser.

The destroyers and the Syndic heavy cruiser were almost forty light-minutes distant from the main body of the Alliance fleet at that point. Task Force *Illustrious* had fallen back even farther, more than a light-hour distant, as it braked to pick up Alliance escape pods. The fleet's main body had already swept over and smashed another Syndic heavy cruiser and light cruiser that had been damaged in the earlier battle, and was less than five light-minutes from a crippled Syndic battle cruiser, which seemed to be awaiting its fate with grim determination.

Unable to intervene at this point, Geary watched lines go across to the Syndic heavy cruiser from his destroyers, watched the very distant figures of sailors in survival suits sailing across on the lines, then after an agonizing wait more figures in survival suits came out of the Syndic cruiser, making their way to the destroyers. Eventually the suits stopped, and the lines were reeled in, then the destroyers accelerated away. "How many?"

"Fleet sensors counted thirty-six more coming off than boarded, sir."

"Thirty-six." He shrugged to Desjani. "Looks like a Syndic kept her word."

"We'll see what the commanding officers of *Rifle* and *Culverin* report when their message gets here in another forty minutes," Desjani grumbled.

Five minutes after that, as the Alliance light cruisers and destroyers raced back toward the main body of the fleet, and the Syndic escape pods kept heading for safety, the Syndic heavy cruiser vanished in a flare of light. "The power core did overload. Why then?" Desjani wondered. "A mistimed booby trap?"

"Maybe. If so, lucky it happened after everyone was clear." He wondered what had happened to the Syndic commanding officer who had promised to remain aboard her ship.

Less than twenty minutes later the Alliance fleet raced across the track of the first damaged Syndic battle cruiser. With no time or fuel cells to waste, Geary simply ordered a half dozen battleships to divert their courses enough for close-in passes on the crippled Syndic warship. Even though the Syndics still had some weapons firing, the Alliance battleships easily crashed the enemy shields as point-blank hell-lance fire methodically smashed the battle cruiser to scrap. "All systems dead on enemy battle cruiser. Crew abandoning ship."

Desjani hummed a little tune as she watched the wreck of the Syndic battle cruiser tumble in the wake of the Alliance fleet.

Soon afterward, a report arrived from *Rifle*. The destroyer's captain seemed bemused as he reported. "We have fifteen liberated prisoners aboard, Captain Geary. Several have serious injuries that have only received triage treatment. We also have the commanding officer of the Syndic cruiser. She requested to be taken prisoner.

Request instructions on where to deliver her and the injured Alliance personnel."

Desjani was staring at the message window. "First some of our own liberated prisoners ask us to arrest them, and now a Syndic officer asks to be taken prisoner. Has the universe gone mad?"

"She must have had a reason," Rione insisted. "Captain Geary, we need that Syndic on this ship so she can be interrogated. I have a strong suspicion that we need to know what ever she does about what happened here."

Geary looked a question at Desjani, who immediately nodded. "*Dauntless* can take care of the wounded, and we have a cell available for the Syndic."

He sent a reply, ordering *Rifle* to close on *Dauntless* so a shuttle could transfer the personnel, then sending *Culverin* to *Amazon* since that battleship had relatively few injured personnel.

"We paid a price for this," Desjani noted. "The light cruisers and destroyers we sent on that jaunt are going to be well under twenty percent fuel-cell reserves when we jump out of here. *Rifle* may be down to fifteen percent." She flipped one hand in a dismissive gesture. "Oh, well. Once our ships get to zero, they can't get any lower."

"I hope that was intended as a joke," Geary said.

"Yes, sir. Whistling past the black hole."

"What were your orders?"

The Syndic commander who had been captain of the heavy cruiser gazed back levelly at Lieutenant Iger from her seat within the interrogation room on *Dauntless*. "I am a citizen of the Syndicate Worlds."

"Was your ship part of the reserve flotilla?"

This time the reply took a moment. "I am a citizen of the Syndicate Worlds."

The chief at the interrogation panel chuckled softly. "Got you. Lieutenant," he said into the comm link, "brain patterns and physiological reactions show surprise and worry. She's wondering how we know about the reserve flotilla."

"How long was your ship attached to the reserve flotilla?" Iger asked the commander.

"I am a citizen of the Syndicate Worlds."

The chief frowned slightly at the readouts. "Lieutenant, I can't get a good call from that. Emotional responses, but hard to tell what they mean. Try baiting her with a characterization of the reserve flotilla."

Lieutenant Iger nodded again as if acknowledging the Syndic commander's last statement, but also responding to the chief. "Is it true," Iger stated, "that the reserve flotilla is made up of the most elite elements of the Syndicate fleet?"

Even Geary could see the emotional responses that statement evoked.

"She didn't like hearing that," the chief reported. "Looks like resentment and anger."

Desjani snorted in derision. "That cruiser wasn't part of the reserve flotilla, then. It looks like the reserve flotilla thinks highly of itself and didn't hesitate to let others know that."

Lieutenant Iger was speaking again. "What are the reserve flotilla's plans once it reaches Varandal?"

"I am a citizen of the Syndicate Worlds."

"Lieutenant," the chief reported, "I didn't see any deception centers light up." He looked toward Geary. "If she knew those plans, then she'd be thinking about how to lie about it, even if all she said was that 'I'm a citizen' junk."

"Thanks, Chief." Geary glanced at Desjani and Rione. "If her ship wasn't part of the reserve flotilla, she probably wasn't told the plan. Chief, have Lieutenant Iger ask her why no one in her crew objected to her surrendering her ship."

A moment later, Iger did so. The Syndic commander's jaw visibly tightened, and the chief at the interrogation panel whistled as the brain scan lit up. As the Syndic commander sat silent this time, Lieutenant Iger prodded her. "We know Syndicate Worlds regulations prohibit surrender. Weren't you worried about what would happen to you?"

The chief nodded as more lights flared on the scan. "She was worried, but it doesn't seem self-preservation centered, Lieutenant."

Lieutenant Iger pursed his mouth as if something had just occurred to him. "Weren't you worried about what would happen to your family?"

"Direct hit, Lieutenant," the chief reported. "Looks like she's very worried about that."

"Why did you surrender your ship?" Iger pressed, while the Syndic commander glared back at him, saying nothing.

Desjani's mouth twisted as she looked at the image of the Syndic officer. "Chief, have the lieutenant ask her if *she* has any questions."

The chief seemed startled but passed on the instructions.

The Syndic commander stayed silent a moment longer after Iger had asked, then spoke reluctantly. "Are my surviving crew members safe as agreed?"

Geary understood then, nodding to Desjani, who seemed grimly satisfied. "She wanted to save her surviving crew. The only way to do that was to agree to surrender, but she couldn't let her crew know she'd done that. Even if none of her officers had objected, she still would have been worried about what the Syndic leaders would do to her family if it was known she'd surrendered her ship."

He tapped the control to allow his voice to sound in the interrogation room. "Commander." She and Lieutenant Iger looked toward the bulkhead from which Geary's voice came. "Your crew is safe. Do you have any messages for them?"

A low whistle from the chief. "Major fear spike. Not self-focused, though."

The Syndic commander took a deep breath. "No. I prefer that they believe I died on my ship."

"Was that what you told them?" Geary asked. "That you were staying behind to die? Did you lie to your crew?"

The chief nodded. "Looks like it from here."

The Syndic commander glared furiously at Lieutenant Iger. "Yes, I lied to my crew. I told them that I'd stay behind and trigger a core overload when the Alliance ships got close enough. But I knew if I really did that, then you'd kill the rest of my crew. I lied to them so they'd abandon ship, and so they'd report that I'd died in the line of duty." Her angry gaze shifted, as if searching for the point from which Geary was watching her. "I would have fought my ship to the death if it would have made any difference, but we were helpless. Even then, I wouldn't have reached an agreement with anyone but Captain Geary, because I've seen too many Syndicate Worlds' escape pods destroyed for sport!"

Geary saw Desjani's face redden. "Self-righteous bitch," Desjani spat. "She's probably shot up some of ours."

Looking for something to change the topic, Geary triggered his mike. "Ask her how her ship sustained that damage to the bow."

After the question was relayed, the Syndic officer just stared at Iger, her face as pale as death.

"Wow," the chief commented. "Huge reaction. She's very upset thinking about what ever caused that damage, Lieutenant."

Iger repeated the question.

She glared back at him. "You know what caused it."

"No," Iger replied in a steady voice. "We don't."

"My ship came here from Kalixa! Does that give you the answer you want?"

Lieutenant Iger looked startled and puzzled, though Geary suspected he'd let those feelings show on purpose. "No, it doesn't answer the question. Something happened at Kalixa?"

"Don't play games with me! You must have caused what happened at Kalixa!"

Geary activated the comm circuit again. "What happened at Kalixa, Commander?"

The Syndic glared around her for a long moment, not speaking.

The chief whistled. "Markers all over the place. Like she's real upset but can't decide whether to lie or tell the truth or just start throwing things."

But the Syndic officer must have made up her mind not to get violent. Instead, her glare deepened. "Fine. We'll pretend you don't know that the hypernet gate at Kalixa exploded, devastating the entire star system."

Geary stopped breathing for a moment. Rione made a choking sound. Desjani just stared rigidly at the Syndic commander.

Lieutenant Iger spoke slowly. "This fleet was not responsible for that. We had no idea it had occurred. No unit from this fleet went to Kalixa."

The Syndic stared back at him, her distress clear now.

"How does she know what happened at Kalixa?" Rione wondered. "This must have been fairly recent."

"That's obvious," Desjani said. "The damage to her ship's bow, as if from a single massive blow. Her heavy cruiser must have been far enough from the gate to survive, but took a lot of damage. That cruiser wasn't shot up in Atalia fighting the Alliance ships from Varandal, it arrived here badly damaged." She seemed to be thinking for a moment. "That amount of damage to a heavy cruiser. The energy discharge from the collapsing gate must have been significantly stronger at Kalixa than it was at Lakota."

"But what made it collapse?" Geary demanded.

Lieutenant Iger was asking the same question at that moment. "Commander, were there Alliance warships in Kalixa Star System when its hypernet gate collapsed?"

"She's considering a lie, Lieutenant," the chief reported. "No. Going for truth."

"No," the Syndic officer said.

"Which warships were near the hypernet gate when it collapsed, then?"

"There weren't any warships near it!" the Syndic screamed, her nerves suddenly breaking at the memories. "Nothing was near it! It just began collapsing, its tethers failing! A merchant ship elsewhere in the star system had seen images, from... from Lakota, and it sent out warnings. It asked for help. Everyone started asking for help! We were far out, near the jump point for Atalia. We went bow on and reinforced our shields and we barely survived! Kalixa..." She took a deep breath and shuddered. "It's gone. Everything. Everybody. Dead. Gone."

"Truth," the chief reported to Iger in a small voice.

"No wonder she looked shell-shocked when we saw her," Desjani commented softly. "Worse than Lakota. First time I ever pitied a Syndic."

Iger was gazing at the commander, his own face pale now. "We didn't do it."

But the Syndic kept talking, her voice wavering with stress. "We jumped here. Orders. Go to Atalia. We found a lot of ships waiting here. Reserve flotilla, they said. Told the CEOs what happened. They didn't believe us, insisted on seeing my ship's records. Then they told us to proceed on duties assigned and turned and headed for the jump point for Varandal. Just left us. Then the Alliance appeared, and there was a fight." The Syndic commander gulped and breathed deeply. "Afterward, our track crossed some Alliance escape pods. Standing orders. Take prisoners when possible. We did."

Iger waited, looking slightly helpless as the Syndic sat shivering, her eyes haunted. Geary motioned to the chief. "Tell the lieutenant to give the Syndic a break. See if she needs any medical care. Captain Desjani, Co-President Rione, please come with me."

They followed him out of the intelligence spaces, none of them speaking again until they reached the fleet conference room and Geary had sealed the hatch. "There only seems to be one possibility for what happened at Kalixa."

"They did it," Desjani said with a scowl. "The aliens thought we were going to Kalixa, or might go there. They eliminated a gate we could use."

"Why not wait until we went there to do that? Then the gate's energy discharge could have hit this fleet."

Her scowl deepened. "They'd have to know... Sir, that's the answer. They can't track us anymore. They're used to knowing where we are or where we're going in something close enough to real time to be usable. But since we discovered the alien worms in the navigation and communications systems on our ships and scrubbed them out, they can't do that. They made an estimate of when we'd arrive in Kalixa if we went straight there and blew the gate accordingly."

"Do the travel times work for that?" Geary ran out the calculations, then shook his head. "Maybe your idea is correct, but they blew that gate long enough ago for the Syndic cruiser to have jumped here with the news before we arrived. That would've been too early to catch us."

"Not if we hadn't uncharacteristically lingered at Dilawa." Desjani brought up the travel times and pointed to the result.

He started to answer, but no words came. The figures didn't lie. A quick transit of Dilawa followed by a jump of the fleet directly on a path for Kalixa would have brought it there a little less than a week before now. Perfect timing.

Rione was shaking her head. "Even when you screw up, it turns out to be a good thing."

"He's guided," Desjani insisted.

"Perhaps," Rione replied. "Though I understand that good planning can have all the benefits of divine intervention without the arbitrary and capricious drawbacks. Be that as it may, uncharacteristic hesitation and characteristic avoidance of Syndic star systems with hypernet gates seems to have served this fleet well." Her expression tightened. "An entire star system and every human in it wiped out. The aliens have started what we've feared, triggering the collapse of hypernet gates."

"We've still got time to defuse this," Geary insisted. "It was a shot in the dark, and it missed. By the time the aliens confirm that our fleet wasn't at Kalixa—"

"This isn't just about the aliens! Don't you understand yet?" Rione glared at both of them. "The Syndic reserve flotilla was waiting here for this fleet, then when it received the report from that heavy cruiser about what happened at Kalixa, the reserve flotilla headed for Varandal. Obviously the news of the collapse of the hypernet gate at Kalixa triggered some modification of their orders. Now think! Why would they go to Varandal after hearing about Kalixa?"

Desjani answered first, her voice strained. "The Alliance hypernet gate at Varandal. They're going to try to collapse the gate in retaliation for Kalixa because they think we did it."

"Exactly." Rione was almost trembling with suppressed emotion. "The cycle of retaliation has already begun what may be humanity's last offensive. The aliens have gotten their wish. It's already in motion. We're too late."

11

"It's not too late!" Geary snapped. "The Syndics haven't blown that gate at Varandal yet, and if we can there get fast enough, we can stop them. We can stop this whole thing, and we will!"

"How?" Rione demanded.

"Captain Cresida has reported that she's been able to make enough progress on her design to protect against gate collapse. We'll need to get one installed on Varandal and every other hypernet gate we can as fast as we can and hope the aliens don't realize what we're doing until too late."

"What about Captain Tulev's list?"

"It's been overtaken by events. We don't have any time left, and a priority list would be too complicated to get across in the time we have available. If we spread the word that the hypernet gates are threats, everyone will start putting up those systems of Cresida's."

Desjani pressed her palms against her forehead. "Even if we do stop the Syndics, why wouldn't the aliens blow the gate as soon as they know we're in Varandal? No, they won't know. It'll take them a while to learn. Long enough to install Cresida's system?"

"We'll have to hope so. We're lucky we picked up that Syndic," he added. "If not, we wouldn't have known about Kalixa."

"If her ship hadn't survived and told the Syndic reserve flotilla about Kalixa," Desjani pointed out coldly, "then they wouldn't have gone off to collapse the Alliance gate at Varandal. I personally could have waited to hear about Kalixa if it would have avoided that."

"She told us something else important." Rione's eyes were still hooded with gloom. "A Syndic merchant ship there had copies of our records from Lakota. That confirms that the information is being spread throughout the Syndicate Worlds, even though the Syndic leaders are doubtless trying to stop it."

Geary walked to the comm panel. "We need a meeting. Now." Less than ten minutes later he was facing the virtual presences of Captains Cresida, Duellos, and Tulev, as well as Desjani and Rione. It took only a couple of minutes to explain what they'd learned from the Syndic commander, then Geary turned to Cresida. "You told me the basic work was done. How close are you to having a design that can be fabricated and installed as soon as we reach Alliance space?"

"Close enough, sir." She shrugged apologetically. "It can be refined, but it's done. It's got a lot of estimates factored in, but it should be effective enough to dampen the shock wave to levels low enough not to threaten a star system. There's a basic emergency level add-on that will at least lower the intensity of the energy discharge so it won't cause significant harm, and a more elaborate system that can be installed afterward on top of the other. That should guarantee the gate collapse is completely harmless."

"How fast can they be made and placed on hypernet gates?" Rione asked.

"As fast as their priority level, Madam Co-President." Cresida shrugged again. "We just need to convince the Alliance political authorities and our military chain of command of the urgency."

The sarcasm in her words didn't need to be emphasized. Rione looked angry but not at Cresida. "That may not be a problem if we lose Varandal, but it would be best not to have that kind of example to point to. We've already got Lakota and Kalixa, but since those occurred in enemy territory, their significance will be debated. We need to go around the Alliance bureaucracy."

"Captain Geary could order it."

"That's no guarantee it would happen," Geary interrupted. "Especially if it becomes a matter of people arguing about me instead of installing the..."

"Safe-fail systems," Cresida supplied.

Tulev smiled without humor. "We just tell everyone. Broadcast it. Here's what happened at Lakota and Kalixa. It could happen to *your* star system. At any minute. Unless you get this modification installed on your hypernet gate as fast as possible. People will pick it up, carry it onward."

Desjani was shaking her head. "We have to maintain security."

"If you do," Tulev stated calmly, "then the political and military authorities will classify it *divine eyes only*, then sit on it and study it and consider it until Alliance star systems are destroyed by the score. All in the name of security and avoiding a panic, of course."

Rione nodded. "Captain Tulev is right. We need to generate a level of urgency to get this done, hopefully get these systems on our hypernet gates before the aliens realize what we're doing and before the Syndics collapse any of them. The only way to do that is to make sure as many people as possible know of the danger."

"Urgency and hysteria may be hard to tell apart. Won't the authorities still attempt to downplay the danger?" Duellos asked.

"Of course they will. They'll try to claim that the gates are one hundred percent safe, perhaps by saying our hypernet gates are different from Syndic gates."

"That's nonsense," Cresida objected.

"Yes, it is. They'll say it anyway, and also try personally to discredit anyone saying the gates are a threat." Rione paused, then turned a sardonic smile on Geary. "Fortunately, the person declaring the gates to be a threat and offering the means to deal with that threat will be Black Jack Geary, returned from the dead to save the Alliance fleet and the Alliance."

All of the others nodded in a satisfied way. "She's right, sir," Desjani added.

He should have expected that if Rione and Desjani ever started agreeing with each other, it would be on things that he didn't like. But as Geary thought about it, he realized the truth of Rione's statements. This was no time to try to hide from the legacy of Black Jack. "All right. As soon as we arrive at Varandal, we start broadcasting our reports to anyone and everyone as well as the instructions on how to build Cresida's safe-fail systems. With my name on them."

Then Cresida surprised them all. "What about the Syndics?"

"I'm sure they'll hear about it eventually," Duellos offered.

"No, I mean, do we give it to them, too? Before we leave this star system." Cresida looked around at the shocked expressions that greeted her question. "I've been thinking about it. Sure, the Syndics are the enemy. But their hypernet gates are being used as weapons against *us* by a third party. There's less and less chance that any Syndic CEO would blow one of their own hypernet gates because word is getting around about what happens. But the aliens can still do it, like they did at Kalixa. If they know we're in a Syndic star system with a hypernet gate, they'll target us, and they'll keep collapsing Syndic gates in an attempt to goad the Syndics into trying to collapse more of our gates."

Tulev watched her intently. "You're suggesting the Syndic gates are now weapons that would only be employed by an enemy common to us and the Syndics."

"That's right. In which case, humanitarian considerations completely aside, we still need to disarm those weapons. And the surest way to do that is by giving the safe-fail system design to the Syndics."

"But you're talking treason," Desjani objected.

"It... could be interpreted that way."

Silence stretched for a moment before Duellos spoke again. "I believe that Captain Cresida has a good point. She's talking about neutralizing a hugely dangerous weapon that could be employed against us. If we don't provide it to the Syndics, we and they both suffer."

"The Alliance grand council is unlikely to see it in those terms," Rione said in a quiet voice. "They'll want to reserve the ability to use those gates as weapons against the Syndics."

"And how do you feel about that?" Geary asked.

"You know how I feel. They're too horrible and too dangerous to employ."

Tulev's head was bowed, his eyes on the deck, as he spoke. "As an officer of the Alliance fleet, I am sworn to protect the Alliance. It's not always easy to know the best way to do so, especially when that could be interpreted as aiding the enemy." He raised his eyes and regarded the others, his expression as impassive as it had ever been. "I have no love for them, but this is as much a matter of self-interest as it is humanitarian. Our leaders are unlikely to accept that argument without extended debate and delay, which could be fatal for billions. As I have nothing left to lose, I can be the one to release the information to the Syndics."

Desjani turned an anguished look on Tulev. "You've given enough to the Alliance! I won't hide behind you!"

"How do you feel about it?" Geary asked her.

She looked away, breathing heavily. "I... Damn. Damn the Syndics and their leaders to hell. After all the misery they've inflicted, now they require us to commit treason in the name of protecting what we care for." Desjani turned her gaze on Geary, her expression intense. "The Syndic hypernet key."

"What about it?"

"It's useless right now. We've been considering it a warwinning advantage if we could get it back to Alliance space and duplicate it, but right now it's *useless*."

Cresida laughed bitterly and nodded. "Of course. I hadn't gotten that far yet. We can't employ the Syndic hypernet using that key because we don't dare go into Syndic star systems with gates. If we did, the gate could collapse as we approached and wipe out the entire fleet. In order for the key to provide us a war-winning advantage, the Syndics have to own hypernet gates that the aliens can't collapse on command."

"We have to give the Syndics the safe-fail system in order to ensure we can beat them?" Duellos laughed briefly, too. "And the Syndics will be forced to install such systems on their gates because the alternative to having the Alliance fleet arrive by using them is having the gates exist as bombs capable of going off at any moment and annihilating the star systems they're supposed to serve. That should be an easy question for even a Syndic CEO to answer. The living stars love irony, don't they?"

"Why wouldn't the Syndic bureaucracy balk at installing the safe-fail systems?" Desjani asked.

"Oh, they would. They'd try even harder than the Alliance bureaucracy to keep it very, very quiet until star systems started going out like bad lights and the Syndic leaders had to start pretending they had no warning or idea why it was happening prior to that time. Unfortunately, that's already begun." Duellos gestured to Rione. "But what's good for the Alliance is just as effective for the Syndics. Broadcast the events at Lakota, as we already have elsewhere, along with the design for the safe-fail system, and it will all spread virally. Local leaders will find ways to justify installing the systems, either voluntarily or to prevent mass rioting on their worlds. By the time the Syndic leaders at the home star system hear of it, there will probably be safe-fails on most of the gates in the Syndic hypernet."

"Will the Syndics trust our design?" Desjani pressed.

Cresida answered. "Any team of halfway-competent engineers will be able to see that it's a closed system that does what it's advertised to do and nothing more. Hell, the Syndics are probably already working on their own safefail system, but odds are it's caught up in that bureaucracy and the bureaucratic mania to keep things secret from your own side."

Desjani exhaled slowly. "Then my answer is yes. Give it to the Syndics. Because ultimately that decision protects the *Alliance*."

"All right." Geary looked around, knowing what he had to do. "Thank you for volunteering, Captain Tulev, but I won't ask you to take an action that's my responsibility. I'll—"

"No, you won't." Rione interrupted, then sighed. "I should lecture you all on your duty and remind you of your oaths and the laws of the Alliance and regulations of the fleet. But I'm a politician, so who am I to speak of honoring oaths? Enough has already been asked of you all, and of your ancestors, in a hundred years of war. Let this politician prove to you that all honor is not dead among your elected leaders. *I* will release the information to the Syndics."

"Madam Co-President," Geary began, as the other officers present looked at Rione with varied looks of surprise.

"I am *not* under your command, Captain Geary. You cannot order me not to do it. The arguments made here are convincing, but we don't have time to try to convince the authorities back home. Not just the fate of this fleet but the lives of untold billions of people ride on this decision being made quickly. If it is seen as treason, you must remain unstained by it for the good of the Alliance. Unless you are prepared to arrest me and openly charge me with treason,

I will do this." Rione turned to Cresida. "Captain, is your design within the fleet database?"

Cresida nodded, her eyes on Rione. "Yes, Madam Co-President. Under the file name 'Safe-fail' in my personal files."

"Then I will acquire it without your assistance since I have the means to access those files. Your hands will be clean."

"Clean? But we know you're going to do this," Duellos pointed out.

"No, you don't."

"You told us."

"The words of a politician?" Rione smiled again, almost as if she were enjoying this. "You have no reason to believe anything I say is true. You probably think I'm just trying to entrap you by urging a course of action I won't actually carry out. You can't be absolutely certain I'm not doing that."

She left quickly, before anything else could be said. Cresida, a pondering expression on her face, suddenly nodded, looking from Geary to the door by which Rione had left. "I finally understand why—"

Biting off the words and reddening slightly, doing her best not to look at Desjani, Cresida rose to her feet, saluted hastily, then her image vanished.

Tulev rose with unusual speed, saluted as well, and also departed.

Desjani, a look of weary resignation on her face, stood up. "I'll get back to the bridge."

"But—" Geary began.

"I'll see you up there, sir." Desjani saluted with careful precision, then stalked out of the room.

Geary frowned at Duellos. "What was that about? What Cresida said?"

Instead of replying, Duellos held up a warding hand. "You're not getting me involved."

"In *what*?"

"Talk to your ancestors. Some of them must know something about women." Duellos paused before leaving, then shook his head. "Oh, I can't leave you hanging hopelessly. I'll give you a hint. When two people get involved, however briefly, other people who know at least one of them naturally wonder what they saw in each other."

"You mean Rione and me? You all wondered what I saw in her?"

"Good heavens, man, how can that surprise you?" Duellos cast a bleak look at the deck. "We humans are a strange bunch. Even in the midst of dealing with a threat to our entire race, we can be sidetracked for a moment by the oldest and smallest of personal dramas."

"Maybe we're trying to avoid thinking about all of this," Geary suggested. "The consequences if we fail. Before, failure could mean our deaths, the loss of our ships, perhaps eventually the defeat of the Alliance. Now, it could mean the loss of everything. What do you think of our chances?"

"I didn't think we'd make it half this far home," Duellos reminded him. "Anything is possible."

"Why? Why are they doing it?"

"The aliens? Perhaps, before all is said and done, we'll have the chance to ask them directly." Duellos's face grew uncharacteristically harsh. "And when we do, perhaps we'll have hell-lance batteries pointing at their faces to ensure we get a reply."

"Another war?" Geary asked.

"Maybe. Or maybe not. The aliens don't seem to like stand-up fights."

"But we do."

"Yes." Duellos smiled unpleasantly. "Maybe that's why they're acting already. Maybe right now they're getting scared."

Seven more hours until they reached the jump point for Varandal. About six more hours until the fleet crossed the path of the second badly damaged Syndic battle cruiser, the one hurt by *Intractable*'s final blows. Geary wandered restlessly through *Dauntless*'s passageways, exchanging brief words or conversations with the crew, acutely aware that in some critical ways events were coming to a head. A successful battle at Varandal was the key to saving the fleet and the Alliance, even though getting the fleet back to Alliance space would still leave some critical issues to resolve. Without victory at Varandal, there could be no next step. So he strode through the now-familiar passageways of the battle cruiser, speaking with the hell-lance battery crews, the engineers, the cooks, the administrative personnel, the specialists of every kind, and all of the other individuals who made *Dauntless* a living ship.

For the first time, he realized that even though he wasn't her captain, losing *Dauntless* would hurt at least as much as losing *Merlon*.

He went down to the worship spaces and consulted with his ancestors, finding small comfort this time. If only his ancestors could warp time and space, bring the fleet to Varandal *now* so the Syndic reserve flotilla could be confronted *now*. Decide it now, end it now. But space was huge, and there were still six hours to jump for Varandal, then almost four days in jump space afterward.

Finally, he made his way back to the intelligence spaces. "Where's the Syndic commander?" Geary asked.

"On her way to the brig, sir," Lieutenant Iger responded. "Captain Desjani is accompanying her there."

Something about that felt odd. "Is there something unusual about that?"

Lieutenant Iger nodded. "Yes, sir." He looked toward the interrogation room, making an expression of distaste. "We don't allow physical harm to be inflicted on prisoners, sir. But, they get escorted to and from their cells through the same passageways the crew uses. The crew reacts by making those trips as unpleasant as possible."

"The prisoners have to run a gauntlet."

"Yes, sir." Iger shrugged. "No physical harm, but words, gestures, noninjurious things thrown at them and their uniforms. Emotions run high, sir. The Marines do have orders to protect their prisoners, but certain things are accepted."

Easy enough to understand. Ships' crews rarely saw the hated enemy face-to-face. Geary looked at the hatch through which Desjani had gone. "But the crew won't do those things to this prisoner if Captain Desjani is with her."

"No, sir, I wouldn't think so."

Odd. A chivalrous gesture toward the enemy. Geary waited a decent interval, then requested that Desjani visit his stateroom at her convenience. "I didn't get a final assessment from you on our plans," he said when she arrived.

"My apologies, sir," Desjani replied. "It's the best of a bad situation. That's my assessment. I can't think of any better courses of action."

"Thank you. I wanted to be sure of that." He paused. "I understand you escorted the Syndic commander to the brig."

Desjani gave him an impassive look, betraying nothing. "Yes, sir."

"It's strange, isn't it? If we ever want a chance at ending this war, officers like that are the people we need to deal with. Officers willing to keep their word with us and who care enough about their crews to put aside uncompromising orders. But in order to get the Syndics to the negotiating table, we need to keep doing our best to kill officers like that."

"I suppose 'strange' is one word for it." Desjani's expression was still impossible to read. "If people like that weren't fighting so hard for a government that they fear, then the war might have ended a long time ago. It's not like we can trust the Syndics as a group to negotiate in good faith anyway. You know that now, after seeing how many times they tried to double-cross this fleet as we headed toward home."

"That's true," Geary agreed. "Can I ask a personal question?"

Desjani looked down, then over at him and nodded.

"Why did you escort that Syndic commander through the passageways of your ship?"

Instead of answering immediately, Desjani looked down again, then eventually shook her head. "She acted with honor. I was granting honorable treatment in return. That's all."

"She was willing to sacrifice herself to save the surviving members of her crew," Geary pointed out. "I know that impressed me as a former ship captain myself."

"Don't push me on this." Desjani met his eyes, her own expression hard. "I still hate them for what they've done. Even that one. I'm certain she hates us, too. If she were truly honorable, why did she fight for the Syndics?"

"I can't answer that. I just see some common grounds, that's all. With her, anyway."

"Did we kill her younger brother?" Desjani closed her eyes after that slipped out, then drew in a long breath through clenched teeth. "Maybe we did. At what point do the hate and the killing no longer make sense?"

"Tanya, hate never makes sense. Killing is sometimes necessary. You do what must be done to protect your home and your family and what's precious to you. But all hate does is screw up people's own minds, so they can't think straight when it comes to knowing when they have to kill, or when they *don't* have to kill."

She gazed back at him, her face still hard, but her eyes searching his. "Did the living stars tell you that?"

"No. My mother told me that."

Desjani's face slowly softened, then she smiled with one corner of her mouth. "You listened to your mother?"

"Sometimes."

"She—" Desjani broke off the sentence, her half smile vanishing.

Geary didn't have any trouble knowing why. What ever Desjani had been planning on saying about his mother, she'd realized that Geary's mother had been dead for a very long time. Like so many others in his life, Geary's mother had aged and died while Geary drifted in survival sleep amid the wreckage of war in the Grendel Star System. Because the Syndics had attacked, because the Syndics had chosen to start this war.

"They took your family from you," Desjani finally said. "They took everything from you."

"Yeah. That's occurred to me."

"I'm sorry."

He forced a smile. "It's something I have to live with."

"Don't you want revenge?"

It was Geary's turn to look down for a moment as he thought. "Revenge? The Syndic leaders who ordered the attacks that started this war are themselves long dead and beyond any vengeance I can manage."

"Their successors are still in power," Desjani argued.

"Tanya, how many people do I kill, how many people do I ask to die fighting, in the name of avenging a crime committed a hundred years ago? I'm not perfect. If I could somehow get my hands on the Syndic bastards who started this war, I'd make them suffer. But they're all dead. Now I'm damned if I can figure out what this war is still about aside from avenging the latest defeat or atrocity. It's turned into a self-sustaining cyclic reaction, and you and I both know the Alliance as well as the Syndicate Worlds are starting to crack from the pressure of a war without end."

Desjani shook her head, walking over to a chair and sitting down, her eyes on the deck. "I spent a long time just wanting to kill them. All of them. To get even and to stop them from killing anyone else. But it's never even, it just goes back and forth, and how many Syndic deaths would it take to equal my brother's life? Every single one of them dead wouldn't bring Yuri back, and then at Wendig I saw a Syndic like Yuri, and I wondered what the point would be of killing somebody else's brother to avenge my own. To make them hurt, too? Once that would have been reason enough. Now, I'm starting to wish that no one else's brother or sister or husband or wife or father or mother had to die. But I don't know how to make that happen."

Geary sat down opposite her. "We may have a chance, once we get home, and you'll have played a big role in making that chance happen."

"Once we get home, you'll have other things to deal with, too. I wish I knew how to make that easier."

"Thanks." He gazed to one side, eyes focused on nothing. "It still doesn't feel real to me, that everyone I once knew is gone. At home, I'll really have to face it. I wonder if I'll hate the Syndics then as much as you have."

She gave him an annoyed look. "You're supposed to be better than us. That's why the living stars gave you this job."

"I'm not allowed to hate the Syndics?"

"Not if that gets in the way of your mission."

He looked back at her for a moment. "You know, Captain Desjani, it has just dawned on me that every once in a while *you* give *me* orders."

Desjani's annoyed expression deepened. "I'm not giving you orders, Captain Geary. I'm just telling you what you need to do."

"There's a difference?"

"Of course there's a difference. It's obvious."

Geary waited a few moments, but Desjani didn't elaborate on what was apparently obvious to her. Debating the issue didn't seem likely to produce a win for him, so he finally made a noncommittal face. "All right. But..." He hesitated, wondering if he could bring up something that had haunted him, then deciding that if he could ever speak of it, then it should be now with Desjani. "I'm worried about how I may react. It hasn't really hit me, I think, on some level. I was so stunned when I was awoken from survival sleep, and I went numb when I learned what had happened, how long it had been."

"You looked like a zombie," Desjani agreed, her voice much softer now. "I remember wondering if Black Jack really still lived."

"I don't know about Black Jack, but I did." Geary looked down at his hands and inhaled deeply before being able to speak again. "But I had to put that aside when I had to assume command of the fleet. I put it aside. I don't think I really resolved it. What's going to happen when we get home, when the reality of everyone I once knew being dead and gone hits me because I'll see the changes and know that I'm alone?"

Desjani's voice was very low, but he could hear her very clearly. "You won't be alone."

That statement came far too close to a subject they could never speak of or even acknowledge existed. Startled, he looked up and caught her eyes.

Desjani looked away. "You needed to hear me say that." She stood up, straightening her body to the posture of attention. "By your leave, sir, if there's nothing else, I have some matters I should attend to."

"Certainly. Thank you, Captain Desjani."

He checked the time after she left. Five hours to jump for Varandal.

* * *

The ball of wreckage that had been the last Syndic battle cruiser in Atalia Star System fell away in the wake of the Alliance fleet as it neared the jump point for Varandal.

"Captain?" The face of *Dauntless*'s systems-security officer floated in a window before Desjani. "There's been some uncleared transmissions from our ship."

"Uncleared transmissions?" Desjani asked mildly.

"Yes. Unencrypted broadcasts to anyone in this star system. I'm trying to identify the source within *Dauntless*."

"Is the information within the broadcasts classified?"

The systems-security officer blinked as he considered the question. "No, Captain, not as far as I can tell. There's no formal classification attached, and the security review scans didn't match the contents of the broadcast to any known classified material."

"Then I don't see any need to make it a priority," Desjani said. "We need to ensure the ship's systems are as close to optimum as possible when we arrive in Varandal."

"But... Captain, any broadcast to the enemy is prohibited."

"Of course," Desjani agreed. "But since no classified material is involved, the damage assessment from this incident will surely place it as a low-priority matter. Let's focus on preparing for battle, Commander."

"Uh, yes, Captain."

After the security officer's image vanished, Desjani gave Geary an enigmatic look. "I wonder what that could have been about."

"Probably nothing important, like you said," he replied.

She was studying the information forwarded to her by the systems-security officer. "The same records from Lakota that this fleet already broadcast, a description of something at Kalixa, plus some kind of equipment schematic and a narrative. No transmission authorization code." Desjani tapped her controls. "Nothing that threatens my ship or the fleet. I have more critical issues to deal with."

"Agreed." He wondered how Rione had managed to trick the communications system on *Dauntless* into sending a broadcast without an authorization. Despite the things that Rione had already admitted she could do with the supposedly secure systems throughout the fleet, Geary suspected there were plenty of other capabilities available to Rione that she had never disclosed.

He studied his display, taking a last look at the situation in Atalia. Task Force *Illustrious*, now a good two light-hours behind the fleet's main body, was still collecting escape pods. The survivors from *Intractable* weren't far from the fleet's main body, but picking them up would be impossible at the speed the fleet was traveling. They'd have to wait for *Illustrious* and her companions to get here.

Fuel-cell reserve levels were hovering around 20 percent on most of the warships, though some like *Rifle* were significantly lower. Only three specter missiles were left in the fleet. Grapeshot inventories were at 60 percent.

On the fringes of Atalia Star System, Syndic HuKs, couriers, and merchant ships were still heading for jump points, racing either to escape or carry word of the Alliance fleet's movements. Most of them would receive the broadcasts from *Dauntless* before they jumped.

There hadn't been any communications from the Syndic authorities in Atalia. No demands for surrender. Nothing. He wondered if the highest-ranking CEOs in this star system knew about the reserve flotilla's mission, if they had been told about Kalixa. They'd know now.

"Five minutes to jump."

Geary tapped his controls. "Captain Badaya, we're about to jump for Varandal. We'll see you there. Good luck." He couldn't think of anything else to say, and in any case Badaya wouldn't receive the message for close to two hours.

"Four. Days." Desjani closed her eyes in resignation.

"Yeah. It's going to be the longest four days in jump that I've ever spent," Geary agreed. The Syndic reserve flotilla was still in jump space, still headed for Varandal. So were the Alliance warships ahead of the Syndics. Now the fleet would join them. The maneuvering system flashed an alert, and Geary sent another message. "All ships, jump at time two zero four nine. We'll see you in Varandal. Be prepared for combat immediately upon arrival."

A few minutes later the stars vanished, and Geary was gazing upon the drab gray of jump space again. Thinking of the Syndic reserve flotilla's mission and their superiority in numbers, and the state of the Alliance fleet, he couldn't help wondering if this would be his last jump.

Four apparently endless days later, they sat in their seats on the bridge of *Dauntless* again, counting down the minutes until they left jump. Geary took long, slow breaths to relax, rolling his shoulders as if preparing for hand-to-hand combat. Desjani sat with her eyes glued to her display, her face calm, her eyes lit with excitement. At the back of the bridge, Rione remained silent, but tension seemed to radiate from her. The watch-standers were poised at their stations. *Dauntless*'s entire crew stood on duty throughout the ship, ready for action.

"All weapons ready. Set to fire on automatic," Desjani said with a coolness that felt eerie amid the stress-filled atmosphere.

Ahead of them, in the gray emptiness of jump space, one of the mysterious lights seemed to bloom across their path. It could have been close or immensely distant, but it hung there a moment as if waiting for *Dauntless*. Geary heard almost everyone's breath catch at the mystifying omen.

"Exiting jump space."

The endless gray and the inexplicable light before them vanished as the stars appeared.

Dauntless yawed around, seeking to avoid possible mines and enemy fire.

Braced against the maneuver, Desjani was still eyeing her display. "They're not at the jump point."

Geary stared at his display, unable to speak for a moment as he looked upon Varandal Star System.

After so many jumps, so many light-years crossed, so many Syndic-controlled star systems transited, the Alliance fleet had finally reached Alliance territory. Varandal, home of a regional fleet headquarters and many fleet installations along with strong defenses. He'd studied the database on *Dauntless*, seen how those installations and defenses had multiplied since the last time he had been to Varandal a hundred years before, but seeing it now for real still felt disorienting. Familiar and yet greatly changed.

Alerts sounded and symbols pulsed. Geary watched updates

rapidly proliferating across his display as the fleet's sensors evaluated everything they could see. "We're in time."

The hypernet gate still stood, just under six light-hours distant.

Three light-hours away, the Syndic reserve flotilla orbited the star Varandal. Seven light-minutes from the box of enemy warships a small formation of Alliance warships hovered, the survivors of those who had attacked Atalia, then tried to defend Varandal. "Two battleships, one battle cruiser, six heavy cruisers, one light cruiser, nine destroyers," Desjani read off. "That's all that's left."

Geary looked at the display, feeling a growing sense of unease. "Why haven't the Syndics destroyed everything? A lot of the defenses in this system have been hit by kinetic bombardment, but the Syndics haven't hit a lot of other things. All of the other facilities seem intact."

"What are they up to?" Desjani muttered.

"Alliance fleet!" The incoming transmission surprised Geary, who only then realized that a destroyer had been positioned near the jump point as a scout, the lone Alliance ship lost in the midst of the scores of warships that had just arrived. Now the voice of *Howitzer*'s commanding officer rang out. "Praise the living stars!"

Desjani turned to her operations watch. "Get a full record from that destroyer of what's happened here since the Syndics arrived. We need to see it now."

"Linking to their combat systems now," the watch reported. "On your display."

"Maintain station, *Howitzer*," Geary ordered, then concentrated on his own display, where historical events were playing at an accelerated pace. The Alliance defenders had made a stand half a light-hour from the jump point, losing another battle cruiser and a battleship along with numerous escorts. "Odds that bad, and they charged right at the enemy again," Geary grumbled.

Admiral Tethys had commanded that action, but had died when *Encourage* was destroyed. Captain Deccan on the *Contort* had assumed command then, until *Contort* was blown apart during another Syndic firing pass. Then Captain Barrabin on the *Chastise* took charge, but *Chastise*'s power core had overloaded during another clash well over two light-hours from the jump exit.

According to the records from *Howitzer*, since the destruction of *Chastise*, the remaining warships in Varandal had been commanded by Captain Jane Geary on *Dreadnaught*. Aside from *Dreadnaught*, only the battleship *Dependable*, the battle cruiser *Intemperate*, and their surviving escorts still faced the enemy.

Between those events, the Syndic reserve flotilla had launched kinetic bombardments, leveling the Alliance defenses in the star system. But they hadn't launched any subsequent bombardments, nor had the reserve flotilla yet closed with the few surviving Alliance defending warships even though to Geary it seemed that there had been opportunities to do so.

Why hadn't the Syndics finished off the defenders? Why hadn't they destroyed more of the Alliance facilities here? Of course the images they were seeing of the enemy were three hours old. It was possible that had happened by now.

"What the hell." Desjani had been watching her display intently, and now her hands moved rapidly, replaying part of the record. "Look at this. After the last clash with the Alliance defenders here."

Geary peered at the detail she was highlighting, zooming in on the Syndic reserve flotilla. The fleet's optical sensors were sensitive enough to pick out small details across immense distances of airless space. "Shuttles? What are they doing?"

"From heavy cruisers to other ships," Desjani murmured, then she entered more commands, and the view tightened even more, showing the access points where shuttles had been next to one of the heavy cruisers. "Personnel. See? They're taking personnel off the heavy cruisers."

"Why?"

Rione answered, her voice stressed. "Automated controls. You told me the Syndics can automate their ships and command them by remote."

"But why would they want to automate heavy—" The reason hit him and Desjani at the same moment.

"They're going to use those heavy cruisers to take down the hypernet gate," Desjani said. "It makes sense. It all ties together. Look. The Syndics have penetrated deep within the star system, but they haven't wiped out the Alliance defenders or heavily bombarded the Alliance facilities here."

"Bait," Geary breathed.

"Right. If they'd wiped out the defenders and destroyed most of the facilities in this star system, we might well hang around this jump point when we arrived, knowing that the Syndics would have to come back here through us sooner or later. But if there's still someone and something to save—"

"We're going to come charging at them." Geary ran a finger across his display, imagining the fleet movements. "When they see us, they wait until the right moment, then they hit the remaining defenders hard enough to wipe them out and send those heavy cruisers toward the hypernet gate. The rest of their force heads for the jump point, tearing past us. By the time we know what's happening, the shock wave is on its way, and the Syndics can jump out just ahead of it. If we hadn't already figured out they intended to collapse the hypernet gate here, their plan might well have worked."

"They get us and the entire star system." Desjani looked ready to kill Syndics with her bare hands. "How can they be sure the gate does enough damage though? That's the flaw in their plan."

"It's possible to scale up the level of an energy discharge from a gate collapse just like it's possible to scale it down," Geary replied. He didn't look back at Rione. When Cresida had worked up the calculations on how to scale down a gate energy discharge, she'd had to work up the reverse solution as well. Geary had entrusted that doomsday program to Rione, hoping it would never be used by anyone. "We have to assume the Syndics have figured out how to do that, too."

They'd already been here for fifteen minutes. The enemy wouldn't see the fleet for another two hours and thirty minutes, but he couldn't afford to waste another second of that time, since any orders he sent would require the same amount of time to reach the remnants of the defenders in this star system.

The first priority had to be orders to the remaining defenders of Varandal. "This is Captain John Geary, acting commanding officer of the Alliance fleet, to Captain Jane Geary, commanding the Alliance task force defending Varandal. The Syndic objective is to collapse the hypernet gate in this star system by destroying enough of the tethers on the gate. If the gate collapses, the resulting energy discharge will annihilate everything within this star system. We assess that the Syndics plan to collapse the gate using uncrewed heavy cruisers operating on automatic controls since any ship near the gate when it collapses will be destroyed. You are ordered to protect that gate," his voice caught for an instant before he could say the next part, "at all costs. Protection of the gate takes priority over all other actions, including the destruction of Syndic warships not menacing the gate and protection of other Alliance assets within this star system. Do not allow your force to be eliminated as a threat unless that is required to protect the gate. Hold out. Help is on the way. To the honor of our ancestors. Geary out."

He'd made it back, reached the star system where his grandniece was located, and his first words to her had been orders to sacrifice herself if necessary to defend the hypernet gate here.

"Are you sure your orders won't be overridden?" Rione asked. "There may still be a surviving admiral within this star system."

"No one's asserted command over Jane Geary yet," Desjani pointed out as if answering something that someone else had said. "But we're back in home territory, and someone might try to order senseless assaults by the defenders or by this fleet." Desjani turned to face her communications watch. "Should any orders come for Captain Geary from any officer senior to him within this star system, I want to ensure that this ship does not develop a serious problem with receipt and relay of incoming messages. Any error would be unacceptable. Under the circumstances, I will personally screen all such messages before receipt is acknowledged and before they are relayed to any other ships in the fleet to ensure they aren't garbled and that Captain Geary isn't distracted at an inopportune moment."

The communications watch-stander seemed momentarily

startled, then nodded with a serious expression. "I understand, Captain. If I see such a message, I should pass it on to you alone so that you can see how badly garbled it is."

"Yes. Exactly. You are not to bother Captain Geary with anything like that until we've finished with the Syndics in this star system." Desjani settled back in her captain's seat and saw Geary's expression. "Is there a problem, sir?"

"Only that I may still have been underestimating you, Captain Desjani."

She raised one eyebrow at him. "That can be dangerous, sir."

"I won't argue that." Geary turned, looking toward Rione. "Madam Co-President, while I'm engaging the Syndics, I'd appreciate it if you could find out what we're dealing with in this star system on the Alliance side."

Rione made a noncommittal gesture. "That's already under way. As far as I can tell at this point, I'm the senior political figure present, so you need not worry about additional political thorns in your side for the time being."

"That leaves the Syndics. How do we short-circuit their plans, Tanya?" He already knew the answer, the only one available. "We have to reinforce the defending task force and bring the rest of the fleet against the Syndics. Stop them from collapsing the gate and hurt them badly enough that they can't carry out their plans."

Desjani gave him a challenging look. "You know what battle cruisers do, Captain Geary."

"Yeah." He had twelve battle cruisers left with the fleet, several of those still bearing significant damage. But they had the firepower he needed, and they could get it where it was needed.

"How fast can we go without running out of fuel cells once we get to the Syndics?"

She ran the calculations. "Point one four light speed. *Dauntless* is accompanying them?" The question was tinged with worry and hope.

"You bet she is." He started working up new formations. "We need to split the fleet. One formation consisting of the twelve battle cruisers accompanied by the light cruisers and some of the destroyers. The other made up of the battleships, the heavy cruisers, and the rest of the destroyers."

"Got it. I'll make sure the Twelfth Light Cruiser and Twenty-third Destroyer Squadrons stay with the battleships. They're too low on fuel cells to accompany the battle cruisers."

"Good catch." They worked frantically, double-checked their work against each other's, then Geary transmitted the orders. "All units in the Alliance fleet, execute attached maneuvering orders at time two one zero five." He paused, eyes running down the list of battleships. *Warspite.* She'd done very well. "Captain Plant, you are designated the commander of the battleship formation. If something happens to me, you are to make every effort to prevent the Syndics from destroying the hypernet gate here."

"I understand," Plant replied several seconds later. "Good hunting, sir."

Rione was by his side again, speaking urgently in a hushed voice only he could hear. "Captain Geary, you can't send *Dauntless* into that kind of danger."

"Madam Co-President," he responded in equally quiet tones, "if that hypernet gate collapses, then *Dauntless* will be in peril no matter where in this star system she is located. We have to stop the

Syndics from succeeding in that, and *Dauntless* is now one-twelfth of my battle-cruiser force. She is needed with her sister ships."

Rione exhaled in exasperation but didn't argue further, going back to her observer's seat.

"Thank you, sir," Desjani breathed.

"We need to beat the Syndics and survive, Captain Desjani. Can we do that?"

"We'll do our damnedest, sir."

On the display the smooth shapes of the Alliance subformations came apart, roughly half of the ships collapsing in toward a single disc holding every surviving battleship and the heavy cruisers along with a healthy number of destroyers. The battle cruisers, most of the light cruisers, and the rest of the destroyers surged forward, sliding together into their own smaller disc as all of them accelerated along a vector aimed at reaching a projected position between the Syndic reserve flotilla and Varandal's hypernet gate.

Geary felt a thrill as the battle cruisers surged forward, hurtling toward the enemy at an acceleration that battleships could never match. He'd never really experienced the charge of a massed battle-cruiser formation, and even though the rational part of him saw the weakness of the armor and shields in the battle cruisers and knew this force couldn't sustain much more damage, his emotions watched the display as the battle cruisers charged and felt an irrational thrill at the courage and glory of it all.

It wasn't smart, but by his ancestors, it was magnificent.

He wondered how many of the battle cruisers would survive this charge.

12

More messages to send, one to the enemy. "Give me a link to the Syndic flagship." A moment later, the link established, Geary put on his best "hero out of legend" look as he sent his message. "To the CEO commanding the Syndicate Worlds reserve flotilla, this is Captain John Geary. We know from whom your flotilla has been defending Syndicate Worlds space on the border on the far side from the Alliance. You know that the Alliance did not collapse the hypernet gate at Kalixa. You know who did. Don't serve their aims. You will not be permitted to carry out your orders in this star system. To the honor of our ancestors. Geary out."

It probably wouldn't work, but it was worth trying.

Another message. "To the Alliance command center in Varandal, this is Captain John Geary, acting commanding officer of the Alliance fleet. I will attempt to defeat this Syndic flotilla and request any assistance you can provide. Be advised that the Syndic goal is to collapse the hypernet gate here, producing an energy discharge of nova-scale intensity. To the honor of our ancestors. Geary out."

Desjani got his attention. "Cresida is broadcasting her package. It's going out to everyone in the star system."

"Good." He took a moment to think, watching his ships move through space, the arcs of their paths forming a brilliant web on the display. The battle cruisers were swinging out wide, the battleships cutting in through the star system, aiming to reach positions on either side of the Syndics.

Should he have said something else to his grandniece? But what could he say in the middle of battle? *You've probably noticed that* Repulse *isn't with the fleet. That's because your brother probably died covering the fleet's retreat from the Syndic home system. He gave me a message for you, by the way.*

No. Anything personal would have to wait. Jane Geary didn't need the distractions. Neither did he. Until this engagement was over, he was the fleet commander first, Captain John Geary second, and the granduncle of Jane Geary a distant third.

The battle cruisers were settling into formation with their light cruisers and destroyers, the battleships already falling behind. After the rush of activity, there would be a long period of waiting. Even at their higher velocity, it would take the battle cruisers twenty-five hours to reach their goal, an orbit between the Syndics and the hypernet gate. In about two and a half more hours, the Syndic reserve flotilla would see the arrival of the Alliance fleet. It would be a little less than three additional hours before the Alliance fleet saw how the Syndics reacted to that.

Geary called the fleet. "Stand down from combat imminent status. Rest your crews."

"Sir, *Howitzer* is requesting instructions."

He accepted the message, seeing *Howitzer*'s commanding officer's jaw drop as she saw Geary. "What were your orders, Captain?" he asked.

It took *Howitzer*'s commanding officer a moment to recover. "Uh, sir, we had orders to maintain position near this jump point, acting as scout and courier as necessary."

"Very well. I understand that's not the most glamorous assignment, but it's a very important one. Remain on station. If the Syndics succeed in causing the collapse of the hypernet gate here, you'll see them destroying the tethers. Do not wait to view the collapse of the gate. If you do, you'll be destroyed by the wave front coming out of it. You'll be able to tell when it's close to collapse. You'll have to jump before that and report that Varandal has probably been destroyed."

"Y-yes, sir."

"Thank you." Geary sat and gazed at the display after the image of *Howitzer*'s captain vanished, thinking of everything that could go wrong. "Tanya, what should the battle cruisers' fuel-cell reserves be at when we meet the Syndics?"

"Roughly fifteen percent, sir, more or less depending on what the Syndics do."

"How many fuel cells does the fleet use in a typical engagement?"

Desjani spread her hands. "One of your typical engagements or one of the engagements before you assumed command, sir?"

"Mine."

"You don't have a typical engagement, sir." She smiled encouragingly. "We can do it with fifteen percent."

"If faith were fuel cells, Captain Desjani, you could power this entire fleet."

"I'm not the only one with faith, Captain Geary." Her eyes indicated the watch-standers on the bridge, who were calmly or excitedly discussing events. None of them betrayed dread or uncertainty. "They don't fear the outcome here."

About five hours later Geary watched his display. In a window there, Captain Jane Geary was acknowledging her orders, her posture and voice stiff, her eyes blazing. She had a haggard appearance, obviously worn by the extended battle that had been fought here before the Alliance fleet arrived. He'd known that because of the century he'd spent in survival sleep, Jane Geary had aged more years than he despite being his grandniece, but it was still odd to see her a bit older than he, her great-uncle. "This is Captain Jane Geary, acknowledging orders from the acting fleet commander. Understand we are to fight to the death to prevent the Syndics from destroying the hypernet gate. Geary out."

She avoided saying his name, but she wasn't disputing his authority. For a moment Geary felt a twinge of resentment that Jane Geary hadn't saluted, then recalled that no one outside of the fleet would use a gesture that he had reintroduced to the fleet. Her omission hadn't been an insult.

Jane Geary had clearly understood the orders to stop the Syndics at all costs. Had she also understood that she had to keep her task force from being destroyed for as long as possible consistent with that?

"Are you all right, sir?" Desjani asked casually.

"I'm just wishing my family reunions could take place under less stressful circumstances. Wait. The Syndics are reacting." Two and a half hours ago, the Syndic reserve flotilla had altered course, angling down and over toward the hypernet gate. Geary ran the courses out, seeing that the Syndics would reach the gate before his battle cruisers could. "It's up to Jane Geary. Can she slow them down?"

"Let's hope so."

The remaining defenders in the *Dreadnaught* task force had fallen back before the Syndics, maintaining their distance as the enemy headed for them and the hypernet gate. Geary watched as the retreat continued for almost half an hour, wondering what Jane Geary would do.

The answer came as the display reported mine strikes against ships of the Syndic reserve flotilla. "Nice," Desjani approved. "They waited until the Syndics were fixed on a course pursuing them, then laid mines in their wake. Look. That Syndic battle cruiser took three hits."

"They lost one of their heavy cruisers, too," Geary noted. None of the other Syndic warships seemed crippled, but even that small blow helped even the odds a bit.

But the Syndics kept coming, until fifteen minutes later another flurry of mine strikes took out two HuKs and damaged several other ships. "How many mines has she got?" Desjani wondered.

"The Syndics are probably asking themselves the same question."

This time the Syndic reserve flotilla didn't hold course, instead accelerating and climbing to alter its intercept of the *Dreadnaught* task force. But the Alliance ships responded by coming around and dodging to one side, putting the Syndics into another stern chase, this time at an angle away from the hypernet gate. "She's trying to draw them off," Desjani noted approvingly. "She is a Geary."

But the entire Syndic reserve flotilla didn't pursue. Instead, the Syndic box split, with a half dozen battleships, two battle cruisers, and a bevy of escorts wearing around to go after *Dreadnaught* while the rest of the Syndics continued toward the hypernet gate.

"What's she—?" Before Geary could finish the question, *Dreadnaught, Dependable, Intemperate*, and their escorts had come around again, charging at the Syndic warships pursuing them. The odds were still far too bad, though. He waited with a sick feeling, knowing that whatever had happened had taken place two hours ago.

Then the two groups of warships were diverging again, with no losses visible on either side. "She avoided them. They expected her to charge straight at them and instead she dodged enough to one side to avoid any hits on her force." Desjani was watching the display with an intrigued look. "Sir, *Dreadnaught* is deliberately avoiding the Syndics. She's figured out that as long as her warships are anywhere near that hypernet gate, the Syndics can't send the heavy cruisers to collapse it while the rest of them run, because *Dreadnaught* and her companions could finish off the heavy cruisers easily."

"Some of the Syndics would have to agree to a suicide mission," Geary agreed. "This isn't like at Lakota. Those ships know what will happen when they drop that gate. Could the Syndic reserve flotilla commander convince enough ships to stay near it anyway to protect against the *Dreadnaught* task force?"

"I doubt it. A small group of Special Forces commandos on suicide missions are one thing, but ships' crews? That's not in the job description."

He called down to Lieutenant Iger. "I need to know your

assessment of whether or not Syndic ships would knowingly undertake a suicide mission."

Iger shook his head. "Not typically, sir. Fighting to the death, yes. But Syndic ships usually are not known to conduct suicide missions." He paused. "There's something that may bear on this, sir. The Syndic prisoner aboard *Dauntless* has been receiving medical care. The doctors tell us she's traumatized by witnessing the destruction of Kalixa Star System and needs sedation to sleep."

"I'm not too surprised to hear that, Lieutenant," Geary said, "but how does that bear on the current situation?"

"Sir, remember that she told us that the Syndic CEOs in the reserve flotilla ordered her to send them copies of her cruiser's records of that event. That means Syndic officers in the reserve flotilla, some of them anyway, have seen the events at Kalixa that had such a strong impact on our prisoner."

"I see." If viewing the relatively less horrible scenes at Lakota had created revulsion in his own officers, what effect would viewing something worse have on the Syndics?

"I assume the reserve flotilla CEOs are keeping those records under wraps, though."

Iger smiled. "They're surely trying, sir. But Syndic systems are just like ours, riddled with back doors and unofficial subnets. You can't build and maintain nets that complex without creating the means for such things, and we know personnel in the Syndic forces exploit them just like our people do."

"So maybe a lot of Syndics in that flotilla have seen those records from Kalixa. Thank you, Lieutenant." He looked back to Rione and filled her and Desjani in on what Iger had said.

Desjani nodded when he finished. "I know seeing what happened at Lakota cured me of any lingering desire to collapse a gate using *Dauntless*."

"Can't the Syndic CEOs in command of the flotilla assume automated control of any ship?" Rione asked. "They did that at Sancere."

"They could," Geary agreed, "but the crews of those Syndic ships at Sancere managed to regain some control before they were destroyed. I think it's safe to assume the crews of these Syndic ships are primed to override any automatic controls. They already know the consequences if they don't."

"Then as long as *Dreadnaught* avoids destruction, we've got a chance," Desjani exulted.

"Looks like it." Geary sent another message to *Dreadnaught* summarizing their latest assessment. "I have to admit that I'm surprised that Jane Geary is avoiding engaging the Syndics. It's exactly what we need her to do, but it's not characteristic of, uh..."

"The way this fleet fought before you came back?" Desjani asked. "It isn't. We wondered why a Geary was in command of a battleship rather than a battle cruiser, remember? There's your answer. Insufficiently aggressive."

Meaning she thought about tactics instead of relying upon head-on charges against the enemy. *Dreadnaught* and *Dependable* were both living up to their names, but *Intemperate* wasn't. Geary felt a renewed hope that he'd get a chance to know Jane Geary. He checked the time remaining until the Alliance battle-cruiser force's arrival in the vicinity of the Syndic flotilla. Nineteen hours. "Captain Desjani, have we heard anything from the authorities in Varandal?"

"No, sir."

"Not even any 'garbled' messages?"

"No, sir. We haven't picked up any orders sent to *Dreadnaught*, either. It looks like they're going to let you run this battle."

"Lucky me. How much longer until the *Illustrious* task force shows up here, do you think?"

Desjani frowned in thought. "Another several hours at the earliest. After picking up the escape pods in Atalia, they couldn't accelerate up to anything near point one light without nearly draining their last fuel-cell reserves. Badaya's no genius, but he isn't stupid enough to do that."

Geary adjusted the courses of his battle cruisers to reflect the movements of the Syndics, then sent a similar adjustment to the battleships. There wasn't anything else he could do at the moment except watch the Syndics keep trying to engage the *Dreadnaught* task force while the Alliance ships kept dancing out of reach.

They were still ten hours from reaching the vicinity of the Syndic reserve flotilla when the Syndic CEO apparently lost all patience. The Syndic box formations came apart as nearly every ship within them went after the *Dreadnaught* task force independently. Only four Syndic battleships remained in a formation, positioned around ten heavy cruisers with a cluster of light cruisers and HuKs providing additional escort. "There are the heavy cruisers they're going to use against the gate. Dodging all of those other ships is going to be hard for *Dreadnaught*," Geary commented with a tight feeling inside. Against faster and more maneuverable battle cruisers, cruisers, and HuKs coming from multiple directions, battleships couldn't hope to evade for long.

The *Dreadnaught* task force didn't try. Instead, the Alliance defenders accelerated onto a vector aimed at the small Syndic battleship/heavy-cruiser formation, boring right through the swarm of Syndic combatants between themselves and their targets.

First one, then two, then three Alliance destroyers blew apart or reeled away, all systems dead. The sole light cruiser with *Dreadnaught* came apart under fire from a dozen Syndics racing past. An Alliance heavy cruiser shuddered as numerous missiles hit, then exploded. *Intemperate* took hit after hit, but kept going. Another destroyer shattered into fragments.

Then the Alliance task force was through the enemy throng and bearing down on the small Syndic formation.

The four Syndic battleships threw out missiles and grapeshot, but the Alliance ships had split and managed to avoid too many hits. Another Alliance heavy cruiser and two more destroyers blew up under the barrage, though.

The *Dreadnaught* task force tore through the Syndic formation, the battleships *Dreadnaught* and *Dependable* screening the battle cruiser *Intemperate* from the fire of the Syndic battleships, while every Alliance ship focused its fire on the Syndic heavy cruisers.

Geary watched the formations diverge, waiting with a sick feeling to see the display update as the fleet's sensors evaluated the results.

"Wow," Desjani commented. Eight of the ten Syndic heavy cruisers were gone, either blown apart or knocked out. "Give that woman command of a battle cruiser. So much for the Syndic plan. They're going to need to decrew some more heavy cruisers."

"Yeah." Geary shook his head as he looked at what was left of the *Dreadnaught* task force. *Dreadnaught* and *Dependable* had both taken damage but remained formidable. Hits to *Intemperate* had taken out almost half her weapons and slowed her to the point where she could just keep up with the battleships. Of the escorts, only two heavy cruisers and a sole destroyer had survived the latest firing pass. "She can't do that again."

"Maybe one more time," Desjani disagreed. "But only the two battleships would make it through. If she's smart, she'll try to avoid the Syndics for a while."

The mass of independently maneuvering Syndic warships had come around and was trying to intercept the *Dreadnaught* task force once more, but the diminished Alliance formation had kept on toward the hypernet gate. "It'll take them a while to catch those ships," Geary said, "but not nine hours." The engagements with Varandal's defenders before the fleet arrived had cost the Syndics as well as the Alliance. But after the latest clash, the reserve flotilla still boasted fourteen battleships, eleven battle cruisers, eight heavy cruisers, thirty-three light cruisers, and eighty-five HuKs. "Eight heavy cruisers left. Would that be enough for the Syndics to collapse the gate?"

"That depends how long they had to keep shooting." Desjani shook her head. "That CEO has got to be realizing that he or she can't stick with the original plan. *Dreadnaught* and her companions are buying us too much time. The Syndics are going to do something different."

Geary's unease suddenly crystallized. "They're going to try to defeat this formation, then take out our battleships when they get here. After that, they can take as long as they need to nail what's left of the *Dreadnaught* task force, then blow the gate at their leisure."

Desjani nodded. "It's what I'd do."

"But we don't have enough fuel-cell reserves to run rings around the Syndics until the battleships catch up."

"Do the Syndics know that?"

"Let's hope not."

Seven hours out. Four Syndic battleships had continued in pursuit of the *Dreadnaught* task force. The rest of the Syndic reserve flotilla was re-forming into the conventional box formation, the surviving heavy cruisers well protected in the center. Geary pondered options, knowing that if he tried ramming his battle cruisers through the center of that Syndic box to get the heavy cruisers he might succeed, but that none of his battle cruisers might survive to exit on the other side of the Syndic flotilla.

Six hours from contact. The Syndic reserve flotilla, its box formation tight and compact, turned toward the oncoming Alliance battle cruisers. "You called it, Captain Desjani. We're outnumbered two to one in capital ships, but more importantly with all those battleships, the Syndics have at least a three-to-one advantage in firepower and armor." His eyes went to the four Syndic battleships that had been chasing the *Dreadnaught* task force but had altered course to form a screen between the Alliance ships and the main Syndic formation.

It was as if Desjani read his mind. "Four battleships. We can take them."

"If we do it right." He looked at the position of the Alliance battleships, coming on steadily but over an hour behind the battle cruisers. Fuel-cell reserves were dwindling on every ship. Geary focused on *Rifle*, now at 6 percent reserves, the lowest in the fleet.

"I should have left *Rifle* at the jump point."

"Her crew would never have forgiven you."

He set up the approach carefully, adjusting the battle cruisers so they seemed to be heading straight for a clash with the Syndic box, bringing the battleships' vector over a little so they'd reach the Syndics at the right time, finding the right point at which to change course again.

"How much longer?" Rione asked. She'd been sitting so quietly for so long that it was easy to forget she was there at the back of the bridge.

"The Syndics are coming at us now," Geary explained "Two hours, forty minutes to contact, give or take a few. They'll get their surprise at two hours, twenty minutes."

"They may expect it," Desjani pointed out. "*Dreadnaught*'s been doing the same thing."

"Good point. We'll dodge in an unusual way."

At one hour from contact, the *Dreadnaught* task force had altered course to close the four Syndic battleships, which in turn had come around to confront the small Alliance task force. With *Dreadnaught* only about fifteen lightminutes distant, Geary sent more orders. "Captain Geary, this is... Captain Geary. Avoid closing on the four Syndic battleships at this time. We're coming that way and will see if we can even up the odds for you."

No acknowledgment came back even though the transit times for messages between *Dreadnaught* and *Dauntless* were only fifteen minutes each way now. With less than half an hour to contact with the Syndic reserve flotilla, Geary couldn't spend time worrying about whether or not Jane Geary would do as directed. "All units in Alliance formation Indigo One. We're going to bypass the main Syndic formation this time, hit those four battleships, then come back and hit the flotilla. Save your remaining expendable munitions for the firing pass against the flotilla."

Twenty minutes to contact, the Syndic reserve flotilla and the Alliance battle cruisers were only four lightminutes apart as they tore toward each other at a combined pace of point two light speed, the Syndics having cut their velocity to point six light speed to keep relativistic distortion from reducing their chances of hitting the Alliance warships. Geary waited, not yet happy with the maneuvering solution.

Fifteen minutes to contact. Ten minutes. "All units in Formation Indigo One, turn port two zero degrees, down one five degrees at time zero four zero nine."

The Alliance battle cruisers and their escorts yawed left, away from the star Varandal, and down, aiming below the plane of the star system. It had literally taken a minute for the Syndics to see the light showing the Alliance fleet dodging, by which time the two forces were less than seven minutes from contact. Geary tapped his controls again.

"All units in Formation Indigo One, turn up two zero degrees at time zero four one three."

The Syndics would be altering course themselves, angling down and to the side to intercept the Alliance battle cruisers, but the battle cruisers were already bending their track upward as the minutes to contact spiraled down to seconds. "The Syndics have fired missiles and grapeshot," the combat-systems watch reported.

The Syndic firing pattern had been aimed at where the Alliance force was going, and had assumed that if they evaded further, it would be to continue downward at a steeper rate. As a result, the Syndic weapons shot by well beneath the Alliance battle cruisers as Geary leveled them out again, aimed at the four isolated Syndic battleships.

Behind the Alliance battle cruisers, the Syndic flotilla's box began coming around so hard that a light cruiser suddenly came apart under the stress as its inertial compensators overloaded.

"Make them mad, make them stupid," Desjani commented. "You know, not too long ago I would have been really upset at just playing tag with these guys instead of hitting them head-on, but imagining what that Syndic CEO is saying right now is great compensation."

"Thanks." The four Syndic battleships would be waking up to their peril right now, realizing that twelve battle cruisers were coming straight for them from one angle while the *Dreadnaught* task force was boring in from the opposite direction as well. "This is what happens when a commander keeps compromising in an attempt to follow an original plan even though the situation is changing drastically. That CEO never should have split his forces that way instead of focusing on either us or the *Dreadnaught* task force."

The Syndic reserve flotilla was still coming around fifteen minutes later when the Alliance battle cruisers braked heavily down to point one light speed and swept past the four Syndic battleships, hammering the closest battleships with repeated volleys of hell-lances, followed by null fields from the rearmost battle cruisers.

"Two down," Desjani announced triumphantly as one of the Syndic battleships exploded and the second drifted helpless. *Dauntless* was still shaking from several hits on her shields.

Despite the overwhelming local superiority in Alliance firepower, *Leviathan*, *Implacable*, and *Brilliant* had taken significant damage, too. "*Dreadnaught*, the other two battleships are yours for now," Geary sent as he brought the Alliance battle cruisers around again.

As the battle cruisers steadied out on a vector aimed at the Syndic reserve flotilla's box, which was coming back toward them at a full point one light speed, an alarm sounded on *Dauntless*'s bridge. "Captain, we just hit ten percent on fuel-cell reserves," the engineering watch reported. "The ship's maneuvering and combat systems are recommending we disengage and refuel immediately."

"Why didn't I think of that?" Desjani remarked sarcastically. "The systems' recommendation is noted."

"Uh, Captain, the systems are warning that if their recommendation is disregarded they will enter an automatic note in the log that the commanding officer is hazarding the ship."

"Tell the systems where they can stick their warning, Lieutenant."

"Captain? How—?"

"Use the override!" Desjani glanced at Geary. "You might want to try wrapping up this battle before too much longer."

"I'll see what I can do." Ahead, the Syndic reserve flotilla was coming on fast. Behind the Syndic box, the Alliance battleship formation was closing the distance to the engagement.

"The *Dreadnaught* task force is engaging the two isolated Syndic battleships, but they're trying to rejoin the main Syndic formation."

The Syndic box still contained ten battleships and eleven battle cruisers, though two of the battle cruisers had taken beatings earlier. Six of the battleships were in the center, around the remaining heavy cruisers, with the other four posted one to a corner along with either two or three battle cruisers.

Judging from the movements of the Syndic flotilla, which showed that its commander was angry and frustrated enough to be reckless and impulsive, Geary duplicated his previous dodge down and to the left, but then brought the battle cruisers up and right enough to aim for where a corner of the Syndic box should pass if its commander assumed the Alliance ships were trying the same maneuver.

The maneuver worked, the Syndic missiles and grapeshot this time passing over the track of the Alliance battle cruisers as they flashed into contact with a corner of the Syndic box anchored on one battleship and two battle cruisers.

The opposing forces shot past each other in a fraction of a second, automated systems aiming and firing. As they drew apart again, Geary saw that the two Syndic battle cruisers were out of action and the battleship significantly damaged.

It took him a second longer to notice the gap in the Alliance formation. The gap where *Furious* had been. Back where the forces had engaged, a spreading cloud of fragments marked her remains.

Desjani's voice came out flat. "They must have concentrated their fire on *Furious*. She suffered a core overload. Nobody could have gotten off. Damn."

For a moment Geary had visions of Captain Jaylen Cresida as he'd first seen her, in the Syndic home system, unhesitatingly backing him against the opposition and doubts of others, and as he'd last seen her in Atalia, with the design she'd created to save humanity from its own follies in building the hypernet without understanding the risks posed by the gates.

Then he shook it off. *Not now.* There'd be time to grieve later. "*Dragon* is seriously damaged, and *Implacable* took more hits." Eleven battle cruisers left and half of them with seriously degraded capability owing to damage.

Geary's eyes went to his battleships, one light-minute distant as the Syndic box came around again. Eighteen of them, with plenty of escorts. His mind worked instinctively to adjust the vector of the battleships given the small time delay remaining between them and *Dauntless*. "Formation Indigo Two, come right zero zero three degrees, down zero two degrees."

The Syndic flotilla commander, focused on the Alliance battle cruisers, must have been rudely shocked when he or she realized that the Alliance battleships had reached the engagement. The Syndic box had barely steadied out to pursue the Alliance battle cruisers again when the Alliance battleships went through one side of it, their massive firepower ripping into the two Syndic battleships and six Syndic battle cruisers anchoring the flotilla there.

In the wake of the Alliance battleships, all eight Syndic capital ships were knocked out, some of the battle cruisers literally blown apart in vengeful counterpoint to the fate of *Furious*.

But Geary's jubilation was cut short by a report from the operations watch. "*Rifle* has exhausted her fuel cells. Her power core has shut down. *Culverin's* power core has begun shutting down. The rest of the Twenty-third Destroyer Squadron has less than five minutes' power estimated remaining. The ships of the Eighth Light Cruiser Squadron report fuel-cell exhaustion and power-core shutdowns imminent."

On the display, the two Alliance destroyers were drifting, their primary systems off, helpless. "How long can the emergency backups maintain life support?" Geary asked.

"Twelve hours," Desjani replied immediately. "I thought we might need to know that. This engagement should be decided before then."

"Damn right." He ordered the battleships back around, watching their formation shed increasing numbers of power-deprived destroyers and light cruisers, whose momentum was carrying them along the former track of the Alliance ships.

He felt everyone's eyes on him, and he didn't have to view the fleet-status readout to know how close his battle cruisers and battleships were to running out of fuel cells, too. At that point the Alliance's advantage in numbers would be meaningless as almost all of its ships in Varandal would be sitting ducks.

The Syndics were between the Alliance battle cruisers and the Alliance battleships now, the battle cruisers between the Syndics and the jump point for Atalia, but the Syndics weren't making any major course alterations, just trying to re-form their flotilla's box after its side had been smashed in.

"They have to know we're running out of fuel cells," Desjani muttered.

"They've only seen escorts run out. We have to make them think our capital ships still have plenty of reserves." Geary punched his controls. "Formation Indigo One, immediate execute come left one nine zero degrees, up zero one two degrees, accelerate to point zero six light speed." *Dauntless*'s structure groaned as the ship whipped around in as tight a turn as the inertial compensators could handle. All around her, the remaining Alliance battle cruisers followed suit, steadying out aimed at the still-ragged side of the Syndic box. "Concentrate fire on the leading Syndic ships!"

They blew past the edge of the Syndics, *Dauntless* shuddering again from hits. "*Valiant* reports heavy damage. *Daring* has lost all weapons but hell-lance battery three bravo and her null-field generator. *Implacable* has lost propulsion and maneuvering control."

Geary kept his eyes on the display, watching the results of the latest firing pass. One of the surviving Syndic battleships had been pounded into scrap, and the single Syndic battle cruiser wearing toward that side of the formation was gone.

The Alliance battleships were coming around, Geary's display flashing warnings about their low fuel-cell reserves, but to all external appearances still a hammer ready to bludgeon the Syndics again. The Alliance battle cruisers, now on the same side of the Syndics as the battleship formation, kept on toward the Alliance battleships as more light cruisers and destroyers fell away not from damage but from core shutdowns. *Dreadnaught*, *Dependable*, and *Intemperate* were only two light-minutes distant now, but though they had plenty of fuel-cell reserves, all three ships had suffered from their earlier encounters with the enemy.

Another alert pulsed. Geary's eyes went to the flashing symbol on his display. "Friendly ships at the jump point from Atalia. We just got light showing the arrival of the *Illustrious* task force." He looked back at the Syndics, waiting to see their reactions.

They swung a short way right, then accelerated, leaving some crippled ships behind to spit out escape pods. "They're running." Desjani was grinning. "They saw the ships with *Illustrious* but haven't evaluated how damaged they are. The Syndics just saw more Alliance battleships and battle cruisers arriving, they see us behind them looking ready to kick their butts again and positioned between them and the hypernet gate, and they're *running*."

He couldn't believe it, watching to see if the Syndics turned again, but they kept going, accelerating as fast as they could. Seven Syndic battleships and two battle cruisers, with their surviving escorts, heading for the jump point for Atalia like bats out of hell.

"Tenth Light Cruiser Squadron and Third Destroyer Squadron report all ships reaching fuel-cell exhaustion. Heavy cruiser *Camail* reports fuel-cell exhaustion."

Desjani began laughing, and Geary looked at her in amazement.

She was pointing to her ship's fuel-cell reserve status, which was fluctuating between 1 and 2 percent. Abruptly Desjani stopped laughing and made an abortive lunge toward him, then caught herself, made a fist, and swung a punch onto Geary's shoulder. "*You did it!* By the grace of the living stars you did it!"

"*We* did it," Geary corrected, rubbing his shoulder and suddenly feeling on the verge of hysterical laughter himself. "Everyone in this fleet." He became aware of cheers resonating through *Dauntless*'s hull. The crew celebrating.

For a moment Geary felt his memories of *Merlon*'s last moments crowding in again. He hadn't been able to save his heavy cruiser, he hadn't been able to get her crew home. No matter what anyone else said of the battle at Grendel, long ago for them and all too recent for him, he had always felt that he had failed. Failed his ship. Failed his crew. But not this time.

"Sir?" Desjani asked, still grinning but now puzzled as she looked at him. "Is something wrong?"

He smiled back. "No, Tanya. I was just remembering something." Somehow he knew that even if the flashbacks to *Merlon*'s last moments came again, they would never hold the same pain.

"Captain?" the operations watch reported. "There are three fast transports towing some construction platforms on their way toward the hypernet gate."

Desjani sobered, taking a deep breath. "Captain Cresida's safe-fail system. They're getting it installed. May your ancestors welcome you with the honor you deserve, Jaylen. Say hello to Roge for me."

"Her husband?" Geary asked, trying to control his voice. The stress and emotions of the moment, good and bad, felt almost overwhelming.

"Yeah. Ever since he died she'd always been sure he'd be waiting for her." Desjani wiped one eye with a rough gesture and turned to her watch-standers. "Initiate maximum energy conservation measures until we get more fuel cells aboard."

Stung into remembering more critical tasks left to do immediately, Geary hit his controls. "All units in the Alliance fleet, brake down velocity as much as possible without going below one percent fuel reserves." He called up another circuit. "All Alliance assets within Varandal Star System, this is Captain John Geary, acting commander of the Alliance fleet. The fleet's ships are extremely low on fuel cells. Some of our ships have already been forced to shut down their power cores. Request all available assets assist in providing fuel cells to the fleet's ships on a maximum-priority basis. To the honor of our ancestors. Geary out."

Another message. "*Dreadnaught*, shadow the retreating Syndics with your task force." *Dreadnaught* wouldn't be able to catch the Syndics with the lead the fleeing enemy had, but it wouldn't hurt to keep the Syndics under a little pressure.

One more. "Captain Badaya, the Syndics are fleeing toward the Atalia jump point. They may try to sweep you up on their way out. Avoid contact with them. We'll get them all another day, and I want the ships with you along with the fleet when we do."

Rione had been sitting still, staring blankly before her, but she finally came out of her daze, looking at Geary as if not sure what she was seeing. "Congratulations. The fight's not over, but you've already done the impossible."

The war wasn't over, but the Lost Fleet was home.

Geary stood in his stateroom, facing the display now centered on Varandal, the ships of the fleet orbiting in a swarm about the star. For the first time since he'd assumed command of the fleet, it was in friendly territory with no immediate threat to its existence. The planets and cities and facilities he saw would help the fleet, not pose a danger to it.

Twenty-four hours had made a big difference. Two hours ago the retreating Syndics had jumped out of Varandal, still running as if the demon from inside a black hole was pursuing them. While the Syndics still fled, in the wake of Geary's message for assistance, spacecraft of all types had swarmed out from Varandal's worlds, colonies, and orbital facilities hauling what ever fuel cells they could carry. Now none of his ships were in danger of running out of fuel cells, and those that had run out were powered up again. The most badly damaged warships were already reaching the extensive space docks and repair facilities Varandal boasted.

He felt a heaviness inside thinking about the warships and sailors who had died on the very threshold of home. *Furious* hadn't been the only loss, though it had struck him most deeply. The heavy cruisers *Kaidate* and *Quillion* had sustained too much damage to be saved, the light cruisers *Estocade*, *Disarm*, and *Cavalier* had been blown apart during the battle cruisers' firing passes against the Syndics, and the destroyers *Serpentine*, *Basilisk*, *Bowie*, *Guidon*, and *Sten* had either been shattered or exploded during the engagement. Those had just been the ships attached to the fleet, not counting those that had died in the earlier defensive battles at Varandal and alongside *Dreadnaught*. And it didn't include the sailors killed or wounded on ships that had "only" been damaged during the battle. Numerous other warships would only be saved because they had been so badly hurt in friendly space.

But the fleet was home. Not exactly safe, and too many ships, men, and women had been lost along the way, but it was home.

There'd been a time when he'd imagined this moment and seen himself gratefully relinquishing command of the fleet. Exactly what he would have done then had always been vague. Aside from a wistful desire to see the planet Kosatka again, Geary hadn't had any idea where he might find any peace or refuge from the legend of Black Jack.

That had changed. He'd seen where duty led, where honor required him to go, and he'd sworn an oath to someone who mattered a great deal to him. He could still try to walk away from it, try to leave behind his concepts of honor and duty, cast aside his promise. But if he did, the killing would surely go on, the war would continue as it had for decade upon decade, and he would lose the one thing, the one person, whose presence made this hard and violent future a place where he nonetheless wanted to be.

Looked at that way, the decision wasn't all that hard. Perhaps he was being delusional, suffering from the Geary Syndrome doctors had defined in decades past, believing only he could save the Alliance. But people he trusted told him he was the only one with a chance to end the war. He believed them in everything else. He had no choice but to believe them in this.

So he looked on the fleet and wondered if he could retain command of it and convince his superiors of what needed to be done.

"It was worse than I feared," Rione was saying. "My contacts here say that in the last few months, as the Syndics broadcast claims that they'd destroyed the fleet and word leaked out that the fleet actually was presumed lost in enemy territory, civil disobedience and demonstrations erupted in a great many star systems. The people of the Alliance are losing hope." She paused. "They *were* losing hope. If Varandal is any measure, your return with the fleet is generating tremendous optimism."

"Great." He remembered some of the public newscasts he'd seen relayed from the cities on Varandal's inhabited worlds, happy faces declaring the latest information they'd been able to acquire. *Officially, the military and the government refuse to confirm anything, but our contacts within the fleet have assured us that the rumors are true! Black Jack has returned just as legend foretold! He saved the fleet! He saved Varandal! Can he save the Alliance as well? After his miraculous return, anything seems possible for the hero of the Alliance!*

Followed by images of tense official spokespersons. *The government has nothing to add at this time.*

What about the messages Captain Geary transmitted during the fight with the Syndics at Varandal?

The government has no comment at this time.

What about the statements from Syndic prisoners from the flotilla that attacked Varandal that Black Jack Geary led the fleet through the heart of the Syndicate Worlds and almost totally destroyed their naval forces?

The government will provide more information when it is available.

The broadcast from the fleet about the threat posed by hypernet gates has caused considerable concern. Can you confirm that the safe-fail system described in it has been installed at Varandal?

The hypernet gate at Varandal is safe. For security reasons we cannot provide any further details.

Observations of the hypernet gate here do reveal that some new equipment has been very recently installed. Can you comment on that?

No. The hypernet gate is safe.

"Why doesn't the government just admit what everybody knows?" Geary asked. "This way they just look stupid."

"Governments often end up looking stupid when they try to control information. I hope you're not expecting me to defend their approach this time. Given the number of ships that have left Varandal by jump and hypernet since your arrival, the news must be spreading at a phenomenal rate. And it is good news," Rione insisted. "The Alliance needs hope, and you embody that hope. Don't bother looking annoyed. You know it's true, no matter how irrational you think it is. By definition, hope usually is irrational."

"I guess I can't complain about that, considering what I intend proposing to the government," Geary admitted. "I'm not sure it qualifies as rational."

"Are you still planning on asking for permission to lead the fleet back to the Syndic home star system?"

"Yes, when I get somebody to talk to me." Geary turned to look at her. "Any idea how long that will be?"

"It's hard to say." Rione appeared thoughtful. "It's possible the grand council itself will come here to speak with you."

"That's ridiculous."

"No, it's not." She exhaled in exasperation. "You're more powerful than they are. You have to realize that and yet not act as if it is true. They need to see you, hear you in person, decide if you're a threat to the Alliance or its deliverance. If the grand council comes here, you and I can convince them that you're not that threat and get approval for the attack on the Syndics. Even I can see that your plan isn't irrational. I thought Bloch's plan was unlikely to succeed, but after all of the damage inflicted on the Syndics, if you can get approval within a short time to strike at the heads of the Syndicate Worlds, there's a chance we might decapitate the beast. But it has to be soon, and it has to be a swift victory. If it's drawn out long enough for the Syndics to rebuild their own force of warships, I foresee renewed stalemate until both governments collapse."

Geary nodded. "That's a real possibility. How do you think they'll take the news of the aliens?"

"Poorly. But we have strong evidence. They'll understand that we need to deal with the aliens as well as the Syndics, and as soon as possible. We have no idea what other attractive traps the aliens could come up with."

"The aliens have to know that another Kalixa will cost them dearly, and I wouldn't mind making them pay for Kalixa. I'll do my best to convince our leaders, then win that victory over the Syndics so we can go have a firm talk backed up by substantial firepower with the aliens."

"If recent history is any measure, your best may well suffice." Rione turned to leave, but as she opened the hatch Desjani was just arriving. The two women passed with impassive glances and no words.

"Captain Geary." Desjani walked to his comm panel and activated it. "You'll recall those garbled messages I didn't want you to be bothered with. One came through clearly a short time ago." She punched receive, and Geary saw an admiral with an outwardly placid expression but nervous eyes gazing out.

"This is Admiral Timbale with a personal communication for Captain John Geary. Everyone in Varandal and the Alliance is naturally overjoyed at your return with the fleet. Overjoyed and... uh... astounded." The admiral hastily looked slightly to one side.

"He got off script," Desjani murmured.

Geary gave her a sardonic look. "Just how did you happen to see a message marked personal for me?"

"I'm the captain of this ship," she reminded him. "That doesn't make me a god within the confines of *Dauntless*, but it's damned close to that. You'd better listen to the admiral."

"You are to remain in command of the fleet until further notice," Admiral Timbale continued. "Those warships in Varandal not previously assigned to the fleet are hereby officially transferred to your control." The admiral flashed an anxious smile. "You have full authority and top priority for arranging resupply and repair of your... of the fleet's ships."

The admiral hesitated again for a moment. "In light of your many responsibilities at the moment and the continuing imminent attack alert within Varandal, the normal courtesy call on your superior officer is waived. I'll let you know when we can arrange a meeting. Until then, I hope Varandal can provide everything the fleet needs. Timbale, out."

Geary frowned at the comm panel. "He doesn't want to meet with me?"

"He's probably afraid to," Desjani remarked. "If he does, he might be accused of plotting with you to overthrow the government. Or he's afraid you might ask his help in that. Or demand it. Or he might offer his support for a coup and find out that Black Jack's loyalty to the Alliance wasn't overstated at all. Avoiding meeting with you and avoiding talking to you is far safer for him."

"Hell. After all the times I didn't want to deal with admirals and had to, now when I need to talk to one, he won't talk to me. Is Timbale the senior admiral at Varandal?"

"He's the only admiral left at Varandal," Desjani explained. "As you'll recall, the battles at Atalia and here before we arrived were pretty hard on the admirals commanding the Alliance warships. Tagos died at Atalia and Tethys here. That just leaves Timbale."

"Tagos, Tethys, and Timbale all assigned to Varandal," Geary grumbled. "Why do I suspect the personnel assignment bureau was playing one of its silly games again? Do they still do that?"

"They do." She rolled her eyes. "One ship a few years back kept getting officers with the same last name. More than once I've vowed that if the war ever ended, I'd drop big rocks on the personnel bureau on my way home."

"I'll help."

Desjani waved at the display. "At least you've formally picked up some new ships. Not many escorts survived among the Varandal defenders, but you've got two more battleships now and another battle cruiser. *Dreadnaught*, *Dependable*, and *Intemperate* are all beat to hell, but that just means they'll fit in with the rest of the fleet."

"Yeah, I guess they will. If I can't talk to any admirals, at least with these orders we can get the fleet back in shape as fast as possible. Can I oversee that with the automated systems available?"

Desjani shook her head. "That's too many worms crawling in too many directions. Just tracking repairs on the capital ships is going to be hard. Keeping a handle on work being done on the destroyers is going to be a nightmare given how many there are and how little time we have. Even with every automated assistant available, you'll still need human assistance in tracking things. I recommend drawing on some of the engineering officers on the auxiliaries, but with *Dauntless* not facing the immediate prospect of battle, I can second you a few officers to help out here."

"That won't be a problem?"

"Not at all, sir," Desjani assured him. "My junior officers love extra challenges." The edges of her lips quivered, but she managed to suppress a smile.

"I bet they do. I know how much I loved them when I was a junior officer." Geary stared at the stars, trying to get his mind around everything that needed to be done. "Is there anything else?"

"We've confirmed that a basic form of Captain Cresida's safe-fail system has been installed already on the hypernet gate here. The more sophisticated version is being prepared. We can't know how the information package Cresida put together is being received in other star systems, but the quick response here is a good sign. The safe-fail design should be spreading exponentially through the hypernet, and from what we've seen in public sources within this star system the images from Lakota are scaring the hell out of people."

"Good. Very good. What about the Syndic hypernet key?"

"It's off *Dauntless* and was delivered to a key-fabrication facility on the habitable world here. They should be duplicating it as we speak."

He shook his head. "I can't believe we got it here. But we're going to need that Syndic hypernet key."

"Which is why we're going to get it back," Desjani added, earning an approving look from Geary. "Once all of the manufacturing data has been confirmed, they'll be returning the Syndic hypernet key to *Dauntless*. Estimated time to return is thirty-six hours. We won't have to keep its location on board a secret anymore, because the Alliance will be able to build as many copies as we want. But we'll have the original again."

"That's great. I was afraid I'd have to kick up a storm to get the thing back." He looked down, steeling himself for the next question. "There haven't been any other messages for me?"

"No, sir. The only messages we've received from *Dreadnaught* were official status updates. Sir." Geary glanced over at her. "She needs time. Jane Geary has to adjust to everything. Then she'll respond to your personal messages."

He closed his eyes for a moment. "We may not have a lot of time."

"Everyone knows that, including her. Remember that Michael Geary had weeks to learn to deal with the fact that you were still alive before you first spoke with him."

Geary opened his eyes but kept them on the stars. "And he still hated me."

"Not at the end! You told me that. I have had communications from *Dreadnaught* monitored in a few unauthorized ways, and I know her commanding officer has been contacting some of the other commanding officers in this fleet. Officers whom Jane Geary knows. Officers whom know you. They'll be telling her about you, about who you really are. Give her time, and she will contact you."

"Those other officers are telling her that I left her brother in the Syndic home star system, and that he's likely dead."

Desjani took a step closer, her voice getting sharper. "Jane Geary is a fleet officer. She knew the risks as well as the rest of us, the same risks we all run. She can't blame you for her brother's death in combat, if that happened."

He breathed a short, sad laugh. "You're assuming she's going to address the issue logically."

"And may the living stars forbid that any Geary act logically!" Desjani shook her head. "Biologically you're younger than she is even though you're her great-uncle. You're the mountain that has shadowed her entire life. *Give her time.*"

"Okay. It's not like I won't have plenty to keep me busy while I wait."

"That's right." Desjani looked around. "Do you want me to bring the junior officers to your stateroom so you can start coordinating repair and resupply activity? There's room here."

"Sure. How soon?"

"Give me half an hour to find a couple of junior officers who seem underemployed." She studied him for a moment. "Have you prayed to your ancestors yet on Jaylen Cresida's behalf?"

Geary felt a stab of guilt. With so much else going on, that had kept being forgotten or pushed aside. "Not formally, no."

"Why don't you go down to the places of worship and do that while you're waiting for me to get back here?"

The suggestion sounded more like an order, but that didn't mean it wasn't a good idea and an overdue obligation. For Jaylen Cresida in particular, and for a lot of other sailors who had fallen in this latest engagement. "Yes. I'll do that." He headed for the hatch along with her.

Desjani faced him before walking away, though. "We're still going back, right?"

"As soon as we can," Geary agreed. "If I can get approval for it." He remembered Rione's words, which summarized the situation perfectly. "We have to win swiftly, or we won't win at all."

"Then we'll win swiftly."

"Yeah. We will."

Or die trying.

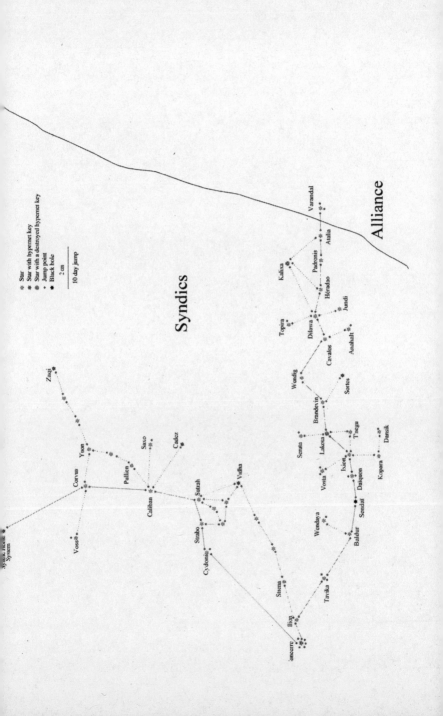

* Star
* Star with hypernet key
* Star with a destroyed hypernet key
• Jump point
* Black hole

2 cm

10 day jump

Syndics

Alliance

Ziaqi
Yuon
Corvus
Saxo
Pullien
Cadez
Voss
Caliban
Sutrah
Strabo
Vidha
Cydonia
Strena
Ilion
Simcerre
Tarika
Wendova
Baldur
Sendai
Kopara
Dansik
Daiquon
Vesta
Ixion
Taegu
Lakota
Seruta
Brandevin
Wendig
Sortes
Cavalos
Anahalt
Jundi
Dilawa
Topira
Heradao
Padronis
Kalixa
Atalia
Varandal

Syndic Home
System

ACKNOWLEDGMENTS

I remain indebted to my agent, Joshua Bilmes, for his ever-inspired suggestions and assistance; to my editor, Anne Sowards, for her support and editing; and to Cameron Dufty at Ace, for her help and assistance. Thanks also to Catherine Asaro, Robert Chase, J. G. (Huck) Huckenpohler, Simcha Kuritzky, Michael LaViolette, Aly Parsons, Bud Sparhawk, and Constance A. Warner, for their suggestions, comments, and recommendations. Thanks also to Charles Petit, for his suggestions about space engagements.

Read on for an extract from the next book in the series:

The Lost Fleet: Victorious

1

He had faced death many times and would cheerfully do so again rather than attend this briefing.

"You're not going to face a firing squad," Captain Tanya Desjani reminded him. "You're going to brief the Alliance grand council."

Captain John Geary turned his head slightly to look directly at Captain Desjani, commanding officer of Geary's flagship, the battle cruiser *Dauntless*. "Remind me again of the difference."

"The politicians aren't supposed to be carrying weapons, and they're more afraid of you than you are of them. Relax. If they see you this tense, they'll believe you really are planning a coup." Desjani made a face. "You should know that they're accompanied by Admiral Otropa."

"Admiral Otropa?" Geary had literally been out of the loop for a century, so his knowledge of current officers was limited to those in the ships of the fleet itself.

Desjani nodded, somehow investing the simple gesture with

disdain that obviously wasn't aimed at Geary.

"Military aide to the grand council. Don't worry about the grand council trying to hand command of the fleet to him. No one would accept Otropa the Anvil as fleet commander in place of you."

Geary looked back at his reflection, feeling nervous and uncomfortable in his dress uniform. He had never enjoyed briefings, and a hundred years ago he would never have imagined that he would be called upon personally to brief the grand council. "The Anvil? That sounds like a strong nickname."

"He's called the Anvil because he's been beaten so often," Desjani explained. "With his political talents far exceeding his military skills, Otropa finally figured out that the position of military aide to the grand council was risk-free."

Geary almost choked as he tried to swallow a laugh. "I guess there are worse nicknames than Black Jack."

"Many worse ones." Out of the corner of his eye, Geary saw Desjani cock her head to one side questioningly. "You've never told me how you picked up the Black Jack name or why you don't like it. Like every schoolkid in the Alliance, I learned the official story in your biographies, but that story doesn't explain your feelings about the nickname."

He glanced her way. "What's the official story?" Since being awakened from survival sleep in a lost and damaged escape pod, he'd made an effort to avoid reading the authorized accounts of his supposed heroic nature.

"That you never got a red deficiency or failure mark in evaluations of yourself or any units under your command," Desjani explained. "Your marks were always 'meets or exceeds expectations' black, hence Black Jack."

"Ancestors preserve us." Geary tried to keep from breaking into laughter. "Anyone who really looked at my records would know that wasn't true."

"So what is the truth?"

"I should have at least one secret from you."

"As long as it's a personal secret. The captain of your flagship needs to know all of your professional secrets." She paused before speaking again. "This meeting with the grand council. Have you told me everything? Are you going to do as you told me?"

"Yes, and yes." He turned to face her fully, letting his worries show. As commander of the fleet, Geary had been forced to project confidence publicly no matter how bad things got. Desjani was one of the few people to whom he could reveal his qualms. "It'll be a tightrope act. I need to convince them of what we have to do, convince them to order me to do it, and not make them think I'm taking over the government."

Desjani nodded, seeming not the least bit concerned herself. "You'll do fine, sir. I'll go make sure everything is ready at the shuttle dock for your flight to Ambaru station while you straighten up your uniform." She saluted with careful precision, then pivoted and left.

Geary kept his eyes on the hatch to his stateroom after it had shut behind Desjani. He'd have the perfect professional relationship with Tanya Desjani except for the fact that he'd done the incredibly unprofessional thing of falling in love with her. Not that he'd ever openly said that, or ever would. Not while she was his subordinate. It didn't help that she apparently felt the same way about him, even though neither of them could openly speak of it or act on it in any way. That should have felt like a small problem in a universe a century removed from his own, where the Alliance believed him to be a mythical hero returned from the dead, where an unwinnable war had been raging for that entire century between the Alliance and the Syndicate Worlds, and where the worn-out citizens of the Alliance were so disgusted with their own political leaders that they would have welcomed him declaring himself dictator. Sometimes, though, that "small" personal problem felt like the hardest thing to endure.

He focused back on his reflection, not able to spot any imperfections in his uniform but knowing that Desjani wouldn't have dropped that broad hint about straightening up if she hadn't seen something. Scowling, Geary moved a few things a fraction of a millimeter, his eyes going to the multipointed Alliance Star hanging just beneath his collar. He didn't like wearing the medal awarded him after his supposed death in a last-stand battle a century ago, not feeling that he had really earned such an honor, but regulations demanded that an officer in dress uniform wear "all insignia, decorations, awards, ribbons, and medals to which that officer is entitled." He couldn't afford to pick and choose which regulations to follow because he knew that he had the power to do just that, and if he started, he had no idea where it might end.

As he began to leave, his comm alert sounded. Geary slapped the acknowledgment and saw the image of Captain Badaya appear, smiling confidently and apparently standing before Geary even though Badaya was physically still located aboard his own ship. "Good morning, Captain." Badaya beamed.

"Thanks. I was just about to leave to meet with the grand council."
He had to handle Badaya carefully. Although Badaya technically
was simply commanding officer of the battle cruiser *Illustrious*,
he also led the faction of the fleet that would, without a second
thought, back Geary as military dictator. Since that faction made
up almost the entire fleet now, Geary had to ensure they didn't
launch such a coup. Since assuming command of the fleet, he had
gone from worrying about mutiny against himself to worrying
about mutiny against the Alliance itself in his name.

Badaya nodded, his smile getting harder. "Some of the captains
wanted to move some battleships over near Ambaru station just to
remind the grand council who's really in charge, but I told them
that wasn't how you were playing it."

"Exactly," Geary agreed, trying not to sound too relieved. "We
have to maintain the image that the grand council is still in charge."
That was the cover story he was using with Badaya anyway. If the
grand council ordered Geary to do something the fleet knew Geary
wouldn't have chosen to do, Geary would feel obligated to follow
those orders or resign, and all hell would probably break loose.

"Rione will help you handle them," Badaya noted with a
dismissive gesture. "You've got her in your pocket, and she'll keep
the other politicians in line. Since you say time is tight, I'd better
let you go, sir." With a final parting grin and a salute, Badaya's
image vanished.

Geary shook his head, wondering what Madam Co-President of
the Callas Republic and Senator of the Alliance Victoria Rione
would do if she heard Badaya saying Rione was in Geary's pocket.
Nothing good, that was certain.

He walked through the passageways of *Dauntless* toward the shuttle dock, returning enthusiastic salutes from the crew members he passed. *Dauntless* had been his flagship since he'd assumed command of the fleet in the Syndic home star system, the Alliance fleet trapped deep inside enemy territory and apparently doomed. Against all odds, he'd brought most of those ships home, and their crews believed he could do anything. Even win a war their parents and grandparents had also fought. He did his best to look outwardly calm and confident despite his own internal turmoil.

But Geary couldn't help frowning slightly as he finally reached the shuttle dock. Desjani and Rione were both there, standing close together and apparently speaking softly to each other, their expressions impassive. Since the two women usually exchanged words only under the direst necessity and often had seemed ready to go at it with knives, pistols, hell lances, and any other available weapon, Geary couldn't help wondering why they were getting along all of a sudden.

Desjani stepped toward him as he approached, while Rione went through the hatch into the dock. "The shuttle and your escort are ready," Desjani reported. She frowned slightly as she examined him, reaching to make tiny adjustments to some of his ribbons. "The fleet will be standing by."

"Tanya, I'm counting on you, Duellos, and Tulev to keep things from going nova. Badaya should be working with you to keep anyone in the fleet from overreacting and causing a disaster, but you three also need to make sure Badaya doesn't overreact."

She nodded calmly. "Of course, sir. But you do realize that none of us will be able to hold things back if the grand council overreacts." Stepping closer, Desjani lowered her voice and rested one hand on his forearm, a rare gesture, which emphasized her words. "Listen to her. This is her battlefield, her weapons."

"Rione?" He had never expected to hear Desjani urging him to pay attention to Rione's advice.

"Yes." Stepping back again, Desjani saluted, only her eyes betraying her worries. "Good luck, sir."

He returned the salute and walked into the dock. Nearby, the bulk of a fleet shuttle loomed, an entire platoon of Marines forming an honor guard on either side of its loading ramp.

An entire platoon of Marines in full battle armor, with complete weapons loadout.

Before he could say anything, a Marine major stepped forward and saluted. "I'm assigned to command your honor guard, Captain Geary. We'll accompany you to the meeting with the grand council."

"Why are your troops in battle armor?" Geary asked.

The major didn't hesitate at all. "Varandal Star System remains in Attack Imminent alert status, sir. Regulations require my troops to be at maximum combat readiness when participating in official movements under such an alert status."

How convenient. Geary glanced toward Rione, who didn't seem the least bit surprised at the combat footing of the Marines. Desjani had obviously been in on this, too. But then Colonel Carabali, the fleet's Marine commander, must have approved of the decision as well. Despite his own misgivings at arriving to speak to his political superiors with a combat-ready force at his back, Geary decided that trying to override the collective judgment of Desjani, Rione, and

Carabali wasn't likely to be wise. "Very well. Thank you, Major."

The Marines raised their weapons to present arms as Geary walked up the ramp, Rione beside him, bringing his arm up in a salute acknowledging the honors being rendered him. At times like this, when he seemed to have been saluting constantly for an hour, even he wondered at the wisdom of having reintroduced that gesture of respect into the fleet.

He and Rione went through to the small VIP cabin just aft of the pilots' cockpit, the Marines filing in behind them to take seats in the shuttle's main compartment. Geary strapped in, gazing at the display panel before him, where a remote image showed stars glittering against the endless night of space. It might have been a window, if anyone had been crazy enough to put a physical window in the hull of a ship or a shuttle.

"Nervous?" Rione asked.

"Can't you tell?"

"Not really. You're doing a good job."

"Thanks. What were you and Desjani plotting about when I got to the shuttle dock?"

"Just some girl talk," Rione said airily, waving a negligent hand. "War, the fate of humanity, the nature of the universe. That sort of thing."

"Did you reach any conclusions I should know about?"

She gave him a cool look, then smiled with apparently genuine reassurance. "We think you'll do fine as long as you are yourself. Both of us have your back. Feel better?"

"Much better, thank you." Status lights revealed the shuttle's ramp rising and sealing, the inner dock doors closing, the outer doors opening, then the shuttle rose, pivoted in place with jaunty smoothness, and tore out into space. Geary felt himself grinning. Autopilots could drive a shuttle technically as well as any human, and better in many cases, but only humans could put a real sense of style into their piloting. On his display, the shape of *Dauntless* dwindled rapidly as the shuttle accelerated. "This is the first time I've been off *Dauntless*," he suddenly realized.

"Since your survival pod was picked up, you mean," Rione corrected.

"Yeah." His former home and former acquaintances were gone, vanished into a past a century old. *Dauntless* had become his home, her crew his family. It felt odd to leave them.

To find out what happens next, pick up *The Lost Fleet: Victorious.*
Available from Titan Books.

ABOUT THE AUTHOR

John G. Hemry is a retired US Navy officer and the author, under the pen name Jack Campbell, of the *New York Times* national bestselling *The Lost Fleet* series (*Dauntless, Fearless, Courageous, Valiant, Relentless,* and *Victorious*). Next up are two new follow-on series. *The Lost Fleet: Beyond the Frontier* continues to follow Geary and his companions. The other series, *The Phoenix Stars*, is set on a former enemy world in that universe. Under his own name, John is also the author of the *JAG in Space* series and the *Stark's War* series. His short fiction has appeared in places as varied as the last Chicks in Chainmail anthology (*Turn the*

Other Chick) and *Analog* magazine (which published his Nebula Award-nominated story 'Small Moments in Time' as well as most recently 'The Rift' in the October 2010 issue). His humorous short story 'As You Know Bob' was selected for *Year's Best SF 13*. John's nonfiction has appeared in *Analog* and *Artemis* magazines as well as BenBella books on *Charmed*, *Star Wars*, and *Superman*, and in the *Legion of Superheroes* anthology *Teenagers from the Future*.

John had the opportunity to live on Midway Island for a while during the 1960s, graduated from high school in Lyons, Kansas, then later attended the US Naval Academy. He served in a variety of jobs including gunnery officer and navigator on a destroyer, with an amphibious squadron, and at the Navy's anti-terrorism centre. After retiring from the US Navy and settling in Maryland, John began writing. He lives with his long-suffering wife (the incomparable S) and three great kids. His daughter and two sons are diagnosed on the autistic spectrum.

Read on for the fifth extract of our exclusive interview with Jack Campbell (John G. Hemry), in which he talks candidly about writing, space travel, his influences and inspirations and much more.

1. How do you go about researching the technology that features in *The Lost Fleet*?

A lot of that took place over the years. I have experience working with sensors of different kinds, for example, so I can understand how different sensors would be integrated to produce a single picture. I know how radar works, so it was obvious that over distances in space, radar doesn't make much sense given the time lags required compared to strictly optical sensors. A lot of the technology in the books evolves from that. Navigating on the Earth's surface grows into the kind of issues you would face navigating through space. Working with Doppler effects in sonar gives a feeling for the impact of movement on the perceptions of other ships.

A big part of the technology issue was the logistics problem. You can't divorce the two issues. You need spare parts. You need fuel to make your ships go. You need food for the crews. All of that can be ignored by using magic technology that makes food out of nothing and engines that only need to be refuelled once a century or so. Maybe we'll develop such

" YOU NEED SPARE PARTS. YOU NEED FUEL TO MAKE YOUR SHIPS GO. YOU NEED FOOD FOR THE CREWS. ALL OF THAT CAN BE IGNORED BY USING MAGIC TECHNOLOGY THAT MAKES FOOD OUT OF NOTHING AND ENGINES THAT ONLY NEED TO BE REFUELLED ONCE A CENTURY OR SO. "

capabilities some day. But my technology needs support. It needs people to fix it, and it needs care and feeding, because that's the technology I've worked with and (as far as I can tell) that's how technology has always worked. It's not magic. It always brings its own work and requirements. That sort of trade-off is a critical part of imagining future technology, I think. It's ironic that fantasy usually has magic users who get tired and can't cast spells until they rest, while SF often has technology that never faces such limitations. But I've learned through experience that limitations are the flip side of capabilities, so that goes into everything that I come up with.

And speaking of limitations, like real technology, the neat stuff in *The Lost Fleet* doesn't always work when you most need it to. As we all know, that's just when something is most likely to break.

My previous series was set only a century in the future, confined to space inside our solar system. A lot of what I applied in *The Lost Fleet* was sort of tested out in the JAG series, where I had a lot fewer ships to deal with and a simpler level of technology.

I try to keep aware of trends in science, and have some practical and theoretical knowledge of physics, for example. What kind of weapons would work in space? I had previously worked with concepts like particle beams. Grapeshot is an old weapon, known to anyone who studies the age of sail or land battles during that period, but in space at short range it could deliver effective blows to other ships. As I've mentioned before, I take the approach that this is real, so I look for what would really work given the technology that I've established. Knowing that the current Vulcan cannon system was created when some technicians decided to see what would happen when they hooked a nineteenth century Gatling gun up to a drive motor in place of its hand crank, helps you realize that old systems can have some simple but highly-effective upgrades to work in environments that were never envisioned for them originally.

One thing I do usually avoid is detailed descriptions of how things work. There are three reasons for that. Anyone who reads SF classics quickly notices is that the more detailed a description is provided of how something works, the more likely that description is to be woefully wrong today. I don't know how the stuff works. Why write a detailed explanation that won't hold up in ten years? Then there's the fact that, in real life, no one stops to explain how something works before they use it. "As you know, Bob, this TV remote employs infrared technology and light emitting diodes to generate coded pulses of light…" No, they just change the channel, or start the car or pull the trigger. Finally, it slows the story down. Anything that happens has to advance the story. Stopping the story dead to offer a detailed description of some high-tech device, information which in no way impacts the story, wouldn't be doing the readers any favours. It's different if something about how that tech works is important to the story. Then describing that aspect of it advances the story.

2. Did you feel it was important to include a form of religious belief amongst those on the Fleet? Why did you choose ancestor worship specifically?

Religion appears to have been a part of every human society. It seemed right to include it in a future society, especially one under the kind of strains that I was writing about. There are times when human efforts fail and prayer is all you have left, and many of us look for something a lot wiser than we are to give us guidance.

Ancestor worship seemed an interesting contrast to the high-tech civilization. I had read an account of the excavation of what might be the oldest worship site found (it was somewhere in the Middle East). That apparently involved ancestor worship and the burning of candles, and I thought, wouldn't that be something to show how, despite everything that has changed, despite all of their equipment, these are still men and women who feel the need for something more, something bigger than them. And so they are doing the same kinds of things that their distant forbearers did. It gives them comfort even when so many have died. At one point Geary asks Desjani if she truly believes, and she answers that if she didn't, she couldn't go on.

Even cultures that don't worship ancestors can revere them. In the United States, the founding fathers of the country are regarded as especially wise and admirable, and people search their writings for wisdom that can guide solutions to problems today.

Of course ancestor worship worked into the story as well, since reverence for ancestors gave Geary extra perceived authority when he appeared among them. He wasn't just speaking for the ancestors. He was one of the ancestors.

3. Have you ever killed a character in a book and regretted it?

I regret it every time I kill a character in a book. I see it as something I have to do, because in real life the only people who die aren't some guest actor who you never saw before he showed up in this episode wearing a red shirt. The characters I kill feel real to me. If I later wish that character was still around to solve some problem or do some deed only they could do, well, that forces me to deal with my own form of reality. That person is dead, so the other characters have to figure out how to handle things without that person. They might say "I wish she was still alive,"

"I REGRET IT EVERY TIME I KILL A CHARACTER IN A BOOK. I SEE IT AS SOMETHING I HAVE TO DO, BECAUSE IN REAL LIFE THE ONLY PEOPLE WHO DIE AREN'T SOME GUEST ACTOR WHO YOU NEVER SAW BEFORE HE SHOWED UP IN THIS EPISODE WEARING A RED SHIRT" but that's what we would all say, and then we'd have to figure out what to do.

One time I did some work and thinking about a story where a character I was fond of had grown old and lost everyone she loved (also characters I had created). It would probably have been a strong story, but I couldn't keep on. She deserved a happier ending, with those she cared about around her when her time ended. So I never wrote that sadder story.

I haven't gone through the problem of killing someone whose death created unsolvable problems with the story after that. But I do miss some characters.

4. Who would play you in a film of your life?

Brad Pitt, of course.

I hope no one took that seriously.

Though Brad Pitt is good at playing the geeky guy who embarrasses his wife, like the scene in *Mr. and Mrs. Smith* where his character starts singing along to Air Supply and Angelina Jolie gives him that look which many husbands would recognize (*You're not really doing that, are you?*).

My wife, whose opinion in this matter must have considerable weight, claims the best actor would be either Hugh Laurie, James McAvoy or Paul Rudd.

So perhaps if Hugh Laurie, James McAvoy or Paul Rudd could act like Brad Pitt being a geeky guy…

"MY WIFE, WHOSE OPINION IN THIS MATTER MUST HAVE CONSIDERABLE WEIGHT, CLAIMS THE BEST ACTOR (TO PLAY ME) WOULD BE EITHER HUGH LAURIE, JAMES MCAVOY OR PAUL RUDD."

5. What's the most blatant lie you've ever told?

Thank you for the opportunity to do this interview...

Well, seriously, that was probably a few months before I left my first ship. My destroyer was tied up in Norfolk, Virginia, across the pier from one of our aircraft carriers. I would have command of the duty section aboard our destroyer on Saturday. On Sunday morning, Prince Charles was scheduled to briefly visit our Navy base at Norfolk, flying in a helicopter to the deck of the carrier. On Friday afternoon, my ship's executive officer called me in and told me to make sure the upper decks of our destroyer were painted on Saturday, so that if, during the brief moments that Prince Charles was airborne over our Navy base, he happened to fly over our destroyer and happened to look down, he would see shiny decks.

I pointed out to the executive officer that it was already starting to rain and that the weather forecast called for rain all day Saturday and into Sunday. He told me that didn't make any difference. The captain wanted Prince Charles to see shiny decks, so they would be painted on Saturday.

Now for some unknown reason that particular destroyer had been afflicted with a number of senior officers who thought it made perfect sense to paint outside in the rain no matter how many times they ordered it done and the result turned out to be atrocious. My second commanding officer never would have ordered that, but the first and third thought this was perfectly reasonable and no amount of experience would convince them otherwise.

I was about two months from leaving the ship for my next assignment. I knew my job well. I knew painting the decks in the rain would produce an awful sight if Prince Charles happened to look down the next day, as well as wasting the time of crew members who had a lot of other and better things to do. I also knew that no amount of further arguing would convince either the executive officer or the commanding officer of that.

I said "yes, sir."

And then, on Saturday, as it rained, I "forgot" to tell my duty section to paint the decks. Instead, they spent the day doing things that made sense.

Come Sunday morning, with lowering, gray skies and drizzle coating every surface with water, we heard the chop of the rotor blades overhead as the helicopter carrying Prince Charles made its way to the aircraft carrier. If the Prince looked down, he might have caught a glimpse through the overcast of our upper decks, and they would have been shining as well as anything could shine that morning, because they were wet.

Neither the commanding officer nor the executive officer ever asked me about it, and I didn't see any sense in bringing it up since everyone seemed happy enough about what had happened on Sunday morning and we all had plenty of other things to worry about anyway.

I'm certainly glad that I finally got that one off of my chest.

Check out the next book in the series – *Victorious* – for another exclusive interview extract!

JACK CAMPBELL'S
TOP TEN SF MOVIES

(1) *Star Wars*

The original, now officially titled *A New Hope*. That title works in a larger sense, because by the late 1970s SF had become mired in a swamp of new wave literary experimentation in which anti-heroes foundered amid dystopias in which nothing mattered and nothing would succeed, not that you could always tell because plot was one of those things that sometimes wasn't "in" anymore. If economics is the dismal science, SF had become the dismal genre. Then *Star Wars* hit, filled with retro concepts like adventure, heroics, action, and lots of things blowing up. SF became fun again. It was okay for the good guys to win, for effort to matter, to dream of rocketing among the stars.

(2) *The Empire Strikes Back*

If *Star Wars/A New Hope* made SF fun again, *The Empire Strikes Back* showed that it could be serious and well-written along with being heroic and positive. *Empire* bears the unmistakable fingerprints of the great Leigh Brackett, who knew space opera and drama. She had not only written a lot of SF, but had done a lot of screenplays, including being one of the screenwriters for *The Big Sleep*. How did Han Solo become a fully fleshed-out character with Humphrey Bogart's mix of bravado and pathos? Because that's how Leigh wrote him. In some alternate universe, Leigh Brackett lived to write more *Star Wars* movie screenplays, and that universe is a much happier place than our own.

(3) Aliens

For me, *Alien* was too much a standard horror movie, with the cliché of everyone going off alone to get taken out one by one. It did a tremendous job otherwise of telling the story of people trapped with a monster, but that particular element didn't work for me. *Aliens*, though, not only dumped people back into being besieged by some very nasty monsters, but had them handling it in what seemed to be the best way they could. Nobody was wilfully stupid, everyone went down swinging (except that venal corporate type) and the movie also took on the extra dimension of forcing Ripley to face her greatest fears. I was surprised to learn how much US Marines liked *Aliens*, given that the Marines in the movie get almost wiped out. But the movie presented a realistic picture of those Marines, treating the entire thing not as "it's just a sci-fi movie" but as "what if this was really happening?" That attention to realistic portrayals of the characters and actions made the movie stand out. *Aliens* also stands out as an example of "that's enough." This universe would have been fine without enduring the next two sequels.

(4) Twenty Thousand Leagues Under the Sea

In 1954, Walt Disney invented steampunk. Seriously. This isn't just a great telling of Verne's story, and doesn't just feature performances by fine actors like James Mason, it is also the only video version of Verne's work that really took the mechanics of the submarine *Nautilus* seriously. The attention to detail is astounding, and it's all perfect, from the elaborate quarters of Captain Nemo to the smallest hatch and porthole. If the

Victorians had built a nuclear-powered submarine, it would have looked like the *Nautilus* in Disney's movie. Disney and his engineers made people really think about what that kind of tech would be, and it's steampunk. Kids who saw that movie grew up and ran with the concept even if they no longer recalled exactly where they had first seen it.

(5) Tron

Most people don't realize that *Tron* (1982) not only came out when desktop computing and the internet were in their infancy, but that *Tron* also predated the book *Neuromancer* (1984) by two years. *Tron* didn't have the best script, but in terms of vision it stands out for creating the whole idea of cyberspace as a virtual world in itself, complete with hackers and security programs waging a hidden war for access. Check out any film or story set in cyberspace that has been done since *Tron*, including many being done today, and see how many elements that first appeared in *Tron* are still used. The movie didn't do that well when it was released, but arguably that's because it really was ahead of its time.

(6) Wall-E

It's hard to single out any one Pixar movie for greatness, but *Wall-E* is the most SF of the bunch, and it's brilliant. The entire first half, virtually dialogue-free, showing a dead Earth literally covered with junk, is breathtaking. The main character is without a face, its emotions and reactions shown by subtle movements of lenses and crude mechanisms, and that's done so well it makes you care deeply about Wall-E's fate. And it features a musical soundtrack built in true post-apocalyptic fashion from a fragment of the past, the songs from the old movie version of *Hello Dolly*. Despite his utilitarian body and "face," despite his inability to speak beyond the simplest utterances, there wasn't any need to stretch the imagination to see Wall-E as human.

(7) Nausicaä of the Valley of the Wind

Most of the Studio Ghibli movies produced by Hayao Miyazaki are fantasy, but *Nausicaä* is SF. It's another post-apocalyptic world, as dwindling pockets of humanity react to the threat of a huge, toxic jungle but continue to try to kill each other. The vision is remarkable, from the chilling prelude about the days of fire to the strange toxic jungle and the creatures within it, and the almost-steampunk fortress aircraft with which humanity continues to wage war. It also has in Nausicaä an early version of the strong yet human anime heroines who in the decades to follow took over much of Western movies and literature.

(8) The Planet of the Apes

No, not the awful 2001 remake, and not the increasingly cheesy sequels, but the 1968 original with Charlton Heston. It's hard to convey now the impact this film had back in '68. The ending has become well-known, a cliché, a matter for parody. But in 1968, when mutual assured destruction still hung over us like the Sword of Damocles, and you didn't know what was going to happen in the movie, when Heston's character discovered the remains of the Statue of Liberty it was an incredible punch to the gut. His "you blew it up!" melt-down of rage, condemnation and remorse hit hard and really made you think. An SF movie that made you think. It does happen.

(9) *On the Beach*

Speaking of punches in the gut, this movie version of the novel didn't pull any punches at all. In 1959, when it came out, nuclear weapons were still seen as something with a bigger bang. I've read a lot of military papers from that period, and the concepts in them involve tossing around nukes like they were just bigger versions of conventional explosives. *On the Beach* was built around the impact of radiation from fallout. Its end-of-the-world scenario didn't have the US being nuked. Instead, a major attack by the USSR on China produced clouds of radiation that had killed everything in the northern hemisphere and were slowly coming south. Much of the story takes place in Australia, where people are waiting for the end, but there are also scenes where you see the empty cities of the US, intact but hauntingly devoid of life. In the end… everybody dies. Depressing indeed, except for the last thing you see, a tattered revivalist banner waving in the breeze with its motto "There's still time." Time to make sure this didn't take place. And, so far, it hasn't. Too often these days SF movies gorge on special effects to show overblown events like the out-of-control weather in *The Day After Tomorrow* or a nothing-you-can-do-but-die fantasy like *2012*. Instead, *On the Beach* uses science to say "this is the outcome if we do that." And *On the Beach* was the kind of SF that says this could happen, but it doesn't have to, and we can make a difference.

(10) *Galaxy Quest*

Snark is easy. Affectionate parody, the sort of thing even fans of something can laugh at, is hard. *Galaxy Quest* nailed an entire generation of SF TV shows and movies, using great actors and a well-written story to hammer some of the silliest things which had appeared in SF shows and among fans. It's hard to settle on a favourite line: "That ain't right." "Try to determine its motivation." "I've got one job on this ship, and it's a stupid job, but I'm going to do it!" And, of course, the wonderful "Whoever wrote this should be shot!" It's probably not surprising that those things parodied in *Galaxy Quest* still appear in "serious" movies. When my wife and I were watching the latest *Star Trek* reboot movie we kept saying to each other "that's like that scene in *Galaxy Quest*."

Check out the other books in the series to discover Jack Campbell's Top Ten Sci Fi books and TV shows!

ALSO AVAILABLE FROM TITAN BOOKS

THE LOST FLEET
BY JACK CAMPBELL

After a hundred years of brutal war against the Syndics, the
Alliance fleet is marooned deep in enemy territory, weakened,
demoralised and desperate to make it home. Their fate rests
in the hands of Captain "Black Jack" Geary, a man who had
been presumed dead but then emerged from a century of
survival hibernation to find his name had become legend.

DAUNTLESS

FEARLESS

COURAGEOUS

VALIANT

VICTORIOUS

BEYOND THE FRONTIER: DREADNAUGHT

BEYOND THE FRONTIER: INVINCIBLE

BEYOND THE FRONTIER: GUARDIAN (MAY 2013)

"Black Jack is an excellent character, and this series is the
best military SF I've read in some time." *Wired*

"Fascinating stuff… this is military SF where the military
and SF parts are both done right." *SFX Magazine*

"*The Lost Fleet* is some of the best military science fiction
on the shelves today." SF Site

TITANBOOKS.COM

ALSO AVAILABLE FROM TITAN BOOKS

THE LOST STARS
BY JACK CAMPBELL

For the first time, the story of the *Lost Fleet* universe is told through the eyes of citizens of the Syndicate Worlds as they deal with defeat in the war, threats from all sides, and the crumbling of the Syndicate empire. In the Midway Star System, leaders must decide whether to remain loyal to the old order or fight for something new.

TARNISHED KNIGHT
PERILOUS SHIELD (OCTOBER 2013)

"Campbell maintains the military, political and even sexual tension with sure-handed proficiency... What emerges is a fascinating and vividly rendered character study, fully and expertly contextualized." *Kirkus Reviews*

"As can be expected in a Jack Campbell novel, the military battle sequences are very well done, with the land-based action adding a new dimension." SF Crowsnest

"[In] this brilliant sidebar new series... Jack Campbell runs a strong saga shown from the viewpoints of the Syndicate at a time when the vicious totalitarian military regime teeters on the brink of total collapse." Alternative Worlds

TITANBOOKS.COM

ALSO AVAILABLE FROM TITAN BOOKS

STARK'S WAR
BY JACK CAMPBELL
(WRITING AS JOHN G. HEMRY)

The USA reigns over Earth as the last surviving
superpower. To build a society free of American influence,
foreign countries have inhabited the moon, where Sergeant
Ethan Stark and his squadron must fight a desperate enemy
in an airless atmosphere.

STARK'S WAR
STARK'S COMMAND
STARK'S CRUSADE

"A gripping tale of military science fiction, in the tradition
of Heinlein's Starship Troopers and Haldeman's Forever
War… The characterization is right on… the plot is sharp
and crisp…Give this one a try." *Absolute Magnitude*

"The *Stark's War* trilogy has great action scenes, interesting
characters and an original concept." The British Fantasy
Society

"Solidly written, action-packed mil-SF… a good page-
turner that will amply satisfy fans of John Scalzi's *Old
Man's War* series, Jack McDevitt, David Weber or John
Ringo." SFF World

TITANBOOKS.COM

ALSO AVAILABLE FROM TITAN BOOKS

JAG IN SPACE
BY JACK CAMPBELL
(WRITING AS JOHN G. HEMRY)

Equipped with the latest weaponry, and carrying more than two hundred sailors, the orbiting warship, USS *Michaelson*, is armored against the hazards of space and the threats posed in the vast nothing between planets. But who will protect her from the threats within?

A JUST DETERMINATION
BURDEN OF PROOF
RULE OF EVIDENCE
AGAINST ALL ENEMIES

"Superior military sf... The last third of the book recalls nothing so much as *The Caine Mutiny Court-Martial* in an sf setting, and it attains the same high level of achievement." *Booklist*

"Fascinating and addictive... Young Paul Sinclair is exactly the kind of guy you want to serve with, and exactly the kind of reluctant hero that great series are made from." SF Revu

"Intelligent and engrossing legal drama... something of a tour de force." SF Reviews

TITANBOOKS.COM

ALSO AVAILABLE FROM TITAN BOOKS

THE CLONE REBELLION
BY STEVEN L. KENT

Earth, 2508 A.D. Humans have spread across the six arms of the Milky Way galaxy. The Unified Authority controls Earth's colonies with an iron fist and a powerful military—a military made up almost entirely of clones...

THE CLONE REPUBLIC
ROGUE CLONE
THE CLONE ALLIANCE (APRIL 2013)
THE CLONE ELITE (MAY 2013)
THE CLONE BETRAYAL (JUNE 2013)
THE CLONE EMPIRE (JULY 2013)
THE CLONE REDEMPTION (AUGUST 2013)
THE CLONE SEDITION (SEPTEMBER 2013)
THE CLONE ASSASSIN (OCTOBER 2013)

"Fans of Jack Campbell should find plenty here to enjoy."
SF Revu

"A smartly conceived adventure." SF Reviews

"Harris is an honest, engaging protagonist and...Kent is a skillful storyteller." *Science Fiction Weekly*

"Offers up stunning battle sequences, intriguing moral quandaries, and plenty of unexpected revelations... fast-paced military SF... with plenty of well-scripted action and adventure [and] a sympathetic narrator." SF Site

TITANBOOKS.COM

ALSO AVAILABLE FROM TITAN BOOKS

WITHOUT WARNING
BY JOHN BIRMINGHAM

March 14, 2003. In Kuwait, American forces are locked and loaded for the invasion of Iraq. In one instant, all around the world, everything will change. A wave of inexplicable energy slams into the continental United States. America as we know it vanishes. As certain corners of the globe erupt in celebration, others descend into chaos, and a new, soul-shattering reality is born..

WITHOUT WARNING
AFTER AMERICA
ANGELS OF VENGEANCE

"A blockbuster... replete with full-throttle action."
Booklist

"This well-thought-out alternate history will appeal to fans of hard SF and techno-thrillers." *Publishers Weekly*

"An absolutely cracking read." SF Site

TITANBOOKS.COM